Passionate Affairs

KAT...

NICOL...

NATALIE ANDERSON

All the characters in this book have no existence outside the imagination of the author, and have no relation whatsoever to anyone bearing the same name or names. They are not even distantly inspired by any individual known or unknown to the author, and all the incidents are pure invention.

Published in Great Britain 2013
by Mills & Boon, an imprint of Harlequin (UK) Limited,
Eton House, 18-24 Paradise Road, Richmond, Surrey TW9 1SR

PASSIONATE AFFAIRS © by Harlequin Enterprises II B.V./S.à.r.l 2013

Breakfast at Giovanni's, *Purchased for Pleasure* and *Bedded by Arrangement* were first published in Great Britain by Harlequin (UK) Limited.

Breakfast at Giovanni's © Kate Hardy 2007
Purchased for Pleasure © Nicola Marsh 2007
Bedded by Arrangement © Natalie Anderson 2007

ISBN: 978 0 263 90571 7
ebook ISBN: 978 1 472 00144 3

05-1113

Harlequin (UK) policy is to use papers that are natural, renewable and recyclable products and made from wood grown in sustainable forests. The logging and manufacturing processes conform to the legal environmental regulations of the country of origin.

Printed and bound in Spain
by Blackprint CPI, Barcelona

BREAKFAST
AT GIOVANNI'S

BY
KATE HARDY

Kate Hardy lives on the outskirts of Norwich with her husband, two small children, a dog—and too many books to count! She wrote her first book at age six, when her parents gave her a typewriter for her birthday. She had the first of a series of sexy romances published at twenty-five, and swapped a job in marketing communications for freelance health journalism when her son was born, so she could spend more time with him. She's wanted to write for Mills & Boon since she was twelve—and when she was pregnant with her daughter, her husband pointed out that writing Medical Romances would be the perfect way to combine her interest in health issues with her love of good stories.

Kate is always delighted to hear from readers—do drop in to her website at www.katehardy.com.

For Jim—
who has taught me much—
with love

CHAPTER ONE

SHE looked as if the world had ended, hunched over an empty coffee cup, staring out of the plate-glass window but not seeing anything.

Gio couldn't leave her sitting there in such obvious misery. So even though he should've locked up ten minutes ago, he did exactly what his father would've done. He made a cappuccino and slid it on to the table in front of her. 'Here,' he said softly.

She looked up, her eyes widening in surprise. 'I…' She'd obviously been about to protest that she hadn't ordered the coffee. But then she smiled ruefully and cupped both hands round the mug, clearly taking comfort from its warmth. 'Thanks.'

'No problem.' He handed her a chocolate dipper. 'You look as if you need this.'

'I do,' she admitted. 'Thanks. I appreciate this.' She rummaged in her handbag for her purse. 'How much do I owe you?'

He waved a dismissive hand. 'Nothing.'

She frowned. 'Won't you get into trouble with your boss?'

'Doubt it.' He smiled. 'Anyway, you're a regular, so call it a refill.'

Those beautiful blue eyes—the same blue as the sky on a

summer evening, he saw, now that he was this close to her—narrowed slightly. 'Regular?'

He shrugged. 'On Wednesday mornings, you order a cappuccino and an almond croissant to go at ten past nine.'

The suspicion on her face morphed into nervousness. 'How do you know that?'

Oh, lord. Obviously she thought he was some kind of weirdo—that he'd been watching her or stalking her. He shouldn't have mentioned the time. 'Work here long enough and you get to know the customers,' he said lightly, hoping it reassured her. 'I'm out of croissants or I would've brought you one—hence the chocolate.' He spread his hands. 'Because that's what women need when things get tough, right? Or so my sisters always tell me.'

'Right. And thank you.' She looked very close to tears.

'Want to talk about it?'

She looked around, as if suddenly realising she was the only customer. 'Oh, lord. Sorry. I'm holding you up.'

'Not at all. Though would you mind if I put up the closed sign and put the bolt on the door, so I don't get a sudden rush and end up staying open a lot later than usual?'

Fran thought about it. He'd actually asked her first, to make sure she didn't feel threatened. And a man who'd brought her a coffee and a chocolate dipper couldn't be all bad, could he? OK, so he knew her Wednesday-morning order—but, as he'd said, you got to know your regulars in business. Just as she did: she recognised voices on the phone and knew even before they asked which ones would be asking for a last-minute panic job and which ones would be booking slots for weeks ahead.

'Sure,' she said.

He bolted the door, turned the sign over to read 'Closed' from the outside, turned off one of the banks of lights, and came to sit opposite her. 'Gio Mazetti,' he said, holding out his hand.

She took it, and was surprised at the sudden tingle in her fingertips when her skin touched his. 'Fran Marsden. And thank you for the coffee, Joe.'

'Gio,' he corrected with a smile.

Now she was listening properly, she heard it. The soft *G*, the *I* and *O* sliding together almost after a pause.

'Short for Giovanni,' he added helpfully.

And then the penny dropped. Of course he wouldn't get into trouble for making her a coffee for no charge. Because the café was called Giovanni's. 'You own the place.'

He lifted one shoulder. 'It's a family concern—but, yeah, I'm in charge.'

'I, um…' She shifted in her seat, embarrassed at her naïvety. 'Sorry.'

He laughed. 'Don't apologise. I'm glad I come across as one of the baristas—there's nothing worse than having the boss supposedly doing a shift and just throwing his weight around instead of doing something useful.'

He had a nice laugh. Good teeth, even and white—no fillings, either, she noticed. A guy who took care of small details. But he also didn't look like the type who went in for cosmetic dentistry. She'd put money on him not going to the gym, either—she had a feeling that Gio Mazetti was in perfect shape from hard work, not from pumping iron. He was good looking, but far from being vain about it.

'So. Want to tell me about it?' When she said nothing, he added softly, 'My *nonna*—my Italian grandmother—always says that a problem shared is a problem halved.'

Homespun wisdom. Just the sort of thing her mother would come out with.

Her mother...

Fran's smile faded before it had had a chance to start. She was going to have to call her parents tonight and admit to them that she was a failure. Not only was she the only one of their children not to get a degree, now she was the only one who didn't have a decent job. And it went right with the territory of not being their real child, anyway—the only one of the four Marsden children who was adopted.

She sighed. 'I lost my job today.'

'I'm sorry. That's tough.'

It wasn't his fault. And he was right—it felt good to unburden herself. Lose some of the sick feeling of failure. 'My boss decided he wanted a new challenge, so he sold the business to go travelling for a year and to work out what he wanted to do with his life.' She shrugged. 'A competitor bought the business. And you really don't need two office managers when you're merging two companies and need to cut your running costs. So one of them has to be made redundant.'

'So you're an office manager?'

'Was.' She pulled a face. 'Ah, ignore me. I'm whining.' She waved a dismissive hand. 'I'll find something else. It's just that I really loved my job—and there aren't that many opportunities in the market because there aren't many voiceover studios around.'

He looked interested. 'What does a voiceover studio do?'

'Record jingles for radio stations, produce radio advertising and audio books, and do audio special effects—you know, like horses' hooves or fireworks going off on bonfire night, that kind of thing.'

'So you get all the famous actors and actresses coming in?'

She smiled. 'They're not always household names—but, yeah, I've booked a few in my time.'

'You were in charge of booking?'

'I didn't make the final decisions on who we booked for each job,' Fran said, 'but I made suggestions and I did the organising. I made sure everyone knew what they were supposed to be doing and when.' And she'd fitted in, right smack in the middle of things. She'd *belonged*. And that, to her, had been way more important than her admittedly good salary. 'We had a sales guy handling the sales side of things, a sound manager to do the technical stuff, and my boss did the copywriting and most of the schmoozing.' She bit her lip. 'I'm going to miss it. Horribly. But, hey, life moves on. I'll get over it. Find something else.' She glanced at her watch. 'Sorry. I'm making you really late.'

Gio shook his head. 'It's really not a problem, Fran. My evening's my own. Though I do need to clean the machines so they're ready for tomorrow morning—so, if you don't mind me sorting that out while we're talking, come and sit by the bar.'

Fran looked at him properly for the first time. Gio Mazetti would get a definite ten on the scale of gorgeousness. Olive skin, dark straight hair that flopped across his forehead and which he'd obviously pushed back with one hand at various times during the day because it stuck up in places, a sensual mouth—and the most stunning eyes. With his colouring and his Italian name, she'd expected them to be dark brown. Instead, they were blue.

A mesmerising deep, almost midnight, blue.

She followed him to the bar.

'So when do you finish?' he asked.

That was what had knocked her for six. 'It all happened

today and I cleared my desk this afternoon. I'm on five months' gardening leave, as of now,' she said.

'Five months is pretty generous,' he commented, starting to strip down the coffee machine.

'I worked at the studio for five years, so I guess the terms are one month for every year I spent there,' she explained. 'But the terms of my leave also mean that I can't contact any of my former clients during those five months.'

'So if you go to a competitor, you can't take your contacts with you.'

He'd hit the nail right on the head, and Fran's spirits took another nosedive. 'In five months' time, my contacts will be out of date, because things change so quickly in advertising and radio and publishing. And that's assuming I can get another job in a voiceover studio—as I said, it's not that huge an industry, so even in London there aren't many openings.' She shrugged. 'On the plus side, my skills are transferable. I dunno. Maybe I'll try some of the advertising agencies, see if I can work on the client management side. *If* that doesn't break the terms of my gardening leave, that is.'

'Tell me about what your job involved,' Gio said.

'I kept the schedule for the studios so I knew which slots were free if we were doing a rush job, and which actor was working on which job. I used to talk to the radio stations and audio publishers to sort out timescales, and to the agencies so we had the right voice for the right job. Plus a bit of PA work for the boss and keeping up to date with invoicing and payments.'

'Hmm.' He finished cleaning the machines and leaned on the counter opposite her. 'So you're good at organisation and you're used to keeping track of lots of different projects at the same time, and dealing with lots of different people at lots of different levels.'

That pretty much summed it up. And there was no point in false modesty: she might as well get used to stating what her skills were. She needed the practice for interviews. 'Yes.'

'And you understand finances.'

There was a difference between being honest and sexing it up. She wasn't going to claim to be an accountancy whiz-kid. 'I can do basic book-keeping and set up spreadsheets and produce graphs,' she said.

'Can you read a P and L statement?'

'Profit and loss? Um—I might need to ask some questions, but, yes, I think so.'

'And you understand how profit margins work, the difference between fixed and variable costs?'

She nodded.

He smiled. 'Excellent. In that case, I might have a proposition for you.'

'What sort of proposition?'

'A business proposition.'

Well, of course—it wouldn't be anything else, would it? Some of the actors at the studio had flirted mildly with her, but Fran knew from experience that men basically saw her as a colleague or a friend, not as dating material. She was the one they came to asking for help to woo the girl of their dreams, rather than being the girl who'd caught their eye in the first place. And she was fine with that. Right now her life was complicated enough, without adding in all the muddle of a romantic entanglement.

'It's something that might solve a problem for both of us,' he added mysteriously. 'Have dinner with me tonight and I'll explain.'

Dinner? Didn't he have a wife and family waiting for him at home?

The question must have been written over her face, because his smile broadened. 'Before you ask, I'm single. My *nonna* says that no girl in her right mind will sit around waiting for a workaholic to notice her existence. She also says it's time I settled down, before I hit thirty and I'm on the shelf.' He laughed. 'I've seriously been considering telling her I'm gay.'

A *frisson* of disappointment slid down Fran's spine. Where a gorgeous man was concerned, there was always a rule of three: he'd been snapped up at an early age, he was a rat, or he was gay.

'But apart from the fact I'm not—'

Oh. Not attached and not gay. So did that put him into the rat category?

'—she wouldn't believe me anyway. Because I'm a hopeless liar,' he added with a rueful smile.

So maybe the rule of three didn't apply in this case. Gio might just be the exception that proved the rule.

He smiled at her. 'Don't look so worried. What I'm trying to say is that you're safe with me. I'm not trying to hit on you.'

Which was true, Gio thought—up to a point. He'd noticed Fran Marsden weeks ago. There was something about her: she was quiet, maybe even a little shy, but she always knew exactly what she wanted instead of dithering over the menu, always had the right money, and always had a smile for the barista who made her cappuccino, not taking the service for granted. Efficient and courteous. He liked that. So he'd made a point of working a morning shift in the Charlotte Street café on Wednesdays, when he knew she'd be in; even if he hadn't served her himself, seeing her put a sparkle into the middle of his week.

But he'd never intended to act on that attraction. He knew

better than to mix business with pleasure, and he'd never overstep the boundaries with a customer.

Besides, Nonna was right. There was no point in asking her out because no woman would put up with the hours he worked. And it wasn't fair to suggest a relationship to someone who was just trying to pick up the pieces of her life after some bad news. Especially the way he was feeling right now—restless, at the point where the chain of coffee shops had stopped being a challenge and started being a burden. Though he'd invested so much of his life in Giovanni's, he had no idea what he wanted to do instead.

Except...

No. That particular dream had crashed and burned. He wasn't going back.

But if the idea that had been spinning round in his head for the last few months worked out, he could help Fran pick up the pieces and maybe help stop his restlessness at the same time.

He knew he was acting on impulse, but he'd always been a good judge of character in the past. And he was pretty sure that Fran Marsden was just the kind of woman he needed to help him. 'I think this could be good for both of us,' he said. 'So, will you have dinner with me this evening? I happen to know the best pizzeria in London.'

'Pizza,' she said, the tiniest sparkle in her eyes.

He laughed. 'Well, what else would an Italian suggest for dinner?'

To his pleasure, the sparkle turned into a full-wattage twinkle. And, lord, she was lovely when she smiled properly. It lit her up from the inside, transforming her from average to beautiful.

'Grilled scamorza,' she said. 'Panna cotta. And dough balls with garlic butter.'

Oh, *yes*. A woman on his wavelength. One who actually enjoyed food instead of nibbling at a celery leaf and claiming she was too full to manage anything more—one who saw the pleasure in sharing a meal instead of the misery of counting calories. One who might just understand what he wanted to do. 'That,' he said, 'sounds pretty much perfect. So we have a deal? I'll feed you and you'll listen to what I have to say?'

She shook her head. 'I might not have a job right now, but I can still pay my way. We'll split the bill.'

Not a yes woman, either; he warmed to her even more. Fran was exactly what he was looking for. 'Deal,' he said. He still had a pile of paperwork to do, but he'd done the banking an hour before and the float would be fine in the safe. 'Let me lock up, and we'll go.'

CHAPTER TWO

TWENTY minutes later, Fran and Gio were sitting in a tiny Italian restaurant in Fitzrovia, halfway between Euston Road and Gower Street. The décor was classic: a black-and-white chequered floor, walls colour-washed in amber, marble-topped bistro tables, wrought-iron chairs with thick burgundy-coloured pads on the seats, a chalk board with the day's specials written in European-looking handwriting, and candles set in raffia-covered chianti bottles.

Gio was clearly known here, because the waiter bantered with him before showing them to what looked like the best table in the house.

'So, are you a regular here?' she asked.

'This place does the best food in London. It's where my family comes for birthdays, red-letter days and every other excuse we can think of.'

The waiter materialised beside them and handed them a menu. 'Except you're always late for dinner, Gio, because you're busy working and you have no idea of time. Nonna would tell me to box your ears.'

Gio laughed. 'Ah, now, Marco, she would also tell you that the customer is always right.'

'*You* don't count as a customer,' Marco said, laughing back.

'But you, *signorina*, do.' He set a plate of tiny canapés in between them. 'Don't let him talk you into giving him your share.'

'As if I would—oh…' Gio's eyes widened '…don't eat those cheese discs, Fran. They're inedible. Better let me handle them.'

Marco pretended to cuff him. 'I'll be back in a minute for your order. And behave yourself, or I'll tell Mama what you just said about her cooking.' He winked, and left them with the menus.

'Are the cheese discs really…?' Fran asked, eyeing the plate of gorgeous-looking canapés.

'No, they're fabulous. They're my favourite and I was teasing you. Actually, I was trying to be greedy,' Gio admitted with a smile. 'I'm sorry. I should have said—Marco's my cousin.'

She glanced at the waiter, who was serving another table; now Gio had mentioned it, she could see the family resemblance. But although Marco was good looking and charming, there was something else about Gio. Something that all the other women in the room had clearly noticed, too, because Fran could see just how many heads he'd turned.

'Marco's mother—my Aunt Annetta—is the chef.' Gio's smile turned slightly wry. 'I'm afraid my family's terribly stereotyped.'

'How do you mean?'

'My grandparents moved to London from Milan in the 1950s, and they opened a trattoria,' he explained. 'Their children all went into catering, too—Dad opened a coffee shop, Netti started the pizzeria, and my Uncle Nando is the family ice-cream specialist. He makes the best *gelati* in London.'

'And you're all still close?'

'As I said, we're stereotyped. Typical Italian family.' He spread his hands. 'Big and noisy and knowing way too much of each other's business. Dad, Netti and Nando all live in the same street—the same place I grew up with my sisters and my cousins. Though none of us lives at home now; my generation's spread a bit.' He shrugged. 'Sometimes it feels a bit crowded, and it drives me crazy when they try to organise my social life and find me the perfect girlfriend. But if things get rough it's good to know there's a bunch of people looking out for you, people you can rely on.'

Fran suppressed the feeling of wistfulness before it had a chance to take hold, and tried one of the tiny discs. 'Oh, *wow*.'

Gio smiled. 'Told you they were good.'

'Do you recommend anything in particular?' she asked, scanning the menu.

'Netti's a genius in the kitchen. You could pick anything and it'd taste superb. But you mentioned grilled scamorza, panna cotta and dough balls.'

'They're not on the menu,' Fran pointed out.

'For us, they will be.' He said it without a trace of arrogance; it sounded more like he knew he was getting special treatment, and appreciated it. 'Would you prefer red or white wine?'

'White, please.'

'Pinot grigio all right?'

'Lovely, thanks.'

When Marco returned to take their order, Gio leaned back against his chair and gave him a wicked smile. 'Ah, *cugino mio*. In fact, oh, best cousin in the world—best cousin in the universe…'

Marco groaned. 'You're going to ask for a Giovanni special, aren't you?'

'Yup.' Gio spoke in rapid Italian. Fran couldn't follow the conversation at all, but Gio's accent was incredibly sexy. And he had the most gorgeous mouth. Even when he wasn't talking, there was a permanent tilt to the corner of his lips, as if he were smiling. A real knee-buckler of a smile, too. Yet, at the same time, there was a sense of suppressed energy and restlessness about him. Gio Mazetti was a puzzle. And she found herself wanting to know more about him.

'*Basta*—enough. I'll ask. But as you're her favourite nephew…' Marco rolled his eyes.

'I'm Netti's *only* nephew,' Gio corrected with a grin.

'As I said. Her favourite. So there's a pretty good chance she'll say yes.' Marco smiled. 'One bottle of pinot grigio and a jug of iced water coming up.'

'What's a Giovanni special?' Fran asked.

'Ah.' Gio coughed. 'It's just the topping I like on my pizza. I went through an—um—let's say *experimental* phase in my teens. This one stuck.'

'Experimental?'

'Blue cheese—preferably dolcelatte—and mushrooms.'

She frowned. 'That doesn't sound particularly experimental.'

'No. That would be the other ingredient,' he said drily.

She was intrigued now. 'Which is?'

'Avocado.'

She blinked. 'Avocado on *pizza*? Cooked avocado?'

'Don't knock it until you've tried it,' he advised.

He was full of energy, full of ideas, a little offbeat—and the more time Fran spent with Gio, the more she liked him. His good humour was infectious.

What she couldn't work out was why he'd asked her to dinner. What his proposition was going to be.

When the wine arrived, he didn't bother tasting it; simply thanked Marco, poured out two glasses, and raised his own in a toast to Fran. 'To us—and the beginning of what's going to be a beautiful friendship.' Again, that mischievous half-smile appeared. 'Horribly corny. But it's true anyway. I think we're going to suit each other.'

'How do you mean?' she asked, slightly suspicious.

'I'm sure you're used to dealing with confidential material at the studio,' he said. At her nod, he asked, 'So I trust you'll keep my confidence now?'

'Of course.'

'OK.' He took a deep breath. 'I'm at the point in the business where I need to make some decisions about expansion—either I can open more branches or I can franchise Giovanni's so we open outlets in other cities besides London. There's a fair bit of day-to-day admin in running a chain of coffee shops, so I need to free up some of my time to let me move the business forward.'

It all sounded perfectly logical.

'So I need to find someone who has fabulous organisational skills. Someone who'll be able to be my number two in the business, who can take over from me in juggling rotas and sorting out time management issues, maybe hiring temps or talking people into doing overtime if we have staff off sick. Someone who can sort out the admin, ring the engineers if one of the coffee machines breaks down, help keep the team motivated and not be fazed by dealing with figures and statistics. Someone who's fantastic on the phone and good with people.'

A new challenge. One where she'd be working with people. Using all her skills. This sounded right up her street.

As if he'd read her mind, he added softly, 'And I think that person's you.'

'You've only just met me. How do you know I'm what you're looking for?' she asked. 'For all you know, I'm not really an experienced office manager. I could be a pathological liar.'

'I've worked in this business long enough to be a good judge of people,' he said simply. 'I trust my instinct. You're no bunny-boiler. And if you were a pathological liar, you'd have told me that not only could you read a P and L statement, you could do business projection modelling and write your own computer programs, while juggling six flaming torches and tap-dancing on a tightrope all at the same time.'

She couldn't help smiling at the picture he'd painted. 'Juggling, tap-dancing and tightrope walking aren't quite my forte. Though I can use a computer and I know where to get help if I'm stuck.'

'Exactly. You're straight and practical and honest.'

Which wasn't quite what a woman wanted to hear from a man, but this wasn't a date anyway, she reminded herself. This was business.

'In short, you're exactly what I'm looking for.' He paused. 'Though, since you brought it up, how do you know that *I'm* not a pathological liar?'

'Because if you didn't own or at least run the coffee shop, you wouldn't have been the only one there after closing time, you wouldn't have the keys and you probably wouldn't be called Giovanni.'

'He isn't. His real name's Fred,' Marco interposed, bringing them the scamorza.

'Just ignore him. He's only jealous because his coffee's not as good as mine,' Gio retorted with a grin. '*Cugino mio*, any time you want a lesson on getting the perfect crema on an espresso—'

'—I'll ask your dad,' Marco teased. 'Enjoy your *antipasto*, *signorina*…?' He waited for a name.

'Fran,' she said with a smile.

'Fran.' He looked thoughtful. 'Short for Frances?'

'Francesca.'

'An Italian name. Hmm.' Marco gave Gio a knowing look, and was rewarded with a stream of Italian.

Fran, judging it wiser not to ask, tried her scamorza. 'It's gorgeous,' she said.

'Course it is. My aunt Netti's a fabulous cook.' Gio gave her another of those knee-buckling smiles. 'So, Fran. *Francesca*. Your family has Italian blood?'

'No idea.' And she really wasn't comfortable talking about her family.

He didn't seem upset that she'd been a bit short with him. 'So we've established that we trust each other, yes?'

She wasn't quite sure how to answer that.

'Trust has to start somewhere,' he said softly. 'And if you see the best in people—expect the best from them—they'll give you their best.'

'Is this another of your Italian grandmother's sayings?'

'Yup—she's a very wise woman, my *nonna*. When I was a teenager, I used to think she was just rabbiting on. But, the older I get, the more I realise she knows what she's talking about.' He raised an eyebrow. 'Actually, you remind me of her in a way.'

'I'll take that as a compliment.'

'It was.' He ate another mouthful of scamorza. 'As I said, this job's got your name on it. But you'll also need to understand the business from the bottom up.'

'Running a coffee shop?'

He nodded. 'Specifically, Giovanni's. What makes us different from the competition. What makes us special. What makes people come to us instead of one of the national chains or the independents. So I need someone who understands about coffee.'

Fran shook her head. 'That counts me out. I know what I like—cappuccino and latte—but when it comes to all these complicated orders…'

Gio took a sip of wine. 'Firstly, all coffees are based on espresso. And Giovanni's doesn't go in for coffee that takes half an hour and a degree in rocket science to order. We make it easy for the customer. A basic espresso for those who like black coffee; latte, cappuccino and Americano for those who like varying degrees of milk or frothiness. Hot chocolate, mocha for those who like a mixture, tea with milk or lemon, and iced coffees and smoothies in summer.' He ticked them off on his fingers. 'Pastries and biscotti in the morning, paninis for lunch and cakes for the middle of the afternoon. It's a matter of knowing what our customers like and second-guessing the right quantities so that we don't run out, but also don't have to throw away too much.' He looked thoughtful. 'I suppose it's like you'd book your studio slots so you weren't empty half the time and double-booked the rest of the time.'

She could appreciate that. But the coffee thing… 'I don't even have an espresso machine at home.'

He groaned. 'Don't tell me you drink instant coffee?'

'No, I use a cafetiere. Same at work—well, used to,' she corrected herself. She really had to get her head round the fact that she didn't work at the voiceover studio any more. 'I like my coffee fresh, not stuck in a filter pot stewing for half a day.'

'Then you already have a feel for what we do. Fran, the best way to understand a business is to work in it for a while— and I'm short-staffed right now. I'm about to lose one of my baristas because she wants to go travelling.'

She flinched. 'Like my boss.'

He smiled ruefully. 'I'm sorry. I didn't mean to rub salt in your wounds. But—to quote Nonna yet again—when one door closes, another opens. This is an opportunity for both of us. I need someone with your skills, and you're on garden leave for five months. It strikes me you're the sort who enjoys being busy and rises to a challenge, so if you work with me this will solve both our problems. I get an office manager who can take some of the weight off me and let me plan where to go next with the business and maybe let me bounce ideas off her, and you get a job that you can stretch to suit you.'

It sounded as if he had it all worked out.

'And the coffee thing isn't a problem. I can train you as a barista, teach you what you need to know. If you work a few shifts in one of the coffee shops, you'll understand the business more and you'll be able to bring that to the office manager job too.' He looked thoughtful. 'You'll need a food hygiene certificate, but the course only takes a few hours and the exam's pretty straightforward.'

Exams? Oh, no. This was where it all went pear-shaped. 'I'm not good at exams,' she told him. 'I tend panic. I failed my A levels.'

'But in day-to-day practical things, you're fine.'

It was a statement, not a question. She nodded.

'Then think of the exam as just another day-to-day practical thing.'

'That's what my parents said about the driving test. It still took me four goes—and Suzy and the twins all passed theirs first time.'

'Suzy and the twins?' he asked.

She shifted in her seat. 'I'm the eldest of four.' Sort of.

'The same as me.' He smiled. 'Now I know why you're

brilliantly organised. You've had years of practice, bossing your siblings about.'

'They're a trainee dentist, a PhD student and a forensic scientist. Bossing them about wouldn't work,' she said with a rueful smile. They were all academic and brilliant at exams, unlike her. They all excelled in sports, too, had always been picked for the school's first team, whereas she'd been hopeless—in sixth form she'd opted to do voluntary work at the local old people's home on Wednesday afternoons rather than sports.

She was the eldest. And most definitely the odd one out.

Probably because she didn't share the same gene pool.

Marco took away their empty plates and returned with pizza and a bowl of salad. 'Mama says panna cotta would take too long, but crème brûlée is on the specials board and she can do you some with raspberries.'

'Fabulous.' Gio smiled. 'Tell her she's the joint best mother in the world, along with mine.'

'Tell her yourself. There are big hints in the kitchen that she hasn't seen her favourite nephew for months.'

'It hasn't been anywhere near that long,' Gio protested.

'Eat your pizza. Then go see Mama, if you want pudding,' Marco advised. 'Fran, would you like pepper? Parmesan?'

'I'm fine, thanks.' She smiled back at him.

'*Bene.* Enjoy,' he said, and left them to it.

'You have to try this,' Gio insisted, and cut a small piece from his pizza. 'Here.' He offered her a forkful across the table; it felt oddly intimate, leaning across to take a bite, and when her gaze met his she felt a weird shifting in the region of her heart, as if it had just turned a somersault.

Oh, lord. Don't say she was falling for Gio Mazetti, a man she barely knew and who was just about to become her boss?

'Well?' he asked. 'So what do you think of avocado on pizza?'

'It's…different.'

He laughed. 'That's the diplomatic answer.'

She shifted the conversation back to business before it drifted on to personal ground. *Dangerous* ground. Because if she was going to work with Gio, any other sort of relationship was definitely out of the question. 'You said you were thinking of expanding or franchising. How big is Giovanni's?'

'We have four outlets in London,' he said. 'So I'm at the stage where I need to decide what to do next. Well, I say "I".' He waved a dismissive hand. 'Dad started the business.'

'But you're in charge now.'

He nodded. 'Though I need to consider Dad's feelings. Franchising's a possibility, but I need to do some proper research into what it all means and whether it's the right way for us to go. And at the moment I simply don't have the time.'

The pizzeria was another of his family's businesses, and his aunt was clearly still hands on. Gio's father couldn't be that much older than Annetta, surely; so why wasn't he hands-on with the coffee shop? 'You seem—well, pretty young to be heading a chain of coffee shops,' she commented.

'I'm twenty-eight. But I've worked in the business for half my life. And I learned how to make decent espresso at my father's knee.'

'And because you're the eldest, you were groomed to take over from your dad?'

For a brief moment, his face was filled with bleakness. And then, before she had the chance to ask him what was wrong, he smiled. 'Something like that.'

She was pretty sure there was something he wasn't telling her. 'Your *nonna* said that trust has to start somewhere,' she reminded him softly. 'So why don't you fill me in on the story?'

He toyed with his pizza for a while before answering. 'I planned to go to college, ten years ago. I was going to study music. I helped out in the business while I was at school—we all did, whether it was washing up or baristaing or clearing the tables for Dad and washing them down when the shop closed—but this one night I was meant to be working a late shift when I had a chance to play in a concert. A concert where I knew a scout for a record company was going to be in the audience. Dad said I had to follow my dreams, and he'd do my shift for me, even though he'd been working all day and it meant he'd be doing a double shift. I was eighteen. Head full of stars. So I went. I played. The scout had a word with me and my guitar teacher. And I came home by the coffee shop to tell Dad my news.' He dragged in a breath. 'Which was when I found him lying on the floor. He'd had a heart attack while he was shutting up the shop. The ambulance got there in time to save him, but no way was I going to make Dad cope with the stress of the business after that.'

'So you gave up music to take over from him?' she guessed.

He grimaced. 'I probably wasn't good enough to make it commercially anyway. There isn't that much scope for a clas-sical guitarist.' He spread his hands. 'A bit of session work, a bit of teaching, the occasional gig in some arts club. It's a bits-and-pieces sort of life, whereas running Giovanni's means I can do pretty much what I like, when I like. It wasn't a hard choice.'

The momentary flicker in those blue, blue eyes told her that he was lying. That even now he wondered, *what if?* But it hadn't stopped him making the decision. He'd given up his dreams for his family.

Fran realised with a pang that Gio was the kind of man who believed in commitment. Who believed in his family.

A belief she so wanted to have. Except she didn't share his certainty in belonging, the way that he did. Even though her parents had told her years before that she was special, that they'd chosen her to be part of their family, she wasn't sure she belonged. Because they'd chosen her when they didn't think they could have their own children, and she'd always thought that they regretted their decision when it turned out to be not the case. It was an unspoken fear, but one that still surfaced from time to time. Like now, when she'd stopped fitting in at work and she'd been the one to be made redundant rather than the other office manager.

Gio came from a large family. One that teased and drove him crazy, but clearly loved him to bits. If she accepted his offer of a job, would she fit in to his world any better than she fitted into her family?

'What was the news?' she asked. 'The news you called by to tell him?'

Gio took a sip of wine. 'Nothing important.'

She didn't quite believe him. Hadn't he said that the scout had had a word with him? But she had a feeling that if she pushed, Gio would clam up completely.

'Besides, I've enjoyed managing the coffee shop. Dad believed in me enough to let me run it without interference. The one on Charlotte Street is the original café, but he was fine about me expanding it.' He looked at her. 'I said earlier about trusting people. I also need to be honest with you. Right now, it's not so much the business that's at a crossroads, it's me.' He sighed. 'I don't know whether it's because I'm heading towards thirty—a kind of early midlife crisis—but right now I feel in limbo. I don't know what I want from life.

And I need to find out while I'm still young enough to do something about it.'

That accounted for the suppressed restlessness she'd spotted earlier. 'Music?' she asked. Did he want to follow the dream he'd given up ten years before?

'I'm too old. Too out of practice. I only play for myself nowadays, anyway.' He shook his head. 'I don't know. I can promise you one thing, though—I'm not intending to sell the business or make you redundant. I just need…time. To sort a few things out in my head. And I need someone to help me. Someone to give me that time.'

He needed someone.

And he'd asked her.

'How about we have a month's trial, with a week's notice on either side?' she asked.

The smile he gave her was like that of a drowning man who'd just been thrown a lifeline. 'Sounds good to me. When do you want to start?'

CHAPTER THREE

'How about tomorrow?' The words came out before he could stop them. Too eager. Stupid, Gio berated himself mentally. If he wasn't careful, he'd scare her off.

'Straight from one job to another, without a break?' she asked, raising an eyebrow.

Very stupid, he amended silently. Hell. Now she was going to say no. Because he'd rushed her. Of course she'd want a break between jobs. Time to recharge her batteries. Would he never learn not to jump in feet first?

And then she smiled. 'Well, it beats sitting around feeling sorry for myself. Tomorrow it is.'

He could've kissed her. Except officially, they were working together now. And Gio had seen too many good business relationships messed up when sex had got in the way of business. He wasn't going to make that mistake. Even though he was definitely attracted to Fran and every time he looked at her he felt that low, humming excitement in his blood.

A feeling he'd just have to keep in check.

He settled on taking her hand and shaking it, instead. 'Thanks. You have no idea how much I appreciate this.'

Time to let her hand go, now.

Now.

Because this was teetering on the very fine line between being a handshake and holding her hand. And he was aware of a tingling in his palm where her skin touched his.

This wasn't the time. And in the middle of his aunt's restaurant was definitely not the place. As it was, Marco had assumed that Fran was his girlfriend, and despite Gio's denial the family grapevine was probably already buzzing.

He knew he'd get a call from his mother tonight, asking him how come he'd taken his girlfriend to meet his Aunt Netti before meeting his mother. Not to mention texts from Bella, Jude and Marcie staking their claims as bridesmaids, demanding full details of their new sister-in-law-to-be, and offering dinner invitations so they could meet her and grill her for themselves: his family didn't seem to believe in taking things slowly.

Just as well he'd switched his mobile phone to 'discreet' mode. Pity he couldn't switch his family to 'discreet' in the same way.

'Appreciate what?' Marco asked, overhearing Gio's last comment.

Gio resisted the temptation to wring his cousin's neck, and let go of Fran's hand. 'Perfect timing, *cugino mio*. I'd like you to meet my new office manager.'

Marco stared at Fran, and then at Gio. 'Office manager?'

'Yup.'

'You're telling me you've just been conducting a job interview—over dinner?' Disbelief filled every note of his cousin's voice.

'It's the civilised way to do things.' Gio gave a wry smile. 'And as I have to eat anyway…'

'You decided to multi-task it.' Marco made exaggerated quote marks with his fingers around the word 'multi-task', and rolled his eyes. 'You're unbelievable. Fran, he did warn you he's a workaholic and his favourite phrase is "multi-task it", didn't he? Don't let him take advantage of you.'

'She's too efficient to do that,' Gio retorted.

Fran coughed. 'And I'm also quite capable of speaking for myself, thank you very much.'

'Indeed. And I apologise, Fran. My family's bad habit—' well, one of them, Gio thought '—is that we talk too much.' He spread his hands. 'Speaking of which…I'd better sneak into the kitchen to see my aunt. If you'll excuse me for a little while?' No way was he taking Fran with him to meet Netti. He needed to stop the family rumours before they spread: and he didn't want his new office manager frightened off by the idea of his family claiming her as his new girlfriend.

Which she wasn't.

Because he didn't have a girlfriend.

Didn't want a girlfriend.

Didn't *need* a girlfriend.

OK, so his life wasn't absolutely perfect at the moment. He couldn't shift this restlessness, this feeling that there was a black hole in the middle of his life. He had no idea what he was looking for or what might fill that black hole—but he was pretty sure that it wasn't settling down, getting married and having babies, whatever his family might think.

The second he walked into the kitchen, he was greeted with a hug and then a cuff round the ear by his aunt.

'I'm too old and—at nearly a foot taller than you—too big for that,' he said with a grin.

'That's what you'd like to think. I'm older and wiser and I know better. So where is she, then?' Annetta asked.

'Who?'

'This *bella ragazza* Marco's told me about. Francesca. This nice Italian girl.'

'Netti, *dolcezza*, you know I adore you. But you're jumping to conclusions.' He kissed her cheek. 'First of all, Fran's not Italian.'

'With a name like Francesca?' Annetta scoffed. 'Come off it.'

'She's not Italian,' Gio repeated. 'Secondly, she happens to be my new office manager. You lot have been nagging me for months and months and months to pace myself and take some time off—aren't you pleased that I'm finally taking your advice and hiring myself some help?'

But his aunt refused to be diverted. 'Marco says she's nice. She has a pretty smile. And that you don't look at her as if she's a colleague.'

'Yes, she's nice,' Gio agreed. 'But Marco's just become a dad and he's sleep-deprived. He's seeing things that aren't there. She's my *colleague*. And I'm not looking to settle down.'

'You're not even looking at going out with anyone, let alone settling down! And you need a social life as well as your work,' Annetta said, pursing her lips. 'You need someone to take you in hand. Why not this so-called "new office manager" of yours?'

'Because.' Gio knew better than to get drawn into this argument. He'd be here all night. 'Netti, *cara*, I should get back to Fran, before she decides I'm going to be a terrible boss and changes her mind. And Marco did say you'd made us crème brûlée with raspberries…'

'Don't think you're getting out of it that easily,' his aunt warned, but she smiled and handed him the two dessert dishes. 'Ring your mother tonight. You don't call her enough. And you work too hard.'

'*Sì, mia zia.* I know. That's the way I'm made. It's how Mazetti men are.'

She threw up her hands. 'You're impossible.'

He kissed her cheek. 'Thanks for the pudding.'

'My pleasure, *piccolo*.' She shooed him towards the door. 'Off you go, then. Back to the *bella ragazza*.'

Uh-oh. She clearly hadn't listened to a word he'd said. That, or she'd decided not to believe him. 'Please remember, Netti, Fran's my office manager, *not* my girlfriend. Whatever you, my mother or Nonna would like to think—or dream up between the three of you,' he said.

Annetta laughed. 'You can tell Nonna that yourself. You know she's coming over from Milan in about three weeks.'

'I'm not sure,' Gio said, 'whether that's a threat or a promise.' He laughed, and fled from the kitchen before his aunt could flick a wet tea-towel at him.

Gio placed the dish of crème brûlée in front of Fran. 'This will be the best you've ever tasted,' he told her.

It certainly looked good. 'How was your aunt?' she asked politely.

'Fine. I was told off for not taking you to meet her. But…' He shook his head. 'As one of four kids, you've got a better chance than most people of coping with the Mazettis. But you've only just agreed to be my office manager. I don't want them scaring you off before you've even started.'

'How would they do that?'

'The women are—how can I put this nicely?—bossy. I grew up in a house with four women, so I can just about hold my own with my mother and my sisters—and my aunt. But when they add Nonna to the mix…' He groaned. 'She's coming over from Milan in three weeks' time. So I'm going to have to go into hiding.'

'Your grandmother's really that scary?'

'No-o. Not exactly. She's very straightforward—she tends to tell things like they are. I don't think you'd have a problem with that. But…' he sighed '…as I said, she's got this thing about wanting me to settle down. Mum and Netti are her sidekicks, and they've got Marco on the team now—his wife had a little girl two weeks ago, and he's just besotted with his wife and daughter. He thinks I should do what he's done: find the perfect wife for me and have babies.'

He looked utterly horrified at the idea.

So was he the odd one out in his family, too? The one who didn't want to do what all the others had done?

She smiled wryly. 'I suppose that's the good thing about being from a family of academics. Nobody expects you to settle down until you're at least thirty. So I'm safe for the next four years or so.'

'Is that what you want?' Gio asked. 'To settle down and have babies?'

A family to belong to. Where she'd fit smack into the middle of things. Be the hub.

She suppressed the shiver of longing. 'Right now, I'm quite happy being single and fancy-free,' she said lightly.

'Hallelujah. Finally I've found someone female who's on my wavelength—who actually understands where I'm coming from. You're going to be on my side on this, right?' Gio raised his glass to her. 'To us. And we're going to make a brilliant team.'

The pudding was indeed the best Fran had ever tasted. The coffee was good, too. And when they'd settled the bill and left the pizzeria, she was shocked to realise how late it was—how long she'd been chatting to Gio at the restaurant.

A man she'd only just met.

And yet, weirdly, it felt as if she'd known him for years. She couldn't remember feeling so comfortable with someone so soon—ever.

'I'll see you home,' Gio said.

She shook her head. 'Thanks, but there's really no need. I can look after myself.'

'Remember, I was brought up the Italian way—it doesn't feel right just to abandon you at the door of my aunt's pizzeria and let you find your own way home. Let me at least walk you to the Tube station.' Clearly he sensed that she was about to refuse, because he added, 'Besides, we need to discuss when you're going to start tomorrow and which branch, so we might as well—'

'—multi-task it,' she finished.

His eyes crinkled at the corners. 'See. You can even read my mind.'

'Hardly. Marco did tell me it was your favourite phrase,' she reminded him with a smile. 'OK. As long as it's not taking you out of your way.'

'I live within walking distance of the station,' he said. 'And it's a warm, dry evening. The fresh air will do me good.'

By the time he'd walked her to Goodge Street station, they'd agreed to meet at the coffee shop on Charlotte Street at half past nine, and she'd checked the dress code—the baristas all wore black trousers or skirts and a white shirt, so she'd do the same. Gio insisted on waiting with her on the platform until she'd got on to the Tube, and then sketched a wave before striding off again.

When one door closes, another opens.

And how. She'd lost her dream job, stared failure in the face, then only a few hours later, she'd been offered something that might turn out to be even better. Something where she'd have free rein.

Gio was prepared to take a chance on her. So she'd take a chance on him. And she had a month to find out if she'd made the right choice.

The following morning, Gio had just finished signing for a delivery when Fran walked in.

He was used to seeing her on a Wednesday morning—but not this early, and only for the couple of minutes it took her to order her cappuccino and almond croissant. Seeing her now and knowing that she was going to be spending the day in his office, sitting at his desk, in his chair, felt…weird.

'Good morning,' she said.

Lord, she had the sweetest smile. A smile that did things to him. Things he hadn't expected. He tried to ignore the flutter at the base of his spine and strove for casualness. 'Hi.'

'Sorry I'm a bit early.'

'Well, you have to make a good impression on your first day,' he teased. He introduced her swiftly to the baristas. 'This is Fran. She's our new office manager. And, no, before you ask, it *doesn't* mean you can all go swanning off inter-railing like Kelly and let me cover your shifts.'

Sally clicked her fingers. 'Damn. And there I was, planning to spend the summer on a beach full of gorgeous Italian men.'

Gio laughed. 'That's easy. Just go to one of my family's back gardens on a Sunday afternoon.'

'A sandpit and a horde of boys under the age of seven isn't *quite* the same thing, Gio.'

'They're male, Italian and gorgeous, yes?'

She groaned. 'Yes.'

'And there's sand.'

'But no sea.'

'That's a minor detail. Plus, everyone has a freezer full of Nando's best ice cream. What more do you need?' he teased.

Sally rolled her eyes. 'Welcome to the madhouse, Fran.'

'Thanks. I think.' Fran smiled back.

'Let me show you round,' Gio said. He gave her a tour of the coffee shop, then showed her into the small staff kitchen, rest room and office at the back of the shop.

Judging by the papers piled in a haphazard mountain on the desk, filing clearly wasn't his thing—and he obviously knew it, because he looked slightly embarrassed. 'I do know where everything is. I'm just not that good at putting things away.'

'And I bet your computer's the same. All the files lumped under one directory.'

'I'm not quite that bad.' Gio's blue eyes softened. 'I've just been too busy lately to keep on top of the filing. I did tell you I needed someone to sort me out. I'll get you a coffee and then I'll talk you through the computer systems.'

He reappeared shortly after with two mugs of coffee.

'You need these.' She handed him an envelope. 'Details for your personnel records.'

He opened the envelope and looked through the files. 'CV, emergency contact details, NI number, bank details—great, thanks—hmm, no, don't need these.' He handed the references back to her without even a cursory scan of the text.

'Why not?'

'The new studio owners are probably going to feel guilty about pushing you out so they'll have written you a very glowing reference to make up for it. On the other hand, they're also too short-sighted to see what they've passed up—so I doubt if their views are worth the paper they're written on.'

He smiled to take the sting from his words. 'Besides, I told you yesterday, I'm a good judge of character. So even though one or two of my baristas came with less-than-glowing reports from previous employers, I went by my gut instinct and I was proved right. They came good.'

'One of your grandmother's sayings?' she guessed.

'If you see the best in people, they'll give you their best.' He nodded. 'Actually, there was one thing we didn't discuss yesterday. Money. You're working for Giovanni's, so you need a salary. What were you on at your last place?'

She told him.

He sighed. 'I can just about match that, but I'm afraid I can't raise it. You'd probably get a lot more from a financial services company or one of the big ad agencies.'

'But you,' she said, 'promised me free rein.'

He smiled. 'I trust you not to make changes just for the sake of it.' He talked her through the different systems on the computer, showing her how the information was coded for each of the four branches and how they fed into an overall system. 'Your username is "marsfran", and this is your password.' He scribbled her initials and a series of numbers on to a piece of paper.

'You sorted this out for me already?'

He shrugged. 'It didn't take long. Besides, I'd left some papers here that I needed last night.' He hadn't stayed particularly long. In peace and quiet with no interruptions, you could get a lot done in a couple of hours. Which was why he was usually in not long after dawn. Before the rush started.

'I'm beginning to see what your cousin means about you being a workaholic,' Fran said dryly.

'Don't tell me you're going over to their team. I need you on my side.' He smiled at her. 'Well, the best way to get used to new systems and what have you is to play with them. If you get stuck, just give me a yell. I'll leave you to it to book yourself on the food hygiene course—the place I normally use is in the address book under "food hygiene course"—and take a look through the systems.'

'And do your filing?' she asked, raising one eyebrow.

Gio pantomimed innocence. 'I didn't ask—but as you've just offered…'

She laughed. 'I'll see what I can do.'

'Give me a yell if you need anything or you get stuck. Otherwise, I'll bring you some coffee and an almond croissant.' He smiled at her. 'I haven't forgotten about the barista training, but the morning rush is probably *not* the best time to introduce you to the delights of the espresso machine and the milk frother. Maybe if there's an afternoon lull? Or just before I strip the machines down after we close?'

'You're the boss,' she said lightly. 'You tell me.'

'Later,' he promised, winked, and left her to it.

The day went surprisingly quickly. Fran sorted out the filing and worked through the different systems, making a list of questions for Gio as she went. He came in a couple of times, bearing a cup of coffee or a cool drink—and one time bringing her a list of what he needed ordering from the suppliers for delivery to each branch, the following morning—but for the most part she was on her own in Gio's office.

The wallpaper on his computer screen was a family photograph. His parents, she guessed, plus three younger women who had to be his sisters, and an older woman who was probably his Italian grandmother. Gio was standing right in the middle of them, with a huge smile on his face. Whatever his protests about not wanting to settle down, he clearly loved his family. And he'd given up his dreams for them. He was a man who wasn't afraid to make sacrifices. Who'd give everything for those he loved.

At the end of their shifts, Sally and Ian put their heads round the door to say goodbye. Fran felt a weird glow spread through her. Her first day, and already she was accepted as part of the team. Just as she'd been at the voiceover studio. Maybe this was going to work out just fine.

She logged off the computer, and then Gio walked in. 'Wow. Are you Mary Poppins in disguise? You know, waving a magic wand and everything tidies itself up and marches in the right order into the right file in the right drawer?'

She laughed. 'All you needed was a system. And it wasn't actually that bad. There was a kind of order to the chaos.'

He perched himself on the edge of the desk. 'The office looks better than it has in years. I normally don't let Dad anywhere near here—in his day he kept things absolutely spotless, and seeing it in a mess would be an excuse for him to get back in here and start working stupid hours again.'

Considering the hours Gio worked… 'Like father, like son?'

'But I'm twenty-eight, not fifty-eight. And I haven't had a heart attack.' Gio made a face. 'I just want him to take things easy and not worry.' He waved a dismissive hand. 'But we need to sort out this barista training. We said we'd do it now, after closing, but you were in early this morning. So tomorrow I don't want to see you until eleven, OK?'

She blinked. 'But…'

'No buts.' He held up one hand to forestall any protest. 'Your hours are Monday to Friday, nine to five with an hour for lunch. If you work more than that, you take time in lieu or you fill out an overtime form. I don't expect you to work the same hours I do.'

Reminding her—in a nice way—that he was the boss and she was the employee. And she'd better keep that in mind. This was an employer–employee relationship, nothing else.

'So how's your first day been?' he asked.

'Good,' she said. 'I like Ian and Sally. And the people in the other branches were fine when they spoke to me.'

'That's a point,' Gio said. 'I need to take you to the other cafés so you can meet the staff there, too. Maybe tomorrow afternoon, or Friday morning.'

'So this is where you're based, most of the time?' she asked.

'Most of the time,' Gio agreed. 'Though I try to do a shift in each of the outlets, once a week. It gives the team a chance to talk to me about any problems that need fixing or any suggestions they have for improvements or innovations—and it gives me a chance to make sure everything's ticking over as it should be and there aren't any problems that need sorting before they get unmanageable. But this was the first branch Dad opened, so the office space is here.' He spread his hands. 'Ready to learn what it takes to be a barista?'

'Sure.'

He talked her through how to use the machines and the steps needed to make an espresso. And then it was her turn. Despite taking notes, she'd forgotten one or two points—but Gio was standing behind her, ready to show her what to do. Not close enough to touch, but she was aware of how near his body was to hers. She could almost feel the heat of his body. And when his left arm reached out to the grinder, his bare skin brushed against hers, for just the tiniest fraction of a second, but it felt as if electricity zinged through every nerve-end.

Mentally, she went through the steps. Grind, dose,

tamp—she tapped the filter gently and watched the contents level, then pressed it down as he'd shown her—fit the filter into the machine, flick the switch and let it pour... She counted for twenty seconds in her head, then turned the tap off.

'Looks good,' Gio said, looking over her shoulder. His breath fanned her ear, and she felt a shiver of anticipation run down her back.

Stop it, she warned herself. He's your *boss*.

So why couldn't she stop thinking about him on a personal level? Why couldn't she stop wondering how his mouth would feel against the curve of her neck? Why couldn't she stop thinking how easy it would be to take one tiny step backwards so that her body was in close contact with his, and his arms would curve round her waist, holding her to him...?

'Stir it,' Gio said softly.

She did, half-expecting the coffee to stay black with just a tiny bit of foam clinging to the edges of the cup, but the crema reformed. 'Wow.'

'Now watch and wait.'

She watched as the thousands of tiny, tiny bubbles began to disperse. And as the caramel-coloured foam started to dissolve, so her awareness of Gio's nearness grew. To the point where she was having a seriously hard time keeping her cool. It wasn't that he was invading her personal space—it was that she *wanted* him to.

Which was a seriously bad idea.

He was her new boss.

Which meant hands off.

She'd seen what happened with office romances. The way the working relationship turned so awkward that one of them had to leave—and until that happened everyone was walking on eggshells. Messy. Complicated. Not something she wanted to happen here.

Gio glanced at his watch when the crema had almost vanished. 'Just over a minute. Good. OK, you can do a second one. This time it's for tasting.'

When he'd tasted it, he said, 'Good. Just the right amount of smoothness. Try it.' He held the mug to her lips.

Her mouth was right where his had just touched. Oh, lord. This was getting ridiculous. She'd spent years working without ever falling for a colleague or a client. So why was she reacting this way to Gio? Besides, he probably taught all his baristas this way, standing close to them so he could reach out and guide them where necessary.

This wasn't personal.

It just felt like it.

'Good?' he asked.

'Good.' Her voice sounded very slightly squeaky; she really hoped he hadn't noticed.

'Excellent. Thus endeth your first lesson. We'll do lattes tomorrow.' He smiled at her. 'See you tomorrow. I'm over in Holborn first thing, but you can buzz through to me if you need anything. And I'll take you round the other branches tomorrow afternoon.'

Class most definitely dismissed, Fran thought, even though he'd done it in the most charming way. 'Do you want me to stay and help clean the machines?'

Ouch. That sounded like an attempt to be the teacher's pet.

'No, that's fine. I've kept you here long enough. And, Fran?'

'Yes?'

He smiled at her. 'Thanks. I appreciate what you've done today.'

'No worries. See you later.' She replaced her notebook in

a tray in the office, collected her handbag from the bottom drawer, and lifted her hand in a casual wave goodbye as she left the coffee shop.

Putting distance between herself and Gio Mazetti was a good idea, she thought. And hopefully by the time she saw him again, she'd have it fixed in her head that they were colleagues only—and staying that way.

CHAPTER FOUR

THE next morning, Fran felt awkward going in to work so late—especially as Gio wasn't there—but Sally and Ian, the baristas, greeted her cheerfully enough. Sally had a mug of coffee ready for her just the way she liked it before she'd even reached the office. Gio had emailed her from Holborn, asking if she'd get some information for him about specific aspects of franchising, so she spent the rest of the morning researching, and the afternoon setting up a spreadsheet that would do automated graphs showing the figures for each coffee shop.

She knew the second that Gio walked into the coffee shop; even though she couldn't see him from the office, she was aware of his presence. Something that made the air tingle.

So much for her pep talk, the previous evening, spent in front of the bathroom mirror, repeating over and over again that Gio Mazetti was her boss and way off limits. It wasn't as if she'd been bothered before about being single or on the shelf. Why should things be different now?

'Hi.' He walked into the office and leaned against the edge of her desk. 'Good day so far?'

'Yes. You?'

'Pretty good. I've got a new supplier coming to see us

tomorrow morning—someone who does organic cakes. So we'll need to do a taste test and, if we like it, work out what we're going to have to charge to keep the same profit margin and where the break-even points are. She left me the price list.' He handed her a folder. 'Tomorrow, can you sort me out some suggested figures for a trial?'

'No problem.' She flicked into her tasklist and typed rapidly.

'Thanks. Are you still OK for another half-hour lesson on baristaing, tonight?' he asked.

So he was still going to teach her, not get Sally or one of the others to take over? A warm glow spread through her. 'Sure.' She tried for a light tone. 'This is where I get to do the milk, yes?'

'Yep. Have you got the orders from Holborn and the others?'

'Yes, and I was just about to ring the supplier,' she said with a smile.

He smacked his palm against his forehead. 'Sorry, sorry. I'm teaching you to suck eggs.'

'No. But you've been doing this for years. It must be hard to give up control.'

'A bit,' he admitted. 'You've got your course booked?'

'I was going to ask you about that. I can go on Tuesday or Thursday next week. Which one would fit in best with whatever you've got planned?'

'Either. And I'm not expecting to see you in here before or after, whichever day it is,' he said firmly. 'Straight to college from home—and straight back home from college, OK?'

'Yes, boss.' She saluted him. 'Though I assume you'd like me to let you know if I pass?'

'When,' he corrected. 'Of course you'll pass.'

She'd already told him she wasn't good when it came to exams, so it felt good that he had that much confidence in her.

'When you've phoned the order through, come out the front and I'll take you on a whistle-stop tour of the Giovanni's empire.' He smiled at her, and left her to it.

When she emerged from the office, a few minutes later, she was surprised when Gio led her to a car.

'Wouldn't it be easier to go by Tube?'

'With all those line changes? Even Holborn, all of two stops away, means a line change. If you add in Islington and Docklands…' He grimaced. 'It's a lot less hassle to do it this way.'

The car wasn't what she'd expected, either. It must have shown on her face, because he said with a grin, 'Just what were you expecting me to drive, Fran?'

Well, he'd asked—she might as well be honest. 'A Harley. Or maybe a two-seater.'

He laughed. 'First off, if I had a motorbike, it'd be a Ducati—I'd always pick an Italian make first. But if you've ever tried having a guitar case as your pillion passenger…' For a second, his face clouded. And then he looked wistful. 'A two-seater… Yeah.'

'A Ferrari?' It was the only Italian sports car she could think of.

'Along with taking out a second mortgage to pay for the insurance? No.' He shook his head. 'My first car was a two-seater—an Alfa. I bought her the day after I passed my driving test. Dad went bananas that I'd spent so much money on an old car with a soft top that always leaked, but she was the love of my life. The day the mechanic told me there was no way he'd be able to fix her up to pass the MOT and I'd have to scrap her…' He sighed. 'I rang every car museum I could think of to see if I could donate her somewhere she'd get a kind retirement.'

'And you found somewhere?'

'No.' He opened the passenger door of the estate car for her. 'Dad had to take her to the scrap dealer's for me. I couldn't face it.'

Oh, bless. On impulse, she gave him a hug.

And then wished she hadn't when every single nerve-end started tingling.

And tingled a bit more when Gio's arms came round her to return the hug. 'Thank you,' he said. 'For not laughing at me.'

'Course I wouldn't laugh at you,' she said, hoping her voice didn't sound as rough and croaky to him as it did to her, and she ducked into the car.

She just about managed to recover her composure by the time he slid into the driving seat. 'So how come you've got an estate car now?' It was the complete opposite of a little two-seater sports car.

'Because Marco got really fed up with me borrowing his to do the cash-and-carry run, and nagged me into getting my own. Although my suppliers deliver nowadays, I haven't got round to changing the car to something a bit smaller and easier to park.' He slanted her a look. 'Don't tell me you drive a two-seater?'

'I don't have a car.' She shrugged. 'Don't really need one, for London.'

'What about when you go home to see your family?'

'Train and taxi.'

'So on a bright spring day, you never get up and decide to go to the seaside?'

'No. But if I wanted to, there's a reasonable train service from London to Brighton.' She glanced at him. 'Is that what you do on your days off? Go to the seaside?'

He gave her a non-committal murmur; given what she'd

already heard his family say to him, she interpreted that as meaning that he almost never took time off.

As he turned on the ignition, the car was flooded with indie rock. Very loud indie rock.

'Whoops.' He turned the stereo off. 'Sorry. One of my worst habits. Volume.'

She'd half-expected him to listen to classical guitar music. Or maybe that was too painful—a reminder of what he'd lost. 'No worries,' she said. 'And I don't mind if you'd rather have music on when you're driving.'

'Just not at that volume, hmm?' he asked wryly, but switched the stereo on again, this time lowering the volume to something much more bearable.

The journey was quick, and he parked in a side street near the Holborn branch. The feel of the place was very similar to the Charlotte Street café, but Fran was intrigued to see that it had its own identity. Different art on the walls, for starters. But the staff were just as warm and friendly as they were at Charlotte Street, and Amy—the head barista—seemed pleased to put a face to the voice from the previous day.

Islington was next, and then Docklands; again, Fran noticed that there wasn't a uniform style to the cafés. 'If you're going to franchise the business,' she said to Gio on their way back to Charlotte Street, 'shouldn't the cafés all look the same?'

'Yes and no,' Gio said. 'I suppose there needs to be some kind of corporate identity. A logo or what have you. But I don't want them to be identikit. I want each café to fit in with its surroundings and suit the clientele in the area. Which means they're different.' He lifted one shoulder. 'I want to keep it *personal*. And sell bakery goods produced locally, to local recipes where possible—so if we expand further afield that would mean Banbury cakes in Oxfordshire, parkin in Yorkshire, Bakewell pudding in Derbyshire and that sort of thing. We'll sell the best coffee and the best regional goodies.' He frowned. 'So I suppose that's an argument against franchising.'

'But if you go the other route and open more branches, you're not going to have time to do a shift in every one, every single week, to get feedback from your customers and staff. Especially if some of them are outside London,' she pointed out. 'With four, you can do it. With five, it's going to be a struggle. With ten—no chance.'

He sighed. 'I'm doing the wrong thing. I shouldn't be looking at franchising—I should be inventing a time machine, so I can make the time to visit all the branches myself.'

'What was it your Italian grandmother says about trusting people?' she asked gently. 'If you expand, Gio, you're going to have to learn to delegate. Trust your managers to do what you do and to give you the feedback. You don't have to do it all yourself.'

'I'm trying to delegate. I'm trusting you to sort the admin side.' He coughed. 'Well. Apart from sitting on your case, earlier.' He parked in a little square just off Charlotte Street.

'Where are we?' Fran asked.

'My parking space, near my flat.' He smiled. 'Told you I lived near the café. It's a ten-minute stroll from my flat to work, tops, which makes life very easy.' He glanced at his watch. 'Are you sure you're still OK for a lesson in lattes?'

'Sure.' Which was when Fran realised that she'd actually been looking forward to it. All day. And even though she'd spent most of the afternoon with Gio, most of the time they'd been with other people.

This would be just the two of them.

Alone.

Strange how that thought made her heart beat a little bit faster.

They arrived back at the Charlotte Street branch just before closing. Once Sally and Ian had left, Gio bolted the door and switched off most of the lights. Then he smiled at Fran. 'Ready?'

'Yup.' She fished her notebook out of her handbag.

'OK. Rule one of milk—it has to be fresh and cold, or it won't froth. It's the proteins in milk that make the foam. And the way we do it is with a steam wand—your goal is to get the froth hole in the wand at the same level as the surface of the milk, so you'll get nice small bubbles throughout the milk instead of huge bubbles at the top.'

'Why do you need small bubbles?'

He smiled. 'I'll show you.' He talked her through how to use the steam nozzle on the machine, starting with half a pitcher of cold milk and gradually working it up so it became warm and frothy. 'This is perfect for a latte. And latte art.'

'Latte art?' Fran asked, mystified.

'It's how you pour the milk in such a way that you make a pretty pattern on the top—the crema comes through in the design. You make a rosetta, swirling the leaves out, and you finish with the stem to pull it all together.' He tapped the jug against the table; then, with what looked like a tiny wobble of the wrist, he swirled the milk on and a flower suddenly appeared in the middle of the foam.

'That's pretty,' she said. 'You make it look very easy— would I be right in saying it's quite difficult?'

'It's advanced baristaing—an extra,' he admitted. 'It's what the coffee tastes like that counts most, not what it looks like. If you've made vile coffee, it doesn't matter how pretty it is— the customer won't want to come back. And then again, some people don't even notice; they add sugar and stir, and your rosetta's gone so you might just as well not have bothered. But it sometimes makes the customer's day when they see a heart or an apple or a flower or a rosetta on the top of their coffee.'

'Latte art.' He had to be teasing her.

He spread his hands. 'If you don't believe me, look on the internet. There are pages and pages of photos of latte art.'

She still wasn't sure if he was teasing her or not. But she liked the way his eyes crinkled at the corners when he smiled, the way his eyes glittered.

'OK. Remember how to make an espresso?' he asked. 'Normally, you'd froth the milk at the same time, but as it's your first time we'll do the milk second.'

'Grind, dose, tamp, fit the filter and pour,' she said.

He nodded, looking pleased. 'Go for it.'

To her relief, the espresso came out well.

'Now to steam and froth the milk.' He guided her through the process, just as he had when he'd taught her to make an espresso. When he moved the steam nozzle for her with a clean cloth, his arm brushed against hers, the brief touch of his skin making her temperature sizzle.

This was crazy. She was known for being level-headed at work, good in a crisis. Reliable, calm and efficient. So why did she feel right now as if fireworks were going off inside her head? Why did she want to leave the coffee where it was, forget the milk, twist round in Gio's arms and brush her mouth against his?

Focus, she reminded herself.

'When you turn the pressure down, can you hear the change in the sound of the steam tap?' he asked.

Low and husky—just like Gio's voice. 'Yes.'

'Good. Bring the nozzle up a tiny bit—remember, we're trying to keep the steam coming out almost at the surface of the milk—and let it froth.' He was standing behind her, one arm either side of her, his hands resting on hers to help her keep the jug in the right place. 'When the jug feels hot to the touch, the milk's ready.'

She certainly felt hot right now. Hot and very bothered. Because his hands were strong and capable, and she could smell his clean personal scent, mixed with a citrussy tang which she assumed was shower gel or shampoo. A scent that she found incredibly arousing; she just hoped that Gio couldn't see the way her nipples had tightened under her shirt.

'You're picky.'

'Details are important,' he said. 'My customers expect the best. And I wouldn't produce anything less.'

'And yet your office is untidy. I thought perfectionists were that way about everything,' she said.

He laughed, the smile-lines around his mouth deepening. 'I'm a perfectionist about *some* things.'

For a brief moment—before she managed to suppress it—the idea flickered through her brain. What else would Gio be a perfectionist about? Kissing? Making lo—

They were making *coffee*, she reminded herself. Flirting and what have you was *not* on the agenda.

'What we're looking for is texture. Tiny microbubbles that make the foam and the milk one—so it settles out in the cup, not the jug. It's got a sheen like quicksilver,' Gio told her. 'We're looking for pure silk.'

Silk. Like his skin. Like his voice.

Oh, lord. She was going to drop the wretched jug in a minute.

'OK. This'll do nicely. Now, what I showed you was free-pouring—but that's quite time-sensitive, and you need to build up to that. For now, we'll spoon.'

Her mouth went dry at the thought. 'Spoon.'

'Spoon the froth from the jug.'

Oh-h-h. The picture that had flickered into her mind at the word 'spoon' had nothing to do with coffee or cutlery. She was really, really going to have to watch what she said.

'Let the jug rest for a little while, so the foam and milk separate out a bit. Then you scoop the foam out of the jug and on to the surface of the espresso. A little bit for a latte.'

She did as he instructed.

Spoon. She couldn't get that picture out of her head.

The picture of Gio's body wrapped round hers.

Naked.

'Then you hold the froth back in the jug with the spoon and pour the milk on to the coffee. It should go through the foam and lift it up, and mix with the coffee.'

She'd barely heard a word he was saying. Tonight, she'd have to go and research it on the internet, so she could make some notes—and maybe try again tomorrow when it was quiet and preferably when Gio was on a break.

'Like so.' He smiled at her. 'The perfect latte. Try.'

'It doesn't look as pretty as yours.'

'You can cheat a bit—some people spoon a tiny bit of foam on top of the crema and make it into a swirl with the back of a spoon. Or you can use a needle to make patterns, like starbursts or the kind of feathering a pastry chef does with icing,' he said. 'Or cheat even more and use chocolate syrup and a knife. But free-pouring's the proper art.'

'And it takes weeks to learn, you say?'

His eyes lit up. 'Sounds as if you're up for a challenge. I'll teach you how to do it. And if you can do it by the end of your trial period, I'll take you to Fortnum's and buy you the biggest box of chocolates of your choice.'

'And if I can't?'

'Then *you* buy *me* the chocolates.' He moistened his lower lip in a way that made her heart beat just that little bit faster. 'And I should warn you that I'm greedy.'

Fran had a nasty feeling that she could be greedy, too.

And it took every single bit of her self-control to stop her sliding her arms round his neck and jamming her mouth over his.

CHAPTER FIVE

'LATTE art,' Fran said, rolling her eyes, when Gio set the cup down on her desk the following morning. On the top was a heart—with concentric rings round it. 'You're showing off, aren't you?'

He pantomimed surprise. 'You mean, you noticed?'

'Just a tad.' She'd noticed something else, too—the guitar case tucked away in the corner of the office. But she hadn't brought it up in discussion with him. After what he'd told her about the way his music studies had crashed and burned, she had a feeling that he was sensitive about it. She wasn't going to push him to talk about it unless he was ready. 'Thank you for the coffee. Now, if you want me to sort out these figures for you, go away and leave me in peace.'

'Your wish is my command.' He gave her a deep bow, followed by one of the knee-buckling smiles. 'I'll come and get you when the cake lady's here.'

'Cheers.' She smiled back, then got to work with the spreadsheet.

Gio leaned through the office doorway at the perfect moment: just when Fran had finished the stats. She printed them off and waved them at him.

'I'll look at them afterwards,' Gio promised. 'But come and taste the goodies first.'

He introduced Fran to Ingrid, the baker, who talked them through the samples she'd brought. 'And I'm leaving before you all start trying them,' she said. 'There's nothing worse than doing a taste-test and not being able to give an honest opinion because you don't want to hurt someone's feelings. Give me a call, Gio, when you're ready. Nice to meet you, Fran, Sally and Ian.' She shook their hands, smiled and left.

'Perfect timing,' Sally said. 'The morning rush is over, the lunchtime one won't start for another twenty minutes—and we have chocolate cake. Oh, *yessss*. Those brownies are mine, all mine.'

Gio produced a knife and cut both the brownies into two. 'No, they're not. We're splitting them all four ways. Except for the Amaretti, which are all mine.'

'In your *dreams*,' Fran said, scooping one of them and taking a nibble. 'Oh, wow. Intense.'

'Intense, good or intense, bad?' Gio asked.

'Definitely bad,' she fibbed. 'Let me save you the trouble of eat—' She didn't get to finish the sentence, because Gio simply leaned over and took a bite from the Amaretti she was holding.

The feel of his mouth against her fingers sent a shiver of pure desire down her spine. Bad. Very bad. This was meant to be a tasting session. And they were tasting food, not each other. They were in the middle of his coffee shop, for goodness' sake! Sally and Ian were there, and a customer could walk in at any moment.

This was even worse than their coffee-making lessons. Because this time it wasn't just the two of them. She really, *really* had to get a grip.

'Mmm. Perfect,' he said huskily.

He was talking about the biscuit. Not about her skin, she reminded herself sharply.

'These flapjacks are good, too,' Ian said.

'*Brownies*. Oh-h-h. I need more brownies,' Sally said, clutching her heart dramatically. 'Save me. Give me brownies.'

'Too late, Sal. You'll have to make do with carrot cake.' Gio handed her a piece wrapped in a paper napkin.

Lord, he had a beautiful mouth. Fran knew she should just stop watching him eat. The last thing she wanted was for her new boss to think she had the hots for him. And she could definitely do without Sally and Ian noticing the state she was in and teasing her about it.

When the samples had been reduced to crumbs, they looked at each other. 'Well?' Gio said.

'They're good,' Ian said. 'Better than our current range.'

'And this is Fitzrovia,' Sally said. 'Organic food is definitely on the up in this area.'

Gio nodded. 'Our coffee's ethically farmed, so organic cakes and pastries fit with the ethos of Giovanni's. Especially as these have no packaging. Eco-friendly and caring—that's good. Fran?'

'I checked out the local competition on the net. If we sell organic, that gives us differentiation from the others,' she said. 'Is our coffee organic?'

'No, but you can talk to the supplier and see what they can offer us, so it's a possible option—in the same way that we can do decaf on request,' Gio said. 'Do the figures stack up?'

She nodded. 'We'll need to put the prices up a little bit, because the wholesale price is higher than the non-organic cakes. But, as Sally said, our customers are the sort who put ethics above economics.'

Gio smiled. 'Good. We'll trial fifty-fifty to start with, see how it goes. Starting on Monday. Give it a month, see how it's affecting sales. If they're the same, we'll make a whole-sale switch.'

'I think,' Sally said, 'you should ring Ingrid and say we're not sure about the brownies—we need some more for testing. A lot more. A whole trayful—no, make that a whole ovenful.'

Gio ruffled her hair. 'Yeah, yeah, Sal. She'll *really* believe that. Thanks, team. Fran, I need to go over to Docklands. Can you draft me a letter to Ingrid about the trial?'

'Sure.'

'Thanks. See you later.'

She loved the way he trusted her enough to get her to draft the letter, instead of dictating it to her over the phone when he got to Docklands. Although she'd adored her job at the voiceover studio, this job was turning out to be a real buzz, too. He'd listened to what she had to say about franchising, too. What she thought *counted*.

Though it wasn't just that, she thought as she headed back to the office. It was working with Gio that gave her the buzz. Because there was definite chemistry there—the way he'd eaten that Amaretti from her fingers…

But she needed to keep her feet on the ground. It was stupid even to contemplate any sort of relationship other than a working one with Gio. She already knew he didn't do rela-tionships and he was at a place in his life where he didn't really know what he wanted. Yes, he flirted with her and teased her, but he did that with just about everyone—so she'd better not start getting any ideas.

She drafted the letter for Gio's approval and was just about to ring through the order to the supplier when she was aware that someone had walked into the office. She looked up, and recognised the woman from the photo on the computer.

'Hello. You're Gio's mum, aren't you?'

Mrs Mazetti looked a bit thrown. 'How did you know?'

'Apart from the fact that he has your eyes, you mean?' Fran smiled, and flicked through the computer screens to show her the wallpaper. 'This is how I know.'

'Oh!' She looked pleased. 'I didn't know he had a photo here.'

'Do have a seat, Mrs Mazetti. Can I get you a coffee and a pastry or something?'

'No, but thank you for offering. Is Gio around?'

Fran shook her head. 'Sorry, he's at the Docklands branch this afternoon—do you want me to ring through to him and get him to come back?'

'No, no, it's fine.' Mrs Mazetti flapped a dismissive hand. 'I know I shouldn't really bother him when he's working. He hates being disturbed when he's busy.'

'Is it anything I can help with? I'm Fran, his office manager, by the way.'

'Angela Mazetti.' She took Fran's outstretched hand and shook it. 'I thought you might be Francesca.'

It was Fran's turn to be thrown. 'Why? Has he said something about me?'

Angela rolled her eyes. 'Of course not. I'm his mother. Giovanni never tells me *anything*.'

'Ah. Marco was your mole?' Fran guessed.

Angela laughed. 'Oh, dear. Was it that obvious?'

Fran laughed back. 'Gio says you're all ganging up on him and trying to get him to settle down, Mrs Mazetti.'

'Call me Angela,' the elder woman said. She sighed. 'We don't gang up on him really. We just worry about him. When you have a son of your own, you'll know exactly what I mean.'

Having a child wasn't on her list of immediate plans, Fran thought, but she tried her best to look sympathetic.

'So are you settling in OK?' Angela asked.

Fran nodded. 'Everyone's been really nice. And Gio's lovely to work with.'

'Good.' Angela gave her a speculative look. 'So you're just colleagues.'

'Yes. And he's an excellent boss. He expects a lot from his staff, but he's fair and he's honest—so everyone's happy to make the extra effort.'

'Hmm.' Angela stood up again. 'Well, I can see you're busy, so I won't keep you. It was nice to meet you, Fran.'

'Shall I tell Gio you dropped in?' Fran asked.

Angela raised an eyebrow. 'I could say that I was just passing...but he'd never believe that.' She gave Fran a rueful smile. 'And, from the look on your face, neither do you.'

'Well, of course you'd want to check me out. Make sure I'm not some kind of bombshell man-eater who isn't going to treat your son properly—or some kind of incompetent airhead who's going to cause him extra work to sort out the mess she's made so he'll be under even more stress.'

Angela laughed. 'Consider me suitably reassured. Welcome to Giovanni's, Fran. And if you're ever at a loose end on a Sunday, you're always welcome to come to lunch at our place. Don't ever feel you're intruding, because we normally have a houseful and there's always room for one more.'

'That's very kind of you.' The sheer warmth of the invitation made Fran's throat feel tight. But if she burst into tears she'd have to explain, and she didn't want Gio's mum to

think she was a flake. 'Thank you.' Please, please don't let
Angela Mazetti hear the wobble in her voice.

'*Ciao,*' Angela said, the corners of her eyes crinkling, and
left the office.

Fran was too busy for the rest of the afternoon to notice the
time but, exactly as the previous day, she was aware of the
precise moment that Gio returned: just about at closing time.
She finished what she was doing and saved the file, then
walked into the coffee shop. 'Hi.'

Gio turned to face her. 'Hi. Had a good afternoon?'

'Fine, thanks. I've done the letters for you, a bit of research
on that project you asked about, and all the orders are sorted
for tomorrow and Monday.'

'Brilliant. It's so good to know I don't have to stop what I'm
doing and sort it all out myself. And having this extra time…
You know, maybe my family's right and I do work too hard.'

Did that mean he wanted to skip the barista training this
evening? The sudden swoop of disappointment in her
stomach made Fran realise just how much she'd been
looking forward to it.

But then he asked, 'Do you still have time to stay and learn
about cappuccinos?'

Pleasure fizzed through her—a feeling she tried to damp
down, because she knew it wasn't just the fact she was
learning something new. It was because she'd be close to
Gio. 'Sure,' she said, aiming for insouciance.

Gio was cross with himself for feeling so pleased that she was
staying late again. And crosser still when he realised it was
more than just pleasure at a new employee showing commitment to the café chain.

The real reason it made him happy was because he was going to be close to Fran.

When she'd hugged him yesterday, he hadn't been able to stop himself hugging her back. And it had taken all his strength of will to let her go again.

This was bad. Really bad. Because now was just about the worst possible time to start a relationship, when he was thinking of taking the business up another gear and he had no free time. And Francesca Marsden was just about the worst possible person he could think of to have a relationship with, because she was his new office manager and he was going to need her help in the business. He couldn't afford to lose someone who'd already shown initiative and drive and an ability to second-guess him.

He locked up, then motioned her towards the coffee machines. 'Same as yesterday with the milk and the espresso, but this time you're making cappuccino. That's a third coffee, a third milk and a third froth. You'll need to rock the jug a bit as you pour—or you can spoon the froth on top if you find it easier.'

He watched her as she worked. When she was concentrating, he noticed, she caught the tip of her tongue between her teeth. And it made him want to lean forward and touch the tip of his tongue to hers. Kiss her. Mould her body against his. Feel the weight of her breasts as he cupped them.

He swallowed hard, just as she looked up and slid the cup in front of him. 'Is this OK?'

'Looks good.' He tasted it. 'You need a touch less milk and a touch more froth, but for a first attempt it's excellent.'

'Thank you.'

'When you've done your food hygiene course, you can practise on some customers. In the quiet spots of the day, that is; I wouldn't expect you to handle the morning, lunchtime or mid-afternoon rush, first off.' He smiled at her. 'And now I ought to let you go home.' He didn't want her to go—but on the other hand, it was probably better for his rapidly un-ravelling self-control that she did. 'Your family's going to be beating my door down and yelling at me for making you work too hard.'

'I doubt it. They know I'm a big girl and I can look after myself.'

She'd clearly aimed for a flippant note, but he could hear the underlying hurt. What was wrong? He fished in the tub on the counter, drew out a chocolate dipper and handed it to her. 'Spill the beans.'

'I don't know what you mean.'

'Yes, you do. You're the eldest of four, but you've hardly mentioned a word about your family. Whereas mine are always around—if not in person, then on the phone or texting or emailing.' She'd met more than one of them, too. 'Sally said my mum dropped by this afternoon. Gave you the third degree, did she?'

'She was lovely.'

'Yeah. She's bossy and she's interfering and she drives me absolutely bananas,' he said with a grin, 'but I still wouldn't change her for anything. I *knew* she'd come and check you out. I bet she'd been skulking in the street, wearing dark glasses and hiding behind bay trees in big pots, until she saw me leave and knew the coast was clear to come and vet you.'

Fran laughed, but he could still see the sadness in her eyes. 'Tell me about your family,' he said softly.

She took a deep breath. 'I'm adopted. My parents didn't think they could have children. So they adopted me…and then the twins came along. And then Suzy.'

He reached out slid his hand over hers. Squeezed it. 'Hey.

There's nothing wrong with being adopted. It just proves your parents really wanted you to live with them. They chose you.'

She swallowed hard. 'That's what they said, when they told me the truth about my parentage. That I'm special because they chose me.'

'And then being able to have more children was a bonus for them. An unexpected bonus.'

'Maybe. But I'm not like Suzy or Dominic or Ted. I…' She struggled to pull her hand away. 'Oh, just ignore me. I'm being wet.'

'No.' He refused to let her hand go. 'Have you told your parents how you feel?'

She shook her head. 'I don't want to hurt them or make them feel I don't appreciate what they've done for me over all the years. But I know I'm a disappointment to them. The others were all good at sport and exams, and I'm not.'

'But look at what you *are* good at,' Gio said. 'You've got tons of common sense—something a lot of highly academic people don't have. You're good with people. And you're scarily organised. I'm willing to bet you anything you choose that they don't see you as a disappointment.' He paused. 'Something else Nonna says. You never treat your children the same, because they're all different. But you treat them equally. And you love them the same amount—just for different things.'

She gave him a smile that didn't quite reach her eyes. 'Maybe.'

'Definitely.' How on earth could Fran not fit in to her family? She'd been here less than a week and already she was part of the team. He'd noticed a couple of times this afternoon that the Docklands team had been halfway to dialling Fran to ask for help sorting out a problem before remembering that he was there on the spot.

But maybe being adopted gave you a different perspective. Fran's birth parents had given her away, so no doubt there was a part of her that would always worry her new family wouldn't want her, either. That there was something about her that made her unlovable.

'Have you ever tried finding your birth parents?' he asked quietly.

She shook her head. 'I've never wanted to. I'm sure they had good reasons at the time for not keeping me.'

And if she managed to trace them and they didn't want to know her, Gio knew that a second rejection would shatter her trust in people completely.

Right now, Fran needed security—something Gio knew he couldn't give her in a relationship, given that he didn't know what he wanted from life right now. But he could definitely make her feel part of Giovanni's.

'It's good that you're not judging them too harshly. Not bitter about it.'

'There's no point. Being bitter isn't going to change anything or make things better.' She shrugged. 'Besides, Mum and Dad gave me a stable home.'

She hadn't mentioned love, Gio noticed, something he'd always taken for granted in a large and noisy family where you got hugged and kissed every day and told how special you were. And even though the demonstrativeness had been excruciatingly embarrassing during his teens—especially when his parents insisted on showing all his baby photos to any girl he brought home—he'd always known he fitted in, that he was part of the family.

'Your family's proud of you,' he said softly. 'Maybe they're not good at telling you—maybe they're English and reserved instead of Italian and over-demonstrative like my lot. But my guess is they're proud of you. And they're going to get even prouder when Giovanni's expands and your parents realise that their daughter is the number two in the company.' He squeezed her hand again, and this time let it go. 'Want my advice? Go home, ring them and tell them you love them.'

'I might just do that.'

'No "mights". Do it. It'll make you feel better.' He smiled at her. 'Go home. I'm not going to make you stay really late on a Friday night.' Even though what he wanted to do with her would take the rest of the weekend, let alone the night. Because he was going to be sensible about this. 'I'll see you on Monday, OK?'

'Sure. Have a nice weekend.'

He laughed. 'You'll never know how glad I am that you didn't say, "Giovanni Mazetti, don't you work *too* hard"…'

CHAPTER SIX

'MORNING, Fran. How was your weekend?' Gio asked as she walked into the coffee shop on the Monday morning.

'Fine, thanks. Yours?'

'Fine.'

She'd just sat down when he brought a latte in to her. This time, there was the shape of an apple floating on the crema. 'You're definitely showing off. Flowers, hearts, apples…'

'Just you wait. Tomorrow I'll do you an ammonite,' he said with a grin.

She scoffed, 'No *way* can you free-pour an ammonite.'

'I didn't actually say I'd free-pour it. I said I'd do you one.' He looked thoughtful. 'But as challenges go…that's a good one.' He leaned against her desk. 'Did you do what I suggested, on Friday?'

She nodded. 'Thanks for the advice.'

'Don't thank me—it's Nonna's wisdom, not mine. She says you can never tell people too often that you love them. And no doubt, as she's coming over from Milan soon, you'll get to thank her in person.' Gio sighed. 'I have this feeling she'll be "just passing" the café, like Mum was. And when she's finished grilling you, she'll start on me. Telling me that I work too hard, and I need to find myself some *bella ragazza* and settle down and produce a great-grandchild for her to spoil.' He rolled his eyes. 'I'm really hoping that she gets distracted by her newest great-granddaughter. Lorena's absolutely gorgeous.' He pulled his mobile phone from his pocket and flicked through the photographs. 'See?'

For someone who was so adamant that he didn't want babies, Fran thought, Gio had a very soppy look on his face. She'd bet he had a picture of every single child in his family on his mobile phone. Not that she was going to take him to task for being a fraud. 'She's lovely,' she said.

'Nonna will enjoy cuddling her. But then again, it'll probably make her worse. Once she gets started on this settling-down stuff...'

'You can always try distracting her with latte art,' Fran said, laughing and gesturing to her mug.

'I could even draw her a bat with a long nose, to make the point. But she'd only laugh and say I was trying to get her off her favourite subject. Like when is her youngest grandson going to settle down,' he said ruefully.

The week got better and better. Gio switched to etching pictures in her coffee, from the promised ammonite through to a lion with a shaggy mane and a spider in a web, making her laugh. Fran teased him back by making a rosetta in his latte with chocolate syrup and ignoring his demands to see a proper free-poured rosetta—she was still a long way from being ready for that. Though she'd been practising in secret, coached by Sally in return for a promise of half-share in the chocolates Gio had bet her.

Even the food hygiene course on the Thursday wasn't that bad; everything was practical, common sense, and the multiple-choice exam wasn't as scary as the exam papers she remembered from her schooldays. Thirty questions in forty-five minutes—and, as Gio said, she was organised and practical, and most of it was simple common sense. She just had to wait a fortnight for the results. A fortnight that just sped by so she actually forgot about the wait.

The post hadn't arrived before Fran left for work on the Thursday morning, but Fran came home to find a large envelope on the doormat. An envelope with the logo of the college on it.

Her results.

It had been nearly eight years since she'd taken an exam. And she'd been physically sick afterwards, knowing she'd done badly and furious with herself because the second she'd walked out of the exam room all the knowledge had come flooding back again and she could've answered all the questions after all.

And when she'd opened the envelope containing her results—proof in black and white that she'd messed up her A levels and let everyone down—she'd spent the whole day crying, because she was such a failure. Despite the fact her parents had tried to comfort her and said it didn't matter, she knew she was a disappointment to them. They were academics, living in Oxford: how could they not be disappointed that she'd failed her A levels and wouldn't go on to university?

Would she be a disappointment to Gio, the same way?

On the day of the course, she'd felt she'd done OK. The exam hadn't thrown her.

Now…she wasn't so sure. Not with her track record. And she couldn't bear the idea of Gio losing his faith in her. Of letting him down.

But she wasn't a coward. She took a deep breath and ripped open the envelope. Stared at the piece of paper inside. No, *two* pieces of paper. A letter and a certificate. So she didn't even have to read the letter to know.

She'd passed.

She whooped and did a Snoopy dance on the doormat.

She'd actually *passed*!

Gio's belief in her had been right. She'd come good.

And she needed to tell him. Right now. She grabbed the phone—and then replaced the receiver without dialling. He'd be in the office, she knew; although he was a stickler for sending her home on the dot, he worked until at least half past seven most nights.

Tonight, she was going to take him out to celebrate. And they were going to drink champagne. She locked her front door, took the tube back to Goodge Street and walked down to the café. As she suspected, the closed sign was up and the front of the café was dark, but she could see the faint light from the office in the back of the shop. Gio was still there. Still working.

She banged on the door.

No answer.

She knocked again.

Still no answer.

Third time lucky?

Yes.

The frown on Gio's face dissolved as he saw her and unlocked the door. 'Hi, Fran. What are you doing here?'

'You sent me to learn about and understand the importance of food hygiene and hazards, plus good hygiene practice and controls based upon food safety management systems,' she said. 'So there's something I need to talk to you about.'

'Uh-huh. Come through to the office.' He stood aside, then locked the door behind her again.

She followed him to the office, rummaging in her handbag, then handed him the letter.

He handed it back without unfolding it. 'I don't need to read this.'

'Yes, you do.'

'No, I don't.' He smiled. 'I told you that you'd pass.'

'Gio, it's the first exam I've taken in eight years. Last time I sat in an exam room, I screwed it up. I failed.'

'But this time, you did well. Just as I knew you would.'

His unshakeable confidence in her made her feel warm from the inside out. She smiled wryly and tucked the letter back into her handbag. 'Just for the record: yes, I passed.'

'Well done. You can do the intermediate certificate next, if you want.' He shook his head. 'Actually, no. You're on the management side, so it's probably better if you do the HACCP in Practice course.'

Was he testing her to see if she knew what the acronym stood for? Ha. No sweat. 'Hazard Analysis Critical Control Points,' she said with a grin.

'And you'll pass that one standing on your head because you're organised, practical and sensible. Piece of cake.' He laughed. 'Well, a brownie, maybe—if Sally leaves us any.'

Fran smiled back. Then she noticed that his guitar was out of its case. 'Sorry, was I disturbing you?'

He followed the direction of her gaze, then shrugged. 'I sometimes use it when I'm thinking. Let things work in my subconscious.'

'And you're thinking about the franchise options?'

He nodded.

'Would you play something for me?' she asked on impulse, settling herself on the edge of the desk.

He blinked. 'I don't play for an audience any more.'

'I'm not an audience. I'm your office manager. And I just passed my exam, so I deserve a treat, yes?'

'That,' he said, 'is manipulation worthy of my mother—in fact, it's worthy of my grandmother.'

Maybe. But she had a feeling that Gio had given up his music as a penance for what he believed he'd done wrong. And maybe playing to someone else would help make him see that he'd more than paid his dues. That he could have his music back.

So she simply sat there. Waiting.

He sighed. 'I should warn you, I'm out of practice. Not like I used to be.'

'I've never heard you play before, so I don't have anything to compare it with,' she pointed out.

'Even so.'

But he was wavering. She could see it. 'Just one piece? Something short and simple.'

He was silent for what seemed like a long, long time. To the point where Fran thought maybe she'd pushed him too far.

She was about to slide off the desk, apologise and leave him be, when he picked up the guitar.

The notes rang out, sweet and clear, in the office—a slow, pretty tune that Fran half-recognised. And then he changed it; it was the same tune, but this time it sounded incredibly different, as if it were being played by a Venetian gondolier on a mandolin. Then he switched back to the slow, sweet version.

'Wow,' she said, when he'd finished. 'I've heard that before, but I've got no idea what it's called.'

'"Spanish Ballad".'

'Spanish? That middle bit sounded more Italian than Spanish.'

He shrugged. 'It's a technique called tremolo—and it's used in Spanish music as well as Italian. Tarrega's "Alhambra" is probably the best-known example.'

Not one she knew—at least, not by name. 'You didn't sound rusty to me. I liked it.' She paused. 'Can I be really greedy? More, please?'

He blew out a breath. 'As long as you don't ask me to play "Cavatina". I *loathe* that piece of music. My sisters used to warble it around the house just to annoy me.'

She shook her head. 'I don't mind what you play. Pick something you like.'

He played Bach's 'Air on a G String', and she ended up closing her eyes and letting the music flood through her senses; the sound was so beautiful that it brought her close to tears. She didn't recognise the next two pieces, though the style reminded her of the Mozart piano pieces Suzy used to practise as a teenager; and then Gio launched into a fast, flamenco-sounding piece. It sounded as if there were two people playing different guitars, though she knew that was a crazy idea. She opened her eyes just to check that someone hadn't just appeared out of thin air to accompany him—but, no, it was just Gio.

And he looked as if he were enjoying himself, as if the speed and sudden loud flamenco licks were releasing all the tension that had built up inside him.

'That was incredible,' she said when he'd finished. If this was what he called 'out of practice', he must've been a truly fantastic musician in his late teens. Gio had a real talent for music, she thought; but he'd sacrificed it for the sake of his family.

'That was Albéniz's "Asturias",' he said. 'A bit showy-off.' He grinned. 'But since I'm being a show-off…' He launched into another piece, slightly jazzy.

'I really like that. What is it?'

'"Verano Porteño". It's by an Argentinean composer, Piazzolla.'

The mischievous twinkle was back in his eye, Fran noticed with pleasure. Music definitely brought out the best in Gio. 'Should I have heard of him?'

'Probably not—unless you dance the tango.'

She laughed. 'Not with my two left feet.'

'Dancing a tango's easier than making latte art.' He gave her a speculative look. 'Maybe I'll teach you.'

Being musical and having a good sense of rhythm, Gio would probably be a superb dancer. And the idea of dancing a tango with him—breast to breast and cheek to cheek, their bodies moving as one—sent little ripples of desire down her spine.

'In Argentina, there's a saying that everything may change except the tango…but Piazzolla changed it,' Gio said. 'He fused the old-fashioned style with jazz, to make something called *nuevo tango*.'

Given that saying… 'And it went down badly?' she guessed.

'At the time, yes—though nowadays most people think of him as the Tango King. He ended up living in Italy, where his parents' family came from, in the late nineteen-seventies. Nonna actually saw him play in Rome, and said he was completely amazing.' He smiled wryly. 'I normally only play Piazzolla for Nonna.'

'Then I consider myself honoured,' Fran said. 'What does "Verano Porteño" mean?'

'Summer—well, it's meant to be an evocation of summer in Buenos Aires. It's from his *Four Seasons*,' he said, 'which is sadly not as well known as Vivaldi's.' He played a couple of bars she recognised from 'Spring', then put his guitar back in the case. 'Enough for now.'

'Thank you for playing for me,' she said.

'Well, I guess you earned it. Seeing as you passed your exams.' He smiled. 'And I'm glad you came to tell me.'

'Even though, strictly speaking, it could've waited until tomorrow,' she admitted. 'But you believed in me, Gio. I couldn't wait tell you.' She took a deep breath. 'Actually, what I'd intended to do was drag you off to a bar and buy you a glass of champagne to celebrate.'

'That's very sweet of you.'

At his tone, Fran felt her stomach swoop. Oh, no. Now he'd think she was trying to hit on him. And he was going to be kind about it and refuse very politely.

'But I think champagne is overrated. There's way too much snobbery about a few bubbles in some wine. I'd rather have a good Margaux any day. Or there's this amazing Sicilian red wine Netti found that actually tastes of chocolate. It's fabulous with puddings.' He switched off the computer. 'Have you eaten yet?'

'No.'

'Good. Do you like dim sum?'

She nodded.

'Then how about we swap the champagne for Chinese food?'

'Don't tell me.' She rolled her eyes. 'You know the best Chinese in London, and it's something to do with your family?'

He laughed. 'Yes to the first, no to the second. Actually, there were a couple of things I wanted to run by you.'

'So we might as well multi-task it.' She threw his favourite phrase back at him.

'We want to celebrate your exam. We both need to eat.' He spread his hands. 'And we can talk at the same time, can we not?'

* * *

Jasmine tea really hadn't been the way Fran had intended celebrating, but when they were seated in the restaurant, having chosen a mixture of dishes to share, she realised that this was just about perfect.

'So, what did you want to run by me?' she asked.

'We're just about into week four of your trial. Which is practically a month.' His eyes glittered. 'We said a month's trial, with a week's notice on either side.'

Fran went cold. Her boss had told her about the studio merger over lunch. Was Gio about to tell her that he'd changed his mind about her working with him, over dinner? Was this going to be her week's notice?

Then her rational side kicked in. They were celebrating her exam results. And he wouldn't have suggested having dinner or said that he had some things to run by her if he was about to terminate her contract. 'So we did,' she agreed coolly, and sipped her jasmine tea.

If he noticed that the bowl clattered when she returned it to the saucer, he didn't comment. 'I'm happy with the way things are going. What about you?'

She nodded. 'I'm enjoying the work and I like the staff.'

'So can we consider you a permanent member of the team, now? Don't look so worried,' he added.

'I wasn't worried,' she fibbed.

'Then you'll stay?'

'Yes.'

'Good.'

That was the first hurdle over with. Now for the biggie. Gio decided to wait until they were eating and Fran had filled her bowl with choice morsels.

'There was something else.'

'What?' She paused with the chopsticks held over her bowl.

'You know my grandmother's coming over from Milan at the weekend?'

She nodded.

'It's for our family birthdays.'

She frowned. 'Birth*days*? Sorry, I'm not with you. Are you saying you have an official birthday as well as a normal one—like the Queen?'

He choked. 'Not *quite*. My sisters and I,' he said, doing his best impersonation of the Queen's opening to her Christmas speech, 'well, our birthdays are all within a fortnight of each other. Four family parties in that short a space of time is a bit excessive, even for my family. So we tend to celebrate them all at one really big family party.'

'Makes sense. Though I do hope you celebrate individually, as well.'

'Yes.' Well, the girls did. He hadn't bothered, the last couple of years, though he'd invented dinner out with friends so his parents wouldn't worry about him. 'I was wondering if you're busy, a week on Saturday. If you'd like to come to the party.'

Her eyes widened, but he couldn't quite read her expression: horror or delight?

'Me?' she asked.

Surprise, then. Well, he could work with surprise. 'Yup. I can guarantee the food'll be good.'

'And your birthday is when, exactly?'

He coughed. 'In the next fortnight.'

'That's approximate. I asked for exact.'

'Are you coming to the party?' he asked, trying to evade the question.

'Are you going to tell me when your birthday is?'

He scooped more food into his bowl. 'You're not supposed to answer a question with a question. It's rude.'

She smiled at him. 'Of course, as the office manager, I have access to the personnel records. So if you don't tell me, I can simply go into the system and look it up for myself.'

'That,' Gio said, 'is flagrant abuse under the Data Protection Act, Francesca Marsden. It's *illegal*.'

'I could still do it. Or…I could ask your mother.' Fran was inexorable.

He knew when he was beaten. He leaned back in his chair. 'All right. It's next Wednesday.'

'Thank you.'

He raised an eyebrow. 'I think it's your turn to answer the question.'

'Thank you for the invitation.'

He really couldn't tell if her answer was going to be yes or no, and he was shocked by the way his skin suddenly felt too tight. It really shouldn't matter whether she said yes or no.

But it did.

It mattered a lot.

He wanted her there.

'I'd love to come,' she said softly.

Which was when Gio realised that he'd actually been holding his breath.

Oh, lord. He was already in way too deep.

'What's the dress code?' she asked.

He spread his hands. 'Whatever. It's a party. Wear what you want.'

She rolled her eyes. '*Men*. Do I have to ask your mother?'

'I'm beginning to think,' Gio said, 'that's you're just as

scary as Mum, Nonna and Netti rolled into one.' But she'd said yes, so far.

Would she say yes to the next question?

'There's, um, a bit more.' He took a deep breath. So much for thinking he'd felt tense before. What he was feeling right at that moment was G-force tension—the sort you got on one of those rollercoasters that sent you round a corkscrew spiral and then round a series of loops. 'I love my grandmother.'

Her smile definitely said, *I already know that. Are you going batty or something?*

'And because she lives in Italy, I don't get to see as much of her as I'd like. I speak to her a couple of times a week, but it's not the same as seeing her.'

Fran stopped eating, rested her elbows on the table and propped her chin on her linked hands. 'It's not like you to beat about the bush. What's up?'

There wasn't an easy way to put it. And however he phrased it, it was going to sound wrong. 'You know my family has this thing about wanting me to settle down—especially Nonna?'

'Ye-es.'

She sounded extremely cautious, and Gio just knew she was going to say no. But he asked anyway. 'Would you pretend to be my girlfriend while Nonna's in England?'

CHAPTER SEVEN

'LET me get this straight.' Fran wasn't sure she'd heard him correctly. 'You want me to pretend to be your girlfriend while your grandmother's visiting.'

He nodded. 'No strings. If you say no, that's fine—it won't change anything between us at work.'

'Why on earth do you need a pretend girlfriend?' Gio was gorgeous enough to have women lining up to be the real thing. If they could put up with his working hours and always having second place in his life to Giovanni's, that was. Which was exactly why she'd never have a relationship with Gio for real: she wanted to come first.

'I told you, I'm not looking for a relationship right now. But…' He raked a hand through his hair. 'There isn't an easy way to put this.'

'Try starting at the beginning,' she suggested.

'Just don't get offended by anything I'm about to say. Please.' He sighed. 'My mother doesn't believe you're just my office manager. So she and Netti have been talking to Nonna—who now thinks that you're my secret girlfriend. And when Nonna rang me last night…I don't think I've ever heard her so happy at the idea I've finally found someone and settled down.' He pushed his bowl away. 'Bottom line—I can tell her the truth and make her believe it, but it's going to hurt her terribly. She's only staying for a few weeks. And…' he looked away '…this is going to make me sound either like a sentimental fool or incredibly morbid, but Nonna's not going to be around for ever.'

She knew exactly what he meant. 'And you want to make her happy while you still have the chance.'

He nodded. 'I'm the only one of my generation who isn't settled down. Even Marcie—my youngest sister—is engaged. All my cousins are married, mostly with children or planning them.'

'So all the pressure's on you to follow suit.'

He sighed. 'Yup.'

'This isn't the right thing to do, Gio. If we pretend we're an item while your grandmother's here, what happens when she goes back to Milan?'

'I haven't thought that far ahead,' he admitted. 'We can split up gracefully—it'll be my fault because you can't stand me being a workaholic, or something like that. And then we can get back to normal.' He waved a dismissive hand. 'Look, I'm trying to buy some time. And there isn't much. Nonna's going to be here in two days.'

'I've worked with you for nearly a month. And I've never seen you panic,' Fran said thoughtfully. 'You're panicking now.'

'Because I can't see a way out of this without shattering Nonna's illusions. Hurting her. Which I really, *really*, don't want to do. She's special to me, Fran. She's always been there for me. Listened to me when I wanted to talk about things I couldn't tell my parents.'

She frowned. 'Gio, this is the twenty-first century. It's perfectly OK to be single, you know.'

'Not according to my family.' He drummed his fingers on the table. 'And I've already disappointed them enough.'

Fran guessed immediately what the root of that particular worry was. And why it was so important to him to please his family now. She reached across the table and took his hand. 'Listen to me, Giovanni Mazetti. You're not a disappointment to your family. Look at you: twenty-eight years old, and you've built your dad's business into a chain with the plan to expand it even more. And you were *not* responsible for your dad's heart attack. It could have happened any time—even if he'd been sitting down relaxing at home that evening, it could still have happened.'

Gio didn't look in the slightest bit convinced.

'Gio, you went to the concert because that was the right thing for you to do at the time—if you hadn't gone, you'd have disappointed your teacher and your family because you hadn't tried, and you'd have spent the rest of your life wondering if you were good enough.'

He lifted a shoulder in a half-shrug.

She squeezed his hand. 'I mean it, Gio. It was the right thing to do, to go. And you *were* good enough. You could've made a career in music, if you'd wanted to. But you gave it up for your family. You put their needs before your own. So no way have you disappointed them. If anything, they probably feel guilty that you gave up your music for them— and I bet they think you've sacrificed your personal life, as well as your dreams, to run the business.'

Gio was silent.

'It's true,' she said gently. 'That's why they fuss about you so much. They love you and they worry about you and they want the best for you. So don't be so hard on yourself.'

'Hmm.' He looked her straight in the eye. 'So was that a yes or a no?'

'Yes or no to what?' a voice enquired next to them.

Gio looked up and groaned. 'I don't *believe* this! Why is it, everywhere I go, I run into one of my family?'

'Because we're on a mission to take over London and call it Mazettiville,' the man said with a grin. 'Imagine how many of us there'll be in our children's generation. Or our grand-children's. Or our great-grandchildren's.'

'That's too scary to think about.' Gio rolled his eyes. 'Fran, this is my cousin Ricardo—Netti's eldest son. Everyone calls him Ric. Ric, this is Fran.'

'Pleased to meet you, Fran.' Ric eyed their joined hands. 'Hmm. I'd heard the rumour. I thought your mum was just hoping a bit too hard. But obviously the family grapevine was right, this time.'

'Oh, for pity's sake…' Gio began.

Fran laughed. 'So much for trying to keep things quiet. Pleased to meet you, too, Ric. And, yes, I'm Gio's girlfriend.'

Gio gave her a grateful look. 'As well as my office manager. But relationships at work are a seriously bad idea, so we were trying to keep it to ourselves.'

'You're on a losing streak there, because your mother has spies all over London. Not to mention Nonna's network,' Ric said, laughing. 'So does this mean you're going to announce your engagement at the party?'

'*Engagement?*' Gio looked utterly stunned. He dragged in a breath. '*Porca miseria*, Ric! You'll have me married with twins next.'

'Nothing wrong with being married with twins,' Ric returned equably. 'In case he hasn't told you, Fran, I have twin boys. Patrizio and Oliviero. They were three last month.'

'I have twin brothers,' she said. 'They're two years younger than I am.'

'So twins run in your family, too?' He smiled at Fran. 'I should warn you—there are rather a lot of us. Though no doubt you'll be meeting us all next weekend at the party.'

'So Gio tells me.' She smiled back. 'And you've escaped tonight for a romantic meal with your wife?'

He nodded. 'It's our wedding anniversary.'

'I did send you a card,' Gio said, lifting one hand to forestall a protest.

'And flowers. Which Alison really appreciated.'

'I most certainly did.' A woman joined them and ruffled his hair. 'Thank you, sweetheart. Hello, you must be Fran.'

'Oh, man. Can't I have a romantic meal in peace without my cousins coming over to interfere?' Gio asked plaintively.

'Not when it's the first girlfriend we've heard of in five years. Of course we want to check her out,' Alison said with a grin. 'Fran, it's so nice to meet you. I've already heard a lot about you.'

'From Angela?' Fran guessed.

'Yes.' Alison smiled. 'The family network can seem a bit overpowering at first—but don't worry, you'll soon get used to it. They only do it because they love each other. Gio's primed you about the party?'

Fran nodded. 'Except the dress code—which he said is "whatever".'

'Men!' Alison rolled her eyes. 'The men try and get away with looking as casual as they can, but the women go dressy. Definitely high heels—oh, and you can make your man buy you a *seriously* expensive bag to go with your outfit.'

Ric groaned. 'I take it that was a hint to me, too?'

'Oh, honey. How *sweet* of you to offer,' Alison teased. 'I'll call Bella and we'll go shopping tomorrow. Gio's middle sister is a handbag fiend,' she confided to Fran.

Gio gently disentangled his hand from Fran's and covered his face. 'I can't cope with you lot. I think I'm going to run away.'

'No, you're not,' Ric said. 'We know exactly where to find you. You'll be in the Charlotte Street café at six o'clock tomorrow morning.'

'Seven, actually,' Gio corrected, lifting his head and looking his cousin in the eye. 'Stop stirring.'

'As late as *seven*?' Ric pantomimed amazement. 'Fran, you've just earned yourself a zillion brownie points with Angela. And…' Ric glanced at his watch. 'Yep. You've got him out of the office a good hour earlier than usual. Make that two zillion points.'

'Don't you dare report this,' Gio said.

'Too late,' Alison told him with a wink. 'I've already texted Jude. But we'll leave you in peace now.'

'In peace? Chance would be a fine thing,' Gio grumbled, but he smiled.

'Happy anniversary,' Fran said.

'Thanks.' Alison tucked her arm through Ric's. 'Now stop annoying your poor cousin and let him have his romantic dinner out. Which is what we're supposed to be doing, too,' she reminded her husband. 'See you later, Fran—Gio.'

'I'm *so* sorry about my family,' Gio said when his cousins had returned to their own table. 'They just…take over. They'll be impossible at the party. You won't get a second's peace.' He shook his head. 'OK. This is what we do. I'll tell a white lie on the night and say you weren't able to come because you have a migraine.'

Fran smiled. 'It won't alter a thing. They'll all drop in to Charlotte Street, the same way your mum did, to check me out. One after another. It's probably easier to get it all over with in one go.'

'Are you sure about this?' Gio asked.

'I just told your cousins I was your girlfriend,' she pointed out. 'So it's a bit too late to back out, now.'

'I could kiss you,' Gio said, his tone heartfelt.

She had to drag her gaze away from his mouth. Because it was all too easy to imagine what it would feel like if Gio kissed her. His lips would be warm and sweet and teasing, coaxing a response from her until heat flared between them.

Until they couldn't stand any more barriers between them and had to be skin to skin.

The ultimate in closeness.

His body sliding into hers.

Oh, lord. She was going to start hyperventilating in a minute.

'Have I told you lately that you're wonderful?' he asked.

'No.'

'Well, you are. You have no idea how much I appreciate this.'

'Just as long as nobody gets hurt,' she warned.

'They won't. OK, we're not telling the truth, but it's for a good reason. It's to stop Nonna getting hurt in the first place.' He topped up their jasmine tea and lifted his bowl. 'Well, here's to us.'

'To us,' she echoed.

On Friday morning, while Gio was at the coffee supplier's, Fran intended to make a few phone calls. But Gio's mother beat her to the first one.

By the time she came off the phone, after promising to go over for Sunday lunch, she was beginning to wonder quite what she'd let herself in for. But she wasn't going to renege

on her promise to help him. It didn't take her long to sort out
the rest of the arrangements. And, best of all, absolutely
everyone agreed to be sworn to secrecy.

This, she thought, was going to be Gio's best birthday in
years.

Gio picked her up on Sunday morning at eleven. 'Are you
sure you're up to this, Fran? I'll do my best to protect you,
but I think you're in for a grilling.'

'Relax. I've already met your mum.' And plotted something with her—not that she was going to let Gio know about
that yet. That was a delicious secret she was going to keep to
herself. 'It's going to be fine.'

Though the butterflies in her stomach were stomping rather
than dancing when Gio parked outside his parents' house.

Relax. This isn't for real, she reminded herself. It doesn't
matter if they decide you're not good enough for Gio, because
it's not as if you're planning to get married. This is just temporary. Acting a part.

And then they were right in the thick of things—in a
houseful of people. Gio started on the introductions. 'Fran,
you already know my mum. This is my dad, Giovanni Mazetti
the elder.'

'Less of this "elder" business,' Giovanni said, giving his
son a pained look. 'I'm not a pensioner *yet*.'

'Pleased to meet you, Mr Mazetti,' Fran said politely.

'Giovanni,' he corrected, ignoring her outstretched hand
and hugging her warmly. 'It's good to meet you too, *piccolina*.'

'My sisters, Giuditta, Isabella and Marcella—known as
Jude, Bella and Marcie,' Gio said, introducing her to the three
younger women Fran recognised from the photograph. They,
too, hugged her in welcome.

'And my *nonna*, Isabella Mazetti.'

'Let me look at you, child.' Isabella—who was even shorter than Fran, with grey hair tucked into a bun and deep brown eyes—placed her hands on Fran's shoulders and peered up at her. 'So you are the *bella ragazza* who's made my Giovanni so happy. *Bene*,' she pronounced, and hugged Fran.

'It's nice to meet the woman I've heard so much about, Signora Mazetti,' Fran said.

'Call me Nonna. *Everyone* calls me Nonna,' Isabella said. 'Now, come and sit down and tell me all about yourself. Gio, don't just stand there, get the girl a drink.'

Fran didn't get the chance to ask if there was anything she could do to help prepare lunch. Just as Gio had predicted, she was in for a grilling. And by the time Gio appeared with a cup of coffee, Isabella knew just about everything there was to know about her.

'Nonna, *dolcezza*, give Fran a break.' Gio set the mug of coffee on the side, scooped Fran out of the chair and sat in her place, drawing her on to his lap.

For a moment, Fran stiffened; he hadn't warned her he was intending to do that. But then again, Gio's family was incredibly tactile. Whenever one of them talked to you, there would be a hand on your arm, a gesture, a smile, a patted shoulder. And she was meant to be Gio's girlfriend. Of course they'd expect her to sit on his lap.

So she relaxed back against him, resting her head on his shoulder. His arms were wrapped round her waist, holding her close, and she was acutely aware of the warmth of his body. His strength. His clean scent. The steady, even beat of his heart.

And then it hit her.

This was exactly what she wanted.

Being smack in the middle of a big, warm, noisy family.

Accepted as one of them. With a strong, handsome man holding her protectively.

Oh, lord. If she'd known it would be like this, she would never have agreed to this pretend-girlfriend thing. Because right now she was setting herself up for a broken heart. This wasn't for real, and there was no chance it would turn out that way either—Gio had already told her he didn't want to settle down.

As if he sensed the sudden tension in her, his arms tightened round her, a private signal that everything was going to be fine. No doubt he thought she was just a bit worried about whether his family would believe their story; and that was fine by her. Better than him guessing what she was really thinking.

Lunch was a noisy affair, with everyone chattering and laughing, the clink of glass and the tinkling of cutlery against crockery. A typical Italian Sunday lunch, with a steaming tureen of minestrone followed by beef with crispy-edged fluffy roast potatoes, roasted peppers and aubergines, cavalo nero and all the trimmings.

And pudding… 'Oh, wow,' Fran said as she tasted the first mouthful. 'I've never tasted ice cream this good.'

'Nando's special. Reserved only for the family,' Angela told her. 'Hazelnut.'

Served with a pile of tiny strawberries and a splash of wild strawberry liqueur over the top. 'It's fantastic,' Fran said, meaning it.

And the entire table beamed at her.

After lunch, Fran insisted on helping to clear away.

'No, you're a guest—you sit down with Gio,' Marcie said.

'She's not a guest,' Nonna said firmly. 'She's Gio's girl-friend. One of us.'

Fran had to blink away the tears. How easily she'd been accepted among the Mazettis. And it felt really good to be in this family kitchen, with all the women washing up or drying dishes or putting things away or making coffee, chattering away with half-a-dozen different conversations going on at once and everyone laughing and telling little anecdotes about their week—breaking off every so often to look at a photograph on a mobile phone screen and coo over assorted babies and puppies and kittens.

So different from her own, much quieter and more reserved family.

And the weird thing was, Fran thought with a pang, she felt as if she *belonged* here.

She'd marry Gio tomorrow, just for his family.

And the sudden realisation made her dizzy. If he asked her, she'd marry Gio tomorrow.

For himself.

If Gio's family noticed that she'd gone a bit quiet, they clearly assumed that she was a bit overwhelmed by the experience of meeting the Mazettis, because nobody made a comment. They simply included her in the conversation and asked her opinion on things.

They'd just finished clearing away when the doorbell went. A few moments later, Ric and Angela came in with the twins, who were clearly used to the Mazetti way of doing things because they came to everyone for a hug and a kiss—including Fran.

With their mop of curly dark hair and huge brown eyes, they were irresistible; before she knew it, she was sitting in a chair with both children on her lap, cuddling them and telling them a story.

'She's perfect,' Isabella said softly to Gio.

'Sorry, Nonna?'

'Fran. She's perfect. When you look at her, the emptiness disappears from your eyes.'

'My eyes aren't empty.'

'Sweetheart, they have been for years. I know you've been unhappy. That's why you work so hard, to make sure you don't have time to feel.'

Since when had his grandmother known that?

'But she's the one for you—and she'll make you happy,' Isabella said. 'I like her very much.'

'Good,' Gio told her, striving for lightness. But every muscle felt tight with guilt. He was lying to his family about his relationship with Fran. Worse still, he had a suspicion that Nonna was right—that Fran was the one for him. That she was the one who could make him happy, fill the emptiness.

But on her part this was just for show.

And he'd always said he didn't want to settle down.

So much for his promise that nobody would get hurt. Fran was right: this was going to end in tears. But it was much too late to go back now.

CHAPTER EIGHT

'I REALLY like your family,' Fran told Gio on the way home.

'They're a bit intense.'

'Gio, they're so warm and welcoming. They're lovely.'

Which was what his family said about her, too. His parents and sisters had grabbed him the same way that Nonna had, to tell him privately that they approved of his choice.

No way could he have hurt them by telling them she was just acting a part.

But maybe she hadn't been acting. The way she'd read stories to Ollie and Pat and cuddled baby Lorena... He'd seen a certain softness in her face. A softness that should have made him want to run as hard and as fast as he could, given that he wasn't ready to settle down and have kids—but instead it had made him feel some weird kind of pull. Made him want something he didn't dare put a name to.

'They adore you, Gio.'

And he adored his family right back. He just didn't want them running his life for him. 'They liked you.'

'Good.'

When he pulled up in the road outside her flat, she asked, 'Would you like to come in for a coffee?'

It was a suggestion he couldn't resist. Particularly as he

hadn't yet seen further into her flat than her front door. Her home would tell him a lot about her, he was sure. And he wanted to know more—a lot more—about the things she never talked about at work. Personal stuff. What made Fran Marsden tick?

'Thanks. I'd love a coffee.'

'It's not going to be like the stuff you serve at the café,' she warned, 'so don't expect it.'

He laughed. 'If you had a café-standard espresso machine at home, I'd be a bit surprised.'

'And my flat's very small.'

'Stop apologising. It doesn't matter how big your home is—only how big your welcome is.'

It was her turn to laugh. 'Why is it I can hear Nonna's voice saying that?'

'Probably because it's one of her favourite phrases,' he admitted.

Fran's ground-floor studio flat was very neat and tidy, as he'd expected. The sofa obviously converted to a bed; there was enough room for a few shelves stacked with books and scattered with framed photographs, a small TV and a micro stereo, and a tiny kitchen in one corner with a bistro table and two chairs next to it. There was a small dragon tree in a white pot on the table.

'It's very nice,' he said.

'But it's still very small,' she said ruefully. 'It was either sharing a house or renting a studio flat.' She wrinkled her nose. 'And I wanted my own space. So I chose this.'

Fran didn't like sharing her space? Given the way she'd fitted in so well with the Mazettis this afternoon, that surprised him. Or maybe not—like him, she was part of a large family where having your own space was a luxury. This would be a bolthole for her. Just like his flat was, for him.

He walked over to the window. 'Nice gardens.'

She nodded. 'I'm really lucky that I'm this side of the building and not on the street side. The gardens are communal so the landlord deals with it all—the nearest I have to a garden of my own is my *dracena*.'

He noticed that she used the Latin name—so, was Fran a gardener at heart? Did she have a secret yearning for a house with a garden of her own?

But if he asked her she'd simply deflect the question. He'd already noticed she was very good at that; she rarely gave anything away about herself. He knew next to nothing about her family, other than that she had twin brothers and a sister and they were all academic.

'Go and sit down.' She motioned towards the sofa. 'I'll make the coffee.'

He sat down and watched her as she switched the kettle on and began shaking grounds into a cafétière. Every moment was efficient, economical. Beautiful to watch. But what shocked him was how much he wanted to go and stand behind her, slide his arms round her waist, hold her close and bury his face in the curve of her neck.

This wasn't supposed to happen.

If he wasn't careful, he'd end up believing their relationship was for real instead of a fiction to keep his family happy.

To stop himself thinking about touching her, he twisted round to look at the shelves behind the sofa. There were several framed photographs propped against the books. 'These are your family?' he asked.

'Yes.'

There was one of them all together, very similar in style to the one he had on his computer screen at work—but he noticed immediately that Fran wasn't in it. 'Where were you?' he asked.

'Behind the camera. Which is where I prefer to be.'

'You're worried about posing for a photograph?' Without giving her the chance to answer, he pulled his mobile phone from his pocket, flicked it into camera mode and took a snap of her. He looked at the screen critically. 'It's perfectly OK. You don't take a bad photograph.'

She rolled her eyes. 'I don't have a phobia about having my picture taken, Gio. I just prefer being behind the lens, not in front of it.'

On the outside, looking in? Or was he reading too much into it? He changed tack. 'Is that what you thought about doing when you were a kid? Being a photographer?'

'No, I'm not that arty.' She shrugged. 'I take reasonable snaps, but I'm not under any illusions that I'm the next David Bailey.'

'So what did you want to do, when you were at school?'

'Can't remember.'

Her back was to him so he couldn't read her expression. He had the feeling that she was fibbing, but he didn't want to push her too hard, so he let it go. Instead, he picked up the group photograph and settled back against the sofa to study it more carefully. 'You've met my family. They're going to grill me about yours—and if I say I don't know, they'll smell a rat. Come and tell me about them,' he invited.

'There's not that much to tell.' She brought the coffee over and handed him a mug. 'Obviously that's my mum and dad—Dad's head of the local middle school and Mum's a geography teacher at the local high school.'

Again, he noticed, she'd given him the least information she could get away with. 'Honestly, getting details out of you is like pulling teeth! I ought to take lessons from Nonna. What are their names?' Gio prompted.

'Carol and Warren.'

They looked pleasant enough. Physically, they were nothing like Fran; they were both tall, and, although Warren's hair was graying, he'd clearly been fair, as had Carol. Her siblings were tall and fair, too. So he could see why Fran, being little and dark-haired, felt the differences so keenly.

'Did you take this in your parents' back garden?'

'Yes.'

It was incredibly neat and tidy; clearly someone in the family loved gardening and took pride in the flowers. Something Fran had had in common with them? But he couldn't think of a way to ask without risking her clamming up on him.

'Tell me about the others,' he invited.

She put her mug on the floor, then pointed to the younger woman in the photograph. 'This is Suzy—she's the baby of the family. She's training to be a dentist.'

Again, the bare minimum of detail. What was Suzy like as a person? If anyone had asked him to describe Marcie, the baby in their family, he would've said she was little and funny and noisy and arty—she worked in a gallery and, although she could barely draw a straight line with a ruler, she had a real eye for colour and detail, and the pieces she bought for herself were already worth at least three times what she'd paid for them.

'Does she get more information out of you than anyone else?' he asked.

She frowned. 'How?'

'By pulling…' He stopped. 'Never mind.' It was a poor joke, and he didn't want to annoy her so that she clammed up again. 'What about the twins?' he asked. They were definitely identical; he couldn't tell them apart.

'This is Ted and this is Dominic.' She pointed them out in

turn. 'Ted's a forensic scientist and Dominic's doing a PhD in history—he'll probably go on to teach at uni because he runs a few tutorials and lectures already.'

Again, very little detail. But one thing he had noted: her family were all academic, with three teachers and two scientists among them, and he already knew Fran felt bad about the fact she'd failed her exams. No wonder she felt so out of place—but he'd just bet her family appreciated her other qualities: the way she was unflappable, dealt with things coolly and calmly and was so neat and organised.

And he told her so.

She scoffed. 'There's really nothing to being organised.'

'There is, when you're trying to juggle six things at once.'

She looked at him. 'Gio Mazetti, are you trying to tell me you haven't sorted out your sisters' birthday presents yet?'

How the hell had she guessed that? He hadn't even discussed it with her. 'I'll get there—' he paused '—unless, that is, you're offering help? Because they're at a difficult age.'

She laughed back. 'Rubbish. There's nothing difficult about twenty-seven, twenty-five or twenty-three.'

'Oh, yes, there is. I have no idea what's trendy and what's completely unfashionable.'

'And you think I do?'

He smiled. 'You have a better idea than I have, anyway. Come shopping with me?'

She gave him a searching look, as if trying to work out if his offer was for real; then clearly she decided to take it at face value, because she said, 'Sure, I'll help you find something.'

'Thanks. I appreciate it.' He finished his drink. 'Nice coffee, by the way.'

'Thank you.'

'In cupping terms, I'd say this has a perfect body.' Just like her. Soft and curvy and incredibly sexy. 'I haven't told you about the cupping, have I?'

Cupping.

Little shivers of desire went all the way down her spine. The way he'd held her on his lap this afternoon, with his hands at her waist—if they'd been alone, how easily his hands could have slid up her ribcage to cup her breasts.

Her mouth went dry. 'Cupping.'

His eyes sparkled with amusement. 'It's the coffee world's equivalent of wine tasting.'

Fran could actually feel the colour flooding into her face. Oh, lord. How embarrassing could she get?

Gio's voice deepened slightly. 'Though there is another definition.' The amusement in his gaze was replaced by sheer heat. 'Fran, if I embarrassed you this afternoon when I pulled you on to my lap like that, I'm sorry.'

She wasn't.

He moistened his lower lip. 'My family is…tactile.'

Yes. And she really wanted him to touch her, right here and now. She could see in his face that he was going to touch her. And when he reached out and stroked her cheek, she couldn't help herself. She turned her face into his palm and pressed a kiss into it. 'It's OK.'

'No, it's not.' She could actually feel his hands trembling. 'Because right now I really need to…' In one swift movement, he'd pulled her on to his lap. Except this time she was sitting facing him. He leaned forward and caught her lower lip between his. Nibbled gently until she opened her mouth and slid her arms round his neck, leaning closer. His hands were pressed flat against the curve of her waist. And then his fingers dipped under the hem of her shirt. She quivered as his fingertips brushed her skin, moving slowly upwards. And then somehow he'd unsnapped her bra, pushed the material aside and was cupping her breasts.

And it was even better than she'd imagined, a few moments before.

When he broke the kiss to trace the curve of her neck with his mouth, she made a little noise of pleasure.

And Gio stopped.

Stared at her, shock blanching his face.

'I… Fran. I'm sorry. I shouldn't be doing this.'

Before she could protest that it was OK, that she was there all the way with him, he restored order to her clothes and gently moved her off his lap.

'This wasn't… Fran, I don't do relationships. And I respect you too much to sleep with you and push you out of my life.'

Respect. What was it about her that made men want to respect her, be her friend, instead of seducing her? Most of the time it didn't bother her.

Right now, it did.

Especially because it would be all too obvious how aroused she was.

The only thing she could salvage from this was pride. So she made the effort to sound like the cool, efficient office manager she was supposed to be. This girlfriend business was just for show and what had just happened between them was—well, they'd both been under pressure. 'No worries. We'll just pretend it never happened.'

'Thank you.' He stood up. 'I, um—see you tomorrow.'

She nodded. 'And bring your credit card.'

'Credit card?'

'Your sisters' birthday presents. We're going shopping in my lunch hour.'

And the minute he left, she was going to take a very, very cold shower. Get her brain and her body back to normal.

Shopping? More like a military operation, Gio thought when Fran marched him into the third shop in Oxford Street. 'What did you do—scope things out on the net first?'

She gave him a sidelong look. 'Don't tell me you'd rather spend hours wandering around, not really sure what you want or where to find it?'

'Well, no,' he admitted. 'But I don't understand how you knew the perfect presents to get for my sisters when you've only just met them.'

'It's called looking at people. Noticing things,' Fran said. 'Jude likes really understated jewellery. Very classic, very pretty. Her wedding ring's white gold and her watch is chrome, so yellow gold earrings wouldn't really be her style. The white gold ones with pink sapphires are more the kind of thing she'd like.'

Hmm. Fran didn't wear jewellery. Didn't have pierced ears. Would she…?

No. He wasn't supposed to be thinking about jewellery and Francesca Marsden. The fact he'd love to see her wearing nothing but a string of pearls and a sexy smile.

Kissing her yesterday had been a big mistake. Because he wanted to do it all over again. And this time not stop touching her until they were both naked.

And sated.

As if oblivious to what was going through his head, Fran continued, 'Marcie, on the other hand, loves jewellery that makes a statement. She wears silver bangles set with big chunky stones. That triangular pendant set with a turquoise is the sort of thing she'd choose.'

'And Bella?'

She rolled her eyes. 'Don't you listen to anyone unless it's about work?'

Ouch. That was definitely below the belt.

'Angela told us in the Chinese restaurant that Bella's a handbag fiend. Here.' She looked quickly through the display, picked out an evening bag and handed it to Gio. 'She goes out a lot in the evening, so a bag that's big enough to take her phone, credit card, keys and a coin purse is perfect. And this particular designer does seriously cute bags.'

'That little Scottie dog on the front looks just like her new puppy. She probably showed you the latest pictures yesterday.' Gio shook his head in amazement. 'See, this is why I needed you with me. You understand girl stuff. I'd never have thought of this.'

'Don't flannel me. You normally text them at the last minute and ask them for a list of ideas and exactly where to buy them, don't you?' she asked.

Was he that predictable? Or was she just really, really good at reading people? But he loved the way she teased him. 'It means they get what they really want. But this year, I wanted it to be different. So I told them all I was going to get them a surprise.'

'And if I'd refused to come and help you?'

'Then I'd have given them vouchers for a pamper day at their favourite spa,' he admitted. 'But I prefer giving presents to unwrap. Ones that people really like.'

'So all you have to do is notice the details.'

'I do notice details,' he protested as he paid for the bag.

'And because we did all the shopping in about three minutes flat, we have time for lunch.'

Though what he wanted for lunch definitely wasn't on the menu.

She pantomimed horror. 'Tut, tut. Should we not be heading to a branch of Giovanni's?'

'The nearest one's at Charlotte Street. Which means I'd feel forced to go back to the office—and aren't you joining my family's campaign to make me take more time off?'

She laughed, but let him lead her into a nearby café.

'I meant it about noticing details,' Gio said when he brought their tray to their table.

'Such as?'

'You, for example.' The way her mouth was so full and lush and sexy when she'd just been kissed. Not that he was stupid enough to say that out loud. 'Your eyes are the most beautiful colour—the same as the sky at about ten o'clock on an August evening.'

'Flannel.' She looked away.

'Fran?' He reached over and squeezed her hand. 'I apologise for embarrassing you.'

'I'm not embarrassed.'

The bright pink of her cheeks said otherwise. 'I'll take it away from the personal, then,' he said softly 'The only jewellery you wear is a watch, and it's precisely eight minutes fast—which I'd guess is the amount of time it would take to sort out a voiceover studio between slots.'

'Well deduced, Holmes.'

'Why, thank you, Watson,' he teased back.

But he managed to keep the conversation light and impersonal, and didn't try to persuade her to take a longer lunch break when she said it was time to go back to work.

* * *

On Wednesday morning, just as Gio was about to leave his flat, his mobile phone rang.

He checked the display before answering: the Holborn branch. 'Hi, Amy. What's up?'

'You know I was having problems with the steam wand the other day, and you sorted it out? It's gone funny again. I'm trying to get it to work, but could you pop in on your way to Charlotte Street?'

'Yeah, sure. I'll get Sal to open up here. Be with you in a few minutes.'

By the time he'd got to Holborn, the steam wand was working perfectly again.

'I feel really guilty, dragging you out here over nothing,' Amy said. 'But as you're here, I was wondering if we could have a chat about something? There's a writers' group who'd like to meet here on Wednesday evenings and they asked me if we could open late. I know we don't normally do evenings, but I've got a business plan. It'll only take me ten minutes to talk you through…'

More like half an hour, but Gio knew the Charlotte Street branch was safe in Sally's hands—not to mention Fran being in the office if there was a problem elsewhere.

He didn't think anything of it until he was walking down Charlotte Street and noticed something odd about the exterior of the café.

Red balloons tied to the door, he saw as he got nearer.

Balloons that said 'Happy Birthday'.

And when he walked into the café, spread across the back

of the bar was a huge banner that said 'Happy 29th birthday, Gio', surrounded by balloons.

Before he had the chance to take it in, his mother, father and grandmother stepped out of the office, together with Fran. Fran counted them in, and they started singing 'Happy Birthday to You' to him, along with Ian and Sally.

Even the customers joined in.

He'd barely registered that today was his birthday—the post hadn't arrived before he left, and he never really bothered making a fuss over the day anyway.

'I don't know what to say,' he said. 'Balloons?'

'There are twenty-nine—one for every year of your age,' Fran told him with a grin. 'Count them, if you like. Now sit down and I'll make you a coffee.'

His eyes narrowed. 'When did you do all this?' Then the penny dropped. 'That call this morning from Amy—you set it up, didn't you?'

She nodded. 'I needed you out of the way until we'd put up the balloons and banner. But she was going to talk to you about the writing-group thing anyway.'

'You know about that?' At her raised eyebrow, he sighed. 'You did the business plan, didn't you?'

'It was a joint effort with Amy, but, yes,' she admitted.

She made an espresso, then heated the milk. And Gio watched, open-mouthed, as Fran made him a latte and free-poured a perfect rosetta on the top. 'Happy birthday, honey,' she said with a smile.

He stared at the mug, and then at her. 'You made me a rosetta.'

'Mmm. I should've made it a cake and a candle, really. But that would mean using a needle and cocoa, and I thought you might like this a little bit more.' Her eyes glittered with mischief. 'Not to mention a little wager we had—which had a deadline of this Friday, I believe.'

He groaned. 'Oh, no. You've been practising, haven't you?'

'Yup.'

'Which means you win the chocolates.'

She spread her hands. 'Don't blame me. You're the one who set high stakes. Which were, and I quote, "I'll take you to Fortnum's and buy you the biggest box of chocolates of your choice."'

He noticed Sally was beaming, and leaned against the counter. 'You've been giving her coaching, Sal, haven't you?'

'For a half-share in those chocolates? You bet I have!' The barista chuckled. 'Though, I admit, my pupil worked pretty hard.'

'It's cheating. Absolute *cheating*,' Gio said.

'Ah, no. You merely gave me a time limit. You didn't say that I couldn't get anyone else to help me,' Fran reminded him.

'I don't know what to say.' He gestured at the balloons and the banner. 'I really wasn't expecting this.'

Her smile broadened. 'Well, I haven't quite finished yet. In fact, I'm expecting a delivery—' Gio heard the door click open '—about right now.'

CHAPTER NINE

GIO frowned as he saw Ingrid in the doorway. From the look of the baskets on the counter, they'd already had their cake delivery for the day. Why on earth would their baker need to come back a second time?

The answer lay in the large white box she was carrying. 'One special delivery, Fran,' she said, and put the cake between Fran and Gio.

'Thanks, Ingrid.' Fran removed the lid and opened the box to reveal a birthday cake, in the shape of a cup of coffee, covered in what looked like pure chocolate. 'Happy birthday Gio' was written on it in white icing, and there was a rosetta piped underneath his name.

There were no candles; instead, there were tiny indoor sparklers along the top of the cake. And Gio had to swallow the lump in his throat when Fran lit them.

She'd arranged all this—just for him.

At really, really short notice.

'Sparklers?' he asked.

'Well, with twenty-nine candles, we would probably have set the cake on fire and then the café's sprinkler system would've gone off,' Fran teased. 'Besides, these are meant to look like froth on top of the coffee. Smile!'

Before he'd realised her intention, she'd taken a photograph of him next to his sparkler-topped cake.

'Make a wish,' she said as the sparklers burned out. 'And remember to keep it secret or it won't come true.'

A wish. There was one right in the middle of his heart, but he wasn't quite prepared to name it to himself. Not yet.

She produced a knife from behind the counter and a stack of plates and napkins; he cut the cake into slices and Fran handed them round to everyone sitting in the café.

'Is this pure chocolate brownie?' he asked.

'Special order,' Ingrid confirmed.

'For a special guy,' Fran added, then kissed the tips of her fingers, leaned over the counter and dabbed them on the end of his nose. 'Happy birthday, honey.'

Gio caught the slightly misty look in his mother and grandmother's eyes. Fran was playing her part to perfection.

But he had to remember it was just a part—and it was going to stay that way, because he knew she wanted something he just didn't think he was capable of giving her. Security and a happy ever after.

And he wasn't supposed to be letting his heart get involved.

All the same, when everyone had gone and Fran had disappeared into the office to do her usual magic with the admin, he went out to the back and gave her a hug. 'Thank you,' he said. 'I honestly wasn't expecting this.'

'It's your birthday. What kind of girlfriend would I be if I let it pass without comment?' She fished under the desk and brought out a neatly wrapped parcel. 'By the way—happy birthday.'

She'd bought him a present? But… 'You didn't have to do this,' he said. 'The cake was more than enough.'

'Hey. You said I could choose whatever chocolates I liked in Fortnum's. Of course I'm going to buy you a birthday present.' She grinned. 'You'll be spending a lot of money on me. I'm just as greedy as you are—'

Yes, please, he thought.

'—when it comes to chocolate.'

Oh, lord. He needed to get his mind back to real life, not fantasy.

He opened the parcel to discover a black cashmere sweater that felt like a soft caress against his skin. Like her mouth tracing a path down his throat, all warm and sweet and incredibly sexy. 'Fran, this is… I don't know what to say.' He leaned forward to kiss her cheek in thanks, and somehow ended up brushing his mouth against hers. A soft, sweet, gentle kiss that made his body feel lit up from within, like the sparklers she'd put on his birthday cake.

He broke the kiss, and for one crazy moment he almost marched over to the door so he could lock it behind them and then stride back to his desk and kiss her properly, until they were both dizzy with need and took the kiss to its ultimate conclusion. The conclusion maybe it should've reached on Sunday, when they'd been kissing on her sofa. The conclusion he hadn't been able to get out of his head ever since.

And then common sense washed back in.

She'd agreed to help him out by pretending to be his girlfriend, for his family's sake. And he was really going to need her when he expanded the business. So the last thing he should be doing was taking advantage of her. 'Thank you, Fran,' he said quietly, and left the office while his self-control would still let him.

At the end of the day, Fran stayed behind. 'I forgot to tell you something.'

He went cold. 'What?' That she'd found another job? That

she'd changed her mind about accepting a permanent role at Giovanni's? That she had a prior engagement so she couldn't go to the family party on Saturday night?

'Your parents and Nonna would expect me, as your girl-friend, to take you out to dinner tonight, seeing that it's your birthday.'

He shook his head. 'It's OK. You don't have to do that. I'll get a takeaway delivered.'

'No, really. I have to eat. And I have a couple of sugges-tions about the business, so we might as well multi-task it.'

How could he resist? 'Are you saying you'd make me work late on my birthday?'

'Let you, more like,' she teased back. 'I'll meet you outside your place in an hour.'

'So where are we going?'

'Within walking distance.'

He rolled his eyes. 'That's only half an answer.'

'It's the best you're going to get. And the dress code is whatever you like.'

He loved the way she teased him. The way she'd come out of her shell over the last month. He'd wondered if meeting his family would bring out her shy streak even more, but it hadn't—quite the opposite. And he really, really liked this confident, bubbly woman who'd emerged from her slightly too serious exterior. 'So I could wear really loud surfer shorts and the most hideously raggy T-shirt in the world?' he tested.

'If you don't mind people pointing at you and laughing at you, sure.' She gave him the sauciest wink he'd ever seen, and sashayed out of the shop.

He swallowed the disappointment that she hadn't kissed

him goodbye. Well, of course she hadn't. Nobody was here
to report back to the Mazetti clan, were they? Besides, they'd
agreed to forget about what happened on Sunday.

The problem was, his body refused to forget. He could
almost feel the softness of her skin against his fingertips,
smell her soft floral scent, feel the texture of her mouth against
his.

It drove him crazy.

The more so because he really didn't know how to deal
with this.

An hour later, Gio had just come out of the front door when
he saw Fran walking towards him.

'What, no surfer shorts?' she teased.

He'd opted for plain black trousers and the light sweater
she'd bought him; despite the fact it was summer, it was chilly
that evening. 'I thought this might be more appropriate.'

'It suits you.' She ran her hand lightly over the soft
cashmere. And even though her palm hadn't actually been in
contact with his skin, every nerve end was on red alert.

He was shocked to realise just how much he wanted Fran
to touch him. Properly. Skin to skin.

This wasn't meant to happen.

And he was going to have to be very, very careful.

'Though dressed completely in black, with those dark
glasses on as well…' She tutted and sucked in a breath. 'You
look a bit like a James Bond wannabe.'

'And how do you know I'm *not* James Bond?' he retorted.
'I could be sending out hidden messages in those lattes. Those
rosettas could be a special secret-agent code.'

She laughed, and tucked her arm through his. 'So you're

telling me your car is really super-turbocharged, instead of cornering like a tank and doing zero to sixty in about half a day?'

'That's below the belt,' he reprimanded her, laughing. 'So where did you say we were going?'

'I didn't.'

'No clues whatsoever?' he wheedled.

'Nope.'

He gave in, and just enjoyed the experience of walking through London with her, arm in arm. She switched the conversation to favourite movies, and he hadn't really noticed where they were going until she stopped outside Netti's pizzeria.

'Here?' Talk about bearding the lion in its den.

'It's the best pizzeria in London. And it's where you told me you celebrate red-letter days. So as today is your birthday—which I would say is a red-letter day—it seemed appropriate.'

The second he walked through the door, the room seemed to erupt with party poppers—and then there was a rousing chorus of 'Happy Birthday to You'.

As the paper streamers began to settle, he could see that the middle part of the restaurant was full, the usual small tables pulled together to form one enormous long table. All the staff from the four branches of Giovanni's were there, along with his parents, his sisters and their partners, and Nonna. There were two spare places at the far end; one of the chairs had a helium balloon attached, with the number twenty-nine emblazoned on it.

Marco gave him a hug. *'Buon compleanno, cugino mio,'* he said.

Gio was still too surprised for any words to come out.

When Netti emerged from the kitchen to give him a hug and a kiss, he submitted gracefully. And then he let Fran lead him over to his seat.

'I had absolutely no idea you were planning this,' he said. She'd already made a fuss of him that morning. He really hadn't expected her to plan a surprise for the evening, too.

'That was the plan.' She smiled. 'Though I can't take all the credit. It wasn't just me.'

'Fran is a girl after our hearts,' Nonna said, patting Fran's hand. 'It was all her idea. We just helped a bit.'

'Happy birthday, boss.' Amy produced a large envelope and a box at the far end of the table, and it was handed down to him.

He opened the card to discover that all the staff of Giovanni's had signed it. And the present was the new boxed set of remastered CDs by his favourite band—a gift that only someone who noticed things the way Fran did would've thought to buy him. 'I…this is fantastic. I'm a bit lost for words.' Understatement of the year. It had completely thrown him. 'Thank you—all of you. I had absolutely no idea.' He looked at Fran. 'How did you organise this?'

'Same way anyone would organise an office party.' She shrugged. 'It's not a big deal.'

Oh, yes, it was. She'd gone to a lot of trouble to organise this, in an incredibly short space of time and in utter secrecy.

'People think a lot of you, Gio,' she said softly. 'And they want to make a fuss of you, once in a while.'

A fuss he didn't normally let people make.

He couldn't remember the last time he'd spent an evening like this. Although the staff at Giovanni's always had a Christmas party, he usually stayed long enough to be sociable but left early, reasoning that they wouldn't want the boss around to put a dampener on festivities. Tonight, they were definitely letting their hair down—but they were all there because they wanted to celebrate his birthday with him. Share his special day.

Just before coffee was served, he said quietly to Fran, 'This is the best birthday I've had in years. It's been really wonderful. Because of you.'

'My pleasure.'

For a moment, their gazes meshed and held. Was he seeing what he wanted to see, or did that expression in her eyes mean…?

The moment was lost when Marco brought round the coffee.

'And Amaretti for luck,' Nonna added, fishing a box from under the table and handing it to Marco so he could share them out.

'Why for luck?' Fran asked.

'You don't know the story? About three hundred years ago, the cardinal of Milan went to pay a visit to Saronno, a poor town where two lovers worked, but they had little chance of marrying. In honour of the cardinal, they invented the Amaretti biscuit, and wrapped them in pairs to symbolise their love. The cardinal took pity on their plight—he blessed them, allowed them to marry and presided over the wedding feast. And Amaretti biscuits have always been wrapped in pairs, ever since, to remind people of the importance of true love.'

True love.

What Nonna and his family thought was happening between him and Fran.

Guilt throbbed through him. He was lying to them. For

the best of reasons, but still lying to them. And that wasn't who he was.

It wasn't who Fran was, either.

Nonna cleared her throat, and it was clear everyone was expecting him to kiss the girl who'd made it all happen, because they were all looking at him and Fran with the most soppy expression on their faces.

So what else could he do?

He leaned over towards her and touched his mouth to hers. It felt as if the room was full of erupting party-poppers again, a mass of glittering tinsel strands. And when he broke the kiss and opened his eyes, Fran looked as shell-shocked as he felt, with wide eyes and a white face. But all he could focus on was her mouth. A perfect rosebud. Lips he wanted to feel against his again.

Except they weren't alone, and he could hear catcalls and whistles in the background.

Just how long had he been kissing her?

Oh, lord. This was starting to get really complicated.

The next morning, Fran was still shell-shocked. That kiss should've been for show. So why had it felt so real? Why had it felt as if the stars were dancing when Gio's mouth had moved against hers—even more so than the time when he'd kissed her on her sofa?

But she pulled herself together and headed for work as usual.

'It was a good night, last night,' Sally said, handing her a mug. 'Though you look distinctly hung over this morning, Frannikins.'

'I feel it,' Fran said. Not that she'd drunk a huge amount; she just hadn't slept well, the previous night. Hadn't been able to stop thinking about Gio. Hadn't been able to get the fantasies out of her head.

'Gio said to tell you he's in Docklands this morning, but he'll call you later,' Sally added. 'You know, I've never seen him look this happy before, and I've worked with him for five years now. When I realised you two were an item, I was a bit worried at first—relationships at work normally make things a bit sticky. But you've changed him, Fran. Made him relax.'

'Good,' Fran replied, pinning a smile to her face. At first, she'd worried about how her colleagues would react to the idea of a relationship between herself and Gio, but they'd all seemed really positive about it. Now, Fran was more worried about what was going to happen once she and Gio had 'split up', how they'd react to that.

But there was nothing she could do about it right now, so it was pointless fretting about it. She'd deal with it when it happened.

She was busy with a set of figures when there was a knock on the office door. She swivelled round in her chair, and stared in surprise when she saw a man carrying the most beautiful hand-tied bouquet of flowers. 'Fran Marsden?' he asked.

'Er, yes.'

'Sign here, please.'

Flowers? Who on earth would be sending her flowers? But she signed for them and set them on her desk. They were absolutely stunning: sugar-pink roses, white lisianthus, pink freesias and tiny white matricia. She couldn't resist putting her nose into them and inhaling deeply; the scent was beautiful.

She opened the envelope that was tucked into the cellophane, and recognised the handwriting instantly.

Thank you. For everything. Love, Gio.

Love.

Her stomach clenched. Except this wasn't, was it?

When Gio walked into the office, he could see that Fran's eyes were slightly red. The flowers were on her desk, just as he'd hoped—but why did she look as if she'd been crying?

Or maybe… 'Oh, no. I should've checked before I had them delivered. I didn't realise you suffered from hay fever.'

'I don't.'

He leaned against the edge of her desk. 'What's wrong?'

'Nothing.'

'I have three sisters. So I know that "nothing" never really means that, especially when a woman looks as if she's been crying,' he said softly, and gently tilted her chin with one finger so she was facing him. 'What's wrong?' he asked again.

'I'm just being silly. I can't remember the last time someone sent me flowers,' Fran said, 'and I wasn't expecting these.'

'My intention wasn't to upset you,' he said. 'I just wanted to say thank you.'

'And it's appreciated.'

There was the tiniest wobble in her voice. He wanted to pull her into his arms, hold her close and tell her everything was going to be fine, because he was there—because he'd always be there and he'd never let anything hurt her.

But that was the whole problem.

He didn't trust himself not to let her down, the way he'd let his family down all those years before—the way he'd been selfish and stupid enough to put himself first, and they'd nearly lost his father as a result. How could he make her a promise he didn't know he could keep? So instead he kept things light. Ruffled her hair. 'I'm off to Islington. I only popped in while I was passing to see if there was anything you needed here.'

'No, we're fine.'

'And these aren't in lieu of the chocolates, by the way— Sally's already checked. We'll be getting those tomorrow.'

That at least made her smile. Which in turn made him feel less panicky. 'Catch you later,' he said, and left the office before he did something stupid.

Like give in to the urge to scoop her up in his arms, kiss her properly, and carry her to his bed.

CHAPTER TEN

AND then it was Saturday. The day of the party.

Fran rang Angela in the morning to see if she could do anything to help.

'Sweetheart, that's so kind of you to offer. But there's no need—Nonna, the girls and I have everything under control,' Angela said. 'We'll see you tonight. And the idea is that you and Gio have *fun*, OK?'

'OK,' Fran promised.

Which left her with nothing to sort out except what she was going to wear. Although she had a perfectly serviceable little black dress—one she'd worn to functions when she'd worked at the voiceover studio—it didn't feel quite right for the Mazetti party. She wanted something a little dressier. The kind of thing that Gio Mazetti's girlfriend would wear, not his office manager.

She was browsing in the clothes shops in Camden when her eye was caught by a dress. It was a deep cornflower blue, in floaty organza over taffeta. Absolutely nothing like what she'd intended to buy—she'd always thought herself too curvy to wear a strapless dress—but some impulse made her try it on.

She was looking at herself in the mirror and wondering if

she had the nerve to wear it when the sales assistant appeared with a lapis-lazuli necklace.

'I don't normally bother with jewellery,' Fran said, eyeing it dubiously.

'Try it on and see what you think,' the assistant suggested. 'I reckon it matches the dress perfectly. Here—do you want me to do it up for you?'

Ten seconds later, Fran stared at herself in the mirror. The necklace really was the finishing touch, skimming across the middle of her collarbones and throwing the paleness of her skin into relief.

And the bulges she'd feared she'd see weren't visible. Just curves.

'It's perfect. Don't wear anything else, not even a watch,' the assistant said. 'What about shoes?'

'I was thinking black high heels,' Fran said.

'Patent or suede?'

'Suede.'

The assistant nodded. 'Perfect. You're going to blow his mind when he sees you.'

Not when she wasn't his real girlfriend. 'Maybe,' she hedged.

'There's no maybe about it,' the assistant said with a smile. 'That dress was made for you.'

'I was planning to get a little black dress. Something practical that I could dress up or down.'

'You *could*,' the assistant said, 'but, believe me, nothing's going to be as perfect as what you're wearing right now.'

And Fran knew the assistant was right when she opened her front door to Gio and his jaw dropped.

'Wow.' Then he seemed to recover fast and go back to

their usual teasing relationship. 'You scrub up nicely, Francesca Marsden.'

So did he. In dark trousers and a silk shirt, he looked stunning. And very, very touchable.

He reached out and traced a fingertip just below the line of her necklace. The feel of his skin against hers made every nerve end quiver and her pulse speeded up.

'Your dress is the same colour as your eyes. It's fabulous,' he said softly.

And she knew he meant it.

He wasn't paying his pretend girlfriend a compliment in front of his family.

He was telling her this, here and now. In private.

'Not just the dress. *You* look fabulous.' Then he held out his hand. 'We'd better go. The taxi's waiting.'

She locked up and followed him out to the taxi. He held the door open for her—the perfect manners were typical of Gio—and it seemed as if hardly a minute passed before they were there.

'Are you really sure you're up to this?' Gio asked. 'The Mazetti clan is pretty big. It's not too late to back out.'

'I've already met Nonna, your parents and your sisters, your aunt and some of your cousins,' she reminded him. 'It'll be fine.'

'Then let's do it.' He slid his arm round her shoulders, and they walked into the hall together.

He'd said his family was big. But she hadn't expected the place to be so utterly packed. Gio introduced her to person after person; although she was normally good with names, there were so many that she simply lost track.

And she had no idea who was topping up her glass, but the level of champagne never seemed to go down. It would be way too easy to drink too much and make a mistake—say something she shouldn't. She made a mental note to put her glass down and forget about it.

'Francesca, *cara*!' Nonna came over to her, hugged her and kissed both cheeks. 'You look lovely.'

'So do you,' Fran responded politely.

Nonna chuckled. 'Ah, but I don't have that extra sparkle—the look of a young woman in love.'

Maybe Gio's family were seeing what they wanted to see, Fran thought. Or maybe after all these years she'd finally found her hidden talent: acting. Because she wasn't in love with Gio.

Was she?

Before Nonna could say anything else, the band on stage played a fanfare.

Gio groaned. 'Why do we have to do this every year?'

'Because it wouldn't be a birthday party without it, figlio mio,' his father said, laughing and patting his shoulder.

'You know the song,' the singer said into the microphone. 'Four times. Giovanni, Isabella, Giuditta and Marcella.'

The band played the introduction to 'Happy Birthday to You', and then were drowned out by the entire room singing in Italian. *'Tanti auguri a te, Tanti auguri a te, Tanti auguri Giovanni, tanti auguri a te!'* The song was repeated for Gio's sisters; and finally, there was a rousing set of cheers.

'Your family definitely knows how to party,' Fran said, smiling at Gio when the cheers had died down and the band was playing again.

'Years of practice,' Gio said. 'Let's get some food and escape outside. It's boiling in here.'

Once he'd piled a plate with assorted canapés and dips, they found a quiet corner in the grounds. Gio looked at the bench, then at Fran's dress. 'Some of that varnish is peeling. I don't want it ruining your dress. Better sit on my lap.'

From another man, it would be a cheesy excuse. From Gio, it was practical common sense. So when he set the plate down on the bench beside them, she acquiesced without making a fuss, settling herself on his lap and resting one hand on his shoulder for balance.

The fact that his hand was resting on the curve of her waist really shouldn't be sending these little shivers through her body, she thought. He'd only done it to make sure she didn't accidentally slide off his lap. And she really shouldn't get used to being close to him like this. Close and personal.

Striving to keep her voice normal, she said, 'It's quite an evening.'

'When we were kids, we used to have a bouncy castle and a barbecue in the back garden. But as we grew older and the family's grown bigger, Mum decided to hire a hall and a band.' He sighed. 'To be honest, I'd much rather have a quiet night out somewhere. See a good film or a show. But Mum, Nonna and the girls really enjoy it. They love planning the party and getting dressed up and having an excuse to get everyone together and talk so much that they end up with sore throats the next day.'

'So you put up with it for their sake?' Fran guessed.

'Yeah.' Gio shrugged. 'Just call me Saint Giovanni.'

She gave in to the temptation to stroke his cheek. Freshly shaven. Smooth and soft and sensual. 'You're a good man,' she said.

He turned his head slightly and pressed a kiss into her palm—like the way she'd pressed a kiss into his palm that afternoon when he'd kissed her on her sofa. 'Not really. I let my family down once—at the time when they needed me most. I promised myself I would never do that again.'

'Everyone else forgave you long ago—if they ever blamed you in the first place.' Which, having met his family, she very much doubted. 'Your dad's heart attack wasn't your fault. When are you going to forgive yourself, Gio?'

'I don't know.' He sighed. 'Can we change the subject, please?'

This wasn't the time or the place to push him. 'Sure. What do you want to talk about?'

'Dunno.'

He looked utterly lost, and it made her heart ache. She leaned forward and kissed the tip of his nose.

He looked up at her, his eyes dark, and his hands tightened round her waist. 'Why did you do that?'

She opted for honesty. 'Because you're hurting, Gio, and I want to make you feel better.'

She couldn't help staring at his mouth. Even though he was in a bleak mood, right now, there was still a tiny curve upwards at the corner of his lips. That irrepressible, funny man she'd grown to l—

Whoops. She was getting too much into this role of being Gio's girlfriend. Better remember she was just his office manager, and this was just for show. 'Talk to me,' she said softly. 'Tell me what's wrong.'

He shook his head. 'Just ignore me. I'm in a funny mood.'

She stroked his face again, and her skin tingled at the contact. 'I'm going to quote Nonna back at you. "A problem shared is a problem halved." You helped me when I hit a bad patch. Now you're having a bad patch and it's my turn to help you. So tell me what's put you in that mood. Is it work?'

'No.' He sounded very definite.

'What, then?'

'I don't know. It's just this feeling of something…' He shook his head in obvious frustration. 'Something *missing*, I suppose.

I can't explain it. If I knew what it was, I could do something about it. But there's just this black hole staring at me.'

'Your music?' she guessed.

'No. I still play, for me.'

And he'd played for her, too.

'You could go back to it. You don't have to expand the café chain—it's doing fine as it is. Take a sabbatical,' she suggested. 'Be a musician.'

'How? Busking on street corners?'

She shook her head. 'There's nothing to stop you playing a concert once in a while. An arts centre, a gallery—even in Giovanni's. You're thinking of opening one evening a week in Holborn for the book group. Why not open another evening a week as a classical music night, maybe at Charlotte Street? Play the music you love for people?'

He took a deep breath. 'I don't know. I don't know if I'm good enough, any more.'

'What you played for me was good,' she said. 'OK, so I'm not a music critic and your technique could've been all over the place, for all I know—but none of the notes sounded wrong. I liked it. And there are plenty of people out there who'd like to relax with a decent cup of coffee and one of Ingrid's fabulous cakes and listen to something to help them chill out.'

'Be a musician.' He stared at her, though it was as if he wasn't seeing her. As if he was some place far, far away. 'I don't know, Fran. The more I think about it, the more I'm sure that being a musician wouldn't have been the right life for me. I don't want to be constantly on the road, or doing bits and pieces and trying to scrape a living. I know I wouldn't have had the patience to teach.'

'Are you sure about that? You did a good job of teaching me to make espresso.'

'Which is not the same thing at all as teaching someone who can either sing in tune, but has no sense of rhythm, or can sing with the beat, but is completely tuneless. That's more like nails scraping down a blackboard, and I'm not noble enough to pretend it doesn't matter and gently guide whoever it is into a better technique.' He sighed. 'I just feel I'm looking for something, Fran. Searching. And I don't know what I'm looking for or even where to look.'

'Maybe you'll know when you find it.'

'Maybe. But right now I feel like the most selfish man on earth. I have so many good things in my life. I love my family, I have free rein in my job, I like where I live. So why can't I be satisfied with what I have?'

She held him close. 'I can't answer that. But I do know your family love you, your employees respect you, and you're a good man. Don't be so hard on yourself.'

'Hard on myself? That,' Gio said wryly, 'is most definitely the pot calling the kettle black.'

'But that's not up for discussion.'

He rested his forehead against her temple. 'Now who's being difficult?'

His breath fanned her cheek, and it was, oh, so tempting to turn her head slightly, let her mouth brush against his. Kiss his blues away. But that wouldn't solve anything: that would just put off the problem. Right now, he needed her to keep this light. 'Not me,' she said with a smile. 'Come on. Let's go and dance your blues away.'

After a few minutes of throwing themselves into the music, she was relieved to see that his bleak mood lifted slightly and he was starting to smile again. But somehow they'd moved near to the stage, and the singer had caught sight of them.

'Gio! Come up and play with us, my friend,' he called when the song had finished.

Gio shook his head. 'No, I'm fine in the audience, thanks.'

'Come on,' the singer wheedled. 'You know everyone would love to hear to you play. And sing.'

'I'm fine right here,' Gio repeated.

The singer refused to let it drop, and Gio's face darkened. Considering the conversation they'd just had, for a moment, Fran thought that he was going to walk out.

And then Nonna placed her hand on his arm. 'Gio, *piccolino*, do it for me. Or if you won't do it for me, sing for Francesca,' she said softly.

Tension was coming off him in almost visible waves. But then he nodded. 'All right. I'll do it for Fran.'

He climbed up on the stage, to loud applause and cheers from the audience. 'OK, so it's August and not October, but there's a certain song I want to sing tonight. For Francesca.' He winked at her, as if telling her that it was going to be OK, he wasn't going to make a scene; then he turned and mouthed something to the pianist, who nodded. And Gio made no protest when the guitarist handed him an electric guitar—just checked the tuning.

And then he counted the band in to a soft, jazzy number Fran recognized: 'Moondance.'

It was a song she'd always liked. But hearing Gio sing it somehow gave it something extra. He had the most beautiful voice. So beautiful that it hurt; she found herself wishing that Gio was singing this to her for real, that he wanted to dance with her and call her his love and make love with her.

But his eyes were on her as he sang. And just for a moment she could almost believe that he really was singing this for her. Could imagine what it would be like to run into his arms and dance in a frost-covered garden with him on an October night, the moonlight shining through the almost-bare branches of the trees and turning everything magically silver.

The song ended with him pleading for one more dance with his love. Then he smiled. 'Thank you. That one was for Fran,' he said, and handed the guitar back.

'Oh, come on, Gio—give us another one!' someone called.

'It's my birthday party and you want me to work?' he retorted, laughing. 'Now there's a first. I thought you lot all wanted me to slow down.'

'Just one more song,' someone else pleaded.

'One's enough. Now I'm going to dance with my girl and hand you back to the real singer. Enjoy your evening, everyone.' He stepped down from the stage and joined Fran again.

'I didn't know you could sing that well,' she said. 'That was pretty amazing.'

'Nothing that a thousand pub singers in London don't do every Saturday night,' he said, making a dismissive gesture. 'It's not a big deal. Dance with me?'

The singer had followed Gio's performance with another Van Morrison song, a slow ballad; Fran stepped forward into Gio's arms and swayed with him to the music. If only she could ease his troubles, the way the singer was telling them the love of his life did. But all she could do right now was hold him.

And even when the next song changed tempo and became upbeat again, Fran and Gio remained dancing close, just holding each other and swaying to the beat. Cheek to cheek. So close they could feel each other's heartbeat.

With shock, she realised that this was what she'd been waiting for. To be in Gio's arms. She couldn't pin down the exact moment, but at some point over the last few weeks she'd fallen for Gio—and the whole Mazetti tribe. Which was stupid, because this wasn't for keeps. Their relationship would end when Nonna went back to Italy.

And the knowledge broke her heart.

Gio sensed the sudden tension in Fran, and pulled back slightly so he could see her face. 'OK?' he mouthed.

She nodded and smiled, but although the light was too low to see properly, he could tell the smile didn't reach her eyes. She was definitely upset about something, but she wasn't telling.

Ah, hell.

He wanted to kiss her better.

No. Actually, he just wanted to kiss her again.

And that would complicate matters beyond belief.

He really ought to let her go right now. Put her in a taxi and pay the driver to wait until she was safely indoors. But he couldn't drag himself away from her. So he just wrapped his arms round her again, held her close. Told her silently with his body that he was there, that whatever was wrong he'd do whatever he could to make it right.

Dancing cheek to cheek with her like this meant that he could smell the sweet floral perfume she'd used. Summer roses. Like the candied petals his mother used on a trifle and that he'd always begged for, as a child. So sweet.

His mouth was so close to her ear; he couldn't resist pressing the tiniest kiss to her earlobe. The next thing he knew, his mouth was brushing a trail of kisses along her cheek. Her face turned slightly to meet his. And at last his mouth found hers. A tiny, gentle, questioning touch.

A second's pause.

And then she tilted her head slightly, kissed him back. An equally tiny kiss. The barest touch of her lips against his.

His mouth was tingling. And despite the fact they were in a noisy, crowded hall with people dancing round them, everything seemed to melt away. There was just the two of them. And an overwhelming need to kiss her properly, feel her mouth open beneath his.

He caught her lower lip between his. So soft, so sweet.

His head was telling him that this was a seriously bad idea, but his body wasn't listening. Because this felt as if tiny stars had started to illuminate the black hole in the middle of his heart. The tiniest flickers of light, of hope.

And when her mouth opened beneath his and the tip of her tongue touched his, the lights became brighter. She was warm and soft and her body fitted against his perfectly.

Right here, right now, this was where he belonged. With Fran. No pretence, no act. And the way she was kissing him back made him feel as if he could conquer the world. Walk on air.

'Put the girl down, Gio. There are children present,' Ric teased, slapping him on the back.

Oh, lord. However long had they been kissing? Fran's mouth was slightly red and swollen, her pupils were enormous, and he could feel that her breasts had grown slightly fuller and heavier against him.

He was turned on just as much. And he couldn't get the words of that song out of his head. How much he wanted to make love to her. In a frosted garden. On a swing.

Uh. He couldn't remember the last time he'd fantasised about someone. His life had been too full with work. But Fran…Fran was different.

'Your timing's impeccable, *cugino mio*. Not,' he said ruefully.

And Fran's cheeks were crimson. He kissed the tip of her

nose. 'Sorry, honey. I got carried away. Give me a second to calm down.' He bent his head slightly and whispered in her ear, 'But please don't move until then, because if you do I think we'll both be extremely embarrassed.'

'I was going to ask you if you were enjoying the party,' Ric said with a smile, 'but I don't think I need to.'

'Tact,' Gio said to Fran with a sigh, 'is not a Mazetti strong point.' He coughed. 'Would you mind not embarrassing my girlfriend?'

'I apologise, Fran.' Ric patted her shoulder. 'For embarrassing you. Though not for embarrassing the birthday boy. *Buon compleanno*, Gio.'

'Thanks, Ric. I think.'

When Gio's cousin left them alone again, Gio stroked Fran's cheek. 'Um. That wasn't supposed to…' He swallowed hard. 'I can't even blame it on too much champagne.'

It was just Fran. Her nearness. And how he wanted her.

'Me, too.'

Had he spoken that last bit aloud? Was she saying that she felt the same way?

But right now he didn't trust his judgement.

Right now, he just wanted to get out of here. But the party was a quarter his—he knew he was expected to stay right to the end.

Somehow, they made it through the rest of the evening. If anyone else had noticed them kissing—well, how could they possibly have missed it?—at least they had more tact than Ric and didn't mention it.

They were the last ones in the hall except Nonna, his parents, his sisters and their partners. Just short of a dozen of them: enough to make clearing up easy work.

'Thank you,' Jude said, hugging Fran.

'We know you helped Gio choose our presents. And they're perfect,' Bella said.

Marcie added, 'But most of all, thank you for making our brother human again. I haven't seen him look this happy in years.'

'No pressure, then,' Fran quipped, but inside her heart was heavy. This whole deception had started to avoid Nonna's illusions being shattered. But the way things were going, when she and Gio staged their break-up, an awful lot more people were going to get hurt. His grandmother, his parents and sisters…

And herself.

'Come on, honey. Time to go home,' Gio said, taking her hand.

Once they'd made their goodbyes and climbed into the taxi, Gio let her hand go again.

Well, what had she expected? That kiss earlier—it hadn't been faked, but it hadn't exactly been for real either. A dream that had caught them both up for a while, but now they were back in reality.

They were silent as the taxi took them back to Fran's house, but she was shocked when Gio actually dismissed the taxi. Was he expecting her to invite him in?

As if he could read her mind, he said, 'I just want to see you safely into your flat. And then I'm walking home.'

'But you live ages away.'

He shrugged. 'It's not raining and the fresh air will do me good.'

He followed her into the lobby and she opened her front door. Her tongue felt as if it had stuck to the roof of his mouth, but she managed to get the words out. Even managed to get them to sound light and breezy, as if nothing had happened. 'Would you like to come in for coffee?'

In response, he moved closer and brushed his mouth against hers. 'If I do, we'll both regret it in the morning. Because right now what I want to do is take that beautiful dress off you and carry you to your bed.'

That sexy, husky note in his voice was her undoing. He'd just voiced exactly what she wanted him to do, too.

'Gio.' She reached up to pull his head down to hers. Pressed her body against his, so close that she could actually feel his heartbeat. Hard and fast, like her own.

And he was kissing her back, gently moving her so her back was against the front door. He nudged his thigh between hers, sliding one hand to cup her bottom and bring her even closer to him; she could feel his erection pressing against her, hot and hard.

Fran had never wanted anyone so much in her entire life.

And then he shuddered. Broke the kiss. Disentangled her hands from his hair. Took a step backwards. 'We can't do this. In the morning, I'll feel guilty about taking advantage of you.'

He wouldn't be taking advantage of her. She'd be with him all the way.

'So I'm going to leave now. While I still can.' He closed his eyes. Embarrassment, or because if he looked at her, saw the sheer desire in her expression, his control would splinter?

'I'll see you Monday.' He opened his eyes again, but didn't look at her. 'And thanks for coming to the party with me tonight.' He raised a hand in the tiniest wave goodbye, and left.

He'd done the right thing. The sensible part of her knew that. It would be way too complicated between them at work afterwards if they spent the night making love. Leaving now was the right thing to do—not to mention the complication of this whole fake-girlfriend thing.

So why did it hurt so damned much? she thought as she locked the door behind her. Why did she want to curl up in a ball and cry her eyes out?

CHAPTER ELEVEN

GIO didn't actually see Fran on Monday, because he was visiting a franchise organisation. She was a bit hurt he hadn't asked her to go along with him; but then again, it was probably better if they were apart for a bit. Sensible. It would give them both a chance to cool down and wipe out any lingering awkwardness from Saturday night.

On Tuesday, Gio didn't even call in to the office to see if everything was OK. Which was good, she told herself, because clearly he trusted her to keep everything in the cafés ticking over without supervision. And that stupid longing to hear his voice was just that. Stupid. Teenagery.

Which was even *more* stupid, considering that she was twenty-six and sensible, not fifteen and full of hormones.

All the same, she made serious inroads into the box of chocolates Gio had bought her for winning the bet about making latte art. She needed the sugar rush.

But after work on Tuesday night, things took a dip for the worse. Fran had called in at the supermarket on the way home. But as soon as she pushed her front door open, she could see that she had a problem.

A huge problem.

There was a hole in her ceiling, and bits of artex were scattered everywhere. And from the way her sofa-bed was completely soaked, it looked as if water had come through the ceiling, collected in the gap between the plasterboard and the artex and stretched it out until it burst—sending water cascading straight down. Her carpets were squelchy underfoot, there were stains on the walls from where water had seeped through the gap between the ceiling and the wall, and already she could smell something unpleasant: wet wool, she guessed. Probably the carpet.

For a moment, she just stood staring at the mess, too shocked to move.

And then common sense kicked in. She needed to make a few calls. Starting with the letting agency, to tell them what had happened so they could book someone to come round and start repairing the damage. The insurance company for the damage to her belongings. And work, to say that she'd be in late tomorrow as she had a ton of things to sort out.

Which meant she was going to have to talk to Gio.

Well, this was business and they were both adults. So there was no point in putting it off, was there? She rang his mobile; he sounded slightly absent when he answered, as if she'd interrupted him in the middle of something and he was only paying half attention to the call.

'It's Fran. I'm afraid I won't be in tomorrow—at least, not until late—because I need to sort out a problem.'

Her voice sounded tight and slightly anxious, not her usual cheerful self. Gio, who hadn't really been listening, suddenly snapped to attention. 'What sort of problem?'

'My flat's been flooded. It's a bit of a mess. I just need to sort a few things out.'

She was clearly aiming to sound practical, but the tiny

wobble in her voice told him how upset she really was. Knowing Fran, 'a bit of a mess' was an understatement. And even though he knew it was sensible to keep his distance for a little bit longer and she was perfectly capable of dealing with the problem by herself, he couldn't just stand by and leave her to it. 'I'm coming over.'

'Gio, you really d—'

'I'm on my way *now*,' he cut in. He ended the call, closed the file he was working on, locked the door behind him, collected his car and drove straight to her flat.

Her face was tight with tension when she opened the door to him. Because she didn't want to face him, or…?

Then he glanced over her shoulder and saw the mess.

'*Porca miseria*, Fran! How did this happen? A burst pipe?'

She shook her head. 'The guy above me left the bath running. He was on the phone to someone, had a bit of a fight with them and stomped out. He forgot he'd left the bath running until he came back, three hours later.'

'And by then it had overflowed and soaked through your ceiling.' Gio shook his head in disgust. 'What an *idiot*.'

'I'm afraid I said something far worse than that when he came down to apologise, a few minutes ago,' she admitted. 'I would offer you a coffee, but—'

'No. It'd be dangerous to use your kettle right now,' Gio said. 'The place needs drying out, the electrics all need checking properly to make sure they're safe before you use them again, and then there's the repair to the ceiling. The carpet's probably not going to recover, so you'll need someone in to measure the room and then fit a replacement. And I'm not sure your sofa-bed is ever going to be the same again.' He surveyed the damage. 'It's going to take quite a while to sort this out. And there's no way you can stay here while your flat's in this kind of condition. Where were you planning to sleep tonight?'

She shrugged. 'I'll find a hotel or something.'

'My family would skin me for letting you do that, when I have a spare room. Problem solved—you're staying with me.' It was a rash move, he knew; after Saturday night, having Fran that close would be a major strain on his self-control. But how could he stand by and let her struggle, when such a simple solution was right at his fingertips? 'Just pack what you need for a few days. Clothes and what have you, paperwork and anything that might not cope with a high moisture content in the air.'

'Clothes?' She coughed and gestured to the rail next to the wall. The sodden canvas cover was sagging over the hangers beneath; it was a fair bet that right now the only dry clothes she owned were those she was wearing.

'OK. Have you got some large plastic bags?'

'I've got some dustbin bags.'

'They'll do. Put your clothes in those. I have a washer dryer, so we can deal with the laundry when we get back to my place.'

'We're going to carry bags of wet clothes on the Tube?'

He smiled. 'You know you say my car corners like a tank? Well, it carries like one, too. And it's parked outside. Without a permit.'

Her eyes widened. 'Gio, you'll get a fine!'

'At this time of the evening? I doubt it. And no traffic warden would be hard-hearted enough to give me a ticket when your place is flooded and your visitor permits are probably so much papier mâché.'

She clearly didn't share his certainty, but it was a risk he was prepared to take.

'Just pack your stuff and I'll carry it out for you and load it up,' he said quietly. 'Oh, and when you talk to your letting agency again, you might want to give them my home number. Just in case they need to get hold of you while you're staying with me and for some reason they can't reach you at work or on your mobile phone; the answering machine can take a message if we're not there.'

Her eyes were suspiciously glittery; she looked very close to tears. How could he stay brisk and businesslike when she so clearly needed a hug? So he wrapped his arms round her, resting his cheek against her hair for a moment. 'It's going to be all right, *piccolina*. Really.' And then he let her go before he did something really stupid, like picking her up and carrying her out to his car.

He helped her pack the rest of her clothes into dustbin liners.

'There's no point in packing these. They're dry-clean only. Ruined,' she said and made a separate pile of clothes.

Including the dress she'd worn on Saturday night, he noted. 'My mum's bound to know someone who can salvage them,' he said, picked up the pile and stowed them in a bag. 'I take it you haven't eaten yet?'

'No. I'd just done a bit of shopping on the way home.' She surveyed the squelchy mess around them. 'I don't think I'm hungry any more.'

'Fran, you need to eat properly. I know this is a horrible situation, but skipping meals will only make you feel worse.' He punched a couple of buttons on his mobile phone. 'Mum? It's Gio. I'm at Fran's—there's been a flood.'

Predictably, his mother wanted to know if he was helping Fran clear up and if she was going to stay at his flat. 'Of *course*. Look, some of her clothes are dry-clean only, and they're soaked.'

'And you need help to salvage them. Do you want me to come over to yours?'

He smiled. 'You're an angel. Yes, please. You've got my spare key.'

'I'm on my way now. Tell Fran not to worry.'

'I will.'

'Love you, Gio.'

'Love you too, Mum.' He snapped the phone closed and turned to Fran. 'Sorted. Have you called your parents yet?'

She shook her head. 'No point. They're too far away to help.'

'Don't you think they need to know where you are, in case they try to call you here and can't get through? They might be worried.'

She gave him a look as if to say, why on earth would they be worried? But she shrugged. 'I'll text them later.'

His first instinct in a crisis was to call his family. And yet Fran kept her distance from hers, sorting the problem out on her own. Was it the adoption thing that had made her so self-reliant? Or was it that she was scared to let herself be part of them, in case she was rejected again?

He remembered the way she'd suddenly tensed on Saturday night, but wouldn't tell him what was wrong. Had that been it, the idea of being part of a family and fearing rejection?

But his family had liked her immediately. They wouldn't reject her.

Neither would he.

If he could only trust himself not to let her down.

Angela and Isabella were already at Gio's flat by the time they arrived. And something smelled fantastic.

'I assume neither of you two have had the time to eat yet,' Angela said. 'So you can just sit down right now and eat.'

Fran felt the tears welling up and squeezed her eyes tightly shut. She was *not* going to be wet about this.

Angela gave her a hug. 'Hey, it's horrible when you get flooded out. Especially when you couldn't have done anything to prevent it. Sit down and eat. You'll feel a lot better when you've eaten something.'

Fran didn't quite believe her, but the gnocchi and sauce were gorgeous.

And Angela was right: it was exactly what she needed.

Fifteen minutes later the washing machine was on, Angela had made a pile of clothes she intended to take to a friend who specialised in restoring textiles, and Nonna was brewing coffee to go with the box of Amaretti biscuits she'd brought over.

'Thank you for coming to my rescue,' Fran said. 'I really appreciate it.'

'*Prego,*' Angela said with a smile. 'Of course we would. You're one of us.'

Oh, lord. She really *was* going to cry in a minute. Something inside her felt as if it had just cracked.

Gio ruffled her hair. 'Come on, *tesoro*. Let's put your things in my spare room.'

'Room' was probably a bit of an ambitious description, Fran thought; the space was more like a large broom cupboard. And it was already crammed with a computer, paperwork and three guitars. Even if he moved them all elsewhere, there wouldn't be room for anyone to sleep there.

Gio might have a spare room, but he didn't have a spare bed. She felt her cheeks scorch with heat. Was he expecting her to share his bed? And as for the message *that* would give his family…

As if he guessed what she was thinking, he said, 'I'll change the sheets for you, Fran. You'll be having my room while you stay here—and my sofa turns into a guest bed, so, before you start worrying, let me reassure you that you're not putting me out. Now, I'll show you how the shower works—there's plenty of hot water, so just help yourself whenever you want a bath or what have you. I won't be expecting you to go in to work at the same time in the morning as I do—and you don't need to come in at all tomorrow.' He took a bunch of keys from a drawer and detached one. 'Spare door key. So you don't have to wait around for me.'

She swallowed hard. 'I really appreciate this, you know.'

'Prego.' He smiled back at her.

By the time Gio had changed the bed and she'd sorted out her things in his bathroom—and it felt strangely domesticated to have her face cream sitting next to his razor on the bathroom shelf and her toothbrush next to his—Angela had finished sorting through the dry-cleaning pile. 'I'll take these to my friend tomorrow morning,' she said.

'Thank you.' Fran hugged her. 'Thank you so much. I thought they were beyond saving.'

'My pleasure, sweetheart.' Her voice softened. 'And you've already done a lot for me. If anything, I'm in your debt: Gio's not such a complete workaholic as he used to be, and he smiles a hell of a lot more.'

'Oh, Mum.' Gio groaned. 'Much more of this, and I'll be forced to put on a Derek Bailey CD.'

'Who's Derek Bailey?' Fran asked, puzzled.

'A jazz guitarist from the 1950s and 1960s. He used to do a lot of improvisation work,' Gio explained.

'It's not actually music,' Angela said, grimacing. 'It's the stuff Gio plays when he wants to clear the room.'

'Don't be such a philistine. Of course it's music. Nonna, you tell her,' Gio said.

Isabella put both hands up in a gesture of surrender, laughing. 'I'm staying out of this one.'

'It's music—but not in the traditional sense,' he said to Fran. 'It works on rhythm and texture rather than a melodic basis. What's known as tonal harmonics.'

'What's that in English? Or even Italian?' Fran asked.

In answer, Gio fetched an acoustic guitar from his spare room and demonstrated.

'See?' he said.

'Um…I'm with your mother,' Fran said. 'That's not music.'

'Why can't you play nice things?' Angela asked. 'Like the pretty bits you used to play. Like the stuff you were playing at the party.'

'And I still think you should've gone to college,' Isabella added. 'Studied music.'

Gio put his guitar away again with a scowl. 'Well, I didn't. And it's too late now.'

'Don't be silly. Of course it's not too late. There are plenty of mature students around—and you're not even thirty yet. You probably wouldn't be the oldest one there. You sort him out, Francesca,' Isabella said.

'I think,' Fran said gently, 'Gio's man enough to sort himself out.'

'Exactly. Thank you for the support, honey.' He slid his arm round her shoulders and kissed the top of her head.

Oh, lord. His closeness made her remember Saturday night. The way he'd held her and kissed her then. The way the whole room had dissolved around them. The way he'd kissed her, pressed against the front door of her flat.

'*Prego,*' she said, and hoped her voice didn't sound as wobbly to everyone else as it did to her.

* * *

Given that Gio was always in the office so early, Fran guessed that he'd go to bed reasonably early, too—so even though she wasn't tired, she feigned a yawn and said goodnight, a good hour before she'd normally go to bed.

It was weird, going to sleep in Gio's bed. Even though the sheets were clean, his scent was everywhere; and being wrapped in his duvet felt a bit like being wrapped in his arms.

Right now she could really do with a cuddle. She had no idea when her flat would be habitable again, or how much of her stuff would have to be replaced, or even if the flat would still have the same feel about it when all the repairs had been made.

'Pull yourself together. Stop being so wet. There are plenty of people in far worse situations,' she told herself fiercely. Yet still the tears slid silently down her face. She scrubbed them away and buried her face in the pillow, until at last she fell asleep.

Until a strange noise woke her.

A noise that sounded like the door opening.

For a moment, she was disorientated: then she remembered she was in Gio's bedroom. In Gio's bed. He was asleep on the sofa bed in the living room. She must have dreamed all that nonsense about the door opening. It was probably a floorboard creaking as the building settled overnight or something; and didn't people always misinterpret the noises in a strange house?

She turned over to go back to sleep.

And then she felt the mattress dip beside her.

CHAPTER TWELVE

FRAN'S first reaction was to shriek and switch on the light.

Gio also gave out the most almighty yell—and then sat bolt upright and stared at her in shock. 'Fran? What—why—how—oh, *Dio.*' He groaned and covered his face with his hands. 'I'm so sorry. When I offered you a bed for the night, I didn't mean you had to share it with me. This wasn't meant to happen. I… Look, I'm really sorry for disturbing you.' He started to slide out of the bed—and then stopped.

'Um, Fran, can you turn the light off?'

'What?'

'Turn the light off,' he repeated. 'Unless you want an eyeful. Because I'm not wearing…' He dragged in a breath and looked her straight in the eye. 'Oh, hell. This isn't what you think it is, I swear it.'

She shook her head. 'Right now, I don't have a clue what's going on.'

He swallowed hard. 'I sleepwalk. I haven't done it for years—I used to do it when I was a kid, but I thought I'd grown out of it.'

'You *sleepwalk*?' So he'd walked into her room and climbed into bed with her without realising what he was doing?

He nodded. 'Mum took me to a few doctors when I was

little. They did all kinds of tests, but it seemed there wasn't any rhyme or reason to it. Nobody knows why it happens. I just…sleepwalk.'

'And when I screamed I woke you up.' She bit her lip. 'Isn't it supposed to be dangerous to wake someone if they're sleep-walking?'

'No, that's a myth—they used to think that sleepwalkers acted out whatever they were dreaming, so if someone was dreaming about being Marie Antoinette or something and you touched them on the neck, their head would fall off. Quite how you were supposed to know exactly what they were dreaming about, I have no idea.' He smiled ruefully. 'According to re-searchers, most sleepwalkers do it in the first three hours of sleep, when your sleep's deep and dreamless. So it's not actually dangerous to wake a sleepwalker—it just throws them a bit and they might get a bit stroppy with you, so doctors recommend you just quietly guide them back to bed. If someone wakes me, I'm usually a bit disoriented and don't have a clue where I am. I certainly wasn't expecting to wake up in here.' He rubbed a hand over his face. 'I really had no idea this was going to happen, or I would've warned you. I'm so sorry I scared you.'

'You used to sleepwalk a lot?'

He nodded. 'Especially around exam times.'

'So it was stress that caused it?'

He shrugged. 'It might have been a factor, yes.'

And having an unexpected guest was definitely stressful. He'd given her his room, changed his routine for her. Which was enough, perhaps, to have made him sleepwalk tonight. Given that this was his bed, it was natural for him to return to it. 'So what exactly happens when you sleepwalk? Do you know when you're doing it?'

'No, though my eyes are open. Apparently, I used to just

walk around the house and turn all the lights on and then off again, and then take myself back to bed,' Gio said. 'Mum said they could set their watch by me. It'd be about quarter to ten when I was younger, and nearer midnight when I was in my mid-teens.'

'So that was it? You didn't used to make yourself a midnight snack or straighten pictures or anything?'

He actually blushed and looked away. 'I haven't done anything dramatic like that girl who was in the papers for climbing a crane in her sleep—or the guy who mowed his lawn in the middle of the night.'

There was a reason for the high colour in his face, she was sure. 'But?' she prompted.

'I tend to take all my clothes off first.'

'You're telling me you sleepwalk in the *nude*?' Now her initial shock of being woken had worn off, Fran could see the funny side of the situation. No wonder Gio had asked her to turn off the light. Beneath the duvet, he wasn't just bare-chested—he was stark naked.

'I was hoping for a little sympathy here.' He sounded pained. 'My sisters used to have friends over for sleepovers and they'd stay up to watch me. They knew I'd worry about sleepwalking in front of their friends, and that's exactly what used to happen.' He sighed. 'I even tried putting a lock on my door. Bolting it, too. But it didn't work—somehow I'd unlock it in my sleep and go and switch on all the lights in the house, then switch them all off again and wander back to bed.'

'Naked.' She couldn't repress a smile. 'So all these teenage girls would be getting quite a show.'

'It's not funny, Fran. Jude used to joke that she could've trebled her pocket money by making her friends pay to sleep over at our place. With me as the entertainment. And as for facing them over the breakfast table, the next morning…' He groaned. 'No way could I face a bunch of giggling teenage girls. So I used to set my alarm, go to work early with Dad and have an Italian breakfast of pastries and a latte at the café.'

She tried really, really hard to look sympathetic. But she couldn't stop the gurgle of laughter escaping. 'I'm sorry, Gio. I'm not laughing at you. It's just the thought of all these girls lining up in the playground, begging Jude to let them come and stay at your house.'

'Thanks a lot,' he said dryly. 'That really makes me feel good. Not. I thought you said you'd never laugh at me?'

When he'd told her about his first car. Impulsively, she slid her arms round him and hugged him, just as she'd hugged him that day.

But then his arms wrapped round her and the atmosphere changed.

Became charged.

'Francesca Marsden.' His voice sounded husky. Sexy as hell. 'You do realise I'm completely naked.'

'Mmm.' She couldn't quite get her mouth to move round a proper word.

'And you've just put your arms round me.'

'Uh-h-h.' Someone had glued her tongue to the roof of her mouth.

'And you're in bed with me,' he said softly. 'In *my* bed. Wearing nothing but a very skimpy nightdress.'

The v-necked top was held up by spaghetti straps. But all he had to do was push them down and the soft jersey material would fall to her waist.

She suddenly couldn't breathe.

He grazed his cheek against hers. 'This isn't supposed to

be happening.' His breath was warm against her ear, and then he was nuzzling her neck. Tiny, teasing brushes of his lips against her skin. Everywhere he touched became supersensitive; and she wanted more. So much more. She wanted him to touch her everywhere. Kiss her everywhere. Make her forget the misery of seeing the wreck of her flat.

His mouth moved down across her shoulder, nudging the strap downwards; she tipped her head back and closed her eyes as his mouth found the sensitive spot in the curve of her inner elbow.

She couldn't remember the last time she'd felt this good: but one thing she did know, she didn't want Gio to stop.

He pushed the edge of her nightdress down to bare one breast, and Fran found herself arching towards him. Wanting the touch of his hands, his mouth.

As if he could read her mind, he traced a path of kisses from her collarbone downwards; and when he drew her nipple into his mouth and sucked, she gasped, pushing her fingers into his hair to urge him on.

His tongue flicked against the hard peak, teasing her and inciting her.

And, lord, she wanted more. Wanted him to touch her much more intimately. Wanted to feel his body inside hers. 'Gio,' she breathed. 'Please.'

He stopped. 'Tell me to stop. Tell me to leave,' he said.

She opened her eyes again, but she couldn't speak.

Didn't want to speak.

'Tell me to stop, Fran. Because my self-control's starting to snap,' he warned.

She remembered the way he'd kissed her at the party. The way he'd sang to her. The way she'd wanted to be in his arms, wanted to make love with him.

And in answer she slid her hand out of his hair, hooked a finger into the other strap of her nightdress and slid it down over her shoulder so her nightdress fell to her waist.

He dragged in a breath. 'Fran, we're about to hit the point of no return. So if you want me to stop, you have to say so right now.'

She swallowed hard. 'No.'

He took her hand and pressed the tip of his tongue against the pulse that beat madly in her wrist. 'Fran, this really isn't sensible.'

She knew that. 'Right now, I don't care.' And, from the look on his face, neither did he.

'It's been driving me crazy, since I kissed you on your sofa. I've been having all sorts of fantasies about you and my desk. And then I saw you in that dress on Saturday. Kissed you against your front door.' His breath hitched. 'I wanted to carry you to bed and unwrap you. It was so hard to walk away from you that night.'

'So why did you walk away?' Not to mention staying well away from her for the last couple of days?

'Because until I find what I'm looking for, I can't make any promises.'

She was under no illusion that *she* was what he'd been looking for. Because if that were the case he would've realised by now, wouldn't he?

'And I don't want to lie to you,' he said, his voice hoarse.

She rested her palm flat against his chest, over his heart. The beat was strong and slightly fast. 'You're not lying to me. And this is as true as it gets.'

'I don't do this sort of thing.' He took her hand and pressed a kiss into it. 'I don't think you do, either.'

'No. But since Saturday night I've had this picture in my

head. Of October skies, bare trees silvered with frost under an ice-bright moon, and the heat of your body against mine.'

He hummed a few bars of the tune he'd sung to her on Saturday. 'Me, too,' he said softly. 'So let's do it. Let's have our moondance.'

Fran wasn't sure which of them moved first. Or how. Or when her nightdress disappeared—or the duvet, for that matter. But at last they were skin to skin. The contact they'd both been craving.

'You're beautiful,' she said, sliding the flat of her palm across his shoulder. Perfect muscles. Not a weak couch potato, but not a pumped-up gym freak either. Just perfect. His pecs were equally well sculpted. She loved the sprinkle of hair on his chest—just enough to be sexy—and the way it arrowed down over his abdomen. His washboard-flat abdomen. 'I'm going to paint you on the top of a latte.'

'What, and scandalise all our customers?' he teased.

In answer, she took his hand. Drew it to her mouth. Kissed the pad at the top of each finger. And then sucked the tip of his middle finger—hard.

His breath hissed. 'Fran, you've just put the most X-rated picture in my head.'

She gave him a slow, sexy smile. 'Which is exactly what you did to me when you taught me to make a latte.'

He frowned. 'How?'

'You used the word "spoon".'

His mouth curved. 'Oh, that. It's a technical term for putting froth on top of coffee. Also an item of cutlery that comes in different sizes.'

She folded her arms across her breasts. 'You're telling me you don't know another definition?'

Gently, he unfolded her arms. Bent down to drop a kiss on

each nipple. 'Oh, I do. A rather nice one. Lying curled round your body. Something like…' He shifted on to his side, moving her with him and wrapping one arm around her body to pull her back against him. 'Like this.' He splayed his hand against her ribcage. 'Almost.' He stroked the soft undercurve of her breast, then cupped her breast in his hand, rubbing his thumb over her erect nipple. 'Mmm. That's better.' His mouth grazed the curve of her shoulder. 'Is this what you had in mind?'

Her breath caught. 'Oh-h-h. Yes.'

'Interesting.' He nibbled her shoulder. 'There I was, teaching you about making coffee, and you were thinking about having sex with me.'

'I was *not*.'

'You just admitted it.'

'I was paying attention. I made notes. And might I remind you that I made you a perfect latte on your birthday? With a rosetta. Free-poured.'

'So you did.' He nuzzled the sensitive spot behind her ear. 'But you were still thinking about having sex with me.'

'May I point out that I'm not the one who invaded your bed—stark naked?'

His hand slid downwards over her abdomen. 'I can't help it if I sleepwalk. And sleepwalkers normally return to their own bed. Technically, this happens to be *my* bed.' He smoothed his hand along the curve of her hip. 'And may I point out that you're just as naked as I am?'

Skin to skin. 'So what do you have in mind?'

'Lying here with you in my arms is good.' He gently bit her earlobe. 'But I think I'd prefer it if you faced me.' He moved back slightly to give her room to turn round.

'That's better,' he said, brushing his mouth lightly against hers.

His gaze was even hotter, now.

'You have the sexiest curves I've ever seen.' He stroked the curve of her waist and hip. 'You turn me on, Fran. In a big way.' His hand drifted along her outer thigh. 'And, just so you know, I don't make a habit of this. I can't even remember the last time I dated someone, let alone anything else.' The smile vanished from his eyes. 'I might be a bit out of practice.'

'That makes two of us, then.' The same fear suddenly gripped her. 'Gio. I don't want to disappoint you.'

'You're not going to.' He held her gaze. 'Let me show you why.' His hand covered hers, warm and strong, and gently drew it down to his erect shaft. Curved her fingers round it. 'Feel what you do to me?'

It was obvious that he was in the same state as she was. So turned on that the world was spinning. She wasn't aware of anything else except Gio—the warmth and hardness of his body, the feel of his skin skating against hers, the heat in those oh-so-sexy blue eyes, the way his mouth tilted up at the ends, inviting a kiss.

An invitation she couldn't resist. She wriggled closer, caught his lower lip between hers, nipped gently until he gasped and opened his mouth and let her deepen the kiss. Let her take the lead. Kissing and touching and stroking until they were both at fever pitch.

Fran blew his mind. Simple as that. The way her fingertips skated over Gio's skin made every nerve end shimmer. And the feel of her mouth against his throat drove him crazy.

He took his time exploring her body. Stroking her skin. Kissing. Nuzzling. Nibbling. Discovering the sensitive spots that made her gasp and arch up to him when he touched her.

By the time his mouth had worked its way down to her

midriff, her breathing was shallow and her voice was husky, and she was quivering with the same intense need he felt. Because, good as this was, it wasn't enough. He needed to be inside her. Needed the ultimate closeness.

'I want you so badly, it hurts,' he whispered.

'Then make love with me, Gio,' she whispered back. 'I'm going crazy here too. I need you. Inside. Me.' A tremor ran through her body. 'Now.'

He didn't need telling twice. He rummaged in the top drawer of the little cabinet next to his bed—oh, please let that box of condoms still be there. To his relief, it was. A quick glance at the bottom reassured him they were still in date.

And then at last Fran was leaning back against a pile of pillows, her hair mussed and her lips parted and those beautiful cornflower-blue eyes all warm and inviting, and he was kneeling between her thighs. He dipped his head to kiss her as he eased into her warm, wet heat.

This was what they both wanted. Both needed.

Had he been dreaming about this when he'd been sleep-walking? Was that why he'd come here to his bed?

But it didn't matter. Because the real thing was, oh, so much better than a dream. Watching Fran's eyes widen with pleasure, feeling her breasts tightening against his chest, hearing the little breathy sighs she made as his thrusts took her higher and higher. He was aware of the pleasure rising through his own body, growing tighter and tighter. Of the softness of her skin. Of the way her body rippled round his, the tiny incoherent murmurs of pleasure she made—pleasure that echoed in his own body.

He heard her cry out his name, and then they were both falling over the edge, spinning down and down and down.

Afterwards he lay with her curled in his arms, breathing

in the sweet scent of her skin. It was the first time he'd felt at peace since the day he found his father lying senseless on the floor in the café. The black hole wasn't there any more.

Had he just found what he'd been looking for, all this time?

And, if so…how did he get to keep her?

The questions spun in his mind, but gradually he drifted into sleep. And the last thing he was aware of was the warmth of Fran's body against his. Completing him.

CHAPTER THIRTEEN

THE next morning, Fran woke to find Gio's body curled round hers, and his arm was wrapped tightly round her waist, holding her against him.

Spooned.

Muscles she'd completely forgotten about were grumbling in protest this morning. But she couldn't help smiling when she remembered last night. The promise of his kiss on Saturday night had more than been fulfilled. Incredible.

And then her smile faded. Now it was the morning. What now? Last night, they'd made no promises to each other. It had been the heat of the moment. And now...

'Good morning.' Gio pressed a kiss to the nape of her neck.

'Good morning.' Her voice sounded croaky. Nervous. Lord, this was awkward. What did she say now?

He could obviously feel the tension in her body, because he rested his cheek against hers. 'I think we need to talk, honey. Turn round and face me.'

He released his arm from round her waist; for a moment, she lay still, but then turned on her right side so she was facing him.

'So. About last night.'

Was this where he told her this was all a mistake and she'd

have to find somewhere else to stay until her flat was habitable again?

He kissed the tip of her nose. 'That wasn't supposed to happen.'

Obviously he regretted it.

He smiled. 'Though I'm glad it did.' His eyes were very blue, very honest. 'Very glad.'

So he *didn't* regret it? That was good. But… 'What happens now?'

He stroked her face. 'I don't know, Fran. I can't give you any promises.'

At least he was being straight with her.

'But I would like to find out where this takes us.' He drew her closer. 'Right now, this is just between you and me. It's nothing to do with anything or anyone else. Not my family, not the café—just us.'

The café. 'What about work?' Was she going to have to find a new job?

'Wherever this takes us, it's not going to change things at work. You're still my right-hand woman.' His lips quirked, and sheer mischief glittered in his eyes. 'Though at this precise moment you're perfectly at liberty to use your left hand on me, if you so choose.'

She placed the tip of her index finger against his collarbone, and drew a line along his sternum. 'Like this, you mean?'

He caught her hand and brought it up to his mouth. 'Oh, you tease.' He kissed her palm and folded her fingers over the kiss. 'Actually, you're right—this probably isn't a good idea.' He smiled. 'Because I'll be late for work. I need a shower. And a shave.'

She stroked his face, enjoying the faint rasp against her fingertips. 'Stubble. You look like a pirate.'

'Hmm. Which means I should carry you over my shoulder and then ravish you.' He eyed her speculatively. 'I *could* carry you to the shower…'

'And then you'd definitely be late for work.'

'Want to know something terrible?' His eyes crinkled at the corners. 'I really don't care.'

She laughed. 'Tut, tut, Gio Mazetti. If you're not careful, you'll damage your reputation as a workaholic.'

'I can think of a few people who'd kiss you for that.' His gaze was fixed on her mouth. 'I could always be their proxy.'

'So you still want to kiss me?'

His gaze grew hot. 'I want to do a lot more than kiss you, Francesca *mia*. But I have a business to run, and you need to find out what's happening with your flat.'

He brushed his mouth against hers, and it turned into a long, slow, lingering kiss that heated her blood.

'Hold that thought,' he said huskily when he broke the kiss and looked into her eyes. 'Until tonight. When I'll make it a reality.'

He vaulted out of bed, completely unselfconscious. Well, after what they'd shared, the previous night, there was no reason to be shy in front of each other. She leaned back against the pillows and grinned.

He glanced over his shoulder and raised an eyebrow. 'What?'

'Just thinking. I'd definitely pay your sister to have a sleepover at your place and stress you into sleepwalking naked.'

He groaned. 'Oh, now that's unfair.'

'And it's a ver-r-ry nice view from here. If I were an artist, I'd definitely book you as a life model.'

He raised an eyebrow. 'Is that an offer to come and wash my back in the shower?'

She laughed. 'A moment ago, you told me to hold that thought until tonight.'

'I just changed my mind.' Before she realised what he was going to do, he walked swiftly back to the bed, scooped her up, and carried her to the bathroom.

'You're going to be late,' she warned, still laughing.

'Don't care.' His gaze smouldered as he set her back down on her feet. 'I want you. Wet and naked. And wrapped round me.'

Her heart skipped a beat at the huskiness in his tone. 'That's what I want, too.'

'Good.' He switched on the shower, stepped into the bath and took her hand. 'Come with me.' His eyes glittered. 'And I mean that in more than one sense.'

Oh-h-h. Her nipples tightened at the thought. She stopped thinking and simply stepped into the bath next to him. The water sprayed down, droplets sparkling against his skin. Wet, naked, sexy male. She couldn't resist touching him; she took the shower gel and poured it on to her palm, then started lathering his body. Starting with his shoulders, then his pecs, then down over his ribcage.

'You're playing with fire, here,' he warned.

'Actually, I'm playing with water,' she corrected, and lathered his abdomen. She watched his pupils dilate as she traced the skin on his belly, just a few millimetres away from his erect penis. Just round the outline of his erection. Not quite close enough to touch, but close enough for him to imagine and want and need.

She had every intention of driving him as crazy as he drove her.

'Francesca,' he muttered hoarsely, 'if you keep teasing me like that…'

'You'll what?' She licked her lips, enjoying his shudder of

desire in reaction. And then she poured more shower gel into her hand and slid it along his length.

'Yes.' The word was hissed between clenched teeth. 'Please. Yes. Oh.'

She loved the fact he couldn't even say the words in the right order. And she really hadn't finished yet. She sluiced the lather from him, then dropped to her knees. Bent her head. Breathed on him so he could feel the heat of her mouth, the promise of what she was about to do.

'Fran.'

It was the last coherent word he uttered. In a voice so gravelly, so out of control, that it gave her a real kick.

And then she licked him.

Teased him with her tongue.

Took him deep into her mouth, until he was quivering and tangling his fingers into her hair, urging him on.

And she loved the fact that she could make him lose control to the point where he was babbling.

'Fran.' Gio was torn between letting her take him over the edge and stopping her before it was too late.

The need to be inside her won.

Just.

Gently, he stopped her. Drew her to her feet. Kissed her hard, then lifted her so that her back was to the tiles. He slid a hand between her thighs, pushing one finger and then two inside her.

'Gio.' It was her turn to go incoherent as he found just the right spot with his thumb, circling and teasing until she was quivering, trying to buck her hips against him. Then, and only then, he cupped her buttocks with both hands, lifted her slightly, and eased his body into hers. Pushed deep. Jammed his mouth over hers to swallow her little murmurs of pleasure as his thrusts grew harder, faster, deeper.

He barely noticed that the hot water had run out; all he could think of was the way she felt around him. Like warm, wet silk. A perfect fit.

And as her body started rippling around his, tipping him into his own release, it felt like a thousand sparklers going off around them.

Gio was late for work. And when Fran finally picked up the voicemail message on her mobile phone, she only just made it back to her flat in time to meet the letting agent. Clearly he'd dealt with similar situations before, because he didn't drag out the painful part of seeing just how much damage there was; he was methodical, but thankfully he was also quick. Ceiling, floor, walls, furniture: it was just a mess.

'Keep a note of your hotel bills,' he told Fran. 'Because we'll claim those back for you.'

'I'm staying with a friend.'

'That's OK for now, but be aware that these things aren't particularly quick to sort out,' he warned. 'We have to dry the place out, repair the ceiling and then check that all the utilities work safely before you can move back in. So if you need to move to a hotel at some point, make sure you keep the bills. Now, I'm also going to need a list from you of everything that's been damaged in your personal possessions. Did you take photographs, by any chance?'

She nodded. 'That's what the London Lets office said to do when I rang last night. They're on my mobile phone.' She showed him.

'Good. Can you forward them to my email address?' He scribbled an address on the back of a business card and handed it to her. 'Or if it's easier, print them out and drop them in to the office. I'll be in touch as soon as I hear from the insurer about when we can get an industrial dehumidifier in and when we can start to replace the things you've lost.'

'Thanks.' Though even being here made Fran want to howl. It didn't feel like her home any more. Just a damp, squelchy studio flat. And even when it had dried out, she had a feeling that it would never be the same again.

It was nearly lunchtime when she walked into the café.

'Hey, we weren't expecting you today.' Sally gave her a hug and pushed a brownie into her hand. 'Gio told us what happened to your flat. Are you OK?'

'Yes,' Fran lied.

Ian handed her a mug of hot chocolate. 'You poor thing. It's a nightmare when you get flooded out. And it takes *ages* to sort out.'

She rolled her eyes. 'Tell me about it. I've spent the morning making a list of everything that was damaged. I can't believe just a bit of water can do so much damage. Or that my neighbour forgot he was running the bath and went out for three hours.'

'At least it was clean water,' Ian said feelingly. 'One of my mates got flooded out when the drains in his road couldn't cope with a downpour. Not pleasant.'

'Too much information. Especially in a café at this time of day,' Sally said, miming a 'zip lip' motion.

Ian smiled ruefully. 'Yeah. Sorry. But if I can do anything to help, Fran, just let me know.'

'Me, too,' Sally chipped in.

'Thanks, guys. I really appreciate it.' She smiled and walked into the office. Gio was sitting in her chair, making a phone call. As soon as he saw her he ended the call, swivelled round in the chair, opened his arms and tipped his head back slightly in invitation.

She couldn't resist the appeal; she leaned over and kissed him.

'No, no, you're too far away.' He pulled her onto his lap, held her close and kissed her again. 'Mmm. That's better.'

She wriggled on his lap. 'Gio, we're at work.'

He glanced at his watch. 'Officially, we're at lunch,' he corrected. There was a mischievous quirk at the corner of his mouth. 'Pity I don't have a lock on the door. Except then I might be tempted to take a very, *very* long lunch.'

'Gio. We *can't*. Not here.'

He stole another kiss. 'I'll just have to take a rain check. Until we get home.'

'Yeah. And I remember the last time you said that. "Hold that thought until later,",' she mimicked.

'Mmm.' He gave her a wide, wide smile. 'And it was worth being late for work for the first time in over ten years.'

'Ten years?' Her eyes widened. 'Gio—'

He put a finger against her lips. 'Shh. Stop worrying. Sal opened up for me and we didn't lose any customers. Though I think it's going to cost me in brownies.' He rubbed his nose against hers. 'So, how did it go this morning?'

'The flat smells to high heaven.' She swallowed hard. 'Like a dog who's been out in the rain, rolled in every puddle he can see and is just starting to dry off.'

He grimaced in sympathy. 'Ouch. Unpleasant.'

'But the agency was really good. They're putting the wheels in motion, getting the insurance company to bring in an industrial dehumidifier to dry the place out.' She sighed. 'The carpet's shrunk already, so I think they're just going to rip it out.'

He stroked her hair. 'You OK?'

'Yes. Well, no,' she admitted, and leaned her head against his shoulder. 'It didn't feel like my flat any more.'

'It will do. When it's dried out, the ceiling's fixed, there's a new carpet and we've painted the walls. It'll be fine.'

She damped down the surge of disappointment. Honestly, how ridiculous could she get? Of *course* she was going back to her own place when it was habitable again. Moving in with him was only temporary; and, had he not sleepwalked the previous night, they wouldn't have shared a bed either.

'But until then,' he said softly, 'I hope you stay with me. And I know I'm being selfish, but I hope they take absolutely ages to fix everything.'

Oh-h-h. If he'd asked her to walk to the moon and back for him, right at that moment, she would've said yes.

'Thank you.' And please don't let him notice that her voice had just gone all croaky.

He kissed the hollow of her collarbones. 'What do you want for dinner tonight? I'll cook.'

She strove for a light, teasing note. 'If you work as late as you usually do, that means we'll be eating at midnight.'

'I'll come home early.'

'Early as in a normal person's "early"?' she tested.

He laughed. 'Probably not.'

'How about I cook for us, then? If you trust me in your kitchen.'

'Of course I trust you.' His smile turned wolfish. 'But there's a condition attached. I get to sleep with the chef tonight.'

'Sleep?'

He nibbled her earlobe. *'Eventually,'* he whispered, sending a thrill of pure lust down her spine.

'Giovanni Mazetti, just how am I supposed to get any work done when you put thoughts like that into my head?'

'You're not.' He brushed his mouth against hers. 'You're going out to lunch with me. And then you're going to play hookey.'

'With you?'

He smiled. 'I'm tempted. Seriously tempted. But, no, what I had in mind is going for a spa afternoon. The sort of thing my sisters do when they've had a rough week.'

'A spa afternoon.'

'Massage, facial, something like that. Bella swears by it. It'll de-stress you.'

She shook her head. 'I'm fine.'

'No, you're not.' He held her just a little bit closer. 'Maybe I'll give you that massage myself, then. I told you to take today off, and I meant it. Go and do something to relax you. Rent some DVDs and spend the afternoon watching films, or what have you. And that,' he added, 'is an order.'

'Maybe.'

But when they'd had lunch out—a bacon, mozzarella and avocado salad in a little restaurant on the South Bank—and Gio had gone back to work, Fran decided to take his advice to do something to relax her. A wander through Kew Gardens went a long way to restoring her equilibrium. Then she went back to Gio's flat via the supermarket, texted him to remind him that she was cooking dinner and it would be ready at half past seven, and enjoyed herself cooking in a decent-sized kitchen for once.

'I might have to change your job,' Gio said when he walked in at quarter past seven. 'Forget being my office manager. You can be my personal chef instead.'

She raised an eyebrow. 'That's a bit rash. You haven't tasted dinner yet.'

'It smells fabulous, so it'll be gorgeous.' He stood behind her and slid one arm round her waist, pulling her back against him. 'And so are you.'

'Behave,' she admonished, though she was smiling.

'Oh, yeah. That reminds me. These are for you.' He brought his other hand round, and gave her a bunch of bright pink gerberas.

He'd bought her flowers. Again. Completely unexpectedly. Her throat closed and she had to blink back the tears. 'Thank you. They're beautiful.'

'Do I get a kiss, then?'

She smiled. 'After you've eaten. I need to put these in water.'

'Ah. There might be a problem.'

'What?'

'I don't actually own a vase.' He rummaged in the kitchen cupboards and came up with a couple of pint glasses. 'That'll teach me to make a romantic gesture without thinking it through first.'

She put the flowers into water and stood them in the middle of the table, then slid her arms round his neck and kissed him lightly. 'Thank you, Gio. The vase doesn't matter. It's…'

'Hey. They were meant to make you smile, not cry.' Gently, he brushed away the single tear with the pad of his thumb.

'I'm being wet.'

'No. You've just seen your personal space ruined. And you've been putting a brave face on it.' He hugged her. 'Everything will be fine. I promise.'

She swallowed hard. 'Go and sit down. I'll serve dinner.'

By the time she'd put the bowl of salad on the table and

spooned the chicken arrabbiata over the pasta, she'd managed to choke back the tears again.

'I'm not sure if I dared cook pasta for an Italian,' she said, placing the plate in front of him.

He laughed. 'You can't exactly ruin pasta.'

'Yes, you can. You can overcook it so it's soggy. Or not drain it properly.'

He took a mouthful. 'This,' he said, 'is textbook *al dente*—absolutely perfect—and that arrabbiata sauce has one hell of a kick.'

'Too hot?'

'Nope. Just perfect. And the wine's good, too. Barolo, yes?'

Trust him to know. She smiled. 'Of course. I can just imagine your face if I'd served you French wine.'

He laughed. 'My favourite wine's French, actually. Margaux. It tastes of vanilla and blackcurrant. Oh, and talking of tasting—want to come with me to a cupping? I normally go with Dad, but he asked me if you'd join us next time. I think he's planning to teach you some of the stuff he's taught me.' He grimaced. 'Sorry. My family really takes over.'

'No, I'd love to.' And it still stunned her how quickly the Mazettis had taken her to their hearts. Made her feel part of them. Her phone had been beeping all day with texts from them. From his sisters, suggesting a night out to see a really girly film with lots of popcorn to cheer her up—and Marcie had also offered to go with her when she needed to buy new furniture. From Angela, saying that her friend could repair all the damage to Fran's clothes. From Nonna, just sending her a hug.

She *belonged*.

Much more than she did in her own family. Here, she fitted in.

After dinner, they washed up together. Something she wasn't used to, and it felt weirdly domesticated. Even more shockingly, she realised that she actually liked it. The whole domestic routine.

Which Gio definitely didn't want.

She was going to have to be really careful here. Gio wasn't offering her for ever. 'For now' was as good as it was going to get. And if she let herself fall too deeply for Gio and the warm, noisy, loving family that came with him as a package deal, she was going to end up with a broken heart.

She needed to keep a distance between them, however small.

'You've gone quiet on me. What are you thinking?' Gio asked.

She shook her head. 'Nothing important.' Nothing she'd admit to. 'Would you play your guitar for me again?'

He leaned against the worktop and stared at her. 'Are you in a conspiracy with Nonna and my mum to make me go to college?'

'No. I just like it when you play.' She smiled. 'As long as it's something pretty and not that tonal harmonics stuff.'

He laughed, but fetched one of the guitars from his spare room, perched on the arm of the sofa and played Mozart to her. She watched him, taking in every detail. How his beautiful hands moved. The passion in his face as the music took over— so similar to the expression on his face when he made love.

Then he looked up, gave her a slow, sweet smile, and played a tune she recognised: an arrangement of 'I Can't Help Falling in Love with You'.

Was he trying to tell her something?

Her heart missed a beat. No, of course not. And she had to remember not to fall for him. Though the song was way,

way too appropriate. 'So you're turning into Elvis now?' she said lightly.

He smiled. 'Hardly. And, for your information, two of the three composers of that song were Italian.'

'Yeah?'

'Yeah.' He played it again, but this time instead of picking out the melody he strummed chords and sang it to her.

Lord, he had a gorgeous voice. A voice that made her melt.

'The simplest tunes are the best ones,' he said when he'd finished, and replaced the guitar in its case. 'So. I've played for you.'

'Sung for your supper.'

He lifted his forefinger. 'Ah, but all good musicians expect payment as well as supper.' He paused. 'A kiss will do.'

'A kiss.' She stood up, reached up to him and brushed her mouth against his.

'Call that a kiss?' Gio tipped her back on to the sofa and gave her a wicked smile. 'Let me show you how it's done…'

CHAPTER FOURTEEN

THE next two weeks were the happiest Fran had ever known. Her days were spent in a job she loved, and her nights in Gio's arms. He taught her about every erogenous zone in her body, including some she hadn't even known existed; the way she responded to his touch scared her, because she'd never felt anything this intense before.

And then Gio really shocked her.

'You're going to be late for work,' she said—her body clock now used to the time he got up to leave for the coffee shop.

'Nope.' He smiled at her. 'Not today.'

She frowned. 'You're in late?'

'Day off.'

She blinked. 'Run that one by me again.'

He laughed. 'You heard.'

'Are you ill?'

He rolled his eyes. 'I just have plans.'

She tried to douse the spark of disappointment that those plans obviously didn't include her. Of course he needed her to be there in the office. That was her job. Running the café chain when he wasn't around.

He didn't offer to meet her for lunch, either. But she shoved it out of her mind and just got on with work, staying late to help Sally lock up the Charlotte Street café.

When she opened his front door she discovered what Gio's mysterious plans were. Something smelled fantastic, and explained the little bistro table in the living-room alcove set with a white damask table cloth and proper silver; there were scented tea-light candles in the middle of the table and the tablecloth was scattered with rose petals.

Gio came to stand behind her and wrapped his arms round her, resting his cheek against hers. 'Good day?'

She nodded. 'And everything's ticking over fine, so you don't need to worry about anything.' She indicated the table. 'You've gone to a lot of trouble.'

'Well, you've done nearly all the cooking while you've been staying here. I thought it was time to even up the balance a little.' He nuzzled the curve of her neck. 'Go and sit on the sofa. I'll bring you a glass of wine.'

Perfectly chilled pinot grigio. Then he fetched one of his guitars and played her some of the pretty Italian divertimenti he knew she liked.

'I feel thoroughly spoiled,' she said with a smile.

And the food was even better. Grilled scamorza, followed by grilled salmon on a bed of garlicky spinach with polenta, and then the most fantastic white chocolate cheesecake.

'This,' Fran said, 'is to die for.'

'I had a rather more, um, *interesting* reward in mind,' Gio said. She grinned. 'Oh, really?'

'Uh-huh. Food of love. I've played to you, I've fed you, we're going to ignore the washing up, and you're going to have to wait for your coffee.' He took her hand and tugged her to her feet, then drew her into the bedroom.

Fran's eyes widened when she saw the rose petals scattered on the bed.

'I told you I had plans,' Gio said, sliding his fingertips under the hem of her top and drawing tiny circles against her skin.

It took him a long, long time to undress her. Every inch of skin he uncovered had to be stroked. Kissed. Licked. And by the time he finally laid her down on his bed of rose petals, Fran was shivering.

'Now. Please, now,' she whispered. Begged. She needed him inside her—right here, right now.

Gio shook his head. 'Tonight,' he told her, his eyes a sultry deep blue, 'we're taking it slowly.'

So slowly that she thought she was going to go crazy. Time and again, Gio brought her just to the edge of climax— then paused for just long enough to keep her on the brink. Her whole body had turned into a mass of sensation, aware of his tiniest movement.

And when he finally entered her—still keeping the pace slow and measured—she came instantly.

'I haven't finished yet,' he whispered in her ear. 'And neither have you.'

She didn't believe him. But when the aftershocks had died away, he began to move again. Stoking her pleasure higher and higher.

'This—' She shook her head. 'I can't…I've never come twice. It's not poss… Oh-h-h.'

He brushed his mouth against hers. 'Something you should know, *tesoro*. I'm aiming for three.'

* * *

Fran's look of shock mingled with disbelief and sheer pleasure gave Gio a real kick. He'd thought it would be good between them, but this was something else. He loved the way she responded to him. The way her body was so in tune with his. The flare of passion in her eyes. The scent of the roses mingled with the musky scent of her arousal. The sound of her little sighs of pleasure. And when his own climax rippled through him, he felt Fran's body quiver in answer. Each beat of her heart matched his own. Two as one.

He wasn't ready to say the words.

But he hoped to hell she knew exactly what his body was telling her.

And that she felt the same way.

'Can I speak to Fran Marsden, please?' the breezy voice asked when Gio answered the phone.

'Sorry, she's not available at the moment.' Jude had annexed her for lunch. Which is how come Gio was left with a panini, a chocolate brownie and a sense of disappointment. Weird how he'd got used to actually taking a proper break. Going for a stroll with Fran in Regent's Park at lunchtime and enjoying the sunshine he hadn't really noticed in years; sitting by the lake, watching the swans and the squirrels with his arm round his girl. Perfect.

'Can I help?' he asked.

'It's London Lets. Can you tell her that the flat's finished? The repairs have been done and checked, the utilities have all been tested, there's a new carpet down and she can move back in again whenever she likes.'

So soon? He carefully schooled his voice to neutral. 'Sure. I'll tell her. Thanks for calling.'

But when he replaced the receiver he sat for a while with his elbows propped against his desk and his chin resting on his hands, staring into space.

Fran could move back home again.

Out of his flat.

He didn't actually *have* to tell her about the call. He could just 'forget'. But she'd find out anyway because the letting agency was bound to ring again to see when she was planning to move back in.

Part of him wanted to give her the message—and then ask her not to go. To stay with him, to move in to his flat properly.

The more sensible part of him knew it was a bad idea. For a start, he didn't know if she'd say yes: Fran had already made it clear that she liked having her own space, and she took up so little room in his flat that you'd hardly know she was staying. Even in the bathroom, her things were kept neatly and separately from his, and could be packed in about three seconds.

But even if she did say yes…he still wasn't sure. Was he simply trying to fit into the role his family wanted for him, settling down at last? Or did he want Fran for himself? And was he the right one for her in any case? Would he end up letting her down, the way he'd screwed up with his family all those years ago?

He didn't have the answers. Needed time to work it out.

Which meant letting her go back to her own place.

And didn't they say that if you wanted someone to stay, you had to give them the freedom to go?

Lord, he hoped she'd decide to stay.

When Fran returned from lunch with Jude, full of smiles and laughter, he couldn't bring himself to tell her the news straight away. It took him an hour to work up to it. And then, keeping his voice light, he said, 'Sorry, I meant to tell you. The letting agency rang while you were at lunch. Your flat's ready.'

'Right.' Her expression went straight into neutral. Which meant he hadn't a clue what was going on in her head. Couldn't read a single signal.

'So I wondered if you wanted a hand. Maybe paint the place the colour you like, before you move back in.' In other words, stay with him a bit longer.

'I… Thanks. That'd be nice.'

He wasn't sure if her smile reached her eyes, because she'd turned away.

'I need to get a new sofa bed, too. And shelving. And curtains.' She shrugged. 'Though the colour's going to depend on what colour carpet they've put in. Something neutral, I hope.'

'Why don't you take the rest of the afternoon off and go have a look?' he suggested. 'You've put in more than enough hours lately to make up the time. And it'd be better to see it in daylight than evening light.'

'Yeah, you're right.' She nodded. 'Thanks.'

He smiled. 'I'll see you later.'

'Sure.'

Though he noticed she didn't kiss him goodbye.

He really, really hoped that wasn't a bad sign. But he had a nasty feeling that everything was unravelling around them.

Well, what did you expect? Fran asked herself as she got on to the Tube. That he'd ask you not to go—that he'd suggest moving in with him properly?

How stupid could she get?

Number one, this had all started off as a fake relationship, to keep his family happy.

Number two, what had happened between them since her flat had been flooded—well, despite that amazing night where he'd cooked for her and made love with her in a bed of rose petals, to the point where she'd felt as if their souls had connected, it was still early days. And the fact that Gio was prepared to let her go so easily showed that he wasn't ready to make their relationship a real one.

He might *never* be ready.

It wasn't necessarily her—if she thought about it rationally, she knew Gio probably wouldn't be ready to commit to anyone for a long, long time, because nothing was going to tame his restlessness—but it still hurt. And it was very clear to her now that once she'd moved back to her own flat and Isabella had returned to Milan, later in the week, they'd be reverting to their original plan.

Ending the 'relationship' quietly.

She knew now that she couldn't face working with him afterwards. Not as his 'ex'. Having to deal with the disappointment of his family and the sympathy of their colleagues would be way too messy. And the idea of watching from the sidelines when Gio was ready to let himself fall in love—with someone else…

It left her no choice.

Quite how she was going to get through Isabella's farewell dinner, she had no idea. But she was going to act as if her life depended on it. No way was she going to let Gio see how much this hurt.

When she got off the Tube again, she called the letting

agency. Yes, the insurance was paying up; they had her claim in progress; and the money should be with her next week.

Which meant she could go and buy new furniture now. On her credit card. Because by the time the bill came in the insurance money would be there. And even if it was late that wasn't a big deal, because she still had her redundancy money in a high-interest account.

Organising was what she did. Really, really well. And keeping busy was a good way of not letting herself think about the way her personal life had just disintegrated. Even so, by the time she reached her flat, Fran was thoroughly dejected. She unlocked the door and took a cursory look around.

Home.

It didn't feel like home. Wasn't her space any more. It was just a very small studio flat. The walls were magnolia, perfectly liveable with. The carpet was beige. Also liveable with. And the neutral décor meant it wouldn't matter what colour she chose for her furniture.

She didn't actually care what colour the furniture was. As long as it was delivered quickly. And there was one way to make very sure that happened. She went to one of the furniture showrooms that let you take things away there and then instead of waiting six to eight weeks for it to be made and delivered. Bought curtains and cushions, chose a sofa bed and shelving and talked the store into delivering it all the following morning.

And one night sleeping on the floor wasn't going to hurt her, was it?

She went back to Gio's flat and packed her things. Called a taxi. And was in the process of writing him a note to explain where she'd gone when the front door opened.

* * *

'Fran?' Gio stared at the suitcases next to her. 'What are you doing?'

'Moving my stuff back home,' Fran said simply.

She was leaving already? But... 'Hang on, don't you need to sort out some furniture first?'

'Done.'

That was the problem when someone was as efficient as Fran. They could sort things out at the speed of light. Anyone else would've had to wait at least six weeks for the furniture to be delivered. Not her. 'What about paint? I was going to help you paint the walls.' It would take at least a day to do that, and they'd need another day to air the place to get rid of paint fumes. That would give him two days—with any luck, enough time to work out how to get her to stay.

'Paint's not a problem. I can live with magnolia walls.'

So he didn't even get the two days he'd been banking on? Oh, hell.

He stared at the suitcases in dismay. 'You're going *now*? Right this very minute?' She'd been planning to leave without saying goodbye to him?

'You've been very sweet to put me up while my flat's been uninhabitable. But everything's fine now. So it's not really fair to put you out any longer.'

She hadn't put him out. Far from it. She'd turned his flat into his home instead of just a place to sleep and maybe eat. 'Fran—'

But what he'd intended to say was cut off by a beep from outside.

'That'll be my taxi,' she said.

He really didn't want her to go.

But she clearly couldn't wait to leave, or else she wouldn't have packed so fast, would she? So although he'd thought that the last couple of weeks had changed everything between them, maybe it hadn't been the same for her.

She was leaving.

And their relationship was back to being a fake. Something to stop other people being hurt.

He hadn't bargained on getting hurt, himself.

And he didn't know if he could go through with this. Pretend in front of his family that everything was fine, when it was very far from fine. He raked a hand through his hair. 'Look, do you want me to make some excuse for you at Nonna's dinner on Thursday?'

She shook her head. 'No, I'll be there. I want to be able to say goodbye.'

Another blast of the taxi's horn. The kind of length that meant, *I do have other fares to pick up, you know, so will you stop messing about and hurry up?*

'I'd better go,' she said, picking up her suitcases. 'Apologies for the short notice, but I'll need to take tomorrow morning off. I'm expecting some deliveries. But I'll work late to make up the time.'

'Whatever.' He was too numb to protest.

'Thanks for everything, Gio.' She picked up her suitcases. 'I'll see you later.'

'Let me take those.' He didn't want her to go—but he wasn't going to stand by and watch her struggle. His hand touched hers as he took the cases from her, and the contact made his heart contract sharply.

This couldn't be happening.

Shouldn't be happening.

If she hugged him goodbye, that would be it. He was carrying her back to his flat and to hell with the taxi driver.

But she didn't. She just gave him a really, really bright smile—as if she were truly delighted to be going back to her own space. 'Thanks for everything, Gio.'

The door closed.

And the taxi drove off.

Gio walked up the stairs to his flat. And even though there wasn't actually that much missing—Fran, being neat and tidy, hadn't taken up much room in the first place—the place seemed empty. Echoey.

The whole heart of it had gone. With Fran.

He couldn't settle to anything that evening. Although he went through the motions of cooking a meal, dinner for one felt completely wrong. Like a discord. In the end, he stopped toying with his food and scraped it into the bin. Music didn't make him feel any better, because he kept thinking of the times he'd played to Fran, the light in her eyes. And there was nothing on television.

He couldn't face going to bed. It was too big, too wide, too empty without Fran in his arms. So he sat on the sofa, flicking channels aimlessly and just wishing. Wishing that he'd never been stupid enough to let her go.

Not home. Not even a flat. After the space she'd shared at Gio's, it felt more like a broom cupboard. Not *her* broom cupboard, either. Fran hadn't yet replaced her ruined books, and although she'd managed to salvage her photographs there wasn't anything to stand them on. So she hadn't unpacked them and the place felt as impersonal as a hotel room.

Her wardrobe rail had dried out, so she mechanically replaced her clothes on the hangers. She had to clench her jaw hard when she unpacked the party dress—the dress she'd been wearing when Gio had first kissed her properly, when he'd sung for her. The dress she'd thought was ruined, but Angela's friend had salvaged. It would definitely have to go to a charity shop. She couldn't handle the memories.

So much for thinking what they'd shared was special. He'd hardly been able to wait to get his space back. He'd even offered to help her paint the walls, he'd been that keen for her to go.

She dragged in a breath. Her world had collapsed before. This time it was going to be a hell of a lot harder to build it all back up again.

But she'd do it. She'd get there. And never, ever again would she lose her heart to someone.

Even turning the shower thermostat to near-on freezing didn't make Gio feel any more awake the next morning. He'd slept so badly that he felt hungover—as if he'd drunk way too much cheap red wine. Paracetamol went a little way to muffling the pain in his head, but he felt lousy.

Today, he'd talk to Fran. Tell her how he felt. Lay his heart on the line and ask her to move back in with him.

But Fran walked into the office dead on nine o'clock, all bright-eyed and bushy-tailed, as if everything was perfectly all right with her world. 'Good morning.'

And the words Gio had planned to say stuck in his throat. She was obviously quite happy with the situation. Pleased to be back in her own space. So if he asked her to move back in with him, it was obvious that she'd say no.

'Morning,' he muttered.

If she noticed he looked like hell, she didn't comment. Simply slid into her seat and started working through the morning's post.

And Gio's world turned just that little bit darker.

How the hell could he stay with her in the office? No way was he going to be able to get any work done. His concentration was shot to pieces. All he wanted to do was wrap his arms round her and kiss her stupid. And she was acting as if nothing had ever happened between them—that they'd only ever had a business relationship.

He couldn't handle this.

'Gotta go to Docklands,' he muttered, and left. Before he did something stupid.

Like beg.

CHAPTER FIFTEEN

GOING to Isabella's farewell party at Netti's restaurant was the hardest thing Fran had ever had to do. To walk in, greet the Mazettis and chat with them as if nothing was wrong, when she and Gio had barely spoken to each other all week and things were decidedly awkward between them.

She knew he found the situation as difficult as she did, because he'd avoided her. There had always been a meeting he'd needed to go to. Or a problem at one of the branches he needed to sort out. Or something to do with the franchise. He hadn't even picked up the phone to talk to her; he'd sent her text messages or emails instead. They'd agreed by voicemail that they'd arrive separately at the party; their cover story was that he'd be 'late' because she hadn't been able to get him out of the office.

And now they had to pretend, for Nonna's sake, that everything was perfectly fine.

Thank goodness everyone kept swapping seats between courses so she didn't have to sit next to Gio. If he'd draped his arm round her shoulders or picked her up and shared her chair—as he'd been doing for the previous few weeks—she wouldn't have been able to resist nestling closer to him.

Which, considering that he'd made it very clear he didn't want to take their relationship further, was completely pathetic.

And Fran wasn't going to let herself be pathetic.

She was just really, really glad she'd dressed up tonight. Posh underwear to make herself feel special, high heels to boost her confidence, and full make-up with a concealer to hide the dark shadows under her eyes.

Tonight she was going to smile and smile and smile.

To hide the fact that her heart was breaking.

How could Fran do this? Gio wondered. How could she sit and chat so easily to his parents and his sisters and his grandmother and his cousins, as if nothing was wrong? How could she laugh at Ric's terrible puns and make a fuss of the kids and filch the last one of Netti's cheese discs from the plate in the centre of the table and just be so damned *normal*?

He was finding it a hell of a struggle.

And then it got worse.

'Gio. You've been sitting too far away—because, as always, you were late to dinner,' Isabella said, tutting. 'Come and talk to me.'

There wasn't a spare seat next to his grandmother. Because Fran was sitting there.

Hell, hell, hell.

His family was used to him scooping Fran up and sitting her on his lap. He'd done it ever since that first Sunday lunch at his parents' house. So he knew they'd expect him to do it now. If he didn't, they'd guess that something was wrong between them. But if he did…would Fran mind?

Then again, she was playing along tonight. Pretending everything was normal, for Nonna's sake.

And playing along with his family's expectations meant that he could hold her again.

It was too much for him to resist. So he walked over with

a smile, scooped Fran out of her chair and sat in her place, settling her on his lap.

He could feel the warmth of her body through the little black dress she was wearing. And he could also feel the tension running through her; her body was almost rigid. As though she'd snap if either of them moved.

Clearly she *minded*. A lot.

But he couldn't see a way out of this without giving some very awkward explanations he'd rather not make. So he simply smiled and chatted to his grandmother as if he didn't have a care in the world—and hoped that nobody in his family was trying to read his body language. Or Fran's.

This was unbearable, Fran thought. Gio had been keeping his distance, and she could cope with that. But now they were up close and personal, sitting on his lap as if they couldn't bear to be any further apart...

Oh, lord. Her body remembered just how his skin felt against hers. Just how his body felt inside hers.

And how she wanted him to touch her. Cover every inch of skin with kisses. Tease her until she was on the knife-edge of climax—and then take her over with him, all the way.

She shivered.

'Are you all right, Fran?' Ric asked. 'You look a bit...'

She felt Gio tense.

Well, she wasn't going to blow their cover at this late stage. Not after all the work they'd put into it. 'A bit sad,' she said. 'Yes, I am. Because Nonna's going back to Milan when I'm only just getting to know her, and it'll be too long before she's back here again.'

Right answer. She felt Gio relax again.

Though his arms were still wrapped round her waist,

holding her close to him. Too close for comfort, and not close enough to satisfy the ripples of desire running down her spine.

But she wasn't going to beg.

He'd made his position clear.

And she'd respect that.

'I'm coming back at Christmas,' Isabella said with a smile, 'though you can always come to Milan. In fact, yes. Gio, you should bring Francesca over to see the rest of the family. And no excuses about being too busy at work. It's time you had a holiday, too.'

'Sure, Nonna. We'll work something out,' he said.

At long, long last the party was over. And Fran couldn't stop herself hugging everyone extra hard at the end of the evening. Because this was going to be the last time she saw them. This wasn't goodnight. Wasn't *ciao*. It was *arrivederci*—a formal and permanent goodbye.

She'd loved having a family to belong to. A family where she fitted in instead of feeling stranded on the edges.

As for Gio—she didn't dare think about what she felt for Gio. Because she knew she'd crumble, right here, right now. At least she'd had the foresight to call a taxi, so she didn't have to deal with the awkward situation of Gio feeling obliged to take her home.

Fran slept badly that night.

By the morning she'd made her decision. This really couldn't go on; there was only one solution. One that was going to hurt like hell—but it was better than letting everything drag on, never letting the scars have a chance to heal.

To her relief, Gio was actually in the office when she walked in.

She closed the door behind her and leaned against it. 'Gio.'

He swivelled round in his chair. 'What?'

'I'm sorry. I can't do this,' she said. Her throat felt as if it were filled with sand. Choking.

She was *not* going to break down and cry. She was going to do this with dignity.

'I know we said a week's notice on either side, but it's not a good idea. I'll forfeit a week's wages in lieu of notice.' Money wasn't the most important thing here. She had her redundancy pay and her 'garden leave' from the studio. But she needed to leave now. Before she made a complete and utter fool of herself.

She was leaving?

Leaving Giovanni's?

For good?

Gio stared at her, so shocked he wasn't capable of uttering a single word.

'Sorry to let you down. I hope the franchise thing works out okay for you. Um, bye.'

And that was it.

The door closed behind her again.

She was gone.

It hurt. It felt as if her heart were being torn out with a rusty spoon to walk away from Gio, to walk away from the colleagues she'd become fond of and the family she'd felt part of.

But Fran knew without a doubt it was the right thing to do.

Because Gio hadn't even tried to stop her.

Quite what she was going to do now, she wasn't sure. But she was going to walk out of the coffee shop with her head held high. And nobody was going to see her tears.

* * *

The black hole was back.

Except it was bigger than before.

A lot bigger, Gio thought savagely.

And throwing himself into work didn't help. At all. Without his perfect office manager to be part of it, the franchise scheme had lost its appeal. He couldn't care less any more about corporate identities and how to blend it with regional specialities.

Without Fran, nothing mattered.

Even his old stress relief—playing technically difficult pieces on the guitar—didn't help any more. Because he kept remembering the nights he'd played to her, sung to her. The time he'd sung for his supper—and she'd rewarded him with kisses. Kisses that were gone for good.

He was sitting in his office after a week in hell, staring into space, when he heard the door close.

Fran?

No, of course not. He pushed the hope down before it had time to grow. He spun round in his chair to see his mother standing there, and pinned a fake smile on his face. 'Hi, Mum. How's it going?'

'That's the question I want to ask you,' Angela said.

'Fine, fine.' He flapped a hand dismissively. 'Just a bit busy with the franchise stuff.'

'Which is why you haven't called home for a week. Why you've ignored every single text from your sisters and you don't answer your mobile phone. Why you take your office phone off the hook every evening and stay here until stupid o'clock. And why you never return any messages from your voicemail or answering machine.'

Gio forced his smile to widen. 'I'm fine, Mum. Just busy.'

'Right.' She walked over to him and traced the shadows under his eyes with the tip of her finger. 'So that's why you have these, is it? And you've lost weight.' Her mouth thinned. 'You haven't been eating properly, have you?'

'Course I have,' he fibbed. Food tasted like ashes. And he couldn't remember what or when he'd last eaten. It didn't matter. He couldn't care less.

She shook her head, mouth pursed. 'Don't try to pull the wool over my eyes, Giovanni Mazetti. When you're *really* busy, you persuade Netti to do you a takeaway and you at least stop for two minutes in her kitchen for a chat. But nobody's seen you for a week.' She paused. 'Nobody's seen *Fran*, for that matter.'

Ah. He should've guessed his mother would work it out for herself.

'Are you going to tell me what happened, or do I have to nag it out of you?'

He shrugged. 'It's like you and Nonna always say. No sensible girl's going to wait around for a workaholic, is she?'

'Fran's sensible,' Angela pointed out. 'And you reformed for her. You actually started taking time out to enjoy yourself. You even took lunch breaks. And yet the day after Nonna went back to Milan, you broke up with her.' She shook her head. 'Something doesn't quite ring true.'

He sighed. 'OK. If you want the truth, it was a set-up right from the start. I know how much Nonna wanted me to settle down. You all assumed Fran was more than just my office manager, despite the fact I told you the truth, so she agreed to be my pretend girlfriend while Nonna was in England.'

'I see.' Angela folded her arms. 'Bit of a drastic measure, don't you think?'

'Nonna sounded so happy at the idea I'd settled down.

How could I disappoint her?' He looked away. 'I've already disappointed my family enough.'

Angela took his hand and squeezed it. 'Gio, you've never been a disappointment to any of us. And if this is about when your dad was ill, that really wasn't your fault. Just for the record, he'd been having chest pains for a few weeks before the heart attack, except being your father he pretended they didn't exist and didn't tell anyone about them. And he was perfectly capable of getting a temp in to cover your shift; he didn't have to do it himself. Nobody's ever blamed you for what happened—except yourself,' she said gently. 'And nothing we could do or say would persuade you of the truth. It drives me crazy that you're still wearing a hair shirt after all these years. The business is doing so well that you can afford to take time out and do that degree in music—and you should have done it years ago. You need to do what makes you *happy*, Gio.'

Gio shook his head. 'You must be joking. Dad's nearly sixty. I don't want to give him the excuse to come back and work himself into the ground while I swan off somewhere with my guitar and indulge myself for a couple of years.'

'That isn't what I meant, and you know it. You had a good office manager. Someone who could run the whole lot while you're studying—and you'll know the business is in safe hands so you won't have to worry about it.'

Gio gestured round the office. 'The only office manager around here is me. So that isn't an option.'

'She's not working here any more, either?'

'Nope.'

She stroked his hair away from his forehead. 'Right now, you look a mess. You miss her, don't you?'

He tried to frame the lie, but he couldn't. 'Yeah,' he admitted, his voice cracking. 'I miss her like hell.'

'Because you're in love with her.'

He took a deep breath. 'It's complicated, Mum.'

'How? You love her. She loves you.' Angela spread her hands. 'What's complicated about that?'

She loves you. He'd so wanted that to be true. But it wasn't. 'She walked out on me.'

Angela frowned. 'Did you tell her how you felt about her?'

Ha. How could he?

At his silence, she sighed. 'You didn't, did you?' She rolled her eyes. 'Sometimes, I wonder how the intelligent, talented son I've always loved and been so proud of can be so *dense*. Gio, the way she looked at you gave her away. You know the reason why your little deception worked so well? Because it had all the hallmarks of truth. I could see by the way you looked at her that you were in love with her. And she most definitely felt the same about you.'

He dragged in a breath. 'Really? So why did she leave? Why did she walk out on me?'

'Because you made this hare-brained arrangement to split up with her when Nonna went back to Milan. And if you didn't tell her how you really felt about her, of *course* she'd leave. Because she's as proud and stubborn as you are and she wasn't going to stick around when she thought you didn't want her.' Angela started at him. 'I can't believe you need me to spell it out for you. Have you called her since she left?'

He gritted his teeth. 'She made it clear it was over.'

'And you're too stubborn to fight for her? Give me strength.' Angela picked up the phone and handed it to him. 'Take it from me, male pride is a very pointless thing. A very *lonely* thing. Call her. Tell her you need to talk to her. And when you see her, tell her how you feel. Be honest with her.'

Easy to say. 'What if she doesn't want me?'

'It's a risk you'll have to take. And it's about time you took it.' She dropped a kiss on his forehead. 'Call her. And then call me later and let me know how things are, OK?'

CHAPTER SIXTEEN

FRAN didn't answer her phone. Didn't call Gio back when he left a message. Ignored his texts and emails.

He considered sending her flowers; then he remembered that she was on garden leave. So she might not even be in London. She might have gone home to see her family. Then again, he knew she didn't think she fitted in with them: so it was unlikely.

So where was she? Had she gone somewhere? Taken a break to get away from everything?

There was only one way to find out. Talk to her, face to face. He went to her flat. Pressed the intercom.

No answer.

So then he pressed her neighbour's buzzer—the one who'd flooded her flat in the first place.

'If you're selling something, I'm not interested,' was the greeting through the intercom.

Charming. Gio resisted the urge to say something rude; if he put the guy's back up, he'd never get the information he wanted. 'I'm not selling something. Actually, I'm trying to get hold of your neighbour.'

'Nothing to do with me, mate.'

'I rather think it is,' Gio said, 'seeing as you flooded her flat in the first place.'

All the belligerence suddenly left the man's tone. 'Oh.'

'She was staying with—with a friend of mine. And she left some things my friend wants to return to her.'

'Well, I can take them in, if you want,' the neighbour said, his voice slightly grudging.

'No, they need to be returned personally.'

'Are you calling me a thief?'

'No, nothing like that.' Gio sighed. Poor Fran, having to put up with such an aggressive neighbour. The sort who'd fly off the handle at the least provocation. Definitely the sort who'd stomp out of his flat in a strop and forget he'd left the bath running. When Fran had had a hissy fit on him for flooding her flat, she was lucky he hadn't flattened her. 'Look, my friend hasn't been able to get in touch with her. Do you know if she's around at the moment or if she's away?'

'Her recycling box was out with the others, this morning. That's about all I can tell you.'

Not a great deal, but it was enough—it proved that she was still in London. She was clearly just avoiding all Gio's messages.

'Thanks.' He stopped leaning on the intercom.

So what did he do now? She obviously wasn't going to return his calls. If his mother was right, this was a defence mechanism to stop herself being hurt, because she thought he didn't want her. Given what he knew of her background, it was understandable she'd be wary of putting herself in a situation where she could be rejected.

But unless he could talk to her, he wasn't going to be able to tell her how he really felt about her. That he wasn't going to reject her.

Flowers weren't going to work. Or chocolates. He needed

something to show her he was absolutely serious about this. That the stakes were as high for him as they were for her.

But how?

He spent the evening brooding about it. And then he remembered her suggestion. Expanding the café chain by adding another branch would mean additional premises costs; whereas if they kept the same number of branches, but opened in the evening, the costs would all be marginal. Starting with the book group in Holborn.

So far, so sensible.

And then she'd suggesting opening the Charlotte Street café once a week.

For an evening of classical music.

With him as the performer.

Her voice echoed in his head: *play the music you love for people*.

And she'd told him to take a sabbatical. Be a musician. His old dream—the one he thought he'd stamped on and crushed years go. But the yearning was still there.

Maybe, he thought, it was time he did.

And maybe, just maybe, if he did it, it would convince her that he was serious.

Courier delivery? She hadn't ordered anything that was likely to be delivered by courier. Fran frowned, but signed the courier's form.

The envelope held no clues whatsoever to the contents. It was just a plain A5 cardboard-backed envelope. Her address was printed on a label, and the postmark was central London. Odd. At first glance, she would have said it was junk mail. But junk mail didn't usually come in a cardboard-backed envelope—and it definitely didn't come by courier.

She opened the flap, and took out the folded A4 sheet.

And blinked as she read the poster.

An evening of music at Giovanni's of Charlotte Street.

She blinked even harder as she read who was playing.

He was taking up her suggestion?

And he'd written something on one of the blank spaces on the poster. *Please come. Gio.*

His handwriting was spikier than she remembered it. As if it was an effort for him to write the note. But the words themselves were so sparse, told her nothing about how he was feeling or why he'd invited her. Was it out of some sense of obligation, because she'd been the one to suggest it? Or was it because he really wanted her there?

Just 'Gio'.

Not 'love, Gio', as his flowers had been.

Just 'Gio'. Impenetrable.

Fran thought about it. Very hard. And she didn't make her final decision until the evening of the concert.

She'd go.

But she'd slip in very quietly. Merge into the background. Once she could judge the situation, she'd know whether to go and talk to him—or whether to leave again, just as quietly.

She wasn't going to come. Gio paced his office. This was the most stupid, stupid idea he'd ever had. He should've called the whole thing off when she hadn't replied to his invitation. He knew she'd definitely received it—he'd sent it by courier so he could check whether it had been delivered and who signed for it. But she'd stayed silent.

She wasn't going to come.

And he had a café full of people out there, waiting to hear him play.

How the hell was he going to do this?

Because it wasn't his reputation on the line, at the end of the day. It was the café's. If he made a fool of himself, so be it. He could live with that. But he didn't want to undermine all the work his father had put in to Giovanni's. Or the ten years he'd dedicated to it himself.

He should have booked other acts, too. So if his own set was a complete waste of time, at least the audience would remember something good from the evening. A string quartet, a small jazz trio, a folk singer. But, no, he was doing this solo. Putting his heart and soul on the line.

And for what?

Because she wasn't going to be there.

Maybe he should've done this as a private performance. Just for Fran. And then if she hadn't turned up he wouldn't have made such a fool of himself.

Why had he been so stupid?

'Gio. You'll be fine, honey,' Angela soothed, coming in and patting his shoulder. 'This is a little bit of stage fright. Perfectly normal. Just relax.'

It wasn't stage fright. At all. 'Is she there? Could you see her?'

'You'll be fine.'

The evasion was all too obvious. She didn't want to say no because she didn't want the knowledge to hurt him. But he knew anyway, and his stomach felt hollow. Adrenalin made his fingers feel heavy and buzzy—no way could they work with the precision he needed to play Bach and Dowland and Tarrega. He was going to screw this up. Seriously screw this up.

He took a deep breath. The last night he'd played a classical concert had been the night his father almost died.

He couldn't do this.

But then his father walked in and hugged him. 'I'm so proud of you, son. Now go out there and show the world what Gio Mazetti is made of. Go and *shine*.'

'We'll be right by your side,' Angela said softly.

He couldn't let his family down. And even though he knew the one person he wanted to play for wasn't there...he'd do it.

He picked up his guitar and walked into the café. Sat down on the stool at the front of the crowd. Heard the buzz of conversation dip to a murmur and then a hush.

He wasn't going to look for Fran. There was no point. But he'd play as if she were there. Play the pretty pieces she'd loved. 'Spanish Ballad', 'Air on a G String', the 'Alhambra', Dowland...

And as the minutes ticked past, he realised.

He could still play.

He could still do this.

And he began to smile.

At last he came to the end of the set. 'Thank you for listening to me tonight,' he said. 'I'm going to play one more song for you. For someone who's very special to me. Someone I love very much, from the bottom of my heart, and I was stupid enough not to tell her so when I had the chance. She's not here tonight, but I'm going to play it for her anyway.' His voice caught. 'Because without her I wouldn't be playing here tonight. Wouldn't be playing at all.'

Tears pricked Fran's eyes. Someone he loved very much, from the bottom of his heart. Did he mean her? But she *was* here. She frowned. OK, she'd slipped quietly into the back, but surely he'd seen her?

And then he began to play. The most beautiful arrangement of a song she knew well—her parents adored musicals and her mother's favourite was *South Pacific*. 'This Nearly Was Mine' was a song that made her mother cry, about the man who was in love with a woman who didn't return his love. And this instrumental version would definitely have her mother in tears. A minute and a half of sheer wistfulness.

It practically had Fran in tears, and she could see how moved the audience was, too.

'Thank you for coming,' Gio said when the last notes died away. 'Goodnight.' And he left the café to wild applause.

Fran stayed where she was, unable to move. That song…had it been for her? A song about nearly having paradise, about the one girl he dreamed of, about kisses he remembered—did he mean her?

She dragged in a breath. Gio had played tonight. A proper classical performance, in front of an audience, for the first time in more than ten years. And he'd asked her to be here.

Maybe she was reading too much into this.

But if she didn't go to see him, here and now, she knew she'd regret it for the rest of her life.

Slowly, she made her way over to the corridor that led to the office.

Gio's parents were there. And when they saw her, Gio's father held out his arms. Hugged her.

'Go to him,' Angela said softly, and pointed to the office.

Fran nodded, swallowed hard, and opened the door.

'Hello, Gio.'

Gio's head whipped round. 'Fran? But…I thought you weren't…' His voice trailed off.

He didn't think she'd been there? 'I was there,' she confirmed. 'I saw you play. Heard you.'

'All of it?'

She nodded. 'That last song—was it for me?'

He dragged in a breath. 'Don't you know that?'

'I wouldn't be asking if I did.'

'Yes. It was.' He looked her straight in the eye. 'I played here tonight, because you suggested it. Because you're right—it's time I forgave myself and played again. Without you, I wouldn't have done this.'

'That wasn't *all* you said.'

A faint smile tugged at the corner of his mouth. 'Ah. The bit about the fact I love you from the bottom of my heart, you mean? I do.' His expression became bleak. 'And when you walked out on me…that was when I realised how stupid I'd been. That I should've told you before. Taken the risk.'

'So why did you let me leave?'

'Because you were so keen to get your own space back.'

She frowned. 'Hang on. You couldn't wait to get rid of me. You even offered to help me paint my flat.'

'Only so you'd stay with me for at least two more days— one while we painted, one for the fumes to go. Maybe one more for luck.'

'So you wanted me to stay?'

He nodded.

And now he was telling her how he felt. Taking the risk. Like he'd taken the risk tonight and played for an audience.

He'd asked her to come along.

He'd said he loved her.

Maybe it was time she took a risk, too. 'I wanted to stay.'

'So why didn't you say something?'

'Because I thought you wanted to stick to your original plan. That as soon as Nonna went back to Milan, we'd end the fake relationship.'

He shook his head. 'It wasn't a fake. It might've started

out that way—but when you stayed at my flat it most definitely *wasn't* a fake. We didn't have sex, Fran. We made love.'

'You let me go.'

'I was wrong.' He took a deep breath. 'The night of my birthday party, I told you there was a black hole inside me. Something missing. Well, now I know what fills it. What makes me complete.'

She waited.

'You,' he whispered. 'You complete me, Fran. I love you.'

'You love me.' She tested the words, almost in wonder. 'You love me.'

'You heard me say it. In front of a crowded room when I didn't even know you were there, I said I loved you from the bottom of my heart. That I was playing for you. And I'm telling you right here, right now, Francesca Marsden, I love you.'

Her breath hitched. 'I…I don't know what to say.'

'The phrase I'm listening for is "I love you, too",' he said wryly.

She did. But saying it… Lord, that was hard.

'When you walked out, I was so stunned that I couldn't even speak. And by the time I'd recovered my wits enough to call you, you'd frozen me out.' He spread his hands. 'I don't know how to prove I love you. But I do. And I know what I want from life, now. I want marriage and babies and a house full of noise and laughter and love. And,' he told her, his voice cracking, 'I want it with you.'

CHAPTER SEVENTEEN

'WAS that a proposal?' Fran asked.

'Not a proper one.' Gio spread his hands. 'I'm Italian. I want to marry you, yes—but I need to ask you the old-fashioned way.'

'The old-fashioned way? What's that?'

He smiled. 'I'm going to ask your father for your hand in marriage.'

She stared at him. 'This is the twenty-first century, Gio. People don't do that any more.'

'Yes, they do. And I want to do it the traditional way.' His gaze grew hot. 'Just for the record, I'm intending to carry you over the threshold as well. And take your wedding dress off very, very, *very* slowly.'

Oh, lord. The picture *that* conjured up. The memories of the night he'd made love with her and insisted on taking it slowly. So slowly that she'd come more than once for the very first time.

Some of her thoughts must have shown on her face, because he added with a grin, 'Spoon.'

She couldn't help laughing back. 'Behave.'

His smile faded. 'Then say the words.'

'Which words?'

'You know which ones. I need to hear them, Fran.'

Words she'd never said before.

She took a deep breath. 'I love you.'

'Didn't hear that.'

'I love you,' she said, more loudly.

'Good.' He wrapped his arms round her and kissed her. Thoroughly.

The next thing she knew, they were sitting in the office chair—and she was on his lap, with her arms round his neck.

'I missed you,' he said softly.

'I missed you too,' she admitted.

'We've been very stupid. We should've been honest with each other. Talked. Taken the risk instead of being too scared.' He brushed his mouth against hers. 'I need to see your parents.'

'No, you don't.'

He sighed. 'Fran, I shared my family with you. Why won't you share yours with me?'

'Because it's *different*.'

'Because you were adopted, you mean?' He stroked her face. 'That doesn't make any difference. They might not be your natural family, but they're still your family—they're the ones who grew up with you. And you refer to your parents as Mum and Dad, so surely you love them?'

She rested her forehead against his shoulder. 'I'm not like any of them. I'm the odd one out.'

His arms tightened round her. 'I don't think you're odd. Well, not very.' He grinned as she lifted her head. 'I thought that would make you glare at me.' His voice softened. 'Meet me halfway, Fran. At least introduce me to them. Because we're going to have a *big* wedding.'

Oh, lord. 'How big a wedding?'

'I'm part of a big family. The Mazettis are close. And even if we disappear with the intention of getting married very quietly at the top of a mountain, they'll all work out exactly where we've gone, and when we get back to base camp they'll be waiting there with a party and more confetti than you'd think could ever be made.'

From what she'd seen of a Mazetti family party, he wasn't exaggerating.

'OK. I'll call them.'

'Call them now.' He leaned forward, picked up the office phone and pushed it into her hand.

She replaced it on the desk. 'Later.'

'*Now*, Fran.'

For a moment, he thought she was going to refuse. But then she sighed, and punched in her parents' number.

'Hi, Mum. It's Fran.' She paused. 'Can I come and see you? There's someone I'd like you to meet.'

Gio couldn't catch the reply on the other end. Why hadn't he thought to switch the phone on to hands-free speaker mode?

'When do we want to come?' Fran asked. 'Um…'

He prodded her so she looked at him and mouthed, 'This Sunday.'

Fran shook her head and turned away.

He grabbed her desk pad and scribbled a note. *Ask for this Sunday or I'll ask them myself.* She'd once threatened to break the rules and look up his personal information on the staff records. He could do the same.

She scowled, but to his relief she said, 'How about this Sunday? Uh-huh. I need to check the train times, but, yes, we'll be there before lunch. OK. Bye.'

No 'I love you', he noticed. All businesslike. So very different from his own family. Well, he'd give Fran all the love she'd been waiting for. And more.

'We're not going by train,' he said when she replaced the receiver.

'Why not? Gio, my parents live in Oxford.'

'Which means it's straight down the M40. That's fine. I like driving.'

'But…'

'Not buts, Fran.' He brushed his mouth against hers. 'By the way, there are two more things you need to know.'

'What?'

'Firstly, I've just discovered I'm *very* traditional. So, much as I want to take you back to my place tonight and spend every single second making love with you, I'm not going to.' He rubbed the tip of his nose against hers. 'No sex,' he whispered, 'before marriage.'

She blinked. 'Gio, may I point out that we've already, um, done it?'

'Uh-huh.' He smiled. 'That was before you were engaged to me.'

'I'm not engaged to you. You haven't asked me to marry you.'

He waved a dismissive hand. 'That's a minor detail. I'm going to. Which makes you as good as engaged. And Italian men are ultra-traditional. No sex before marriage. Not even phone sex.'

'Phone sex?'

'Where I tell you exactly what I want to do with you. What I want you to do.' He nuzzled the sensitive spot just below her ear. 'And I'll hear the change in your breathing. Know the very second that you come—and that you're thinking of me when you do it.'

'Oh-h-h.'

He could see from her expression that the idea intrigued her. And he could feel her heat beating just that little bit faster. He licked her earlobe. 'I might just do that, some time,' he told her, his voice husky with promise. 'But not until we're married. Which leads me to number two.'

She stroked his face. 'I'm not sure I'm ready to hear this.'

'Trust me, you will be.'

'All right. The second thing?'

'Our engagement's going to be short.' He moved back slightly so he could look into her eyes, and moistened his lower lip with the tip of his tongue. 'Really, *really* short.'

'Define "short".'

He stole a kiss. 'Given that organising is your forte—how quickly can you organise a wedding?'

She laughed. 'Is that a challenge?'

'Nope. Wrong tone. I'm not challenging. I'm *begging*. And I'd prefer the answer to be something in nanoseconds.'

'A small wedding we can sort out in however long the notice period is to the register office. Days, probably. A big church wedding—well, you have banns and all sorts of things to sort out. We're talking weeks. *If* the church isn't booked up. And I'm assuming you're Catholic.' At his nod, she continued, 'I'm not. So there's all that to sort out, too.'

'How long?'

She shook her head. 'I really don't know. Can't even guess. Definitely weeks.'

He groaned and leaned his forehead against hers. 'I might have to revise number one.'

'Uh-uh.' She wagged a finger at him. 'You said you were going to do this the traditional way.'

'In which case, I'd better take you home now. And you

need to think about whether you want a big church wedding or a big register office wedding.'

'You haven't asked me yet,' she reminded him. 'And I haven't said yes yet.'

'I will,' he said. 'And so will you.' He kissed her. 'And now I'm going to take you home. Before my very poor self-control snaps. Because I remember what it feels like to be deep inside you, Francesca, and my body's screaming out to do it again.'

He gently nudged her to her feet and led her out of the office.

The café was deserted and locked up, although one bank of lights was on over the counter. Fran blinked. 'I saw your parents and your sisters earlier. I thought they'd still be here.'

Gio smiled. 'Believe me, the second I switch my phone on you'll hear beep after beep from all the text messages asking me if everything's OK and we're together again.' His smile broadened. 'For the first time ever I think they're trying to be tactful. I think they realised we needed some space.'

Her eyes glittered. 'I remember you saying once about needing a lock on your office door. Looks as if we don't need one tonight.'

He dragged in a breath. 'You've just put another of those X-rated pictures in my head.'

She gave him the sexiest smile he'd ever seen. 'Then let's make it real, honey.'

Oh-h-h. It was way too tempting. He almost picked her up in a fireman's lift to carry her back to the office and push the papers off his desk and ease into her body. But he stopped himself in time. '*Not* until we're married. But we can have dinner together tomorrow night.' He sighed. 'And I'll have to put you in a taxi at the restaurant door. On your own. Tonight as well as tomorrow.'

'You're absolutely serious about this traditional bit?'

He nodded. 'Until I've met your family and spoken to your father, I'm not going to ask you to marry me.'

She sucked in a breath. 'What if my dad says no?'

'He won't,' Gio said confidently. 'Because I'll tell him how much I love you. That I want to spend the rest of my life with you. That you're going to be my equal and I won't expect you to give up your career to have babies.' He smiled. 'Though we most definitely are going to have babies. At least one. I want a little girl who looks just like her mum, with big blue eyes I can't say no to.'

Fran gave him a truly wicked grin. 'Can't say no to, hmm?'

He kissed her. Thoroughly. And then called the local taxi firm. 'While I still can,' he said, when he'd ended the call. 'The next time we make love, it's going to be on our wedding night.'

'That,' she teased, 'is a challenge.'

'No. It's a promise.' He smiled. 'And I'll always keep my promises to you.'

CHAPTER EIGHTEEN

ON Sunday Fran was almost sick with nerves. She was awake hours before Gio was due to pick her up, and she couldn't settle to anything.

At last he buzzed through to the intercom.

'On my way down,' she said.

'Good morning, *tesoro*.' He kissed her lightly. 'All set?'

She nodded. 'I just need to get some flowers on the way.'

'Already sorted.'

Oh. Well, it would have been. Gio had impeccable manners. 'Thank you.'

She barely said a word all the way to Oxford. Gio didn't push her to talk—just occasionally reached out to squeeze her hand, letting her know that he was right beside her.

It was completely ridiculous. Of course her parents would like Gio. Everyone who met him liked him.

But—and it was a big but—she so wanted their approval. To know that she'd done something right in their eyes.

When they came off the M40, she directed him to her parents' house. As he parked in the driveway, she frowned. 'That's Suzy's car. And Ted's.'

He smiled. 'So I get to meet all of them, then? Good.'

He didn't mind?

Her thoughts must have been obvious, because he touched her cheek. 'Hey. You had to meet nearly all mine at once. There were rather more of them. And you know I want to meet your family.' He climbed out, undid her door and then collected the most beautiful bouquet from the boot of his car. Pure white roses, lilies and freesias.

Which Fran's mother most definitely appreciated, because she went pink with pleasure when Gio handed them to her. 'How lovely! Thank you.'

'My pleasure, Mrs Marsden. And thank you for allowing Francesca to bring me to lunch.'

'Do call me Carol. Please.' She smiled at him. 'Hello, Fran.'

'Hello, Mum,' Fran muttered.

This was ridiculous. She'd been an office manager for years—firstly at the voiceover studio and then for the Giovanni's chain. Competent, efficient and effective. So why did she turn into a shoe-scuffing, awkward teenager the minute she walked into her parents' house?

'I'll put the kettle on. Tea?' Carol asked.

Gio smiled. 'Thanks. That'd be lovely.'

'Warren—Fran's dad—is at the allotment, but he'll be home soon,' Carol added.

'What allotment?' Fran asked

'He's doing this stuff about eco schools, and he thought having an allotment would fit in really well with it. And he wants us to have home-grown vegetables for lunch. He's dragged the others off with him to help him cut the beans.'

Home-grown vegetables? Then Fran noticed her mother hadn't just made the usual Sunday roast. There was a chocolate cake—her favourite—cooling on a wire rack. And an apple pie ready to go into the oven when the main course was out.

'You've gone to a lot of trouble,' she said, feeling guilty.

Her mother must have spent all morning cooking. 'You didn't need to do all that.'

Carol scoffed. 'Of course I did. You're my daughter. I wanted to.'

'And I didn't think the others would be here today.'

'Dom'll probably tell you he's only here because he can't stand college food—but as soon as I mentioned you were coming today, he was straight on the phone to Ted and Suzy.' Carol smiled at her. 'They wouldn't miss you coming home, love. Though you can expect Suzy to moan about the fact she could've seen her favourite band in Manchester last night and Ted's swapped duty at the last minute to get today off.' She handed Gio and Fran a mug of tea. 'It's nice to meet you, Gio. Fran hasn't told me much about you, but then none of my four are particularly forthcoming.'

Gio smiled. 'My mother has a spy network. If we don't tell her ourselves, someone else does.'

Carol laughed. 'I'll bear that in mind.'

Just then, there was a kerfuffle; the kitchen door burst open and a young springer spaniel bounded in.

'A dog? Since when…?' Fran asked, looking at her mother.

'No, she's mine. Last week. Rescue dog,' Ted explained. 'Fran, meet Bouncer. Bouncer, this is my big sister.'

Fran could easily see how the spaniel had got her name. 'Hello.'

'Muddy paws! Oh, no. Sorry, Mum. Sorry, Fran,' Ted said, looking at the paw-prints on the floor and his sister's dress.

'Hey, mud washes out. It's not a problem.' Gio made a fuss of the spaniel. 'Hello, *bella ragazza*.' He was rewarded with a lick—and muddy paw-prints on his shirt.

'Ted's girlfriend's a police dog handler,' Suzy said. 'She's meant to be helping him train the pup. Not that it's working yet. Hi, Fran.' She gave Gio a shy look. 'And you must be Gio?'

'Pleased to meet you,' he said, shaking her hand.

Fran made quick introductions. 'And this is Dominic, and my dad,' she finished as they walked in together, laden with vegetables.

'Hello, love.' Warren smiled at her. 'I cut extra beans so you can take some home to London with you. And Dom's going to wrap some carrots up for you in newspaper—they keep better with earth on.' He looked at Gio. 'Nice to meet you, young man.'

'And you.' Gio held his hand out. 'May I have a quick word in private, Mr Marsden?'

'Warren.' He smiled. 'When Carol told me Fran was bringing you to see us, I wondered. Come into my study. Bring your tea with you.'

'Does this mean you're getting married?' Suzy asked when Gio followed their father out of the kitchen.

Fran took a sip of tea. 'Possibly.'

'Um, have you sorted out bridesmaids yet? Because if not, I'd really… Well…' Suzy wriggled on her chair. 'You know.'

Fran stared at her sister in surprise. 'You want to be my bridesmaid?'

Suzy nodded. 'I know I'm the scary dentist-to-be and all that, but—you're my big sister. And even if you want me to wear a dress that makes me look like a meringue…I won't mind.'

Carol squeezed her hand. 'And I know you're brilliant at organising, but I'd love to help you choose your dress.'

Fran really hadn't expected this reaction. Her mother and sister wanted to be involved in the wedding?

'And we'll be ushers if you want us to,' Dominic added.

'As the elder twin, I'll make sure he wears a suit,' Ted said, sitting on the floor with a wriggling puppy on his lap.

Which was when Fran realised. They were making a fuss just because she'd come home. So maybe, all these years when she'd thought she was an outsider, she'd been completely wrong. Her throat felt thick with tears and she swallowed hard. 'I'd love that. Gio…being Italian, he wants to ask Dad's permission to marry me.'

'We guessed as much. Because you never bring anyone home,' Suzy said.

'And that's why Ted—' Dominic began.

His brother nudged him hard. 'Shush, or I'll let Bouncer chew your shoes.'

'Ted *what*?' Fran asked curiously.

'Ah.' Ted stared at the floor. 'I, um, bent some rules. Looked him up on the police computer.'

Fran stared at him in shock. 'You didn't!'

He shrugged. 'Well, we just wanted to be sure he was OK. And that he treats you right.'

'He will,' Warren announced, returning to the kitchen. 'Gio and I have just had a very interesting chat.'

Fran squirmed. 'Uh-huh.'

'And I think we all need to disappear for a minute,' Warren added.

Gio shook his head. 'Absolutely not. This is the exactly the right time and the right place—in the heart of your house and the heart of your family.' He took a small box out of his pocket and dropped to one knee in front of her. 'Francesca Marsden. I have your father's permission to ask you a very important question.' He opened the box to reveal a platinum ring set with a heart-shaped diamond. 'Will you marry me?'

A heart-shaped diamond—a ring she hadn't even known

he'd bought—given in the heart of their house and the heart of her family. Fran could hardly see because her vision was blurred with tears. 'Yes,' she whispered. 'I will.'

'I think,' Warren said, 'this means champagne. So we can welcome Gio to the family properly.' It seemed to take only seconds for a bottle of champagne and seven glasses to appear. And as the cork popped, Gio held her very tightly. 'It's just the beginning,' he said softly, 'of the rest of our lives. And a very extended family.'

One that wasn't as tactile as the Mazettis and maybe didn't say it as often, Fran thought—but one that felt the same way.

With love.

EPILOGUE

Thirteen months later

'HAPPY ANNIVERSARY, Mrs Mazetti.' Gio set the tray on top of the bedside cabinet, then climbed back in bed next to Fran.

'Champagne and strawberries for breakfast?' she asked.

'It's our wedding anniversary. And I'd like to draw your attention to a very romantic gesture. There's a single red rose on that tray.'

She smiled. 'For a student, you know, that's terribly extravagant.'

He laughed, leaned back against the pillows and pulled her into his arms. 'I'm not your average student.'

'You're not average *anything*,' she murmured, kissing him.

'Why, thank you, honey.' He held her close. 'It's been quite a year. Getting married, starting up the Thursday jazz and classics nights in Charlotte Street, moving to Greenwich, opening a new branch here...' He sighed. 'Not to mention handing over a lot more of the control to the new partner in Giovanni's. Who's so damned efficient she leaves the office at five every night.'

'Something had to give. Even *you* can't do a full-time degree on top of managing a café chain,' she said. 'Especially as you have a new role to fulfil shortly.'

'Oh?' He frowned. 'What's that?'

'I have an anniversary present for you too.'

He rubbed his nose against hers. 'Mmm. I do hope it's what I think it is.'

She laughed. 'That's for later. And you're going to have to share this particular present.'

He looked at her in puzzlement. 'How? And with whom, precisely?'

'You'll see when you get the present.'

'"When" being the operative word,' he grumbled.

She sat up and opened the drawer next to her. 'Close your eyes and hold out your hand.'

He did so, and she placed a small white rectangular object on his palm.

'OK. You can open your eyes now.'

He looked at it. Stared at her. Stared back at the item on his palm. 'Fran, is this what I think it is?'

'*Sì, papà,*' she confirmed. 'You're going to have to learn to play some lullabies. Maybe compose some.'

'When?'

'About seven months.'

He whooped with joy. 'A year ago, I thought you'd made me the happiest man on earth. But today I've learned I was wrong: it's just going to get better and better. Every day, for the rest of our lives.'

Tears of sheer happiness pricked her eyes. 'I love you, Gio.'

'And I love you too, Francesca—my love, my life.' He

wriggled down the bed and dropped a kiss on her abdomen. 'And the perfect family. Where we belong.'

'The perfect family,' she echoed.

Where she most definitely belonged.

PURCHASED FOR PLEASURE

BY
NICOLA MARSH

Nicola Marsh has always had a passion for writing and reading. As a youngster, she devoured books when she should have been sleeping, and later she kept a diary whose content could be an epic in itself! These days, when she's not enjoying life with her husband and two sons in her home city of Melbourne, she's at her computer creating the romances she loves, in her dream job. Visit Nicola's website at www.nicolamarsh.com for the latest news of her books.

CHAPTER ONE

THE minute Kate Hayden saw Tyler James again, her world turned upside down.

Okay, maybe nothing quite so dramatic, but it sure seemed as if her axis tilted way off kilter as the gut-wrenching desire that had been a feature of their brief relationship eons ago was back, overwhelming in its intensity.

It had been six, long years since she'd last seen him so why were her hormones going haywire at the sight of him now?

She'd gotten over him a long time ago.

She'd prepared for this.

She'd psyched herself up for weeks ever since she'd seen his name on the list of 'Odd Bods', the rather quaint name given to the charity man auction the magazine was sponsoring, and known she had to see him.

So she was curious? No big deal. She'd been nosy her whole life and the trait served her well in her job, giving her a head-start on the next big story, helping her make a name for herself.

But this insatiable curiosity about Ty was different and she'd known it the minute her tummy had tingled at the sight of his name on the auction list.

This wasn't just the natural curiosity of an investigative journalist. Uh-uh.

This was the intense burning curiosity of a woman who'd walked away from the best thing that had ever happened to her.

First loves weren't supposed to last and she'd moved on a long time ago, but somehow seeing his name on that list had brought back a rush of memories, all good, and she had to see him.

She'd hoped he'd be shrunken and balding and his muscles had wasted away. Although where would the fun be in that?

She sipped her champagne, hoping the bubbly liquid would ease the sudden dryness of her throat as the guy she'd once thought she'd spend the rest of her life with strutted across the stage.

Oh, my.

The champagne momentarily soothed her thirst but it did nothing for her erratic pulse, which skipped all over the place at the sight of the sexiest guy she'd ever met standing on display to a room full of women as if he didn't have a care in the world.

Ty looked incredible, far hotter than she remembered—and she remembered a lot! If anything, the years had enhanced his rugged good looks. Fine lines radiated from the corners of his blue eyes doing little to detract from the tanned, hard planes of his face, his high cheekbones hinting at arrogance. Rich brown hair streaked blond by the sun, cut in the traditional short-back-and-sides he favoured. And those finely shaped lips…

Oh, yeah, she remembered those lips all too well, seducing her with their skill, giving pleasure, wreaking havoc.

The memories still lingered, imprinted on her brain, branded there, utterly indelible. She'd deliberately blocked them over the years, concentrating on her career, trying to build a life for herself in a new country.

Leaving Sydney for LA had been a huge decision for a twenty-one-year-old. But meeting Ty shortly after she landed in the US had made that transition a lot less scary; in fact the guy had lit her world back then.

Squirming in her chair, she took another sip of champagne. This wasn't the time to get caught up in memories of Ty. She had to focus her attention for the next ten minutes, at least till she'd given her speech. Senior editors needed to be cool and poised, not hot and bothered while practically drooling over an old flame.

'So, without further ado, ladies, I present our last Odd Bod for the evening. Though from where I'm standing there's nothing odd about this particular bod!'

A soft twittering swept the room as all eyes turned to the stage. Kelly Adams, the glam local TV station presenter, gestured to the man on her right as she continued her spiel.

'I know you'll like what you see, ladies. Tyler James is a Navy SEAL instructor. By the way, SEAL stands for Sea, Air and Land, for those of you who don't know, and they're an amazing bunch of Special Forces guys. Tyler stands at six feet four with muscles to die for, has amazing blue eyes, is equipped to handle anything and likes to take charge!'

Catcalls and whistles filled the air while the man in question squared his broad shoulders and grinned, not in the least embarrassed.

'So, what am I bid for Tyler? Come on, ladies, dig deep. The Ramirez Orphanage is a good cause that needs your help to stay open. Besides, who wouldn't want this man doing their odd jobs for the next week? Perhaps a spot of gardening? Car washing? Cooking? Housework? Your call, ladies. I'd bid myself though I think my husband would have something to say about it. Who'll start the bidding?'

As Kelly's announcement sank in Kate pondered his change in career. Ty had become an instructor? When they'd first met he'd been a proud SEAL, resplendent in his uniform and bristling with macho ideals. No behind-the-scenes action for that guy. He'd been committed and passionate with a genuine love for his career. Why the change of heart?

She stared at the man on stage, questions swirling through her head.

Why hadn't they given it a go?

Had chasing their careers rather than following their hearts been worth it?

Had growing up changed them?

Needing a distraction from her futile questions, she glanced around the table and noticed every woman's attention riveted to the stage. Not that she could blame them, considering what was on show up there.

They were a great bunch of girls to work with, all highly talented in their own right: journalists, editors and photographers. Diane, her personal assistant, had organised this gathering in support of the magazine's sponsorship of the orphanage. In fact, Di had been in charge of choosing this year's worthy cause and had taken care of every detail and all she'd had to do was turn up.

As if sensing her gaze, Di turned towards her.

'Why don't you put in a bid, Kate? About time you had some excitement in your life.'

Excitement? Her? No way. Been there, done that and still had the SEAL scars to prove it.

To her mortification, the rest of the girls turned to look at her so she schooled her features into her best 'I'm too busy to have fun' look.

'Sorry to disappoint, everyone. No time for excitement. What would I do with an Odd Bod anyway?'

Though her voice remained steady the idea of Ty trailing after her for a week did strange things to her insides.

Things she shouldn't be feeling…or remembering…

'My point exactly,' Di smirked. 'If you don't know what to do with a total hunk like that you need more help than I first thought. Why don't you live a little and show us you're human after all?'

The rest of the table joined in, goading her into bidding and she shook her head, chuckling at their enthusiasm.

So Di had a point. She did bury her life in her work, determined to show that effort and dedication were the keys to success. However, being a workaholic had its downside and she hadn't had any fun in ages. She'd been fun and impulsive once, and she was too young to be living the sensible 'all work no play' life. Maybe a brief catch-up off-stage with an old 'friend' could be an antidote to that?

What harm could placing a bid do? It wasn't as if she'd be the only one. Just one look at Ty and every woman in the room would be reaching for their cheque books.

'Okay, okay. I'll do it. Sheesh.'

She held up her hands in surrender and grinned as the girls cheered. Downing the rest of her champagne in two gulps, she raised her hand high in the air and waved it like a cheerleader on a caffeine high.

'Five hundred dollars,' she yelled, buoyed by the alcohol and a sudden rush to do something completely out of character.

Pin-drop silence followed and rather than sinking into her chair with embarrassment she straightened her spine, head up, waiting for the moment Ty laid eyes on his bidder, eager to see his reaction, wondering if they still had a spark.

She had her answer in the next loaded second when Ty focussed that too-blue gaze of his on her, the shock of recognition registering in the imperceptible widening of his eyes across the room as they stared at each other, neither backing down, locked in an invisible battle of wills so reminiscent of the past.

Maybe it was the champagne, maybe it was the number of women packed into the room, but while Kate sat trapped under the intensity of Ty's stare she broke out in a sweat as her body temperature sky-rocketed and she could barely breathe.

'Do I have any further bids?' Kelly queried, surveying the room with a grin on her expertly made up face.

Please. Someone…anyone…

Kate's silent plea preceded complete and utter bedlam as the ladies—and she used the term loosely—in the room erupted.

Maybe her initial bid had been a tad on the high side considering the average guy had gone for around three to four hundred all night. But she'd wanted to prove a point to the girls, show them she could lighten up when needed. Unfortunately, she hadn't counted on the speculative gleam in her ex's eyes or the competitive nature of her fellow bidders.

'Five-fifty!' shouted a boppy blonde.

Kate rolled her eyes. Blondes were so not Ty's type.

'Six hundred,' yelled a willowy redhead who looked like Nicole Kidman, her smug smile indicating she thought she'd won.

'Six-fifty.'

Kate sat up and took notice of the third bidder, a sultry brunette reminiscent of Catherine Zeta-Jones with breasts that could take out a guy's eye at a hundred paces.

Now she was Ty's type.

Di leaned over and muttered behind her raised hand. 'Hey, are you going to let these amateurs beat you?'

Suddenly, Kate knew that was out of the question. Fuelled by a fierce competitive streak she'd had since birth, she downed her newly topped-up glass of champagne and jabbed her hand high in the air.

'One thousand dollars!'

Chaos ceased as curious eyes—and several eyes shooting daggers if she counted the blonde, Nicole and Catherine—focussed on her and she clenched her fists under the table, her heart pounding.

'Going once? Going twice? All done?'

As the gavel in Kelly's hand hit the podium with a resounding thud Kate jumped.

'Sold. To Kate Hayden, whose magazine is our major sponsor today. Well done, Kate. Why don't you come up here and claim your prize?'

'You go, girl,' Di laughed, slapping her on the back. 'Didn't know you had it in you.'

Numbness flooded Kate's body as she walked towards the stage mechanically putting one foot in front of the other as thunderous applause rang out, almost succeeding in drowning out the pounding of her heart, which still reverberated in her ears.

Well, wasn't this just peachy?

She'd envisaged a brief catch up with Ty tonight, but not like this. A short, impersonal meeting off-stage had been her goal, not an up-close-and-personal encounter in front of the whole room.

As she dragged her feet up the steps she looked Ty in the eye and tried not to crumple into a pathetic heap at his feet. Up close he was even more handsome if that were possible. His vivid blue eyes, the spectacular colour of the Pacific Ocean at Malibu on a fine day, had a quizzical edge as his glance raked over her, setting her body alight.

Damn, he was hot. Hotter than hot and she was burning up from the inside out just being this close to him.

'You're looking good, Katie. Long time no see.'

His deep voice flowed over her in a warm caress just as it used to and her knees wobbled, an instant reminder of her foolishness when it came to this guy.

Rattled by her reaction, she aimed for cool. 'Yeah, it has been a long time. Amazing what I'll do for charity, isn't it?'

The momentary warmth in his eyes sparked into fire, the same fire that had scorched her with its brilliance on more than one lucky occasion.

'Now, now. Is that any way to talk to your *fiancé*?'

'Ex,' she muttered, unable to keep her mouth from twitching at the teasing glint in his eyes.

Those incredible eyes…she was convinced they had the

power to make her do crazy things. Why else would she be standing here like a hypnotised chook unable to look away?

Kelly's head swivelled between them, her catlike eyes glowing with interest.

'Well, well. Seems like these two are going to get along famously. They're already chatting. Why don't you say a few words, Kate, before we wind things up?'

Kate tore her gaze away from Ty's mesmerising stare and strode to the podium, hoping that her professionalism wouldn't desert her while her mind was a useless jumble of unexpected memories.

'As senior editor for *Femme* magazine I'd like to thank you all for attending our Odd Bod Man Auction here tonight.'

Glancing at the piece of paper thrust into her hand, she continued, 'Thanks to your generosity we've raised over ten thousand dollars for the Ramirez Orphanage. Well done, ladies.'

Particularly well done to her considering she'd contributed one tenth of that money to 'purchase' the guy she had every intention of cutting loose once this evening was over. The money didn't irk nearly as much as the fact he now knew she'd outrageously overbid to beat every other woman in the room to have him, not once, but twice.

The smattering of applause died down and she forced herself to concentrate on finishing up the speech.

'I'd also like to thank the men who generously volunteered their time tonight and for the next week. I'm sure the ladies will be more than thrilled to have personal Odd Bods for the week ahead. I know I am.' *Not*.

There, that last remark should show him that he hadn't affected her. Not much, anyway.

Squaring her shoulders, she turned to Ty and flashed him an uneasy smile. Once again loud applause filled the room as he blew her a kiss.

Damn it, her knees wobbled again. All it took was one

stupid little gesture and she was acting as she had when they first met: star-struck, smitten and totally unable to control her reactions to him.

Leaning on the podium for support, she fixed a bright smile on her face and turned to the audience.

'Thank you, ladies. We hope to see you at our next fund-raiser.'

As she stepped away Kelly grabbed her arm.

'Not so fast, Kate. Have you forgotten what the last step is after a successful bid?'

Her heart plummeted. She'd been hoping to escape the final humiliation every other woman who'd purchased an Odd Bod had gone through. The goofy friendship bracelets bearing a strong resemblance to handcuffs to shackle the Odd Bods to their bidders were tacky to say the least. And it looked as if she'd have to grin and bear it.

'Come on, you two. Don't be shy. Kate, you can remove this any time you want…if you're game.'

With that final remark, Kelly snapped the bracelet onto her wrist, the other end already securely fastened to Ty's, and dropped the key into his jeans pocket.

'You've got to be kidding,' Kate muttered, silently vowing she would never drink champagne again.

Though deep down she knew it wasn't only the alcohol that had made her bid for Ty. One look into those gorgeous baby blues after all this time and she'd lost it.

Though she didn't have feelings for him any more the thought of some other woman having him trailing after them for a week performing goodness knew what duties had been incentive enough to make her commit the ultimate folly, that ludicrous bid to end all bids.

'No joke, I'm afraid. Looks like the fun's just beginning,' Ty said, swinging their bound arms into the air in a victory salute.

The applause crescendoed, accompanied by raucous hooting and laughter, and light bulbs flashed in a continuous wave as the contingent of photographers lapped up the opportunity. Kate clenched her jaw and grinned, determined to appear in control when in fact she wanted to bolt.

'Yeah, I'm having a real ball,' she said through gritted teeth, keeping her smile in place and giving a subtle yank on the chain binding them.

'Just a little longer. Plenty of time to get *reacquainted* later.'

His subtle, husky emphasis on 'reacquainted' set her pulse racing and she took a deep breath, knowing the faster they got off-stage and unlocked, the happier she'd be.

She lowered her arm forcefully, pulling his down, and Ty tugged on the chain linking them, reinforcing the fact that if he hadn't wanted to lower his arm she wouldn't have succeeded in moving him one inch.

'Let's go.'

She marched off the stage, leaving him no option but to follow.

Now was her big chance.

To do what?

Exchange pleasantries? Make small talk?

Chewing her lip in frustration, Kate picked up the pace. For someone who spent her life making decisions over which words sounded better or which articles went where, she hadn't thought this through at all.

Seeing Ty on stage was one thing, having him attached to her up close and personal another.

She'd wanted to catch up? Well, looked as if she had her opportunity considering she'd spent a small fortune to have him bound to her for a week.

Not that she'd hold him to it. They'd have a quick catch-up backstage and she'd let him go.

Yeah. That was exactly what she would do. Simple.

Then why did she feel as if fate was chuckling and the joke was on her?

Tyler shook his head. Still the same old Kate: proud, gorgeous, independent, with those bewitching hazel eyes that got him every time.

He'd enjoyed teasing her during their brief relationship, the golden flecks in her eyes sparking whenever she reacted to his banter. Those flecks had also glowed when she'd been aroused, as he remembered all too well.

He'd been floored when their gazes had locked across the room, her presence at the auction a sucker punch to the gut when he'd least expected it, and try as he might he'd found his gaze drawn to her repeatedly while she'd acted as if he didn't exist.

Then what had that crazy bidding been about?

Damned if he knew.

'Keep up,' Kate said, giving a none-too-subtle yank on the chain binding them, and he bit back a grin.

She hadn't changed at all, still the same determined woman who wasn't going to wait for anyone, as she picked up the pace.

His gaze travelled to her butt and the way the black linen skirt clung to every sexy, provocative curve. She didn't merely walk. She strutted and then some on long legs, showgirl legs, sensational legs that had wrapped around him so many sweet times.

The great thing about her height was it didn't detract from her curves one iota. In his experience, tall women were usually lean with small breasts and few curves. Kate, however, was the antithesis of this stereotype. For a woman about five-ten, her voluptuous breasts and narrow waist would put an hourglass to shame.

She was a knockout, pure and simple.

He wrenched his gaze away from her butt and his mind out

of fantasy land and focussed his attention on her hair, admiring the sleek, new style. Shorter hair suited her. The burgundy highlights in the chocolate-brown depths drew attention to the shiny mass that now brushed across her shoulders and he itched to run his fingers through it.

Unfortunately, it seemed moving his view higher hadn't dampened his growing desire. If anything, the thought of her luscious locks trickling like soft silk through his fingers inflamed him further.

Looked as if he still had it bad. No great surprise there.

How many nights had he lain awake dreaming about her, wishing he could reach out and touch her? In fact, the fantasies about Kate had been one of the few things that had kept him sane during the agonising year-long knee-rehabilitation programme two years after their split, when dreary days had merged into pain-filled nights as he had tried to come to terms with the fact his knee was bust, no amount of exercise could ever repair the damage and he'd be off Team Eight, removed from active duty permanently.

Life had sucked big-time back then.

Now, it looked as if his fantasy had come to life again. So what was he going to do about it?

From the first minute he'd caught sight of her sitting at a table surrounded by beautiful women yet standing out anyway he'd been stunned. She'd been staring at him, her luscious mouth a perfect little pout, and he'd had difficulty breathing. In fact, his first glimpse of Kate after six long years had been worse than a case of the bends, and no amount of hyperbaric chamber treatment would fix what he had for her.

Lust, pure and simple, had slammed through his body, making him want to leap over tables, grab her and lock his mouth to hers, tasting her, possessing her, reminding her of how damn good they'd been together in the bedroom.

He stumbled and she cast a pitying glance over her shoulder while he sent her a cocky grin.

Staring at his sassy ex strutting in front of him had him re-membering exactly how great they'd been together. Perhaps spending seven days trying to resurrect old times before facing the life-changing appointment next week wouldn't be such a bad thing?

Yeah, that sounded like a plan.

And like any good SEAL, he always stuck to the plan.

CHAPTER TWO

KATE didn't speak till they reached the confines of a dressing room backstage. With Ty's stare boring holes into her back, it took her a while to figure out what to say.

Her plan to have a quick chat and catch up had sounded good at the time. However, now that she actually had him all to herself her plan had hit a snag. A big one.

She hadn't banked on the familiar zing between them, that special something that had prompted her to propose to him in the first place. Back then he'd thought it had been a bit of a laugh and she hadn't disillusioned him.

She'd played it down, they'd joked about being engaged, he'd attributed it to her crazy sense of humour, but deep down she'd known it hadn't been real. They were two crazy kids in love, him fresh out of SEAL training, her fresh off the plane from Sydney. Vegas had been a hoot, hooking up with the fun-loving SEAL even more so, and it had seemed natural to move in with him back in LA.

But life wasn't just about fun and they'd both had places to go, careers to pursue and they'd done the right thing in splitting up.

Hadn't they?

Kate closed the door behind them, determined to make their catch-up short and sweet. Either that or succumb to a sudden hankering for a fix of seal and it sure didn't involve going to the zoo to get it.

'Look, I know this must seem crazy to you, me bidding and all. But I just wanted to catch up. Basically, I've no intention of holding you to this odd-jobs stuff. I'll happily donate the money to the orphanage and we can call it quits, okay?'

He remained silent, a speculative gleam in his blue eyes with the barest glimmer of a smile playing about his sexy mouth.

Disconcerted by his silence and the look in his eyes, she rushed on. 'It's been a while, hasn't it? Guess I just got curious, wondering what you've been up to. Six years is a long time.'

Could she sound any more pathetic?

Standing this close to Ty, having that intense blue stare focussed solely on her, was short-circuiting her brain. Not to mention the nerve-endings firing through her body.

'It is a long time.'

His cool tone was at odds with the banked heat simmering in his eyes and she shivered despite the warmth of the room.

'So a quick catch-up before cutting you loose isn't so bad, right?'

She forced a fake laugh, expecting him to join in and agree.

'No.'

Typical Ty: short, sharp, to the point and the opposite of what she expected him to say or do.

'What?'

'I said no.'

'No, you don't want to catch up or no, you don't want to be cut loose?'

Oh-oh, why did her voice have to do that, go all soft and low and husky? As if she were baiting him? Tempting him?

It was his fault. Less than a few minutes in his company after six years and she'd fallen into flirt mode automatically.

He shook his head, a slight frown appearing between his brows, accentuating the age lines that fanned from the corners

of his eyes. Though little could detract from his good looks
Ty looked older, weary, as if he'd fought a thousand battles.

'I don't want a quick catch-up.'

'Oh.'

She couldn't stand this. He was confusing the heck out
of her just as he'd always done by keeping his emotions
under tight control while burning her up with those 'come
get me' eyes.

'I want a long one. I want to hear everything you've been
doing. Everything.'

His eyes darkened to the colour of her favourite stone, a
deep blue sapphire, and the comparison disconcerted her. She
didn't want to compare him to anything as precious as her
grandma's heirloom ring.

'It's been way too long, Katie.'

His smooth, steady tone did little to placate her as she tried
to ignore the way her heart thumped when he said her name
in that familiar way.

'Uh-huh,' she said, wishing she could think of something
witty to say rather than standing here captured in the intensity of his stare, wondering if he knew the effect he was
having on her after all this time.

'So what do you want to do?'

Fling myself at you?

Tear your clothes off?

Have my way with you?

She had to think of something sensible to say, something
to break the tension.

'What do you want to do?'

Rather pathetic but at least she'd put the onus firmly back
on him. Let him make the decision. She couldn't think straight
and control her impulse to jump him at the same time.

'This.'

His husky tone sent a shiver of anticipation skittering down her spine and before she knew what was happening he had tugged on the steel links binding them, hard.

She fell against his body, the wind knocked out of her, reaching for him to steady her as his head descended, blocking out the harsh glare from the mass of light bulbs around the mirrored walls.

Oh, wow…

His lips crushed hers, frantic, hungry, but oh-so-sweet. Her mouth burned beneath his as his kiss demanded and she gave without thought, without reason.

Pure, blind need shot through her body as she responded to him on some kind of instinctive level.

This can't be happening, flickered through her mind as his tongue nudged her mouth open, urgent, exploring, begging her to match him for pleasure. Not again.

Her stomach dropped away as his commanding kiss deepened, logic fleeing as his tongue ran along her bottom lip, driving her crazy with longing.

She'd missed this, missed him more than she'd realised, and as his teeth followed where his tongue had been, nibbling and nipping with precision, she realised the strange whimpering sounds filling the air were coming from her.

'Ty.' She whispered his name, lost in waves of electrifying sensation as her body trembled under his expert touch, currents of desire shooting every-which-way.

No other man had ever made her feel this way. Only Ty.

And it had been six, long years.

She strained against him, encountering hard evidence of how much he wanted her. Her eyes flew open and she turned her face away, staring at their reflected embrace in the mirrored walls. Reality sank in as she watched him rain kisses up her throat and she pushed him away, barely able to tear her gaze away from the mirrors. He followed her stare, a lazy smile tugging at the corners of his mouth.

'We still look good together, huh?'

His words roused her from the sensual fog that had enveloped them as reality crashed in.

What was she thinking, responding to him like this?

She was a big girl now, not some love-starved, naïve tourist who'd landed in a new country and ended up staying.

'Dream on,' she muttered, hating how she'd melted into a mushy marshmallow under his hot kiss, hating that he was right even more.

They did look good together. Too good. A picture she'd believed in six years ago before realising it was a mirage and mentally ripping it in half.

He chuckled, tracing a finger from her cheek to her jawline with torturous patience.

'Maybe I was out of line with that kiss but I think you wanted it as much as I did.'

Damn him for knowing her almost better than she knew herself.

'I'm tired. I responded without thinking.'

Yeah, and she practically melted into a heap at the feet of the nearest sexy guy whenever she was exhausted—which happened to be often considering the office hours she kept. As if.

He grinned. 'Great response. Maybe this catch-up was meant to be? Maybe your subconscious prompted you to buy me because you still want me? Maybe—'

'You're full of it,' she said, mortified by how easily he could read her, by how that one kiss had resurrected a whole host of sensual memories she'd assumed long forgotten.

The impulse to be fun and spontaneous had not been one of her brightest ideas. She'd end this now if she could get her brain to slip back into gear and her heartbeat back under control.

Ty ran his free hand through his hair, the usual short-back-and-sides that suited him so well, and for an irrational instant she had the urge to do the same.

'Insult me all you want but I'm not going anywhere. Though can we catch up some other time, maybe tomorrow? I've had one helluva week on the job and I'm beat.'

He did look tired and as a grimace of pain distorted his handsome features and his posture stiffened she wondered what he'd had to face over the last few years. When they'd first met he'd been fresh from BUD/S, the intensive training to become a SEAL, and as fit as a Mallee bull back home. Now he looked dead on his feet.

'Besides, I need some sleep if I'm to perform all those odd jobs you probably have lined up for me over the next week.'

Kate heard the teasing lilt back in his voice and sighed, ignoring his innuendo. She'd had a long week meeting killer deadlines at *Femme* and she didn't want to prolong this. Seeing Ty again had her more wound up than she'd anticipated, and as for that kiss…

'You want to go through with this? Are you insane?'

'Not like I used to be.' He grinned, the same smile that had captivated her so many times in the past. 'And, yeah, being your Odd Bod for a week could be interesting.'

Sighing, she said, 'It's not going to happen but we'll talk about this in the morning. I don't have the energy to argue with you right now. I think you're crazy, you don't, so let's agree to differ till I sort you out and we go our separate ways. Now, unlock me, please.'

'Sorry, you'll have to do it.'

'Come on, give a girl a break. No more games. Give me the key.'

His grin widened. 'I can't. In case you haven't noticed, my left hand is connected to your right and the key is in my left pocket. At the risk of dislocating my right shoulder, I think you better do the honours.'

She stared, annoyed at the twinkle in his eyes and the devilish smile, sure that he could remove the key if he really tried. However, he didn't move an inch and continued to watch her as if he was enjoying every minute of her discomfort.

'Well, what's it to be? Do you prefer being linked to me indefinitely or rummaging around my pockets and seeing what pops up?'

Ignoring his laughter, she struggled with the decision. Sink or swim time. Either way, she'd always been lousy in the water.

'You're such a child.'

Kate delved her hand quickly into his pocket; thankfully the key wasn't too deep and she didn't have to feel around. Though it could've been fun.

'Not half as childish as you.' Ty chuckled. 'I'm not the one pouting.'

She thrust the key into the lock and turned. Typical of her luck this evening, it stuck.

'I'm not pouting. Help me with this, will you?'

She jiggled the key to no avail and his chuckles turned to laughter.

'If you're not pouting you must be limbering up those lips for another kiss. They're looking rosy and full and very, very sexy.'

Her patience snapped and heat seeped into her cheeks as his smooth words recalled her attention to the crazy way she'd responded to his unexpected kiss moments before.

'Cut the suave act, sailor boy. I'm not in the mood. Let's open this damn lock so I can get out of here.'

'Here, let me try.'

As his hand enclosed hers she couldn't ignore the heat. It sizzled through her body every time he touched her, even at the innocuous touch of his hand trying to open the lock.

She'd lied. She was definitely in the mood.

'There. You're a free woman.'

I wish.

Unfortunately, seeing Ty tonight, swapping banter with

him, even getting mad at him for that presumptuous kiss had woken her up.

She wasn't as free as she'd like to think.

She might have got over him a long time ago and moved on with her life, but it hadn't taken much more than a kiss to snap her emotions back to attention and right now they were firmly focussed on the sexy SEAL.

The lock snapped open and the bracelet sprang apart, clattering to the floor at their feet, and Kate winced as her wrist freed. She'd been so engrossed in her reaction to Ty turning on the charm that she hadn't realised the hard plastic and steel had bitten into her soft flesh.

'Thanks.'

She glared at him, wishing he didn't look so darn appealing when he smiled, absent-mindedly rubbing her wrist.

'Let me do that.'

Before she could protest, he reached over and captured her wrist between his hands, slowly massaging till the circulation returned to her aching flesh.

'Mmm…that feels good,' she murmured, her eyes drooping with fatigue.

However, as the pain in her wrist eased a deeper, more demanding ache increased, an ache she'd determinedly ignored for years. His hands were warm, firm, attuned and she imagined them leaving her wrist, travelling up her arm to her tight shoulders and then sliding down the rest of her body.

'Better?'

Her eyes flew open as he relinquished her wrist and her gaze locked on his, questioning, hungry, reflecting the need she knew must be visible in her own. That all-seeing blue stare that had captured her so long ago, mesmerising her in the blink of an eye.

'Would you like a lift home?'

She shook her head, knowing the last thing she needed right now was to be holed up with him in the confines of a car.

'Thanks, but I'm fine. I came with the girls and we're headed back to the office.'

He glanced at his watch. 'We've been here a while. Maybe they've gone?'

'Don't worry about it. If they have I'll take a taxi.'

Kate knew she sounded petulant but couldn't bear being this close to him one second longer. If he took her home she'd be tempted to ask him in and, considering her reaction to his kiss, she knew exactly where that could lead.

Her sex life had been one, continuous dry spell since her last brief relationship had ended eighteen months ago and she had no intention of letting Ty be her drought breaker.

He laid a hand in the small of her back and guided her to the door. 'Let's check it out. It's no problem, really. Where do you live?'

'Beverly Hills.'

'Pretty impressive.' He looked at her with admiration and pride filled her.

'My grandparents built the place. We hooked up after you left. They welcomed me with open arms, then died within a few months of each other shortly after our reunion. Amazingly, they left the house to me. Pretty special, huh?'

It had been a beautiful gesture and she liked to think they'd come to love her as much as she'd loved them in the short time they'd had together.

'Sure is. I'm glad you had someone to look out for you.'

He dropped his hand and insanely she missed his warm touch.

This wasn't good. Curiosity was one thing, kissing him and opening up to him about her grandparents was in another realm. She needed to get home before she really lost it and told him a few other deep, dark secrets.

'Look, I really have to go,' she said, her voice harsh and cold considering they'd just been making small talk.

'What's wrong?'

He stared at her and raised an eyebrow as if he couldn't fathom what he was looking at and she hated the traitorous leap of her heart that the hint of concern in his voice might actually mean he cared.

'Nothing, why?'

'You're wound tighter than a spring. You used to be spontaneous and eager and able to laugh at yourself. What happened? Did inheriting the family jewels change you?'

She clenched her fists, barely registering the sting of fingernails biting into her palms when all she felt like doing was kneeing him in *his* family jewels.

'I'm just tired. Besides, you don't know the first thing about me any more.'

He straightened and she had to tilt her head to look up at him. 'That's where you're wrong. We used to have a connection and I intend to use the week ahead to catch up.'

Catch up.

Two simple words that held a staggering array of connotations, of the various ways in which they could catch up, and her heart flipped in a perfect somersault with double pike at the thought.

Sighing, she followed him to the doorway and, before they walked through it, reached out and touched his arm.

'Why are you doing this, Ty?'

He stopped and swivelled to face her, his features softening. 'You haven't called me that in a long time.'

'It's been a long time,' she responded, suddenly saddened by their lack of contact over the years. 'Now answer my question.'

He shrugged. 'A week isn't all that long and I'm a sucker for a good cause. The orphanage is home to those poor little kids and they deserve a chance in life.'

She'd meant why was he doing this to them, insisting they spend a week together when they'd been finished for years.

However, she let it slide for now, the sadness creeping across his face telling her how much he sympathised with the orphans.

'Still the same old Ty? Always out to save the world.'

'It's what I do. Why do you make it sound like I'm on an ego trip or something?'

'Aren't you?'

He swore softly and she changed tack. 'Are you on leave?'

'Yeah, one week.'

'Why didn't you just donate money rather than giving up your week?'

The thought had niggled since she'd seen his name on the list of prospective guys for sale. His job had always come first and she doubted that would have changed. After all, it was one of the things that had driven them apart.

He shrugged and looked away. 'I thought the auction might raise more money than I could give.'

He was lying.

She knew it the minute he glanced away. Ty was as straight as they came. He always looked a person in the eye and called a spade a shovel, which made his reticence to discuss this all the more intriguing. He'd been a stand-up guy when they'd first met, too much so if his blunt declaration their marriage would never work with one absentee partner all the time had been any indication.

'There's more to this. You're hiding something.'

'Still the snoop, eh? You won't find your next story here.'

This time he looked straight at her, something akin to challenge etched in the darkening depths of his eyes.

If there was one thing she thrived on it was a challenge and sailor boy knew it.

'Maybe not, but you can't blame a girl for trying. Perhaps I should just let it all go and agree to this crazy scheme, and then use it to my full advantage.'

Not that she'd seriously contemplate spending the week

with him, but it was nice to gain the upper hand with Mr Confidence.

His voice dropped, low and husky, eliciting a whole host of visceral reactions she'd rather not decipher.

'Now you're talking. If you let it all go this week could be more fun than I thought.'

He ran his hands lightly over her upper arms in a soft caress and her legs trembled, her desire needing little to rekindle. One touch. That was all it took to make her burn for him just as she used to.

So much for gaining the upper hand.

'Goodnight, Ty.'

She spun on her heel and strode away, eager to put as much distance between them as possible.

His taunting laughter followed her down the long corridor. 'You can run but you can't hide.'

'Wanna make a bet?' she mumbled as she lengthened her stride and hoped to God that Di had waited for her.

CHAPTER THREE

'AREN'T you the dark horse? Fancy waiting to the end to bid and snaffling the best of the lot.'

Kate had been grateful Di had waited for her after the auction. And, clearly realising her boss needed some space on the trip back to the office, Di hadn't asked her any questions. Apparently now, though, she was fair game.

'Don't you have work to do?' Kate shuffled papers around, hoping to get rid of Di pronto.

Predictably, it didn't work. The woman had an inquisitive nature worthy of an up-and-comer in the publishing business.

Di perched on the edge of her desk and shoved aside the papers Kate had been fiddling with. 'Nothing that can't wait. Come on, spill the beans. Where did you two disappear to after the show? In a cosy little friendship bracelet, no less.'

Kate sighed, pushing the thought of Ty's dynamic kiss to the far recesses of her mind.

'There's nothing to tell. We unlocked ourselves, had a chat to establish boundaries and that was it.'

Di pounced on her. 'Aha! I knew it. Why would you need to establish boundaries? Did something happen between the dishy SEAL and my intrepid boss?'

'Ex-SEAL,' she corrected automatically.

'How do you know that?'

Great, she thought. Slip up number two in less than a minute. Di was no slouch, which was why she'd hired her.

She could've fluffed her way out of it and rambled on about the announcer saying he was an instructor these days, but she knew Di wouldn't let up until she had nothing less than the truth.

'I know Tyler James.'

A deafening silence followed her revelation till Di let out a squeal. 'Ooh, I knew there was more to you than meets the eye. Here I am feeling sorry for my workaholic old boss and she's out there running around with hot sailors.'

'Hey! Enough of the old stuff and I'm not running around with anybody. I met Tyler about six years ago when he was a SEAL. He isn't just an instructor. He's had his fair share of action.'

Both in and out of uniform and lucky for her she'd been privy to Ty at his best.

'I just bet he has,' purred the younger woman.

'For heaven's sake, get your mind out of the gutter.'

'Why, when it's so much fun?'

Di slid off the desk and wandered around the office, trying to look nonchalant and failing miserably. 'Is that why you put in a bid, boss? Looking for a little action?'

Kate threw a pencil at her. 'Out. Now. Get back to work before you're fired.'

'You wouldn't dare. I'm your right-hand gal.'

Di smirked and flounced out of the room, her bright orange skirt swishing around her ankles.

Kate sat back and laughed. Di was right. She was the best PA she'd ever had and, what was worse, the young woman knew it. However, why did she have to be so accurate in her assumptions about Kate's nonexistent love life?

Seeing Ty had awakened her dormant hormones in a big way; her skin still tingled at the memory of his hands rubbing her wrist. No man had ever affected her as he did.

He'd been a dynamite lover, her first, but despite that mind-blowing kiss earlier she had no intention of revisiting that part of her life.

Though in all honesty if she hadn't been bound at the time there was no telling what her hands would've been tempted to do and she squirmed in her seat at the recollection. For a twenty-seven-year-old at the top of her game, her little 'let's get reacquainted' experience with Ty had hot-wired her libido and how.

The phone ringing brought her back to the present.

'Kate Hayden speaking.'

'So, you did go back to the office. I thought that was just an excuse to escape.'

Ty's husky tone did little to calm her racing pulse. If anything, the sound of his deep voice fuelled the fantasy she'd just been indulging in. Stupid, stupid, stupid.

'You think I was trying to escape?'

His low chuckle fired her nerve-endings. 'Oh, call it a feeling. You weren't exactly falling all over me earlier this evening.'

She kept her voice deliberately cool, trying to ignore the erotic memory of their entwined bodies reflected in the mirror that leaped to mind. If that wasn't falling all over him she didn't know what was.

'It isn't every day a girl acquires an Odd Bod. Perhaps I was just nervous?'

She doodled on the pad in front of her, almost falling off her chair when she realised she was drawing large hearts with the initials K.H. and T.J. intertwined.

'Yeah, right. The Kate I know is never nervous. Confident and bossy maybe. Nervous? No way.'

'You forgot gorgeous,' she murmured, wondering where the breathy voice came from.

She shouldn't flirt with him, she really shouldn't, but somehow he brought out that side of her without trying and she heard a sharp intake of breath on the other end of the line.

'That goes without saying.' He paused for a moment. 'Are you flirting with me, sweetheart?'

The endearment thrilled her, though she knew it was a game with him and suddenly, just like the old days, she joined in with gusto.

'What if I am? I'm a woman, you're an Odd Bod. Why not?'

'Lady, you're a chameleon. One minute you can't get away from me quick enough, the next you're sounding like Mae West. Why don't I come up and see you some time?'

She leaned back in her leather chair, crossed her ankles and stared out at the twinkling lights of downtown LA, spread out like a fairyland forty storeys below. She adored this view, loved the hip city vibe, yet somehow sitting here chatting to Ty inspired her more than the vista she admired on a daily basis.

Playing with him was fun, even if she had no intention of following through, and it had been so long since she'd had any fun. How far could she push him?

'What are you doing right now?'

Once again, silence greeted her.

'Ty, still there?'

'Yeah. Where did you say your office was?'

His voice dropped lower, reminding her of the intimacy they'd shared all those years ago when she'd hung on his every word.

'I didn't. Though if I let it all go like I mentioned earlier, I could invite you for a coffee at my place…'

Yeah, like that was going to happen. There was only so much her hormones could take and teasing him like this, flirting with him, was bad enough.

'Do you mean coffee…or *coffee*?'

A delicious tingle ran up her spine and she knew for a fact he would give her a better buzz than any caffeine fix: rich, warm, addictive. And the high would last a heck of a lot longer.

'Boss, I'm leaving.' Di's voice startled her as she stuck her head around the door.

Kate sat up straight. 'Can you hold on a sec?' she said into the receiver and covered it with her hand.

'Sure thing, Katie,' he murmured, sending heat flooding into her cheeks.

'Who's that?' mouthed Di.

'Nobody important. You head off.'

'Whatever you say, boss.' With a wink and a blown kiss, Di left the office.

Kate took a steadying breath, almost relieved at the reprieve, and removed her hand from the phone. 'Sorry about that.'

'So, I'm nobody, huh? Nice.'

She smiled at the thought of bruising Ty's ego. 'I didn't mean it like that.'

'What did you mean, then? If I'm not nobody I must be somebody?'

His probing question sent doubt spiralling through her. What was she doing encouraging him when she'd already made up her mind to ditch him first thing tomorrow morning when she'd had time to gather her wits?

Damn it, he'd always had the power to do this, to tie her up in knots till she couldn't think straight.

'Look, I'm tired. It's been a long night and I've got one more article to edit before I leave. We'll catch up tomorrow, okay?'

His silence did little to soothe her frazzled nerves.

'Ty?'

'You're running scared.'

She swallowed, trying to ease the sudden dryness in her throat. 'I don't know what you're talking about.'

He chuckled, deep and low, the familiar sound skittering across her skin, raising tiny goose-bumps.

'Yeah, you do. Shame. I thought you might want to pick up where we left off.'

'You wish.'

The image of their parting six years ago flashed into her

mind. It had been touch and go; he'd touched her all over her body, initiating her into pleasures she'd only dreamed about before pulling away from her by running back to his precious job, and she'd gone the same way, burying herself in a new job as far away from him as she could get.

Now he was back. Just as gorgeous, just as charming and just as dangerous to her peace of mind as ever if she was foolish enough to let him in.

'Oh, yeah, I wish.' He paused, as if choosing his words carefully. 'By the way, why are you working after eleven?'

'The usual. Deadlines to meet. Nothing out of the ordinary.' She sounded weary, even to her ears.

'Don't you have a life?'

Her brittle laugh echoed around the empty office. 'This is my life.'

She didn't add that it was about all she had.

'You really need to get out more. I'm going to make it my personal goal to ensure you live a little over the next week. Deal?'

'It's not going to happen.'

Her brisk reply sounded strained and, though the thought of Ty helping her to 'live a little' conjured up some wild images, she'd done enough fantasising for one evening and had to put an end to this ASAP.

He ignored her rebuttal, his low chuckles sounding way too confident.

'I'll call you tomorrow. Pleasant dreams, Katie.'

As the dial tone hummed she knew that dreams would be impossible tonight. She needed to sleep in order to dream and she seriously doubted that she could nod off after the evening she'd just had.

Tyler James was her history.

Then why did he feel startlingly like the present?

* * *

Tyler was too wound up to sleep. Shrugging into a bomber jacket, he picked up his keys and headed out the door.

Living near the base had its advantages. Dropping into the rec hall for a drink meant he was bound to run into someone he knew and, though usually reticent, he felt like company tonight. Perhaps trading a few jokes with the boys might take the edge off?

He doubted it. Only one thing could take the edge off and she was buried in some uptown office, her nose to the grindstone.

Kate's hot little act on the phone had pushed all his buttons. If only her assistant hadn't interrupted he could be holed up in her house right now sharing more than coffee.

And, boy, did he need it.

Seeing her again had him remembering all too well the contours of her curves beneath his hands, the eager sounds she made during sex, the way she made him feel as if he were the only man in the world for her.

Unfortunately, that couldn't be true. He wasn't a total idiot and a vibrant woman like her would have had a string of guys panting after her since they'd parted.

He clenched his hands into fists, hating the irrational surge of jealousy stabbing through him. He'd moved on and hadn't exactly lived like a monk himself in the last six years so what did he expect—for a stunner like Kate to sit around twiddling her thumbs?

Gritting his teeth, he picked up the pace and entered the rec hall. He didn't need this complicating his life. Never had.

What Kate did with her life and who she spent it with had nothing to do with him. He valued his independence and answering to number one suited him just fine and, despite the unexpected pleasure of having Kate reappear at this point in his life, he had no intention of getting sucked back into the confusing whirlpool their relationship had become towards the end.

Instead, he'd consider this chance encounter as a surprise

gift dropped in his lap, one he had every intention of unwrapping and enjoying at his leisure over the next week before he had his annual physical and potentially had his career ripped out from under him.

'Hey, TJ. What's happening?'

He looked up, more than glad to see the big guy in front of him, and stuck out his hand. 'Hey, Bear. What're you doing here? Thought Team Eight was on leave at the moment?'

'Nah, got called back last night. So much for a little R and R.'

Tyler laughed. 'The Chief pushing you too hard these days, huh? Want a beer?'

Bear nodded and pulled out a chair, turning it backwards before sitting. He'd never seen his giant friend sit any other way.

'Yeah, the Chief is always pushing for more. You know the drill.'

Tyler nodded and placed the drinks on the table. 'Yeah, I do. Cheers.'

They clinked bottles and lapsed into silence. As Tyler took a long swig of icy cold beer he thanked the Lord that Evan 'Bear' Bridges had chosen tonight to walk into the rec hall. He could do with a friend.

'What's up? You look like hell, man.'

Tyler set his bottle down. 'That obvious?'

'Uh-huh. Tell old Bear all about it.'

He leaned back and crossed his arms. 'It's the orphanage. Looks like it's going to shut down.'

Bear's eyes widened. 'No way. With the amount of cash you donate out of your wages each year the joint should be open into the next century.'

''Fraid not. Looks like the place is in trouble.'

'Anything I can do?' His friend reached towards his back pocket as if ready to pull out his wallet.

'Not unless you can rustle up a quick half-million dollars.'

Bear shook his head. 'No can do, bro. Sorry.'

'I'm the one who's sorry,' he muttered, feeling helpless for only the third time in his life and not relishing the emotion one bit. The first time had been when he'd walked out on Kate, the second when he'd blown his knee, and he felt just as useless now.

SEALs were renowned for their innovation, their ingenuity, their persistence. So why the hell couldn't he do more for the one cause that meant everything to him?

At that moment, their chief, Jack Crawford, strolled into the bar and headed straight towards them.

'Howdy, Bear. Thought you were on leave, TJ?'

Tyler grabbed the proffered hand and shook it. 'I am.'

'Then what are you doing here?'

Tyler downed the rest of his beer. 'Business.'

'I bet.'

He couldn't fathom the reason behind Jack's sly grin.

'Been to any auctions lately?'

Though the question seemed innocuous enough, combined with Jack's smirk, Tyler knew his secret was out.

'Ha, ha. How did you find out?'

Bear's head turned from side to side as if watching a tennis match. 'What are you clowns talking about?'

Jack's grin widened. 'Didn't you hear the news? TJ's latest mission involves being shackled to a woman for a week doing all her *odd jobs*.'

Bear guffawed loudly. 'You're kidding me, right? Why the hell would you do a fool thing like that?'

'For charity, of course.'

Tyler glared meaningfully at Bear, hoping he'd get the drift. His friend was the only one who knew about his upbringing at the orphanage and he wanted to keep it that way. He'd had enough pity to last him a lifetime growing up, he sure as hell didn't need any from his colleagues now.

Bear cottoned on quickly. He merely quirked an eyebrow and chugged on his beer.

Thankfully, Jack relented. 'Yeah, I agree that the orphanage is a good cause. Though I reckon there's more behind this, TJ. I reckon you like being at the beck and call of some fancy dame.'

'Who told you she's fancy?' Tyler chuckled, envisaging how Kate would respond to being described as 'fancy'.

'Leila was at the auction. She just got home, bursting with the news about you and that magazine editor. Said that sparks were flying and that was before the shackles went on.'

Tyler's gut tightened. The image of being bound to Kate did it. At least thinking about the orphanage had distracted him from her memory. For a good ten minutes, anyway.

He leaned back, trying to instil a measure of casualness into his voice. 'I think Leila has a great imagination. There were no sparks. I'm just donating my time for a good cause.'

'Yeah, right. So what if this editor looks like a supermodel? All part of the job, huh?' Jack's cheesy grin grew wider by the second.

'Damn sure.' Tyler pushed back his chair. 'Sorry, guys. Much as I'd like to hang around, I have to go. Early start. O-six hundred.'

Suddenly, his need for company had vanished. He'd come here to erase Kate from his memory bank, not discuss her, and he knew the boys. Once they got started they would want to hear every last detail. He waved and walked away, leaving his two closest friends grinning in his wake.

'See you in a week, TJ. If you survive, that is.'

Ignoring Jack's final taunt, he headed out into the balmy Californian night. There was no doubt in his mind that he would survive. After all, he'd handled tougher missions and come out unscathed.

Once again, a vision of Kate's gold-flecked hazel eyes

flashed into his mind, closely followed by the memory of their searing kiss.

He just hoped this mission wasn't about to become his nemesis.

Kate prided herself on being cool, organised and professional at all times. To do this she needed at least eight solid hours of sleep a night. Without it she turned into a monster, as all her staff knew. Unfortunately, last night hadn't been conducive to sleeping and she was paying the price now. So would anyone else who crossed her path today.

'Good morning, boss. Sleep well?' Di strolled into her office, all blonde spikes and cheerfulness.

'Is it? And no. Where's that damn article on homeless shelters?'

She shuffled around her desk, sending papers flying in all directions while making a frantic grab for her take-out skinny latte.

What happened to organised and professional? Right now her desk resembled a second-grader's with the writing strewn across it probably making about that much sense.

'Didn't sleep too well? Can't blame you.'

Kate didn't like the twinkle in her assistant's eye. Besides, how could Di be so darn chirpy every morning? Didn't she ever wake up with a sore head?

'What's that supposed to mean?'

Kate finally stopped rummaging around and sat back, draining the last of her coffee, lobbing the cup in the bin and rubbing her temples. She rarely drank and the three glasses of champagne last night combined with the haunting image of Ty looking better than ever had kept her tossing and turning all night.

'Oh, nothing.' Di's grin broadened. 'Though if I had the prospect of some sexy sailor trailing after me all week I wouldn't be able to get any shut-eye either.'

'He's not trailing after me,' she snapped, her headache intensifying by the minute.

'Oh, yes, he is. He's just stepped out of the lift and is heading this way.'

Kate sat bolt upright in time to see Ty honing in on her office. Great. Just great.

Di wiggled her fingers in a saucy wave and strolled away, giving Tyler a similar wave, and Kate tried to ignore the absurd jolt of jealousy that shot through her. Ty was her past and she shouldn't have to remind herself of that fact.

He walked straight into her office as if he owned the place. 'Hi. Got a minute?'

How dared he look so good at this hour of the morning? Faded denim jeans hugged his long legs and a white T-shirt moulded his muscular torso like a second skin, delineating every single layer of taut, hard muscle beneath it. The type of muscle she used to love running her hands over, caressing, skimming, relishing.

Okay, maybe good was an understatement. Try delectable and she struggled not to drool.

'What are you doing here?'

Though she tried to keep her voice cool, it came out all high and squeaky.

A smile tugged at the corners of his delicious mouth. 'Still not a morning person, huh?'

She shook her head and wished she hadn't as the pounding in her brain increased.

'I'm surprised you remember.'

'How could I forget?'

He flashed his trademark killer smile, the one that always made her knees go weak. Thankfully, she was sitting down.

'So, what else do you remember?'

He closed the door and strode across the room in one lithe

movement. She loved how he walked. Correction, how he stalked, all stealth and fluid lines, and her pulse accelerated in anticipation as he perched on the corner of her desk less than two feet away.

'I remember plenty.'

He tipped up her chin, stroking her cheek with his thumb in the barest of touches as she stared, trapped beneath his scrutinising gaze, his thumb doing crazy things to her insides as it grazed her skin slowly, repeatedly.

'Yeah, well, I do too.'

She leaned back, breaking the tenuous contact that was wreaking havoc with her senses. 'But that's all they are, just memories.'

His eyes narrowed to slivers of electrifying blue. 'Yeah, but they were good. Damn good. And you know it.'

She glared, the jackhammering in her head intensifying as she tried to put words together in a coherent fashion , her brain befuddled by his closeness, his touch.

'All I know is I've got a lot of work to do and sitting here talking about ancient history is wasting my time.'

Thankfully, his thumb had stopped stroking her cheek. On the downside, he re-established contact by trailing his index finger along her jaw-line, setting her nerve-endings alight.

'What's with the attitude? You said we'd talk in the morning. Aren't you glad to see me?'

She pulled away from his blazing touch. 'We'll talk later. I haven't got time for this now.'

He grinned, sending her pulse rate into overdrive. 'You didn't answer my question.'

'About the memories, the attitude or being happy to see you?'

There was no way she would answer any of his questions. She'd made a fool of herself last night. Questions only led to answers and they led directly to trouble.

'How about all of the above?'

'Look, I'd love to chat but I've got important deadlines to meet.'

She tried to stare him down. It had been a game with them, a battle of wills to see who would look away first. She'd always lost but not today.

He sat back and folded his arms, looking way too cocky, the corners of his mouth curving into a tempting smile.

'Surely Lois Lane can take a break for a few minutes?'

'Nope, sorry, no can do. I'm busy.'

She picked up a few papers and rattled them for good measure, needing to look away from his intense stare and that sexy smile. He still had the power to reduce her to a blathering mess with just one look—not that she'd let him know that.

'Aren't you the least bit curious?'

'About?'

'Why I'm here. Where I've been. What I've been doing. You must be otherwise you wouldn't have paid a small fortune to have me last night.'

Sighing, she pushed away from the desk, grateful to establish some distance between them. 'You're never going to let me forget that, are you?'

His smile couldn't get any smugger if he tried. 'Not on your life.'

Her heart clenched at the seductive glint in his eyes, the same twinkle that had prompted her to do all sorts of crazy things six years earlier.

He'd always had this power over her, teasing her, infuriating her, making her fall in love when it was the last thing she'd expected.

Unfortunately, it looked as if he still held that same power to make her contemplate all sorts of nutty things, like make her bid for him when the last thing she wanted was to have him trailing after her for a week.

'Okay, you win. Let's get this sorted now so I can get back

to work. You really can't be serious about wanting to go through with this odd-jobs stuff?'

He leaned forward, the depth of his blue eyes leaving her breathless as his voice dropped an octave lower. 'Why not? It'll be fun.'

She didn't have time for fun. Maybe the girls were right, she was stuck in her ways and a workaholic: uptight, frustrated and alone.

Logically, she should never have attended the auction if she hadn't wanted a confrontation with Ty and now that she'd had it, he'd kissed her silly and resurrected memories better left forgotten, she needed to get rid of him once and for all.

'That may well be,' she said, aiming for cool and botching it horribly when heat surged into her cheeks at his triumphant expression, 'but I don't think it's a good idea.'

'I do.'

He slid off her desk and sauntered towards the door, leaving her with a great view of the sexy butt she'd grabbed on numerous lucky occasions, turning to face her before he left. 'It's going to be great catching up. Just like old times.'

Kate stiffened.

Just like old times.

Images of fun-filled days at the beach and long, hot, sultry Californian nights spent making love on top of twisted sheets sprang to mind and she wondered if time had enhanced her memories or if it really had been that good between her and Ty.

'Katie?'

'My answer is no, Ty.'

She blinked several times, hoping he couldn't read her thoughts as he used to.

'I still want you too.'

With that he sauntered out the door, leaving her open-mouthed before she snapped her jaw shut, wishing she'd had the final word.

The guy was infuriating.

The guy was cocky.

The guy was right.

She did want him, with every cell in her oversensitised body, and the feeling was mutual?

Oh, boy.

'You're crazy,' she muttered, sinking into her chair and picking up the overworked stress ball on her desk and squeezing as if her life depended on it. It didn't help. The rubber ball looked a bit like her, worn out, frayed around the edges, with all the life crushed out of it.

She threw the ball into the bin and leaped to her feet. If she rushed after Ty she just might make it. He hadn't accepted her refusal and she needed to ram home her point that the last thing she wanted to do was spend the next week with him.

However, as she yanked open the door she ran straight into her boss.

'Whoa. Where's the fire?'

Henry Kerr, *Femme*'s Chief Editor, settled her back on her feet. He always managed to catch her at a bad time. In fact, she was convinced he had radar for trouble and it was tuned in to her frequency.

'Sorry. In a hurry.'

He quirked an eyebrow. 'So I see. Got a minute?'

She knew by the serious look on his face that it wasn't a question, it was an order. So much for chasing after Ty.

'Sure. What's up?'

He smiled and she knew she was in trouble. Her boss never smiled unless she'd done something wrong. 'Come into my office and I'll let you in on a secret.'

She followed him, slouching along in the same way she usually followed the dentist into his rooms, though she hoped her meeting with Henry didn't involve anything as difficult or painful as pulling teeth. The memory of her first and last tooth removed as a nine-year-old still rankled.

Henry closed the door and gestured towards a chair. 'Have a seat and we'll get down to business.'

Here it comes, the injection and the drill.

Henry sat down behind his desk and rested his folded hands on his paunch. 'Good work last night, Kate. Real good.'

Huh?

She smiled and nodded, not having the faintest idea what he was talking about.

'Buying that Navy guy was a stroke of genius on your part. Unbelievable. Pure gold.'

Okay, now she knew something was up. Her boss was impressed with the stupidest thing she'd done in a long time?

Thankfully, she didn't have to reply as Henry continued, 'The publicity in the papers today is worth a mint on its own, but have you seen the pictures we've got? Amazing. Just what the magazine needs. A real-life story about one of its own. Good one, Kate.'

She didn't like the sound of this. Clasping her hands in her lap, she counted to ten, slowly. 'I'm an editor, not a news story.'

He chuckled, a deep belly laugh that caused his three chins to wobble in succession. 'That's where you're wrong. Our phones haven't stopped ringing all morning. All the reporters want to talk to our newest star and I've told them to back off. They can read all about it in the upcoming issue of *Femme*. Like I said, pure gold.'

She rarely argued with her boss but decided that today was a day for firsts.

'This isn't a good idea. I don't want my credibility to suffer. I've worked long and hard to get where I am. You know that.'

Thankfully, Henry had stopped chuckling but his sly

grin worried her even more. 'Don't worry about your credibility. What could be more credible than being appointed Chief Editor?'

'Pardon?'

She could have sworn that he'd just uttered the words she'd wanted to hear for ever.

'You heard me. The job's yours if you want it.'

He beamed like Santa Claus and for a minute she believed that all her Christmases had come at once. Until reality set in.

'You know how much I'd love your job, Henry. But that's just it. It's *your* job.'

'Not any more. I'm retiring in the next few months and I want you to be the next chief. How about it?'

It wasn't a joke. Though Henry was smiling she knew he wouldn't make her an offer like this unless he was genuine.

'If you're serious, I'll take it.'

She finally allowed her face muscles to relax into what she hoped was a smile. She hadn't realised till that moment just how tense she'd been.

'Good. That's settled.' He leaned back in his chair looking like the proverbial cat that had swallowed the canary. 'Just one more thing.'

'Yes?'

'The magazine has to run that feature story on the auction last night and your acquisition.'

'Are you bribing me? The promotion for the story?'

Kate didn't like bribes. Never had. Not since the early days when her father had tried to buy her love with meaningless trinkets on his all-too-brief visits home.

Henry smiled and rested his steepled fingers on his chest. 'Got it in one. So, is it a deal?'

This was an opportunity of a lifetime. She'd coveted Henry's job for as long as she could remember and here it was being offered to her on a plate. And all she had to do was one story? Why was she hesitating?

Ty.

She didn't want to spend a week with him and had just told him so.

What would he think if she back-pedalled? Would he take it as a sign she did still want him?

Why did this have to be so complicated? She'd wanted this promotion for ever. Why did getting it have to involve Ty? Could she put up with him for a week—and all the possible ramifications—for the job of a lifetime?

Deep down, she knew the decision was a no-brainer. She was a journo at heart, a career girl with places to go, and nothing would stand in her way. Nothing.

'You've got yourself a new chief.'

She shook Henry's hand, crossing her fingers behind her back, for luck with the other.

Ty would come to the party. He had to.

Though did she really want him to?

Doing this story meant spending time with him and possibly more, so much more.

And she had no idea if she was ready for it.

CHAPTER FOUR

TYLER stabbed at the buttons of the elevator, wishing the damn thing would move faster. He hated skyscrapers. Give him rescue operations any day. Buildings stifled him, made him feel bulky and out of place and he'd had a lifetime of feeling like that, of not belonging.

However, his building phobia faded as he stepped into the elevator. Instead, a sexy vision of Kate perched behind her cushy desk, her hair slicked back in some weird bun arrangement and her hot body sheathed in a tight-fitting fire-engine-red suit had imprinted itself on his brain and he couldn't budge it.

She had him squirming, no two ways about it. He couldn't get her out of his head and though he hadn't got a handle on why she'd 'bought' him in the first place only to renege on the week ahead, he didn't care.

Why waste time trying to analyse the female psyche? He'd be better off interrogating terrorists for Intel; at least he'd have more chance of getting answers.

No, he wouldn't question this unexpected gift. For that was exactly what spending a week with his sultry ex would be, especially considering he could be a washed-up ex-SEAL this time next week.

And she would spend the week with him, despite her protests to the contrary. He'd make sure of it.

He might have been out of the action for a while now but his persuasive powers weren't that rusty. And if he could convince his current charges to crash through a burning wall if needed, he was pretty damn sure he could change Kate's mind.

As the elevator doors opened his mobile phone vibrated against his hip.

'TJ here.'

He strode across the foyer, eager to get outside and feel the warm Californian sunshine on his face before he was tempted to head back up to Kate's office and convince her that her fancy-schmancy desk could be used for a lot more fun activities than work.

'Ty?'

Her almost-whisper slammed into his conscious. Damn, why did she have to say his name like that, all soft and breathy as if she'd just woken up? His libido, already fully revved up by the sight of her a few minutes ago, went into overdrive at the sound of her sexy voice.

'Miss me already, huh?'

She paused and he wished for one, irrational moment that she'd say 'you bet'.

Dream on, lover boy. There was about as much chance of that happening as he had of returning to active duty. His knee was blown just like any chance he had of more than a casual, fun week with his luscious ex.

'Uh…I was wondering if you were free for lunch.'

He heard the uncertainty in her voice and wondered what had happened to the feisty, confident 'get out of my life' Kate. He'd been intrigued by her motivation to buy him, still was. Now, after practically shoving him out the door she was asking to see him in a few hours?

Shaking his head, he grinned. He'd never figure her out.

'What did you have in mind?'

She sighed, a small sound that shot straight to his groin. Damn, he had it bad.

'How about meeting at Venice Beach?'

Ty gripped the phone, wondering if she remembered the first time he'd taken her there and how that day had ended in an unexpected explosion of passion when she'd clung to him, soft and needy in the back seat of his SUV, and he'd lost his mind. She'd made him squirm back then and it looked as if nothing had changed.

'Fine. What time?'

'Midday? At Whippy's?'

Yeah, she remembered all right.

'Sounds like a plan.'

Now, if he could keep his cool and not jump her as his instincts had been urging him to since he'd seen her last night he'd be doing great.

'See you then.'

She hung up on him and he snapped his phone shut, confused as hell but looking forward to seeing the cause of his angst much sooner than he'd anticipated.

Kate loved the Venice Beach vibe. Jugglers and buskers vied for attention alongside muscle men and in-line skaters clad in teensy-weensy bikinis, with an eclectic blend of tourists and food vendors thrown in for good measure.

The place was buzzing any time of day or night and she often headed here in her limited down time to soak up the atmosphere and indulge in her favourite pastime, people-watching. It stirred her like no other part of LA, a bit like the guy who had introduced her to this part of town.

As if on cue Ty sauntered towards her, his long strides eating up the boardwalk, and all she could do was stare, feasting her eyes on the striking vision he made in hip-hugging jeans and white cotton T.

'Hi.'

She pasted a smile on her face, willing her heart to stop pounding so she'd have a chance of hearing his reply.

'Hey. You changed.'

His gaze slid up her body, lingered on her breasts for an appreciative second before fixing on her mouth.

And you noticed.

She shrugged, her skin burning from the intensity of his gaze. 'Yeah, well, the corporate look doesn't quite fit in down here.'

He laughed and the rich, deep sound washed over her, warming her better than the sun's rays. 'You can say that again. Besides, I prefer what you're wearing now.'

Kate gulped, trying to ease the tension of her constricted throat muscles. The cargoes, pink T-shirt and sneakers were the only casual items she carried in her gym bag for changing into after a workout. Not exactly seduction material.

But then, who said anything about seduction?

'Want an ice cream?' she blurted, anxious to break the tension that enveloped them, the same tension that caused her to do crazy things like bid on him at a public auction, the same tension that had always zinged between them and amazingly hadn't waned.

If anything, the sparks they generated now were fiercer than six years ago and she knew without a doubt they'd ignite into a blazing conflagration given a little oxygen.

'Yeah, I could do with something to cool me down.'

Great. Was he saying he was hot for her or was it a throw-away comment on the LA weather?

'Same as usual?'

She nodded, wondering how he remembered a small, in-significant fact like her favourite ice-cream flavour and thrilled that he did.

After ordering and paying he handed her a choc-mint

waffle cone and their fingers brushed. An electrifying charge raced up her arm and she would have dropped the ice cream if he hadn't pulled away faster than she could blink.

So much for wanting to touch her. He must have been talking about the weather after all.

'Mmm…' She licked the sticky glob of ice cream, savouring the icy tingle as it slid down her throat.

A strange choking sound came from Ty's direction and she looked up to find his gaze fixed on her mouth.

Letting her know she'd been wrong. It wasn't the sun that had raised his temperature to the point he needed cooling down; given it was his fault she was in this current awful situation perhaps it was time for a little payback.

'Isn't this the best?' she murmured, taking a long, leisurely swipe at the rim of the cone with her tongue.

Desire, swift and fierce, blazed in his eyes as his gaze stayed riveted to her tongue. She licked the rivulets running down the side of the cone before running her tongue along her upper lip, every flick a slow, torturous attempt at teasing him.

He gripped his ice-cream cone, it snapped and as if in slow motion the scoop fell and landed on the pavement, quickly forming a molten mess of rum'n'raisin.

'Oh,' she said, trying to hide her grin behind her cone.

'Too bad. Now I'll have to share yours.'

In an instant he'd wrapped his hand around hers and brought her ice cream to his mouth and it was her turn to squirm as he licked her ice cream in what could only be described as an extremely indecent way to eat a dessert in public.

Watching his tongue, she had a sudden wish to be every flavour under the sun, though the way her body burned she'd be lying in a puddle like the scoop on the hot concrete.

'Not bad,' he drawled, pulling back a fraction but not letting go of her hand.

Kate didn't know how long they stood that way, gazes

locked, hands clenched around the cone. It seemed like an eternity and in a sudden flash of clarity, she knew.

This man was going to rock her world all over again.

He let go of her hand and stepped away, leaving her feeling slightly chilled despite the midday sun.

'So I'm guessing you didn't just want to meet down here for the ice cream?'

She nodded. 'I was hoping we could talk.'

'About?'

'The week ahead. And a woman's prerogative to change her mind.'

'This sounds interesting.' He sat on a nearby bench and patted the space next to him. 'Guess I was right.'

'About?'

She scowled at him; he didn't have to spell it out. The minute his heated gaze locked on hers, she knew he was referring to his parting comment about her still wanting him as much as he wanted her.

Grinning, he said, 'You know you're making too much of this, right? It's no big deal. We get to catch up, maybe have a laugh over old times. Like I said, no biggie.'

She ditched the remainder of her ice cream in the bin and sat beside him, her gut churning. No biggie? Who was he kidding? Spending a week with the sexiest guy on the planet was a big deal no matter how much he tried to play it down.

'Okay, so I change my mind and we get to play catch-up. I was also wondering if you'd do me a favour.'

He leaned back and rested his arm across the back of the bench, the light dusting of dark hair along his muscular forearm grabbing her attention. Most of her friends had a thing for guy's butts. Personally, she had a thing for forearms. The more muscly, the better, and Ty had two of the best.

'Depends on what it is.'

His teasing smile lit up his face and she wondered how long that would last once he heard what she had to say.

She took a steadying breath. 'Being my odd-job guy is going to involve more than you might be prepared for.'

'I think I can handle anything you dish out.'

The lines around his eyes crinkled adorably and it took every inch of will-power not to reach out and smooth them.

She'd always loved this teasing side of him and they'd often bounced off each other, trading quips with incredible speed.

A huge part of her wanted to pick up where they'd left off and swap one-liners like a pro but she couldn't. She wouldn't let her guard down around him completely. She couldn't.

Funny things might happen if she did that, like her falling for him a second time around, and, for a savvy career woman who knew what she wanted these days and went out and got it, that would be very, very stupid.

'I'm not a mind-reader, Katie, so spit it out. It can't be that bad, right?'

As if making it easier on her he looked away and she drank in the sight of the sun skimming his tanned face, etching the hard planes and angles in shades of bronze, and in an instant she was transported back to the first time they'd come here.

Strolling along the boardwalk hand in hand at dusk, sharing fish and chips on the beach before snuggling in the back of his SUV.

Heat surged into her cheeks at the recollection of how far that snuggling had gone, how incredible Ty had made her feel.

'Katie?'

He sat up suddenly and fixed her with a piercing stare that drove all rational thought from her mind as she struggled not to re-enact the erotic images flashing through her mind a second before, wishing she could pick up the conversation thread but coming up a total blank.

Something about the week ahead… The words starting to form turned to dust as their gazes locked, heated and combusted and before she knew how it had happened his hand skimmed her neck and she leaned towards him, powerless to resist the irrational urge to taste him once again.

'This is crazy,' he muttered against the side of her mouth as their lips melded in a blaze of heat, intense, burning, erotic.

She clutched at his chest as if she were drowning, sliding her hands along the hard contours before dropping lower, the familiar ridges of his six-pack tantalising her exploring fingertips through the cotton of his T-shirt, and she itched to touch his bare skin, to feel the smooth, silky hardness she'd known in the past.

Angling her head slightly, she gave him access to her craving mouth, wanting more, wanting all of him. His teeth nibbled her lower lip before his tongue eased into her mouth, tasting and stroking every inch of the way. He tasted delicious, the intoxicating combination of choc-mint and Ty sending her senses spiralling dangerously out of control. And it had been far too long since she'd lost control.

This was no ordinary kiss.

Nor was it the power-packed, spur-of-the-moment kiss of the night before.

It was different and she knew that this time she wouldn't be satisfied with anything less than having all of him.

What seemed a mind-blowing eternity later he broke the kiss, pushing her away and staring at her with a slightly shell-shocked expression.

'You're right. Definitely crazy,' she said, reaching across and running her thumb along his bottom lip before she realised what she was doing and snatched her hand away.

'You'll get us arrested,' he muttered, a hint of a smile tugging at the corners of his mouth. 'But, hey, what the hell? With a bit of luck we'd be locked up together and wouldn't that be fun?'

Rather than the heat flooding her body dissipating, it intensified until she thought she'd dissolve unless she got the conversation back on track.

'Look, I take full responsibility for participating in that crazy moment a second ago, but can we get back to why I asked you here?'

She thought he'd block her sidestep.

In fact, she would've bet on it for the old Ty would never have let her get off that easily. Especially considering she'd labelled an explosive kiss a 'crazy moment'.

However, to his credit he let it slip, though the banked heat in his vivid blue eyes had her struggling to string words together.

'Okay. Shoot. What's this favour about?'

'I've got a job for you.'

Surely he wouldn't balk at the idea of an article for the magazine? He knew what her career meant to her. After all, it had been one of the major factors that had driven them apart, their unquenchable thirst to get ahead, to make their mark on the world.

The SEAL and the journalist, taking on the world, and this time around he could help her secure the job of a lifetime, the job that would keep her occupied when he walked out of her life in a week and she tried to forget this amazing man all over again.

It only took a second for the lust in his eyes to blaze again, swift, scorching, irresistible.

'Does it involve being bound to you again?'

Logic fled yet again as her pulse kicked up another notch and she couldn't resist slipping into familiar word games.

'Only if you're very good.'

He stood up and held out his hand. Involuntarily, she took it and he pulled her flush against his body, taking her breath away and sending her heart rate into overdrive all over again.

'Sweetheart, when I'm good, I'm very, very good. And when I'm bad…I'm even better.'

CHAPTER FIVE

KATE had the whole week mapped out.

She'd work from home, gain the relevant information needed to complete the article on the man auction for the magazine while satisfying the intense curiosity about Ty that had been burning within her since she'd first glimpsed his name on the auction list.

Having an inquiring mind was a godsend in her job, but unfortunately the more time she spent with Ty, the more she wanted to know. If anything her curiosity had intensified with every second they spent together and she couldn't concentrate on anything for thoughts of him clouding her mind.

Why was he doing this?

How far would they go to get *reacquainted*?

If those explosive kisses were any indication neither of them would be satisfied with anything less than going the whole way and, while the very idea sent an illicit thrill through her body, she couldn't help but wonder if there was more behind her need to catch up with Ty than curiosity.

The doorbell pealed, interrupting her thoughts and her pulse quickened in anticipation as she was only expecting one person.

Taking a deep breath, she opened the door. 'Didn't take you long to pack.'

He held up a smallish overnight bag and grinned. 'Didn't think I'd need much in the way of clothes.'

Her heart lurched as he leaned against the doorjamb, looking a million bucks and knowing it.

'Come in,' she managed to say, her breath catching as he brushed against her bare arm. 'Minimal clothes, huh? Sounds like we need to have a little chat about your expectations for this week.'

'Hey, I haven't got any expectations. I'm your odd-job man, you call the shots. Simple.'

He glanced around the room, an appreciative gleam in his eyes. 'Nice place you've got here. Not what I expected.'

'What did you expect?'

She'd hoped he'd like her home. For that was what it was to her: a home. Not just bricks and mortar but a place she loved to be. A place that gave her security, a sense of belonging, two things she'd never had growing up with her grumpy, distant mother who'd never really made a home out of their dreary house.

He dropped his bag at the door and stepped inside. 'Guess I expected something different, being Beverly Hills and all.'

'Just because the post code says 90210 doesn't mean I live in a mansion. I'm definitely not movie-star material.'

'I don't know about that.'

A thread of huskiness wove through his voice as his gaze skimmed her body the way it used to: approving, reverent, with a touch of awe in his blue eyes.

Clearing her throat, she turned away before she did something stupid like fling herself at him before he'd even come inside. 'Why don't you make yourself comfortable?'

'How comfortable do you want me to get?'

She stopped mid-stride, forgetting why she'd been heading to the kitchen. 'Consider this place your home for the next week, so whatever makes you happy.'

That was good. She'd managed to deflect his innuendo right back at him.

Predictably, he lobbed straight back. 'These days I usually walk around naked at home.'

Game. Set. Not quite match.

She managed to keep a straight face, barely.

'That works for me. Though I've taken up fencing lately and I have this really weird tendency to practise in my sleep.'

He laughed, the deep sound rippling over her and wrapping her in familiar warmth.

'Thanks for the warning. Though I have to tell you I'm pretty handy with a sword myself.'

His look of assumed innocence backhanded his *coup de grâce* back at her.

Game over. Thank you, linesmen, thank you, ball boys.

She joined in his laughter. 'It's called a rapier in fencing, not a sword. Want a drink?'

'No, thanks.'

She shrugged, wondering why he was still standing around. 'Anything else?'

'I want you.'

Three little words, spoken so quietly that at first she thought she'd imagined them.

'We definitely need to establish house rules,' she said, unable to move even if she'd wanted to as her knees trembled at the sight of Ty strolling towards her.

'I have to kiss you.'

'Ty, I—'

'I have to.'

Tyler's mouth settled over hers and he groaned. He'd ached for this kiss ever since she'd opened the door and he'd seen her standing there wearing a faded purple Lakers T-shirt over cut-off denim shorts, one bare foot propped over the other, a nervous smile playing about her mouth and uncertainty in her hazel eyes, an intoxicating blend of sexy contrasts.

As she responded, her lips opening beneath his, shock slammed into his gut. He didn't just ache for this kiss. He ached for her, to have her in his arms for more than a fleeting minute, maybe for more than a week.

And it scared the hell out of him.

Besides, he couldn't do it to her. She deserved a life and, by the look of her fancy house and snazzy office, she had one now. Being bound to a guy who had no idea what he wanted out of life any more, especially a guy likely to be booted out of the one job he'd known his whole life next week, wasn't for her.

He wouldn't let it happen. She deserved so much better.

Concentrating on the here and now, he slid his hands under her T-shirt and caressed the soft, silky skin beneath, reaching for her breasts that had teased him since he'd walked through the door. Hell, their memory had teased him for the last six years.

'I've missed you,' he murmured against her hair, inhaling the familiar floral fragrance of her shampoo.

Gardenias. He remembered the scent imprinted on his sheets, his pillowcases, his shirts, wherever she'd rested her head.

He grew dizzy at the memory alone and, combined with the touch of her hands fluttering around his waist and the fresh mint taste of her lips, it drove him to the brink of losing control.

'Tell me what you want, Katie,' he murmured before re-capturing her mouth, nibbling and tasting till she made soft, mewing sounds.

This was how he'd imagined it would be from the minute he'd laid eyes on her again.

This was how it should have been for the last six years.

Damn, he'd never felt like this with any other woman. She turned him on with just a look, a flick of her chocolate-brown hair, a glimpse of those amber flecks in her eyes, and for the few glorious moments when she returned his kiss he could ignore the stabbing guilt of the lie he'd told her when he'd walked away six years ago, the constant emptiness of what that had cost him.

Resting her hands on his chest, she gave a slight push, breaking their kiss.

'I want us to take things slow,' she said, raising her eyes slowly to meet his, and the gut-wrenching vulnerability reflected in her hazel depths hit him—hard.

What was he thinking?

It wasn't her fault he kept kissing her whenever he got within two feet and though she responded it didn't mean she wanted some sex-starved SEAL jumping her every time she turned around.

She obviously didn't want *this,* though for the life of him he couldn't figure out what she did want.

His motivations were simple and he'd take whatever fleeting fun she could give him before his world as he knew it was ripped out from under him, but what did she get out of all this?

'Guess you're right about establishing house rules,' he said, thrusting his hands in his pockets to stop from reaching for her again as she tugged her T-shirt down.

She shuffled her bare feet like a recalcitrant schoolchild. 'Where do we start?'

'Ladies first.'

Nodding, she plopped into a comfy armchair, the furthest one away from him, and he sat on the sofa opposite.

Glancing around properly for the first time, he admired the roomy Spanish-style single-storey that exuded a cosiness that sucked him in and would probably spit him out just as quickly.

He didn't belong here.

This was Kate's home, her sanctuary, and he was an intruder, wanting to take whatever scraps of affection she'd throw his way for the next week. For seven days he would put his own needs over hers. Surely no one would begrudge him this interlude considering what he might face next week?

Her eyes pinned him with a knowing stare as if reading his mind and he slipped his poker face into place while his gut churned.

She had the ability to tie him into knots, always had, and right now one thing was for sure: he was way out of his depth. He'd handled that feeling before in the murky waters of the Pacific and Indian Oceans, but on those occasions he'd been trained for it. This time he'd have to survive on instincts alone.

'Go ahead. You're the boss. I'll take my orders from you.'

Confusion flickered in the amber depths of her eyes and he wondered if she felt as off kilter as he did. From the minute they'd hooked up again last night he hadn't been thinking straight and, combined with a sleepless night where he couldn't get her image out of his head, his logic had gone AWOL.

'Okay, house rule one. You look after yourself.'

'Check.'

'House rule two. I'm working on a big article this week so no distractions.'

'Check.'

'House rule three. You need to curb the catching-up behaviour.'

'Such as?'

He bit back a grin, knowing it was cruel to make her spell it out but enjoying the faint blush that stained her cheeks.

She rolled her eyes. 'You kissing me all the time.'

'You've responded.'

She leaped off the sofa as if he'd prodded her with a machine gun and stalked across the room.

'Yeah, well, maybe I've been spending too much time buried in my work so when the first decent guy came along I lost the plot.'

'You think I'm decent, huh?'

He leaned back on the couch, arms outstretched and resting along the top, grinning like a SEAL at graduation.

'I think you're a pain in the ass.'

She flicked her dark hair over her shoulder and recognition washed over him. Even her defence mannerisms hadn't changed in six years.

'And I think you still have a thing for me but, hey, I won't hold it against you.'

Kate couldn't answer for a second. She wanted to argue that he was wrong, that he couldn't be more wrong, but she wouldn't go there. She couldn't, not when her brain was still befuddled by his scintillating kiss.

She had to think logically, to make sure he understood what this week was about. Though apart from his help with the article she was having a hard time figuring out exactly what that was. The lines had blurred around the time he'd laid his hands on her skin and plastered his lips to hers.

She whirled to face him, tucking her hair behind her ears. 'Think whatever you like, though there is something else we need to discuss about this week.'

'Ah…the mysterious favour we didn't quite get around to discussing earlier. Come on, let me have it.'

'I need your help. Your input actually. My chief wants me to do an article on the man auction.'

'Sounds easy enough. Where do I come in?'

If he still valued his privacy as he used to, she knew he wouldn't like the next part. 'Uh, the article's about you and me.'

A tiny frown creased his brow, not detracting from his handsome face one iota. 'What you and me?'

Hearing him say the words out loud hurt more than she could've imagined. Worse still, he was right.

She tilted her head, staring him straight in the eye. 'There isn't any you and me as such, but seeing as we're playing along with this Odd Bod business for the next week, why don't you play along with me on this too?'

He stood up and walked towards her, stopping less than two feet away, invading her personal space with every inch of his incredible body and tipping her chin up, his touch re-igniting the slow burning fuse deep in her heart. 'Play along with what?'

'I need you to be a part of this article. Without your contribution I can't do it.'

'Depends how far I'd have to go?'

'All the way.'

Her statement hung in the air as heat zinged between them, urging her to close the small gap separating them and bury herself in his arms again.

He arched an eyebrow. 'Are we just talking about the article here?'

'What do you think?'

There she went again, unable to bite her tongue, teasing him with innuendo without intending to, half afraid he'd take her up on it, half afraid he wouldn't. What on earth was she doing? She'd just laid down the rules, yet here she was back-sliding already. What was wrong with her?

After staring at her with burning desire for five, long, exquisite seconds he shook his head, picked up his car keys from the coffee-table and strode to the door.

'Okay, I'll do it, but right now if I don't get out of here this minute I'm going to blow rule three straight away. I'm kind of addicted to the catching-up behaviour, so I'll put myself out of the way of temptation for a bit. Back soon.'

He blew her a kiss and she scowled as he walked out the door.

Okay, she should be ecstatic he'd agreed to help her, but as the eye-popping memory of the way the denim hugged his butt as he walked out the door refused to budge she knew the week ahead had the potential to blow all their rules sky-high.

* * *

Tyler revved the engine of his Porsche and slid away from the kerb. His baby handled like a dream and provided him with the perfect opportunity to hone his driving skills. After all, no harm in practising what he preached to his charges.

If only handling Kate were as easy. They were on a collision course headed straight for a crash that would probably leave them both nursing emotional injuries that could leave them scarred for life.

Whenever he was near her all he could think about was getting physical and rather than push him away she pushed his buttons more.

He slammed the wheel with the heel of his hand. Kate had always given him all of herself unconditionally and by her eager responses to his kisses it looked as if nothing had changed. Sure, she kept singing the 'no catching up' tune but could she be that detached? Could they be together for the next week and walk away unscathed at the end of it?

Maybe she could. After all, he'd only known her for a few brief months and they'd been apart for six long years. Her new sassy attitude screamed confidence while back then he'd been her touchstone, the guy she'd leaned on when she'd left Australia and landed here with stars in her eyes, hopes of finally getting to know her American grandparents and dreams of making it big in the reporting world. Perhaps the new confident Kate could handle anything?

If she could she was braver than him for he had a sneaking suspicion that the week ahead was going to test him way beyond endurance.

At least she'd come clean about why she wanted him for the week. She needed his help with some stupid article. He'd known she couldn't just want him for his charm and personality.

Heading down Melrose, he wondered if she remembered cruising down this strip with him, checking out the vintage-clothing stores, sharing a hamburger at their favourite diner.

They'd been inseparable for a while and he'd loved showing her the tourist sights like the Mann Theatre, Hollywood Boulevard and day trips to Anaheim to visit Disneyland where they'd laughed like a couple of kids on Space Mountain.

He remembered every carefree day they'd ever had back then and he fully intended to recapture that feeling with his sexy ex over the next week.

Grinning, he angled the car into the orphanage's front gates. Yeah, he'd help her out, but if she expected him to stick to all her rules, particularly the crazy one about keeping his hands off her, she had another thing coming.

The kids were playing beneath an old oak, making enough noise to raise the dead as a flashback had him blinking rapidly—the memory of himself entering these same gates as a terrified youngster.

Nothing much had changed, just the faces passing through, and he'd seen a lot of those over the many years he'd spent here.

A petite woman detached herself from the group and walked towards him as he unfolded his limbs from the car, flexed his knee and stiffened as a wave of excruciating pain stabbed deep and low through the dodgy joint. He should've sold the car years ago but his damn fool pride had stopped him. The way he saw it, the low-slung sports car was the last symbol of his strength. Silly but, hey, it was a guy thing. That and the fact that it was the one luxury he'd ever allowed himself, a hangover from the wishes of a poor kid growing up in the city of dreams.

'Hey, you. Long time no see.'

He held out his arms, knowing that however he was feeling Mary Ramone had the power to make him feel a whole lot better. They'd known each other since they were kids and she knew every one of his moods and he wondered what vibe she'd pick up from him today.

She hugged him before playfully punching his arm. 'Yeah, it's been a while. Work keeping you busy?'

'You know how it is. Teaching those SEALs to handle a vehicle is tough work.'

'Is that why you call it the "crash and bang" course?'

He tweaked her nose. 'CTTC to you civilians, smartypants.'

'Oh, you mean the Countering Terrorist Tactics Course? The one that teaches trainees to use a Browning 9mm, a .38 Special and counter-surveillance techniques? And did I forget to mention the counter-terror driving skills?'

'The girl has a memory.' He clapped and glanced pointedly at the kids. 'Though it's about time you used it for something other than the alphabet.'

She linked her arm through his and guided him towards the decrepit sandstone building he'd once called home. 'I hope you didn't come to lecture me. You know I love my work here.'

'But don't you want to broaden your horizons? See what life holds outside these four walls?'

He sure as hell had wanted to. As soon as he could he'd escaped the orphanage and enrolled in the Navy, eager to travel the world and make it a better place than the one he'd grown up in.

'I love the kids. I can't think of anywhere else I'd rather be than running this place.'

'Yeah, but you've spent your whole life here,' he persisted, knowing his advice fell on deaf ears but compelled to continue anyway. 'If we had more money, someone else could run it and you'd be free to pursue anything you wanted.'

A worried expression crossed her face and the knife of guilt embedded in his conscience twisted. He'd left as soon as he could, Mary hadn't and she'd forfeited her life's dreams while he had fulfilled his.

'We do need more cash and soon. Otherwise, these gates

will close permanently. I'll be out on the streets, not to mention the poor little tykes.'

'Isn't there something else we can do?'

She reached up and smoothed the frown from his forehead. 'You do enough.'

He continued as if he hadn't heard her. 'We need to raise the profile of this place, raise people's awareness...'

He trailed off as a smidgeon of an idea hatched in his mind, growing from chick-size to pterodactyl in a second.

'Want a drink?'

Mary bustled around the kitchen, preparing dinner for the children. She'd always looked after him like this from the first day he'd set foot in the orphanage all those years ago. She was a mere eleven months older than him yet she'd mothered him as though the age difference were eleven years and he loved her for it.

He shook his head. 'No, thanks. Look, I have to run. See you soon.'

He dropped a kiss on the top of her head and strode out the door, ignoring her protest of 'But you just got here.'

He had a plan and the sooner he put it to Kate, the better.

Kate lit the final candle and stepped back from the table. So she'd pulled out all stops tonight, but she had a feeling she was going to need all the help she could get.

No matter how much she deluded herself that the week ahead was all part of her job and might provide some light-hearted fun in her workaholic world, she knew deep down that there would come a time very soon where she'd cross the line, throw herself at Ty and there'd be no turning back.

Her almost frantic responses to his kisses proved it.

She wanted him. Badly. Insanely. Desperately.

She couldn't get him out of her head and having him here for a week would be more temptation than she could withstand. More than she wanted to withstand if she was completely honest with herself. What had she been thinking laying down those rules? No catching up—who was she kidding? She wanted to *catch up* with him in a bad way.

And why not?

It shouldn't be a big deal. She was a career girl with high aspirations who lived life to the full. Why couldn't she take what Ty offered and say bye-bye in a week?

It would be so much fun to explore the unresolved tension between them, to see if they still combusted the way they used to. But was she immune to him emotionally? She'd got over him a long time ago but spending one-on-one time could be dangerous.

Could she let him go at the end of the week if they clicked as she expected? They'd already picked up where they'd left off mentally, matching each other quip for quip, teasing, pushing the boundaries. What if the sex was as good as she remembered—or, worse, better?

Was she strong enough to get over him a second time?

Well, there was only one way to find out.

Glancing around, she fiddled with the place settings for the umpteenth time, making sure everything was perfect. Dimmed Tiffany lamps sent muted light over the room, making the candles seem so much brighter. The table setting for two appeared cosier with candles, the shadows cast creating an intimacy that beckoned, reflecting off the coffee-coloured walls, deepening the rich ochre of the sofa and highlighting the turquoise cushions scattered in a casual formation.

Ty would probably laugh his head off if he remembered how they'd shared their meals all those years ago and compared it to this fancy setting. Back then they'd eaten pizza out of a box most nights courtesy of her complete lack of culinary skills, and rarely at the table, preferring the cosiness of cuddling in bed licking mozzarella off each other's fingers before turning their attentions to other parts.

The memory brought a smile to her face and before she could uncork the wine the doorbell rang. Wiping her sweaty palms on a napkin, she smoothed her skirt and opened the door.

'Hi. Care for something to eat?'

She aimed for casual yet her voice came out husky as her pulse galloped at the look in Ty's eye.

'I should warn you. I'm ravenous.'

His intense gaze started at her toes and worked its way slowly upward, leaving her in little doubt that he wanted to start at dessert.

And come back for seconds.

CHAPTER SIX

T<small>YLER</small> thought he knew Kate but the minute she opened the door wearing a slip of material parading as a dress she blew every preconception he'd ever had.

When he'd left earlier with a smart-ass remark about not sticking to rule number three he could've sworn she'd wanted to flay him alive. He'd seen it in the glowing gold flecks of her eyes, in the bunched fists, in the clenched jaw. He could read body language a mile away and hers had screamed, 'Back off.'

So what was with the vamp dress?

Soft blue material clung to every inch of her delicious curves, ending just above her knee and wrapped halter-style around her neck. It tied at exactly the spot he'd wanted to plant his lips the minute she'd sauntered up on stage to join him last night.

If she wanted to tempt him, to drive him wild, to send him to the doc at the base for debriefing, she was certainly going about it the right way.

Rules? What rules? It appeared Kate had a penchant for teasing and the way he was feeling he'd be lucky to last the next minute without shooting down her stupid rules in flames.

'You look amazing. Did you dress up for me?'

'Only if you're lucky, sailor boy. Want some wine?'

'Please. Mind if I take a quick shower?'

She waved towards the back of the house. 'Go right ahead. I put your bag in the spare room, second door on the left. Towels are in the bathroom.'

So much for the faint hope she was planning on going through with her 'going the whole way' taunt. He'd looked forward to waking up next to her despite the fact she'd laid down clear cohabiting rules for the week.

Who was he trying to kid? He'd been counting on it. Instead, he'd be closeted in the spare room, tossing and turning and dreaming of his sexy ex across the hall.

'Thanks,' he said, admiring her long, bare legs accentuated by sexy black shoes with monstrous heels before heading for the shower. A long, cold shower.

He didn't get it.

If Kate was so keen on sticking to rules why was she sending him mixed messages? She responded to his kisses, she joined in his flirtatious banter and now this cosy dinner scenario with her looking like a walking, talking fantasy.

He didn't know what to think, let alone how to respond. Some of the tougher missions he'd faced had been a walk in the park compared with figuring out what made her tick these days.

Kate waited till Ty left the room before sinking into a chair with a glass of wine in hand.

She'd failed.

So much for giving him an obvious sign she was willing to throw rule three out the window and go for it.

He'd obviously liked her outfit, but as for making a fuss about being in the spare room he'd shrugged it off, not appearing to be bothered in the slightest. She'd expected him to make some cutesy remark. Heck, she'd hoped he'd pick up his bag and march straight into her bedroom.

Now she'd have to tell him what she wanted, and how embarrassing would that be?

'Oh, by the way, Ty, remember my hands-off rule? Well, scratch that. I've actually still got the hots for you so why don't we spend the next few days getting reacquainted in every way?'

Yeah, as if she could say that.

Darn it, why was this so difficult? She had no trouble being assertive in the business arena; why couldn't she just tell Ty what she wanted?

It wasn't as if the guy were immune to her. After all, he'd kissed her several times over the last twenty-four hours and flirted incessantly.

Hating her indecision, she tried to ignore the sound of the running shower by turning up the CD player. Unfortunately, once she'd heard the taps turn the image of Ty naked with water sluicing down his toned body sprang to mind and she couldn't dislodge it.

Sipping her wine, she focussed on the soft jazz filtering through the room, though the alcohol and music didn't help. Before she knew it she'd emptied the glass and was still tuned to the sound of running water rather than soulful sax. Leaning back in the chair, she closed her eyes for a moment.

'You work too hard.'

Ty strolled into the room looking delectable in bone-coloured chinos and a casual white shirt open at the neck. The sandalwood soap she kept for guests had been put to good use if the heady scent emanating off him was any indication and she breathed deeply, infusing her senses with it, with him.

'Occupational hazard,' she said, trying not to focus on the tanned V visible at the base of his throat, the area of skin she knew drove him crazy when nibbled on.

Damn memories…

She tried to relax as he rested his hands on her shoulders and slowly stroked and kneaded the knots in her neck muscles, and though she knew his touch was therapeutic the feel of his warm hands on her bare skin sent erotic shivers down her spine.

'I'm pretty tense,' she murmured, leaning her head forward to allow him better access.

How long since she'd had a massage, done something indulgent or just plain taken time out for herself? Too long if her reaction to Ty's touch was anything to go by, though she knew that probably had more to do with who was giving her the massage than the rub itself.

'Just relax.'

He increased the pressure, his thumbs circling into the base of her skull, and she stifled a loud groan of pleasure.

'Ooh…yeah. Right there.'

His hands stilled and she realised how her words sounded. Aiming for light-hearted, she said, 'I didn't tell you to stop.'

'Yes, boss.'

Kate couldn't think straight as his thumbs started stroking the indentations above her collar-bones, rhythmic circles that enticed rather than soothed, liquid heat seeping through her body and turning her bones to mush.

'How do you know all the right spots?'

'Your body speaks volumes.' He wound his way back to her neck, his gentle yet firm touch hypnotising.

'So what do you think it's telling you now?'

Her breath caught as his fingers snagged on the tie of her dress and she wished she hadn't had that glass of wine on an empty stomach. The alcohol had taken the edge off her nerves, given her false courage, and there was no telling what she'd say next.

'The suggestions your body makes, it should be branded with an "R" rating.'

As if to emphasise the fact, he lifted the halter knot at the base of her neck and kissed her, so softly that at first she thought she'd imagined it.

'You're incredible, Katie, but I don't want to be accused

of breaking rules again, and on my first day too,' he murmured against her ear, his breath soft and warm.

Her head snapped up as he walked to the table, her body missing his touch so much it bordered on physical pain, her brain unable to process how he could switch off like that when a second ago he'd seemed about to untie her dress and have his way with her.

'Nice set-up. What's for dinner?'

He pulled out a chair and looked in her direction, a knowing smile flirting around his mouth as if he could read her mind.

Struggling to keep her tone casual, she said, 'Spaghetti marinara. Salad. Nothing too flash.'

Thanks to her bones having dissolved under his expert hands she almost staggered to the table, kicking off her high heels in the process. So much for the illusion of longer legs. At this point she'd settle for both legs staying vertical rather than sprawling on the floor.

'What's so funny?'

He chuckled, a pure happy sound that evoked instant memories of how much they used to laugh together, how much fun they'd had in their too-brief relationship. 'Still a one-glass wonder, I see. Take a seat. I'll get dinner.'

She sank gratefully into the chair as he pushed it towards the table and she avoided the wine bottle. She'd had more than enough for one night.

Besides, if she were to pluck up the courage to tell him exactly how badly she had the hots for him she wanted to remember if they got to the fun stuff later.

'Nice manners. You must've had a good teacher.'

'One of the best.' He strolled into the kitchen, tension etched into the breadth of his shoulders.

Funnily enough, he'd never mentioned family six years ago and she hadn't asked, being so rapt in the throes of first love. In fact, he'd skilfully avoided any questions regarding his childhood, and she knew next to nothing about the man she'd loved apart from the fact he had been raised in LA, how he liked his eggs in the mornings, what side of the bed he liked to sleep on and how many times a night he could please her.

Resisting the urge to fan her flushed cheeks—memories of Ty's prowess in bed combined with wine were not conducive to staying cool—she said, 'Did your mum teach you?'

Silence greeted her question, soon followed by the sounds of pots opening and clanking spoons.

'Ty?'

'No.'

He strode towards the table, bearing plates heaped with steaming pasta and seafood sauce.

'Then who?'

He ignored her once again as he strode towards the kitchen, this time returning with the salad.

'What's with the twenty questions?'

She shrugged, as if his answer weren't important.

'Just wondering. We didn't exactly do lots of talking six years ago.'

She twirled a few lengths of spaghetti onto her fork and managed to shovel them into her mouth, avoiding his eyes the whole time, wondering if her veiled reference to what they had spent their time on might give her the opening to say what she wanted now.

'You're right about that.'

His voice was strangely flat and she sneaked a peek, not surprised to see him concentrating on his pasta as if it hid the answer to world peace.

Taking a deep breath, she plunged in. 'Maybe this is a good opportunity for us to, you know, talk? For old times' sake, see how far we've come.'

He lifted his head, his blue-eyed gaze meeting her dead-on.

'You know what that sounds like?' he asked archly.

She nodded, knowing the rising blush staining her cheeks would be a dead give-away if her leaning so far forward and practically climbing onto his lap wasn't enough of a clue.

'Uh-huh.' Managing a smile, she pointed to her dress. 'Guess I kind of hoped this would be enough of a sign that I'm not so rigid on the rules, but you didn't take the hint so maybe I'll have to spell it out for you.'

His eyes blazed with instant heat before he blinked and reached across the table to capture her hands.

'You don't need to spell anything out. I know you want me as much as I want you. But are you sure? Come the end of this week I'm out of your life. Are you absolutely certain you want to concentrate on here and now?'

Oh, yeah.

She didn't want to think beyond this week, she just wanted for seven days to let her hair down for once and have a little fun with the sexiest man she'd ever known. However, hearing Ty casually stating that their reunion was a one-week-only deal hurt like the devil and it shouldn't.

Damn it, she wanted it that way.

She just didn't need reminding of the fact.

'I'm sure,' she murmured, squeezing his hands, hoping he could read the excitement in her eyes as anticipation blazed a trail through her body.

Shaking his head, he sat back, confusion warring with desire on his face.

'I'll be honest with you, Katie. I don't get this. We both made a conscious decision to end our relationship six years ago. We had careers to forge, places to go, things to do. Then you turn up out of the blue, buy me at some crazy male auction, tell me to take a hike, then change your mind and we've barely kept our hands off each other ever since. What's going on? Do you really think you'll be happy with just a week-long fling?'

Sighing, she disengaged her hands from his and reached for her wineglass. One more sip for courage wouldn't hurt.

'You want the truth? I'm married to my job. I haven't dated in a while. I'm stale, stifled. Then I saw your name on the auction list; I got curious. I thought we could catch up over a drink. Then I had too much champagne, went a little crazy and bought you, tried to fob you off before agreeing to have you trail after me for a week, and here we are.'

His stare didn't waver and she wondered yet again if he could still read her like a book. He'd had a happy knack of doing it back then, honing in on her thoughts with startling clarity. However, this time he'd come up blank because she'd basically told him the truth. Well, most of it anyway.

'So you're bored and you want to have a little fun? And that's it?'

She nodded, hating the logical, cut-and-dried way they were discussing this when he should be clearing the table in one swoop and bending her over it to have his wicked way with her.

'In a nutshell, yes.'

After a few seconds' silence where she felt like the biggest fool in the world for laying her cards on the table, he smiled and shook his head.

'You haven't changed a bit. You never ceased to surprise me back then and it looks like nothing has changed.'

Filled with an indescribable joy that she'd spilt her guts and he hadn't laughed at her—in fact, in a roundabout way he'd agreed to give her what she wanted—she picked up her fork and toyed with her pasta, feigning nonchalance.

'Oh, I think you'd be surprised. I may have changed in all sorts of interesting ways.'

'Is that so?'

His eyes narrowed to slivers of fiery blue as heat flared between them in an instant and she laid her fork down, her appetite vanishing. She couldn't eat when he looked at her like that, as if he'd like to gobble her up rather than the meal she'd prepared.

'Uh-huh, but maybe you should finish dinner? You know, to keep up your strength?'

She had to lighten the mood, say something, anything, to distract herself from the insane desire to clamber onto his lap and ravish him.

'Nothing wrong with my endurance, you should know that,' he said, grinning like a guy who knew exactly how impressive his capacities were in that department.

Struggling to keep a straight face, she said, 'Yeah, but you're older now, probably more decrepit. Maybe a healthy serving of pasta will boost your energy levels.'

Rather than Tyler laughing out loud as she expected, a flicker of unease flashed across his face and she wondered what he'd faced in the line of duty and what changes it might have wrought on him emotionally as well as physically.

'You're right about the decrepit part. Since my knee blew jumping out of a helicopter and I had it reconstructed, I haven't been the same since.'

'I was only kidding,' she said, hating the serious turn their conversation had taken, wishing she'd kept things light-hearted.

The flicker of unease had turned into a sombre expression, with his eyes hooded in mystery.

'Being an instructor just isn't the same as active duty,' he said, almost to himself as he picked up his wineglass and took a healthy sip. 'But, hey, you don't want to hear boring tales of battle-scarred Navy guys, right?'

'I'm interested in hearing about what you've been up to,' she said, hoping he'd open up more to her now than he had six years ago.

Back then he'd been tight-lipped about his job, his training, preferring to concentrate on making her laugh rather than revealing what drove him to take on one of the most dangerous and highly skilled jobs in the world.

He clicked his fingers. 'Speaking of work, I need to ask you for a favour. You know that article about you and me? Well, I'll answer all your questions if you run an article on the orphanage. A big spread. Full coverage. High exposure.'

She sat up, surprised at the swift change of topic, but grateful his expression had lightened up.

'Are you serious?'

His interest in the orphanage was a lot more than he had initially let on and she wondered what was behind it.

'Deadly. Think you can do it?'

'Why?'

'It's personal.'

In a blinding flash of clarity, Kate knew it had to involve a woman. What else could it be? Just because she'd been dateless for a while didn't mean he had. After all, look at the guy. What woman could resist?

She shouldn't care; she really shouldn't.

But she did. And the surprising ache in the vicinity of her heart told her just how much.

She decided to call his bluff, following a masochistic urge to find out more about this cause that meant so much to him—or, more realistically, who was behind it.

'I need to check it out first, see if it's newsworthy. Why don't you take me out there tomorrow?'

'Sounds good.' He picked up his fork and stabbed it into his pasta till it stood vertically. 'Now, maybe I should get back to eating? You know, to keep up my strength and all.'

Kate smiled, though inside her mind churned.

She'd thought she'd had it all a few moments ago with Ty agreeing to a week of fun. But his unorthodox request had taken some of the gloss off what had promised to be the most fun she'd had in ages.

Ty had a life that didn't involve her and suddenly the truth hit home.

She didn't really know this man. She never had.

And a week just wasn't enough to play catch-up.

Not the way she wanted.

CHAPTER SEVEN

KATE pointed at Ty's car and grinned. 'Nice wheels.'

'It's just a Porsche.'

His answering little-boy grin told her exactly how much he loved his car as he opened the passenger door, resurrecting memories of his perfect manners and the way he'd made her feel like a queen. Not many guys did that any more and she liked it. She might be independent and self-sufficient, but she hadn't burned all her bras just yet.

'Yeah, just a Porsche. So what if it's sleek, powerful and built for speed, right?'

His smile widened as he gunned the engine. 'Sounds a bit like me. Apart from the speed thing. I prefer to take things nice and slow.'

She quirked an eyebrow. 'Could've fooled me, the way you've been carrying on.'

No matter how hard she tried she couldn't get the memory of his scorching kisses out of her head. Not that she was trying particularly hard to forget.

Ty concentrated on the road so she couldn't read the expression in his eyes. 'Have we made love yet?'

'No,' she mumbled, heat flooding her cheeks at his typical blunt assessment of the situation.

'See, told you. Slow.'

She barely caught his murmured addition, 'Too bloody slow.'

A flood of heat flowed through her body at the delicious recollection of exactly how slow Ty could take things.

He'd been a master lover, knowing exactly how to please her, to make her want him so much she couldn't think straight. First loves were supposed to be like that, a bit over the top, surreal, almost too good to be true, and she wondered if he'd changed.

Would he still be a great lover?

The thought notched up her temperature another few degrees and she clasped her hands firmly together, suppressing the urge to lean over and stroke his thigh.

She loved him in jeans, the denim hugging in all the right places, leaving little to her already over-stimulated imagination. She'd lain awake all night tossing and turning in her bed while less than twenty feet away had slept her sexy ex. The same ex who flirted whenever he got within two feet of her, the same ex who made her lose sight of the fact he'd be out of her life by the end of this week whenever he talked in that low, husky voice or looked at her with hunger in his blue eyes.

Their dinner had ended on a surprisingly chaste note after her true confessions but in a way she'd been relieved. It had been one hell of a day: seeing Ty first thing, lunch at Venice Beach, having him move in and dinner had left her more drained than she could've imagined.

'Your house is great. It feels like a real home.'

'My grandparents built it when they first married. Apparently they were both actors in Hollywood's early days and nothing's been done to it since then. That's why it's modest by Beverly Hills standards.'

'I like it. It's comfortable, the type of place that feels good to hang out in.'

His praise thrilled her more than it should. Why should she care what he thought of her home? He'd waltz out of it in a week without looking back.

'Thanks. I've felt like that from the minute I stepped into it.'

She'd loved living with her grandparents, the feisty old couple who had fought and made up till their dying day. They'd showered her with love and affection for the brief period they'd known each other.

'How did you meet up with your grandparents?'

'After we split up, I looked them up. I barely knew my dad, who preferred going walkabout in the outback to living in Sydney with his family, and have little to thank him for except that through him I was entitled to American citizenship. But, I knew his parents lived in Beverly Hills so I checked out the phone book, called them and they welcomed me with open arms. I lived with them for a while till they both passed away within a few months of each other.'

Her voice shook at the memory. For some reason, most of the people she loved died or left her and, though she'd come to terms with her loss a while ago, seeing Ty again and knowing she'd lose him in a week ripped open old wounds she'd thought long healed.

'Sorry seems pretty inadequate right about now.'

Ty turned to face her as the car slid to a stop. Compassion shone from his eyes and she was surprised to see something else: empathy.

She'd almost say he knew what it felt like to be shunned by parents, to yearn for love so badly you could almost taste it.

Glancing around, she noted the orphanage's rickety gates, the ancient oak tree, the crumbling stone building, and with a startling flash of insight she knew. A piece of knowledge she'd long forgotten, in fact had barely known, suddenly clicking into place.

This was why he'd dedicated his week off.

This was why he wanted her to feature an article on the place.

'You grew up here, didn't you?'

He nodded, his expression closed, before unfolding his

long legs from behind the wheel. 'Come on. Time to meet the kids and Mary.'

Mary.

Kate's initial relief that Ty's past was motivation for his interest in the orphanage faded as she watched in growing horror as he strode towards a stunning woman standing on the front steps and enveloped her in a hug.

She'd never seen anyone so delicate, so pretty. Long black hair framed a heart-shaped face, the outstanding feature a pair of intense green eyes. The woman couldn't have been more than five-two, had curves in all the right places, giving the impression of a china doll, and Kate could understand why Ty would want to pick up the porcelain princess and cradle her.

Hating the shaft of jealousy stabbing her, Kate waited till they pulled apart before approaching and holding out her hand.

'Hi. I'm Kate Hayden, a friend of Tyler's.'

'Mary Ramone. Nice to meet you.' The doll's handshake was firm, warm. 'Please come inside. Tyler's told me all about you.'

Kate winced, knowing that couldn't be true. Mary obviously had no idea she'd been so desperate for a little fun in her life that she'd stooped so low as to purchase her ex at a male auction.

'Tyler rang me first thing this morning and said you're doing a story on the orphanage? That's great.' Mary sliced freshly baked carrot cake, judging by the delicious aroma filling the kitchen, and set a percolator for coffee, her soft smile warm and friendly the entire time.

A regular little homebody too.

Stifling her bitchy side, Kate deliberately kept her answer noncommittal. 'I'm looking into it. I thought I'd check out the orphanage today and run it past my boss. He makes the final decisions as to what stories the magazine does.'

If it meant that she would have to spend more time at the

orphanage seeing Ty and Mary playing best pals hell would freeze over before *Femme* ran an article on the place.

Ty interrupted. 'Surely your input is valued, though? If you say the story is appropriate, your boss would agree?'

Reluctantly, she nodded. 'It shouldn't be a problem, though all he seems to care about at the moment is the feature on the man auction. However, we can possibly tie the two stories together.'

Mary laughed. 'I heard about that. You're a brave lady, Kate, buying this guy for a week. Good luck.'

Suddenly, shame washed through Kate. Mary seemed like a genuinely nice person. It wasn't her fault that a green-eyed monster the size of Disneyland resided in Kate's head. Or was that her heart?

'Oh, I think I can handle him.'

The man in question merely raised an eyebrow.

Mary dropped an affectionate kiss on the top of his head and Kate's heart clenched, the pain almost visceral. 'I tried looking after him for years and it didn't get me anywhere.'

Kate subdued her aching heart and tried to make polite conversation. 'So you two grew up together?'

Mary nodded. 'Yeah and he was a terror. Still is, if you ask me.'

Ty swatted her butt as she walked past. 'No one's asking you, pest.'

That did it. The sight of his hand on Mary's cute little butt even for one second was one second too long for her.

'Can we look around now? I need to pitch the idea to Henry as soon as possible if the article's to make this week's deadline.' She forced a smile when in fact she felt physically ill.

'Sure. Follow me.'

Mary led the way and Kate felt like an ogre in munchkin land as she followed the petite woman.

Why had she thought Ty could even be remotely interested

in a five-ten giant when he could have cabbage-patch cute? Not that she wanted his interest beyond this week. Right?

She repeated the silent question as Mary led her through the orphanage and introduced her to the children. Their cherubic faces almost broke her heart; that was, if it hadn't already sustained a few blows back in the kitchen.

In under an hour she'd seen enough. The orphanage would make a great human-interest story for *Femme*'s readers.

As they walked back to the car Kate made mental notes about the orphanage, anything to keep her mind occupied and off the topic of Ty and Mary.

Were they involved?

Had they ever been involved?

Did she really think she could have a week with Ty and walk away at the end?

'Thanks for the tour, Mary. Nice meeting you.'

'You too. I'm looking forward to seeing what you come up with for the article. And if you need anything else don't hesitate to call.'

Kate mumbled a vague goodbye and slid into the car, studiously avoiding watching any departing contact between Ty and Mary. No way was she a glutton for punishment.

As Ty backed the car out of the driveway her words fell out in a rush. 'I'm not sure if I can do the story.'

'What?'

'It may not work.'

Ty's hands clenched the wheel and his gaze fixed on the road but she could read the signs. Not happy.

'Why not?'

'Just trust me on this one, okay?'

He would have to because there was no way she could tell him the real reason.

'No.'

He paused for a moment and she tensed, ready for an

argument as he continued. 'Is this some strange jealousy thing on your part? Because I saw the way you looked at Mary and it's totally unnecessary. Mary's like a sister to me.'

How did he do that, read her mind as if it were an open book? Surely six years' absence should've dulled it?

Sister, huh? Sure.

'You're way off base. The world doesn't revolve around you. Besides, I'd have to care to be jealous.'

'Yeah, and your point is?'

'I don't care.'

She expected thunder and a bolt of lightning to strike her down. Or her nose to grow at least another three inches.

'Sure you do, Pinocchio.'

Damn, he'd done it again. The mental telepathy thing he had going on was really starting to annoy her.

She crossed her arms, digging her nails into her upper arms, and her mouth twitched as she remembered doing the same thing years ago whenever she'd stood her ground around him.

'I'm just not sure about the story, okay? Let's leave it at that.'

'No story, no Tyler.'

'Pardon?'

'You need me…for your article.'

He'd left a sufficient pause to insinuate just how he thought she needed him.

She swore softly. He was right, on both counts.

'So what's it to be? My full co-operation in exchange for a story on the orphanage?'

Unfortunately, she had a fair idea what his full co-operation would involve. Which was totally outrageous and yet…

'I don't like being blackmailed.'

He chuckled. 'It's a deal, then. So, when should we get started?'

She didn't know if he meant on the interview, the story or the co-operation.

'I hate it when you're cocky.'

He pulled into her driveway before answering, his blue eyes sparking with the knowledge that he had the upper hand.

'No. You just hate it when I'm right.'

In response, she sent him a haughty glare and slammed the car door. Not that she was particularly annoyed with him when she was the one acting like a jealous schoolgirl.

Logically, she knew there hadn't been the slightest sign of flirtation between Ty and Mary, and even if there had been she had no right to feel this way.

Ty was her past. Just because she had him in her life again for a week didn't mean she owned him. Far from it. He'd always been his own man, independent to the nth degree, and she'd been the same way. They'd parted on civil terms so why was she going all mushy now?

Damn it, this business wasn't turning out the way she'd hoped. What happened to having fun? She needed to lighten up, a lot.

'When are you going to start obeying me like a good Odd Bod should?'

Unlocking the front door and punching in the alarm code, she entered the room, grateful for the familiar rush that enveloped her whenever she came home. No matter how busy or crazy her life got, she always had the comfort of this place.

Ty brushed past her, the soft cotton of his T-shirt scraping against the bare skin on her arm and sending an unexpected tingle racing through her. Taking a seat on the couch, he laid his arms across the back of it and crossed his ankles, long denim-clad legs stretched out in front in a typical, casual, 'I'm in control' pose.

'When hell freezes over.'

To top it off he grinned, that infuriating, sexy smile that notched up the heat all over again.

She stared, unsure whether to kiss him or throw the nearest thing handy, which happened to be an expensive antique vase. Instead, she took a deep breath and walked towards the kitchen.

'Where are you going? Tired of playing already?'

She didn't break stride. She wouldn't give him the satisfaction. Especially when laughter bubbled up within and she almost snorted trying to control it.

'No. Just stocking up on ice blocks, turning up the air-conditioning and ordering a blizzard.'

His warm chuckles wrapped around her, a comforting sound that never failed to raise a smile.

'That's it. Crank up the cold treatment. Not that it's going to do you any good.'

'Want to make a bet?'

She stopped in the doorway and turned to face him, wondering how far she could push him, wondering if this time their banter would lead where she'd wanted it to from the first minute she'd laid eyes on him again, with her cocooned in his arms and his body doing incredible things to hers.

'I'm a SEAL, remember? I can handle anything you care to dish out.'

'Big statement. But can you deliver?'

Ty didn't move a muscle, but she could see the tension in his bulging biceps as he surreptitiously gripped the back of the sofa and the swift flare of fire in his eyes as they darkened to midnight.

Taking a deep breath, knowing this was it, she murmured, 'Dare you.'

He leaped off the couch and walked towards her, sending her new-found seductive powers spiralling out of control as she inadvertently backed away till the breakfast counter digging into her back stopped her short.

Heart pounding with excitement, fear and trepidation, she said the first thing that came into her head. 'How about a swim first?'

'So what I'm hearing is that you want us to get our gear off and get wet?'

His eyes gleamed with challenge and, damn him, he knew she would never back away from one.

They'd always been like this: fiery, spontaneous, playful and challenging. Always trying to get the better of the other, always playing the game, trying to outwit the other.

Well, time to resurrect old times and have her fun in the process.

She tilted her head up, determined to stare him down. 'Yeah, that's exactly what I want.'

He smiled and ran one finger lightly down her bare arm, sending fireworks shooting through her body and liquid heat pooling in all the right places.

'Be careful what you wish for, Katie.'

'Why? Think you can make all my dreams come true?'

She managed to stay upright as his finger slid up her arm, across her collar-bone and towards her ear lobe in agonising slowness.

'I'm here to do whatever you want me to.' He tapped the end of her nose and smiled. 'Me the Odd Bod, you the boss, remember? Meet you out the back in a minute.'

She stared as he turned and strutted out of the kitchen, leaving her hot and trembling and wanting him more than ever.

CHAPTER EIGHT

OKAY, so this hadn't been one of her smarter ideas. When she'd suggested they take a swim she'd imagined cooling off a tad before she took the plunge with Ty in more ways than one.

However, she should've known better. If the thought of Ty wearing nothing but trunks was enough to send her body into meltdown, what hope did she have when confronted with the real thing?

As if on cue he strutted out to the pool, dropped his towel on the nearest chair, flashed a cocky smile and stepped into the water. She'd expected him to execute a fancy dive into the deep end, but it looked as if his knee, which he unconsciously rubbed or flexed at times, must be giving him more trouble than he let on.

'Come on in. The water's great.'

He trod water as his gaze slid over her body, starting at her toes and slowly working its way up, leaving a trail of super-sensitised skin as if he'd physically touched her.

'Nice bikini you're almost wearing.'

He grinned and dived under the water before she could reply, not that she could've given him a coherent response if she'd tried.

The way he'd looked at her, with adoration, with desire, had her insides tied up in knots along with her tongue.

Not that she'd said much of anything since he'd strolled out to the pool, every rippling muscle on display. She'd feasted her eyes, memorising every line and plane of his body to savour and dissect later. Washboard abs, moulded pecs, lean yet hard legs. All that a girl could ask for and he was freestyling in her pool, inviting her in. What was she waiting for?

She knew.

She knew that the minute she entered the water any last semblance of self-control would exit her mind. If they so much as touched, skin to skin, without the flimsy barrier of clothes she'd lose it.

Wasn't that what she wanted?

Her body screamed yes while her heart reserved its better judgment.

This wasn't just a casual fling.

This was her ex she was considering making love with.

And though they'd both made it clear they wanted nothing more at the end of the week, she was scared.

Scared of her memories, scared of how he made her feel, scared of wanting too much and most of all scared of falling for him all over again.

Damn it, why couldn't she let go of her inhibitions and enjoy the week as two friends getting reacquainted before moving on?

Because this was Ty she was talking about and she knew what would happen if she dropped her guard altogether.

She'd spent a lifetime playing it safe thanks to her overprotective mother, and though she'd escaped Doris's influence years ago she still found herself making the right decisions all the time, the conservative choices.

Maybe just this once she could do the opposite?

Bracing herself, she muttered, 'Ready or not, here I come,' and stepped into the tepid water, knowing she was far from ready but willing to take the plunge anyway.

Tyler surfaced in time to watch Kate step into the water.

He'd hoped a lazy five laps would take the edge off his hunger but it hadn't. He'd been aroused the minute he'd spotted her in that barely there bikini, the black triangles held together by flimsy string. One tug and all that lushness could spill into his waiting hands.

Kate had always been temptation personified but the beautiful young woman she'd been had blossomed into a sexy siren and he had to answer her call.

Yeah, she was pure temptation, all right. She'd been toying with him since the auction and it was time to put an end to it. He was a SEAL not a Boy Scout. She'd pushed all his buttons and he couldn't hold out any longer.

Time to see if his smart-mouthed ex stood by her word.

'You were right. The water feels great.'

She hadn't moved far from the steps as if poised for flight and he knew he'd have to take the lead. Not that it bothered him. Taking charge was what he did best.

However, as much as he wanted Kate, and he pretty much knew she wanted him as badly, a small part of him wished she'd make the first move just as she had all those years ago.

'Come in. You'll love it.'

Their eyes locked and he saw her pupils dilate, whether in shock or anticipation he didn't know.

This was it, the moment when she'd flee or stay. God, he wanted her, more than ever.

Suddenly, it happened.

She submerged beneath the water for several seconds and swam towards him, and when she finally stood before him, water sluicing down her luscious body, he couldn't speak.

If his life went belly-up after this week he'd remember this moment for all eternity, treasuring the sight of the gorgeous woman he'd once been lucky enough to share a relationship with staring at him with tentative longing in her expressive hazel eyes.

'Hope you didn't burn up too much energy with all those laps.'

She smiled, a slow, upward turning of her lips that undid him completely and he growled as he reached for her, pulling her close.

'I'm trained for stamina. I was just getting warmed up.'

She wrapped her legs around him, just stopping short of bringing her intimate heat in contact with him, and he gritted his teeth, barely able to restrain himself from tearing off the flimsy barrier of cloth between them and taking her on the spot.

'So, are you?'

In response, he pulled her flush against him, almost groaning aloud as she rubbed against him. 'What does it feel like to you?'

She looped her arms around his neck and snuggled closer. 'I'd say warm-up's over and it's time for the main game to start.'

He stared at her, mesmerised by the glowing gold flecks in her eyes, by the heat that shimmered and flared in her irises.

She'd always been so responsive, so eager, and in a flash he knew he'd missed her more than he'd let himself believe all these years.

Unable to resist a second longer he slanted his mouth over hers, amazed at the instant response of her lips, putting every ounce of feeling into the kiss.

Like the few times they'd kissed already he combusted in an instant, his control shredded as he wanted to devour her, to taste her, to examine every inch of her exquisite body with his hands and his mouth and his tongue.

He cupped her butt as she rocked her hips against him, inflaming the burning heat sizzling between them.

'Ty, I want—'

'I know, Katie. I want you too.'

More than was rational. More than was sane.

He shouldn't want her this much, need her this much.

They were over at the end of this week. His head believed it; the rest of him had some serious catching up to do.

The water lapped around them as he waded towards the steps, eager to get inside quickly before the last of his self-control vanished and he took her here and now without protection.

As he strode towards the house Kate wiggled against him and he cupped her butt tighter.

'Do you have a thing for my ass?' she whispered in his ear, her teasing tongue flicking around his ear lobe.

'Sweetheart, I have a thing for *all* of you.'

He gently squeezed, bringing her in closer contact to the evidence of how much of a thing he had for her, knowing that whatever happened with his career next week, whatever happened with the rest of his life, he'd never regret getting together with Kate again.

She was worth it, every special inch of her.

Kate clung to Ty, her skin on fire. She had trouble breathing with his hands splayed across her butt, holding her so close their bodies were plastered together.

Memories came flooding back, overwhelming in their intensity as she remembered the first time he'd held her like this, the first time he'd undressed her, the first time they'd touched skin to skin.

She would've done anything to have him back then. In a way she had, going as far as proposing to him to hang onto the magic they'd created.

But that had been plain silly. They'd both been too young, too driven, too career-oriented.

And now? Could Ty make her lose her mind over him again?

Sighing, she closed her eyes and shivered with pleasure as his strides ate up the distance to her bedroom.

This wasn't a time for thinking or analysing or remembering the past.

This was about here, now and the pleasure she knew only he could give.

As he laid her on the bed her eyes fluttered open and she gazed into the face of the sexiest man she'd ever known. He was all hers, even if it was only for a week.

'I'll be back. Wait for me.'

He feathered a kiss across her lips and she watched him walk out the door, transfixed by the perfection of his body.

Not that he had to ask. She wasn't going anywhere as long as he came back soon and doused the flames that were threatening to burn her alive. Stretching her arms overhead, she savoured the languorous heat that started at her toes, flowed to her fingertips and all the places in between, luxuriating in the feeling of being a desired woman.

'You're incredible.'

Gazing into her eyes, he lay down beside her, slowly running his hand down her arm, and she trembled beneath his touch and turned towards him, eager to feel him flush against her again.

'Uh-uh. Not so fast.'

He smiled, an intimate, sensual smile designed just for her, the type of smile she'd melted under countless times before as he stilled her frantic hands, capturing her wrists and holding them overhead. Reaching behind her neck, he freed the knot holding her bikini bra up and her breath hitched as the Lycra tumbled onto the bed, baring her breasts.

'Oh, Ty,' she murmured as he blew on her damp skin, the ferocity of his gaze burning her with its intensity. 'Please…'

'I know, sweetheart. I know.'

He nibbled at her mouth, her jaw-line and trailed lower, leaving a scorching line of fire branded against her skin and she caught her bottom lip between her teeth to keep from crying out.

He stilled for an instant, caressing her cheek with the tenderness she'd always found so surprising in a man of his profession, a man who relied on cunning and power and brute strength to obtain a mission objective.

'Is this what you want?'

Another typical Ty trait: honour. He was giving her an out, one she had no intention of taking him up on.

'Definitely.'

She nodded shyly and his cheeky grin sent her heart lurching for cover.

Her heart? Not good.

This had to be just sex. She couldn't risk anything more.

Physical, she could do.

Emotional, no way.

'What else would my boss like?'

He trailed his lips down her stomach, not waiting for an answer, every kiss teasing her, torturing her, making her want him more than she'd ever wanted anything in her life.

'Surprise me,' she murmured, though he didn't seem to hear, all his attention focussed on her body.

She should have been self-conscious as the afternoon sunlight streamed into her bedroom, but with Ty gazing at her body with reverence she felt like a goddess.

'Okay,' he murmured a second before his tongue hit her navel, laving it thoroughly as her hips arched off the bed and her desperate need for him went into orbit.

'So, that's a definite yes, then,' he murmured as he slid his hands under her butt and raised her towards him.

Feather-light kisses skimmed along her bikini line before he pressed his mouth against the wet material and she gasped as the heat of his mouth burned through the clinging Lycra, sending her one step closer to electrifying oblivion.

'Here. Let me.'

He tugged at the side strings, peeling the bikini bottoms away in one fluid motion before returning to exploring her intimate folds with his talented tongue.

Her mind and body took flight as he probed and suckled the swollen flesh of her core, sending her into another plane as she arched into his mouth, yelling his name.

Several mind-blowing, exquisite moments later she lay limp, barely aware as he shimmied up to lay alongside her once again.

Maybe her memories were foggy, maybe it had been too long since she'd had sex, but whatever the reason Ty had just sent her to heaven and back.

They'd always been good together but wow!

'We have lift-off,' he whispered against the side of her mouth, wearing a smile and little else as he draped an arm across her body.

'And how.'

Rousing herself out of her blissful stupor, she reached towards him, the sight of his erection sending shivers through her body all over again.

'When did those come off?' She pointed to the wet trunks lying in a sodden puddle on the floor.

'About the same time yours did—' Ty bit back the rest of his words as she took him in her hands.

'How about we swap roles for now? You're the boss and I'm the Odd Bod. Tell me what you want, Ty.'

She gently squeezed, sliding her hand up and down his shaft, remembering how much he liked foreplay as much as she did.

He groaned as his thumb caressed her nipple. 'You're doing just great on your own, sweetheart. No instruction from me needed.'

Tyler tensed as her fingers lightly brushed over the head of his straining penis, pleasure and pain warring as he barely held onto what little control he had left.

He'd waited for this moment since he'd first laid eyes on Kate again and having her satisfied and hot and horny in his arms was almost too good to be true.

'Sure?'

She wrapped her fingers around his length, moulding to it, blowing his mind, and he stilled her hand before he lost it completely.

'Hell, yeah.'

She'd just shattered whatever self-control he had with her tentative yet firm grip and he reached towards the bedside table, quickly ripping open the foil pack he'd had the sense to grab earlier, and sheathed himself.

'Glad someone's prepared,' she said as she watched him, the gold flecks in her eyes glowing fiery amber, the exact colour of the Sahara at dusk last time he'd been stationed there.

He lowered his weight back onto the mattress, his heart pounding at the need reflected in her beautiful face.

'Why did you think I went out before?'

She draped a long leg over his, tempting, hot, seductive. 'I didn't care as long as you came back.'

His heart clenched at the vulnerable look that flickered across her face and warning bells clanged in his head.

Maybe this wasn't such a great idea.

He didn't want to hurt Kate. What if she wanted more than he was willing to give, more than just this week?

He'd had his doubts about her ability to separate the past and the present but he'd doused whatever doubts he had with a good healthy dose of lust. Maybe he should've listened a little harder to his voice of reason, the same voice that had served him well through the hairiest of missions?

However, his conscience didn't stand a chance when she rubbed against him with her warm, slick entrance that led straight to heaven, sending his good intentions skyward too.

Knowing nothing could ever feel as good as this, he probed gently before sliding into her welcoming heat, the sheer rush of pleasure making him groan.

'Katie, you feel so good.'

She stared at him from beneath long eyelashes, desire blazing in her eyes, and the depth of her passion shocked him, that she should want him as much as he wanted her.

It was written in her eyes, in her face; she couldn't have spelled it out any clearer, and the thought that this beautiful, amazing woman wanted him was humbling beyond belief. He wouldn't disappoint her.

'You've been calling me Katie,' she whispered, something akin to awe spreading across her face as he started to rock.

'Do you like it?'

He increased the tempo, sliding out and thrusting into the hilt, encouraging her to join him on a wild and unrestrained ride.

Her answering moan fuelled his fire. 'I haven't heard it in a while. Only you've ever called me that. I like it.'

'Do you like this too?'

He couldn't wait any longer as her response took him to the next level, striving to give them both the ultimate pleasure, eager to give her the world if he could.

He hadn't thought she could climb any higher after her first shattering orgasm but he'd been wrong. Very wrong.

Her breasts swayed as he pounded into her and her short, panting cries urged him to the end, each powerful thrust bringing them closer to the edge, their voices blending as they tumbled over, clinging to each other.

Collapsing onto the bed, he exhaled slowly. If they'd burned up the sheets six years earlier it had nothing on the heat they generated now.

He'd lost his mind, shot to the stars and was still dazed as he realized that walking away from something this good, again, was going to be harder than any dangerous mission he'd ever had to face.

Silence enfolded them, broken only by the sound of ragged breathing as the realisation hit that this might've been more than just sex for him. Hell.

'Wow.'

She gave a low, husky laugh against his chest as she curled into him and he pushed aside his awkward thoughts and concentrated on Kate.

He snuggled her closer and grinned. 'If this is what being an Odd Bod's all about, shackle me for ever and throw away the key.'

'Be careful what you wish for...'

Her soft voice trailed off, hitting him where he was most vulnerable.

His conscience.

Kate might've said she wanted nothing from him beyond this week, but in the past she'd wanted to play for keeps.

Then what the hell was she doing playing with him now?

'What a dummy.'

Kate stepped out of the shower, aching in places she hadn't ached for a long time, though pleasantly so. The afternoon had been incredible and if the number of torn foil packets in her bin was any indication she would be aching for a while yet.

However, that wasn't the reason she was chastising herself as she towelled dry. The sex had been amazing, it was the aftermath that had her cringing. She'd been stupid enough to snuggle up to Ty, chatting about the years since she'd last seen him and expecting to have a light supper in bed before resuming where they had left off that afternoon.

Wrong. He'd barely lasted thirty minutes, holding her as if she were a ticking time bomb before beating a hasty retreat with a mumbled excuse about meeting someone.

So much for post-coital bliss.

She slipped into a sweatshirt and track pants and padded into the kitchen, needing comfort food. Ice cream or chocolate would do. At this point, anything with sugar in it would pass. Grabbing a pack of choc-chip cookies, she flopped into a nearby chair and tore the top off.

Who had she been trying to kid, convincing herself that one week with him would be enough? The afternoon's horizontal activities had well and truly put paid to that brilliant idea.

One taste and she was hooked all over again.

Being addicted to Ty was way too dangerous and she'd been stupid enough to kick-start the habit.

A knock on the front door roused her and she padded into the hallway to open it.

'Surprise. Thought I'd drop by with that material you were after.'

Though Di smiled at her, Kate watched her PA's gaze wander past her shoulder and into the room behind. No prizes for guessing who she was trying to catch a glimpse of.

Kate opened the door further. 'Come on in.'

Di winked. 'Only if I'm not interrupting anything.'

'You're not.'

'That's not what it looks like to me.' Di wiggled her eyebrows suggestively.

'Huh?'

Kate wondered if she was that easy to read. Surely the fact that she'd just had the best sex of her life didn't show?

'You've got that look, boss.'

Di handed over a pile of work, sat on the couch and folded her legs under her, her cheeky smirk saying it all.

'What look? Want a drink?'

Kate shook her head, hoping her hair would hide the guilty smile that was getting harder to disguise by the minute.

Di waggled her index finger. 'Don't distract me with beverages. I came here for gossip, not coffee. And that look says you've been swimming with the SEALS.'

Heat seeped into Kate's cheeks at the memory of what her afternoon dip with Ty had led to.

'So? What's the harm in that?'

Di ran a hand through her blonde spikes, re-creating her trademark porcupine look with little effort. 'I knew it! You got wet and wild with that guy. Details, I want details.'

'Not much to tell. We're getting along okay.'

Kate shrugged, determined to play down her involvement with Ty.

'What aren't you telling me?'

'Nothing.' Kate's mutinous silence didn't deter Di.

Her assistant hugged her knees and leaned forward, as if she had all the time in the world to listen. 'Spill it.'

What could she say? That she was falling for her ex all over again? How stupid would that be considering he'd made it clear he'd be out of her life again in a few days?

'I don't get it. Looks like you two have hit it off. Why don't you just enjoy the week with Adonis and who cares what happens after that?'

That was just it. Kate *did* care.

She cared a lot and it scared her. And if there was one thing she didn't do it was scare easy.

She'd survived a rough childhood with a bitter mother who blamed her for her father's absence.

She'd survived a new start in a strange country and she'd forged a fabulous career.

She was an Aussie battler and never stayed down for long.

So what was she doing wishing her week of having fun would turn into something more?

Di's squeal broke Kate's silence.

'Oh, no. You've fallen for him, haven't you?' She smacked her head. 'Girlfriend, what are you thinking?'

Kate smiled at Di's theatrics. 'I wasn't.'

'The idea of buying a man is to use him, not the other way round. See what happens when you don't get out much?'

'I get out enough.'

Kate knew that falling for Ty again had nothing to do with the number of men she had or hadn't dated. The minute she'd seen him at the auction she'd wanted him all for herself, past or not. 'Can we change the subject, please?'

'Whatever. Though you call me if you need me, okay? I have to get back to the office. How did you wangle a week to work from home anyway? I thought Henry had you under serious pressure?'

'Henry's not that bad. He knows I'm a professional. I'll deliver the story he wants whether I'm in the office or not.'

She wished she could tell Di about the promotion but she couldn't. Henry would announce his retirement and replacement in his own good time.

Di cast her a strange look. 'If this is what having a man around does to you, perhaps you should go back to being single.' She stopped at the doorway and looked Kate up and down. 'And a word of advice. Lose the sweats. Maybe that's why you're not getting any.'

'I'm getting plenty!' The words flew out of Kate's mouth before she could think.

Di poked her head around the closing door. 'Gotcha. Knew I'd get details out of you eventually. See ya round, chickadee.'

Kate poked her tongue out at Di's retreating back.

So much for not thinking about Ty. Chatting with Di had cemented the thoughts that had been whirling around in her head since he'd left and unfortunately, once acknowledged, the facts couldn't be ignored.

She was falling for him. Again.

And there wasn't one damn thing she could do about it.

CHAPTER NINE

TYLER had never run away from anything in his life. Even as a kid he'd stood his ground and fought his own battles and since joining the Navy standing up for what he believed had become ingrained, entrenched, and unshakeable. It was part and parcel of being a SEAL.

Then why had he run out of Kate's house as if the enemy were on his tail? To make matters worse he'd acted like a complete jerk in the process.

Retreat had been his only defence when he'd held her in his arms and listened to her anecdotes. If he hadn't run he would still be cocooned in her bed, enjoying the feeling of belonging there way too much.

He couldn't do it.

Why build false hope when all they had together was a week?

At least they had that and making love with Kate had blown his mind. She'd been insatiable, matching his needs in every way, as if she remembered all his erogenous zones and all the ways to please him.

Damn it, after a week with her he'd never be the same again. She'd raised the bar in more ways than one.

And what had he done? He'd run.

He could've cradled her in his arms all evening but the minute she'd started talking to him like the good old days he'd bolted.

He needed time out. No use letting their intense attraction get in the way of logic and no matter how Kate made him feel or how much he wished things could be different, they weren't. He'd made a promise to himself and he'd stick to it. He'd just have to stay focussed on the mission at hand— which was to enjoy every precious second with Kate—and not think beyond this week.

Strolling into the rec room at the base, he headed for the corner table where Bear sat nursing a giant coffee. The big guy's call on his cell phone had been welcome. His friend had mentioned something about saving the orphanage and he'd been hooked. Though in fairness Bear could've talked about walking on water and he would've been hooked, anything to wrench his thoughts away from Kate and how she made him feel.

'Howdy, Bear. What's happening?'

Bear shook his hand and kicked out the chair opposite. 'Could ask you the same thing. How's the odd-job business going?'

Tyler helped himself to coffee from a nearby machine and sat down. 'Remember that mission to Liberia? Way easier.'

Bear let out a long, low whistle. 'That bad, huh?'

'Worse.'

'This woman's got your number, huh?'

'Oh, yeah. And she knows just how to punch all the right buttons.'

Bear chuckled. 'Never thought I'd see the day, TJ taken down by a woman. Good one.'

No, it wasn't good. Not by a long shot. The more time he spent with Kate, the harder it would be to walk away. He'd already done it once and it had almost killed him.

This time it would be damn near impossible: he liked being in her cosy house, in sharing simple things like dinner, a swim, a bathroom.

He liked the feeling of belonging, of cohabiting with her, of feeling her gaze on him.

Hell, he liked it all and he was going to pay for it the minute he walked out of her life and the old terror gripped him: the loneliness, the urge to call her and the fear that he'd weaken and wouldn't be able to follow through on his promise to put her needs first whatever the cost to himself.

He'd thought he had a handle on loneliness as a kid, hiding behind a nonchalant façade, acting tough, and the persona had served him well enough as he'd existed within four walls of equally tough kids who'd also turned against the world and all its injustice. He'd survived alone and learned a valuable lesson along the way. Never depend on anyone. Ever. He relied on number one: no disappointment, no expectations, no pain, just the way he liked it.

He'd just have to remind himself of that the next time Kate looked at him with those hazel eyes of hers, drawing him in deeper and swifter than quicksand.

One thing was for sure—handling loneliness as a kid would be easy compared with what he'd have to face losing her this time around.

'What did you want to talk about, Bear?'

'Just wanted to chew the fat over a couple of ideas to save the orphanage. I was wondering if Team Eight could do anything. A marathon? Triathalon? You know the guys. They're always up for a challenge.'

'Thanks for the offer but I'm working on it.'

'How so?'

'I've persuaded Kate into doing some publicity by placing a big article in her magazine.'

Bear grinned. 'I'm not going to even ask what methods you used to *persuade* the lady in question.'

'Can it. I got enough grief the other night from Jack. I don't need it from you too.'

His friend seemed to sense his mood. 'This isn't serious, is it?'

'Depends on your interpretation of serious.' Tyler paused and stared into his coffee, knowing he had to confide in someone before he bust a gut. 'We were engaged once. How's that for serious?'

His friend's jaw dropped. 'What?'

Tyler nodded and managed a wry grin. 'Yeah, told you. Real serious.'

'What the—?'

'We met six years ago. She'd just come over from Australia, I'd just completed BUD/S training. We both kinda lost it for a while there.'

'You, engaged?' Bear shook his head, a stunned expression on his weather-worn face.

'It was a bit of a lark, really. She proposed to me, I jokingly said yeah, but we never got round to making any plans. We were both starting out on our careers; it wouldn't have made sense to stay tied. Not with me traipsing the world on missions never sure if I'd return or not. Anyway, it's all ancient history now.'

History. As in *the past*.

He'd be a damn sight better off if he remembered it.

What they shared now had to be a logical extension of two people who'd once hooked up for all the wrong reasons getting reacquainted. Nothing more. It couldn't be.

Bear opened and closed his mouth several times before managing to speak. '*Engaged*? No way. You never said anything. Does anyone know?'

'No. And I'd like to keep it that way. Besides, we only lived together for a few months. We were practically kids. It's no big deal.'

His friend swiped a hand over his face as if waking from a long sleep. 'Okay, you two were once an item, now you're trailing after her for a week? You gonna explain or what?'

Tyler shrugged. 'Nothing to explain. We've been apart for six years, she turned up at the auction and bought me, we're spending a week together and that's that. End of story. No complications, just two people catching up.'

When he put it like that it sounded so simple, so logical. Then why did his heart feel as if it had been twisted and ripped in half?

Bear paused, downed the last of his coffee and cast a puzzled look his way. 'Why are you still running, TJ?'

Tyler hated when his best friend was right. They'd been dive buddies for a long time before his knee blew out and Bear knew him better than anyone.

'I'm not. I just like to move around.'

'Yeah, I've heard that one before. You've been running your whole life and looks like nothing has changed. Have you told her about the physical?'

'What for?' Tyler glared, annoyed by his friend's accurate assumptions and wishing Bear weren't spot on. 'It's not relevant.'

Besides, he didn't want Kate's pity if he didn't pass and had to leave his beloved Navy behind, nor did he want her sticking around, maybe spending more time with him out of some warped sense of loyalty for what they'd once shared.

She deserved better. He'd always felt that way, which had made walking away the first time around just about bearable. He just had to remember it at the end of this week too.

Bear shook his head. 'If I need to tell you that you're wrong you're dumber than you look. You better do some thinking, man, and quick. Starting now.'

'What's there to think about? Kate's a great girl. She's intelligent, gorgeous and on her way to the top. What would she want with a washed-up SEAL who has no idea what to do with his life?'

There, he'd voiced his inner thoughts out loud, the same thoughts that had driven him out of her house when he'd realised that making love with her had been more about re-establishing emotional links with someone he still cared deeply about rather than a simple physical release.

Bear folded his arms and leaned forward, fixing him with the intimidating glare that had caused many a recruit to take a backward step.

'You're full of trash. In all the time I've known you I've never seen you spend more than a few dates with one woman, let alone get engaged to any of them. Now here you are giving me some spiel about how this wonder-woman is too good for you? Come on, TJ. I know you better than that. You've still got a thing for her and you're running scared, just like I said before.'

His friend stood and shrugged into his bomber jacket, shaking his head. 'Jeez, you've got it bad. I'll be damned. Anyway, I have to report in to the Chief. Later.'

Tyler watched his friend exit the bar and breathed a sigh of relief. If he'd wanted an interrogation he'd have allowed himself to be captured years ago. Bear was no slouch and had him pegged.

He *had* spent a lifetime running away from his demons.

How ironic that it looked as if the past might catch up with him yet?

Kate stretched, rubbed her eyes and looked at the clock in amazement. She never slept as late as nine.

Must've been all the exercise yesterday.

She ignored the thought and pushed out of bed, taking a full minute to realise that Ty wasn't around.

He hadn't returned last night.

So much for getting reacquainted. He'd had one taste and run ten miles in the opposite direction.

Swiping a hand across her gritty eyes and silently cursing herself for being such a fool, she stuck her feet into faded floral flip-flops and padded into the kitchen. Switching on the percolator, she leaned against the benchtop, surprised when the doorbell rang.

Hating the way her pulse quickened at the hope it could be Ty, she opened the door, her traitorous heart lurching at the sight of her errant houseguest wearing tight black jeans and matching T-shirt, a hint of dark stubble covering his jaw. The ultimate bad boy in the flesh; and she was so tired of being good.

'Brought you breakfast.'

He held out a bag of muffins with a slight smile playing about his mouth. That oh-so-gorgeous mouth with lips that had tasted and teased and driven her insane with need yesterday.

'Peace-offering, huh?'

Opening the door wider, she took the bag, opened it and inhaled deeply; apple cinnamon, her favourite—and she was touched that he'd remembered while trying desperately not to show it.

He strolled into the living room as if he belonged there, looking way too relaxed while she stood there feeling like yesterday's news, something he'd read and discarded.

'Didn't know I needed one. Are you angry about something?'

She squirmed under his disconcerting stare. 'Not really. Though you didn't come home last night…'

She trailed off, mentally kicking herself for sounding like a nagging girlfriend. He might be her odd-job guy for a week but he owed her nothing.

'I had some stuff to take care of back at the base, so I crashed there. No big deal, right?'

'Right.'

She stomped into the kitchen, eager to put as much distance between them as humanly possible before she did something stupid like give him a welcome-home kiss. Or hit him for summing up what she already knew but didn't want to hear.

He was right, this wasn't a big deal and she had no right to question him about his whereabouts no matter how much it burned her up inside.

She busied herself with breakfast, ignoring his stare boring into her back as he followed her into the kitchen.

'Going for a run?'

She whirled around to find him lounging in the doorway, looking her up and down.

'No. I slept in these.'

It wasn't as if she had to impress anyone, least of all him.

He smirked. It should've dented his good looks yet predictably it didn't.

'Who made you the pyjama police anyway?'

She tossed her hair in an 'I don't give a damn what you think' action and bit into a muffin, savouring the burst of tart fruit and sweet spice, barely managing to swallow the first bite as he stalked towards her, a dangerous gleam in his eyes.

'Pull over, driver, and show me your licence.'

He placed his arms either side of her, effectively pinning her into a corner between the benchtop and the pantry, his lowered, husky voice rippling over her in a caress.

She shouldn't play this game. Didn't she have any self-respect?

What they'd shared yesterday hadn't meant a thing to him otherwise he would've stuck around, maybe for an all-night encore. Instead, she'd slept alone. Correction, she'd lain awake half the night alone, listening out for his return, hating herself for feeling so needy.

For her, making love hadn't just been about having fun, and now that she knew it she'd be a fool to go there again.

'Licence, driver?'

Desire flooded her body as he leaned towards her and a waft of fresh citrus soap hit her reeling senses, leaving her confused and dazed and yearning.

How could any red-blooded woman resist a sexy male at his teasing best?

'Uh…I don't have it on me,' she said, transfixed by the dark silver flecks in the blue sea of his eyes, captured by the unadulterated lust she glimpsed there.

He lowered his head one infinitely slow inch at a time till his lips brushed hers in a barely there kiss.

'Then I'll just have to frisk you,' he whispered against the corner of her mouth, her heart flipping in sync with her common sense.

Screw common sense.

She'd done the sensible thing her whole life, particularly since Ty had walked out of it. She'd been the epitome of a good little career girl striving straight for the top and where had it got her? Successful in the boardroom, barely a ripple in the bedroom.

In some warped way maybe this was a golden opportunity to show Ty that cosying up to him in bed yesterday hadn't been a sign that she cared, that she could do the casual thing and stay emotionally detached.

If anything, she needed to prove it to herself. She might have fallen for him again but that didn't mean she had to lose the plot completely.

They'd always set the world on fire physically. Why not prove that making love didn't have to involve complication of feelings? Yeah, there was only one way to prove it and that was lose herself in Ty again.

Happy with her self-rationalisation—even if a small part of her recognised that her logic was flawed—she moulded her lips to his, opening her mouth under his increasing pressure.

Their tongues tentatively met, reaching to explore further as heat flooded through her. He nibbled on her bottom lip, sucking gently before dipping his tongue into her mouth once again, teasing her, pleasing her.

Flawed logic? What logic?

The minute his lips had touched hers again she'd been a goner. Wasting precious seconds rationalising anything when it came to this guy was foolhardy.

She was putty in his hands; always had been, always would be.

'So, are you going to arrest me?' she managed to say as his lips trailed towards her ear lobe, planting delicate butterfly kisses along the way and making her melt into a puddle of need.

'Still hung up on being bound to me, huh?'

He licked the delicate skin behind her ear, sending sparks shooting along every nerve-ending in her over-sensitised body as she arched towards him, desperate for more, desperate for him to assuage the growing tension winding her body tighter than a spring.

'Whatever turns you on.' She gasped as he finally reached for her and pulled her flush against him, her body tingling all over at the contact, the remaining muffin clutched in her hand pulverised into crumbs and scattering on the floor like the last remnants of her resistance.

She reached for him blindly, sliding her hands underneath his T-shirt, her fingertips tracing a light path down the warm skin, encouraged by his swift intake of breath.

'Does this turn you on?'

He ground his hips in a slow, undulating rhythm, leaving her breathless and dizzy with need.

'Or maybe this?'

He slid his hands under her top, cupping her breasts as fire streaked from his erotic touch to the very heart of her.

'Or this?'

He trailed a hand across her stomach and lower, much lower…

'I want it all,' she ground out, wondering where all reason fled to when Ty touched her.

She'd always been like this around him: yearning, melting, hungry for him, and it looked as if nothing had changed. Right now she was ravenous and staring in wonder at a virtual smorgasbord of delicacies all wrapped up in one delectable, edible package.

'Greed is good,' Tyler murmured, his hands continuing their leisurely exploration of her body, every sweet curve a precious memory to be stored and savoured when he took the only option available and bailed on her at the end of this week.

Kate held onto him, unsteady on her feet, awakening every protective urge within him to hold her close and never let go.

'You've done something to my bones,' she said, her eyes glowing like polished topaz in the morning light streaming into the kitchen.

'And you've sure done something to mine.'

He leaned into her again to emphasise the point as she smiled, a self-satisfied grin that made him want to tease her for ever as she fiddled with his zipper.

'My, my. So I have.'

Her confident touch belied the feigned innocence on her face as he reached into his back pocket, thankful he'd had enough foresight to keep a condom in his wallet.

'Always prepared, huh?'

She reached for the foil packet, tore it and unrolled the latex over him in an instant. He'd never thought using protection could be erotic but Kate's skilled hands put paid to that preconception.

'Yeah, that's me. A regular Boy Scout.'

He stripped quickly, feasting his eyes on her exquisite body as she shimmied out of the baggy cotton, his erection giving a painful throb as he absorbed every gorgeous inch of her.

'Nothing boyish about you.'

The mischievous glimmer in her eyes as she stared at him

and opened her arms made him feel ten feet tall, as if he were the only man in the world for her.

But he wasn't. He couldn't be.

She needed a man to give her everything and he couldn't be that man no matter how much he wanted to.

Picking her up, he held her close, enjoying the sensation of her full breasts pressed against his chest, soft mounds against hard muscle.

'You make me feel so good.'

She stared directly into his eyes as her hips arched towards him, her legs wrapping around him, urging him on and he slid into her, filling every inch of her slick heat, groaning with the exquisite pleasure of it, watching her eyes widen as he moved within her. Slowly. Very slowly.

'The feeling's mutual, sweetheart.'

Withdrawing, he plunged into her again, the friction of his flesh inside her burning dampness sending him to the edge much faster than he wanted.

'This is so amazing,' she murmured, squeezing him tighter with her legs, egging him on with her low, soft moans, her panting answer spurring him on as he groaned and sank into her again and again, his thrusts reaching fever pitch.

Her ecstatic cries of release undid him completely and he exploded, the quick-fire spasms almost buckling his knees.

But not half as much as the mental detonation in his brain that signalled what he'd known since they'd made love yesterday: this was more than physical.

Hell.

He leaned his forehead against hers, hating how complicated things could get now that he'd finally acknowledged what he'd suspected all along, grasping at words that just wouldn't gel as she slanted her head and kissed him on the mouth.

'If that's a frisk, arrest me, please. With an extended non-parole period.'

'I wish I could, sweetheart. I wish I could.'

But there was no use wishing for the impossible and as he held her close he hoped she hadn't seen his bittersweet smile.

Kate tucked a strand of wayward hair behind her ear, put her glasses on and steadied her fingers over the keyboard.

'We've got to do this today. I have a deadline to meet.'

Ty sat across from her, leaning back in a chair with his hands clasped behind his head. The pose drew attention to his muscular chest, yet another distraction for her wandering thoughts. 'Guys don't make passes at girls who wear glasses, you know.'

She peered at him over the top of trendy rimless frames she'd spent a small fortune on. 'Didn't seem to stop you.'

He laughed, a rich, deep sound that rolled over her in comforting waves. 'Nothing could keep me away from you.'

'Even if you were Superman and I was kryptonite?'

He flexed his biceps, sending her hormones into overdrive again. 'I'd eat you for breakfast and fly you away into the wide blue yonder.'

She blushed, his words conjuring up visions of their morning in the kitchen. 'I think you've already done the first bit.'

His eyes glowed, an endless indigo ocean she could drown in. 'Yeah. And I'm already looking forward to lunch.'

She wrenched her attention back to the keyboard with great difficulty, her breathing coming in short, shallow bursts at the anticipation of what 'lunch' he had in mind.

'Stop it. I need to concentrate. Can we get started?'

She tried a glare on for size, sending him a warning glance she hoped spoke volumes. In reality, she felt like Bambi trying to stare down a tiger.

Thankfully, he got the message. 'Okay, okay. Fire away.'

'Why did you become an instructor?'

'An injury during active duty. Can't tell you the details, though. If I did, I'd have to kill you.'

He grinned and her heart turned over for the hundredth time since she'd first laid eyes on him again.

Yeah, he'd kill her all right, with a smile rather than a stake straight through her heart.

'Okay, funny boy. Why teach driving skills to recruits?'

'Because I've always liked using a vehicle as a means of escape or a weapon of survival. Whether the bad guys are attempting a car-jacking, a kidnapping or a terrorist assassination, our response is the same. Get out of the situation quickly. That's where the expertise in handling a vehicle comes in.'

Her fingers flew over the keys, typing as he spoke. She couldn't resist a peek at his face, noting pride etched into the lines of experience, hearing the enthusiasm in his voice. He loved his work and it showed.

'Do you have any other options as an instructor?'

'I can always quit my day job and concentrate on instructing you in the finer art of—'

'Ty! Just answer the question.' She stifled a giggle at the mock chastised look on his face.

'Sure, I've got plenty of choices. We've got pathfinder school, sniper school, hand-to-hand combat school. And that's just for starters.'

'Do you have any favourite areas of expertise apart from vehicle training?'

He moved the way he'd been trained, with stealth and deadly precision, and wrapped his arms around her from behind before she'd even looked up from the keyboard.

'Yeah, I'm an expert in this area.'

He nuzzled her neck, his lips brushing her skin with the gentlest of touches.

She closed her eyes for a moment and leaned back, relishing the feel of his strong arms holding her tight and wishing that he would never let go. However, that dream was futile and she knew it.

Besides, she had a story to write and a promotion to gain. Despite the pleasant distraction of Ty in her life she couldn't lose sight of her main goal. Being Chief Editor would sustain her in the years ahead, which was more than could be said for the heartbreakingly gorgeous SEAL who would walk out on her any day now.

She broke the embrace with reluctance. 'Okay, point taken. Now, can we get back to work?'

'Slave driver,' he mumbled, resuming his place on the chair opposite.

She instantly missed the warmth and security of his arms. 'And don't you forget it. I'm ordering you to answer my question.'

She smiled as he extended his arms and crossed them, then blinked genie-style.

'As you wish, boss.'

'Well?'

He paused, feigning indifference. 'What was the question again?'

She picked up the nearest cushion and flung it at him.

He caught it with little effort, his reflexes lightning-fast. 'Okay, okay. My other areas of expertise include underwater operations, combat diving and jungle warfare.'

'Are all those courses taught here in LA?'

'No. Some aspects, like hydrographic reconnaissance, underwater demolition and jungle stuff are taught in Puerto Rico.'

'Any chance of you teaching over there?'

She held her breath, suddenly desperate to hear his answer yet simultaneously wanting to place her hands over her ears and yell 'la-la-la' so she couldn't hear him.

Why did she care?

Once this week was over he could go wherever he liked, do whatever he liked, with whoever he liked, just as they'd agreed.

A relationship wasn't for a guy like Ty; he'd proved it last time around. Yet somehow in the last forty-eight hours she'd found herself fantasising just a little too often about what it would be like if she didn't push him out of her life at the end of the week, about what it would feel like to give him another chance.

Apart from her job and her grandparents the last six years had been pretty empty without him. Would it be so bad to let him into her life again?

'You like having me around that much, huh?'

Damn, he'd turned her innocuous question into what it really was—a personal quest for information.

She shrugged, playing coy and hoping he bought it.

'Maybe.'

'I kind of grow on you, don't I?'

'Yeah, like a fungus.'

She hoped her quick retort would hide what she'd been about to almost admit—that she *did* like having him around. A lot.

'And here I was, thinking you'd fallen under my spell again.'

'I wouldn't be stupid enough to do that. Not when you'll be out of here in a couple of days.'

Now that she'd said the words out loud all she had to do was believe them.

He nodded. 'Smart girl. That's why we're having so much fun. We both know exactly where things stand.'

A knifelike pain stabbed at her heart. Smart? More like dumb. Dumb, dumb, dumb.

What had she expected, for him to fall down on his knees and profess he'd never forgotten her and move in permanently after making love a few times?

'Any more questions?'

She shook her head, unable to speak for a moment.

'Good. In that case, care to play hookey for a while?'

Her pulse raced in anticipation at the playful tone in his voice.

'What did you have in mind? I really need to get this article finished.'

'Leave it. Let's go for a drive.'

Willing to do anything to prolong the pleasure of whatever precious time they had together, she threw her pen and notepad down, barely having time to find her keys and lock up before he grabbed her hand and led her outside.

'Where are we going?'

He brushed a kiss across her lips, sending her heart rate into arrest mode. 'Trust me.'

He didn't have to say the words. She did trust him, body and soul. Unfortunately, she also knew that blind trust could end up breaking her heart. Again.

CHAPTER TEN

TYLER didn't like questions.

He always felt as if he were being interrogated by the enemy and the damned thing was they always led to answers. Right now he didn't want to think or analyse. He just wanted to feel, to enjoy the company of his beautiful Kate for the little time they had left and not think about the consequences.

Kate's questions had been easy enough till she'd honed in on the future. He didn't want to think about it, let alone respond to questions he didn't know the answers to.

'This is some view,' he said, leaning both arms against the car roof and taking in the sweeping LA vista he'd come to appreciate in the short space of time he'd spent at her place.

She smiled, pride evident in her face, and it struck him how much she loved her home. 'Yeah, the house may not be up to the usual Beverly Hills mansion standard but the view is to die for.'

They stood in companionable silence as his gaze swept across the rolling hills dotted with cream-rendered movie-star homes, lush greenery and twinkling lights in the descending dusk. If he believed in fairy tales he could quite easily see himself coming home to this view, this house, this woman every day for the rest of his life.

But he'd given up on believing in happy endings a long

time ago and, no matter how much this whole scene tugged at his heartstrings, a guy had to do what a guy had to do.

Straightening, he turned to face her, only to find her staring at him rather than the sensational view.

'Hope you like Japanese food?'

He opened the car door for her and she slid onto the leather seat, her knee-length denim skirt offering him a tempting view of long, tanned legs and resurrecting memories of how they'd felt that morning wrapped around him.

'Love it.'

Gritting his teeth at the pain that ripped through his knee, he braced himself using his arms on the steering wheel before sliding in.

'Your knee giving you trouble?'

Waiting till the wave of nausea that washed over him at the excruciating burning in his knee subsided, he said, 'It's driving me nuts at the moment. Comes with the job, I guess.'

'You should see someone about it.'

'Uh-huh,' he mumbled, needing a change of topic and fast. 'You've only got a couple of days left to order me around. Anything special you want me to do for you?'

'How about nightly foot rubs, a manicure, a night out at the theatre and a five-course meal?'

Kate kept her voice light-hearted, determined to hide the hurt piercing her soul. She'd tried voicing her concern and he didn't want it.

Not that it surprised her. He didn't want her concern or anything else she had to offer beyond this week and though she'd made a conscious decision to live for the moment and walk away at the end, the practice was a lot harder than the theory and she was floundering badly.

If Ty found out she'd fallen for him he'd have a field-day. Or else bolt in the opposite direction before the week was out, leaving her heartbroken into the bargain.

'How about we start with a rub and see what follows from there?'

His low, seductive voice washed over her, warming her better than the car's heater as once again her common sense took a back seat to her treacherous body.

'I think we both have a fair idea.'

Despite her flippant response, she secretly liked the way his mind worked. If the only attention he paid her for their remaining time together was aimed below the belt, she'd take whatever she could get. 'So theatre is out?'

'I'm not great with the fancy stuff. If you need a penguin to take you out, you're playing with the wrong guy.'

'I'd rather have a SEAL.' She paused, biting back the next words but they popped out anyway. 'And who says I'm playing?'

An ominous silence hung between them and she wished he'd say something, anything, to bridge the awkwardness of the moment.

'Don't go getting serious on me, Kate. I'm not the guy for you. I don't play for keeps, as we've already established.'

He sounded more distant than ever, his gaze fixed on the road ahead.

If he'd called her sweetheart or Katie she might have been able to laugh it off. However, he didn't and the use of her proper name reinforced the seriousness behind his words. He meant every word and, boy, did it hurt.

'Yeah, I know. Why do you think I only bought you for a week? It's not like I want to give us a second chance or anything.'

Her laughter sounded forced and she swallowed, trying desperately not to cry. Thank goodness they were having this conversation in the car and he couldn't see her face.

Unfortunately he sensed her distress and pulled the car over to the side of the road at the Gucci end of Rodeo Drive and she nibbled on her bottom lip, keeping her gaze firmly fixed on the designer shops and constant parade of tourists rather than face the inevitable now that she'd been stupid enough to hint at the truth.

Ty grabbed her hand and she had no option but to turn to face him.

'Listen to me. You need a guy to be there for the long haul, a guy who's going to be around for ever. I'm not him. You need stability, someone to give you everything you deserve and more. You need something I can't give you.'

Holding back a sob, she murmured, 'So now you're trying to tell me what I need?'

She tried to pull her hand away but he squeezed tight.

'You're saying I'm wrong?'

She glared at him, tucking a wayward strand of hair behind her ear, her fingers shaking. 'I'm saying you don't know the first thing about me any more.'

He let her go, the sadness in his eyes leaving her bereft.

'Maybe you're right, but I know one thing. There is no future for us beyond this week. If you can handle that, we keep having fun for the next few days. If not, I walk now.'

Taking a steadying breath and trying to ignore the ache in the vicinity of her heart, she said, 'So that's what you're calling sex these days. Having fun?'

'Well, isn't it? What would you call it?'

She wanted to scream 'making love' but managed to hold her tongue. She'd made enough of a fool of herself for one night. She had all the answers. There was nothing left to say.

Lifting her chin and blinking back the sting of tears, she looked him straight in the eye.

'You're right. It's been fun. How about we have dinner and go ho—back to my place.'

If he noticed her slip up he didn't say. She couldn't bear the thought of using his name and 'home' in the same sentence, not ever again.

She would take what little he had to offer for the remainder of their time together, lock away her emotions and throw away the key. One thing she couldn't bear to live with was regret; she'd lived a lifetime of it already, wishing she'd reached out to him six years ago and told him how she'd really felt rather than pushing him away with her own ambition.

She wouldn't make the same mistake with him again. If all he could offer her was the next few days, she'd take it.

'If that's what you want.'

He restarted the engine after staring at her a moment longer. *I want it all.*

She quashed the unbidden reply, knowing she'd never have it. At least not with Ty, the only man who mattered.

Tyler's plan had been an unmitigated disaster. He'd wanted to escape after playing twenty questions with Kate that afternoon.

So what had he done? Taken her to dinner only to have the conversation to end all conversations in the car on the way there. Ironic that it had occurred on Rodeo Drive, with its fancy boutiques and cafés, places Kate was probably familiar with, places as far away from his world as it was possible to get.

They were so different, destined to not be together despite the magnetic physical pull that kept him anchored to her side. As for the emotional bonds they'd reforged…he wouldn't go there.

He'd hurt her, no doubt about it. He'd seen the tears glistening in her eyes when he'd told her there was no future for them. Hell, it had taken every ounce of his self-control not to reach out to her, to tell her he'd like to hold her for ever.

For ever.

Nothing lasted that long and he wasn't about to take a huge risk in finding out if a relationship with Kate could change all that. No way.

She'd surprised him with her bravado all through dinner, making casual small talk as if her life depended on it. However, he hadn't been fooled. He'd seen the sadness in her eyes, the hurt behind her smile that he'd put there with his personal brand of God's honest truth. Honesty had served him well in the past. What the hell had gone wrong now?

He stared at the ceiling, hands clasped behind his head to stifle the impulse to punch his pillow. He knew exactly what had gone wrong. Honesty only worked if you faced the truth yourself and in this case he hadn't. He'd fed Kate all the right lines about not being good enough for her, about not being around for the long haul.

But he hadn't bought it. Not any of it.

Rather than face the truth he'd buried it under a pile of excuses. She'd basically offered him more than a week with her half-veiled hints at playing for keeps and what had he done? Hidden his feelings behind cocky words as usual. After all, a SEAL couldn't show vulnerability. It went against the grain.

A SEAL also kept his promises, yet the more time he spent with Kate the harder it was to focus on what he wanted.

Pity was, he had no idea what that was now.

A week ago it had been easy: get through his physical and if he couldn't, put his thinking cap on and figure out what the hell he wanted to do with his life.

He didn't do emotional entanglements for this very reason. Why let down someone else when he couldn't be the man he'd spent his life trying to be?

Kate deserved more.

She deserved a full, active life, to continue making leaps in her career, not to be bound to some surly tempered has-been with a bust knee. And he knew without a shadow of a doubt that if he couldn't be a SEAL in any capacity following his physical, he'd be a nightmare to be around.

Kate stirred and snuggled into him and he tensed.

With his thoughts a jumbled mess and guilt plaguing him at causing that defenceless look in her eyes, he hadn't laid a finger on her tonight. Instead, he'd cuddled her till she'd fallen into a restless sleep, ordering his libido to behave. Thankfully, it had worked.

Until now.

With her hands skimming his chest and her lips pressed against his neck, he was having a hard time of it. Very hard.

He tried to sidle away, disentangling her arms in the process.

'Ty, don't leave me.'

He stilled at her whispered plea and rolled towards her.

'Are you sure?' He gently kissed her forehead, wondering if she meant now or for ever.

Moonlight slanted through the window, bathing the room in a soft, silvery glow as her eyes glowed like a nocturnal cat in the reflected light, watching and waiting for his next move.

'Love me,' she whispered, her hands spreading over his chest and moving lower, effectively shattering his latent gallantry, which didn't want to make this situation any more complicated than it already was.

He might be a SEAL but he wasn't a saint, and with a muffled groan he pulled her on top of him, slanting his mouth across hers in a hungry kiss.

She shuddered as he parted her lips with his tongue, teasing her with tortured patience, grateful for the opportunity to obliterate his thoughts, to sate his unquenchable need for her, maybe for the last time.

Her lips were warm and soft, coaxing him into prolonging the pleasure. As she parted them and let him in, he kept the kiss slow…infinitely slower than he could have thought possible considering how she turned him on.

He'd always felt this way with her: ready and raring to go, unable to get enough of her, wanting her every minute of every day.

Walking away the first time had been hell and it looked as if he was headed on a one-way return visit.

However, she'd asked him to love her and that was what he intended on doing. All night.

He could give her that much at least.

'You're wearing too many clothes,' he said, playfully tugging at the oversized T-shirt she'd worn to bed, his fingertips skimming the smooth, velvety skin beneath and itching to fill his palms with it.

'So are you.'

She smiled, a coy, sexy upward turning of her kissable lips as she sat up, whipped the T-shirt over her head and threw it on the floor.

'Allow me.' She shimmied down his legs, taking his boxers with her. 'Better?'

His breath caught as her hair draped across his erection. He'd never seen anything so erotic and he burned the memory into his memory bank, knowing he'd never forget the incredible week they'd shared no matter what happened from here on in.

'Come here.' He crooked a finger at her.

'Hey, who said you could give the orders around here?' she murmured, a seductive glint in her eyes. 'Or is that an offer? Because I intend to. Over and over again.'

She flicked her tongue out over her lips and that one little gesture shot straight to his groin.

'That's it. You're in trouble.'

He pulled her down to the bed again and lay on top of her, the sensation of bare skin to skin notching up the heat sizzling between them an extra degree or two.

He'd been in some hot situations before while trapped under enemy fire or extracting civilians from war-torn countries, but nothing had his heart pounding or his body burning up on pure adrenalin as much as getting naked with Kate.

'Mmm…big trouble.'

She wriggled against his erection, driving all conscious thought from his brain.

'You make me crazy,' he said, rolling away for a second to protect himself before returning to one of his favourite positions and lowering his weight on top of her.

'And you make me horny,' she said, sliding her arms around him and raking her fingernails slowly down his back, her smile pure temptation.

'You've got a smart mouth.'

He nudged between her legs as her hips rose to meet him and slipped a finger into the moist curls between her thighs, rubbing softly till she whimpered.

'All the better to—'

He took her mouth, kissing her with all the passion in his soul, knowing that if this was as good as it got he'd die a happy man indeed.

'I love it when you talk dirty,' he murmured against the side of her mouth as she writhed beneath him, her wild, uninhibited cries ringing out before he brushed her lips again, their breath intermingling as she came in a loud scream of ecstasy.

Unable to hold back a second longer he sheathed himself quickly and pushed inside her silken, hot flesh, knowing that nothing came close to this indescribable feeling of being so warm, so tight, with her all around him.

His heart clenched as her eyes fluttered open, their luminous depths almost incandescent in the moonlight and her delicious mouth formed a small O as he started to move, sliding in and out, taking them to the brink.

As he thrust harder, deeper, her eyes widened and he could've sworn he could see right into her soul.

It finally hit him at the same moment as the force of his climax gripped him and sent him spiralling over the edge.

He loved her.

Enough to want to stay here like this, for ever.

But he couldn't do for ever so what now?

Looking down into her face, he pushed away the hair that

clung in tendrils to her heat-dampened skin, in total awe of the unique feeling that flooded every cell of his body and made him crave more.

Tell her.

Yeah, right. She'd think he was totally nuts. Driving her away this afternoon, saying he loved her tonight after mind-blowing sex?

Nah, the timing sucked. He'd have to do better than that. In fact, he needed to get his head around this startling revelation first before blabbing the first words that came into his mind.

Fortuitously, he didn't have a chance to say anything as Kate placed a finger against his lips.

'I know. We had fun. No words needed, James. That's an order.'

Tyler bit back a groan as she slipped out from under him and strolled into the bathroom, her butt glimmering like two perfect orbs in the moonlight.

Shaken to the core by the realisation he loved Katie, the woman he'd planned on walking away from once and for all shortly, he rolled onto his back and closed his eyes.

What the hell was he going to do now?

CHAPTER ELEVEN

As Kate typed the finishing touches to her story Ty strolled into the room and placed a mug next to her.

'Thought you might like a coffee.'

'Thanks.'

She clasped her hands behind her back and stretched, working out the kinks in her neck.

As Ty stared at her she quickly dropped her hands. By the intense look on his face he might take her stretching as an invitation to start massaging her neck again and that was one thing she couldn't cope with right now.

She had to focus her energy during the day to maintain a friendly camaraderie. She'd planned to keep the physical side of their relationship to nights, using the darkness as a shield to hide the emotion written all over her face whenever he touched her.

'Finished?'

He walked towards her, his long, tanned legs looking particularly delectable in running shorts. She noted the slight limp where he favoured his right leg and knew his knee was worse than he let on. He'd avoided talking about it and she hadn't pushed it.

So she had her head in the sand? Nothing new there. It just about summed up her whole attitude when it came to Ty.

Though that wasn't entirely true; he'd made it perfectly clear where she stood in their clear-the-air conversation in the car the other night and it still hadn't dimmed her pleasure in having him around. Go figure?

She sipped her coffee, trying to ignore the heat radiating off his legs as he stood beside her and looked over her shoulder.

'Yeah, all done. I'll drop it off later.' She shielded the laptop screen with a hand. 'And no peeking. If you want to see it, you'll just have to buy the magazine.'

He laid a hand on her shoulder, sending her pulse rate racing. 'Surely the star attraction of the article can take a look before it runs hot off the press?'

She shrugged his hand off, snapped the laptop shut and stood up. 'No. I've got to go.'

He smiled. 'You creative types are all the same. Touchy as hell when it comes to work. Why can't you e-mail it to your boss so we can spend our last day together?'

She shook her head, instantly quelling the irrational leap of joy at his suggestion. She wasn't that good an actress. Spending all day with him would just make it harder to act nonchalant.

Besides, they couldn't spend an hour in each other's company without ending up in the bedroom…or the kitchen… or the living room, without any clothes and having way too much fun. The more time they spent together, the more danger she was in of saying something else she would regret.

'Thanks for the offer but I want to run a few ideas past Henry for the orphanage article so I thought I'd drop by the office. See you later.'

She slung her bag over her shoulder, picked up her keys and walked out the door, trying to ignore the bemused expression on his face and barely acknowledging his wave.

Yeah, the office was the place to be right now, a perfect SEAL-free sanctuary.

However, if she'd thought that she could totally avoid him at the office, she was wrong. Di pounced as soon as she walked in.

'Managed to come up for air, huh?'

Kate wasn't in the mood for banter, though she couldn't fault her PA's inquisitiveness. She did the same thing whenever Di had a new man in her life, which seemed to be every few weeks. In fact, she'd lived vicariously through Di's tales a lot lately and it was nice to be on the receiving end for once.

Kate wiped her brow and flicked away imaginary perspiration. 'Yeah, though it's tough keeping up with a SEAL. All that training, you know. Gives them incredible stamina.'

Di's eyes widened and she leaned closer. 'Ooh, tell me more.' She paused, before placing her hands over her ears. 'On second thoughts, I don't want to hear. I'm jealous as hell. It's no fun when my old boss is getting some and I'm not.'

Kate patted her on the head, her hand not making a dent in the gelled blonde spikes. 'Tough luck. Some guys just go for the more experienced type.'

Di perked up at this. 'Hey! If it's experience he's after, I'm—'

'Too busy meeting deadlines to think about anything else. Now get back to work.'

Di saluted. 'Yes, boss,' and goose-stepped her way into the copying room.

Kate smiled and knocked on Henry's door, which opened in record time and Henry ushered her in. 'How's my replacement today? Got anything to show me?'

She couldn't believe it. Not only had her boss opened the door but he was smiling at her. Usually, he barked an instruction to enter from behind his desk and frowned through the whole interrogation, for that was what it was whenever anyone was summoned to his office, a succession of sharp questions that left you feeling as if you had faced a firing squad. He must be getting mellow as he neared retirement. Amen to that.

She handed him a printed copy of the article. Though she'd already e-mailed it to him, she knew he liked reading hard copies.

'All done. I'm also doing another piece to tie in with this one for the next issue.'

She took a steadying breath as Ty's image popped into her head, driving his deal home so she would run the story on the orphanage. 'The man auction was to raise money for the Ramirez Orphanage. However, it wasn't enough. The SEAL in this story believes that raising the profile of the orphanage will ultimately save it. I happen to agree.'

Henry speed-read the article she'd handed him. 'This is good stuff, Kate.'

He scratched his balding head for a moment. 'You've got yourself a promotion, girly. I'll announce you're my successor at the next staff meeting.'

He shoved the article on top of a pile of paperwork in his in-tray, signalling the end of the interview.

'About the other article?'

He waved her away. 'Since when have you needed my opinion on a story? If it's good enough for you, it's good enough for me. Now get back to work…Chief.'

Kate smiled and thanked him, desperately trying to keep her legs steady as she walked out of his office.

She'd done it. The dream job was hers and she couldn't wait to take up the position. Throwing herself into a new job would be the only way to distract herself from the heartache of losing Ty.

By the way her heart clenched and splintered at the thought of losing him, she was going to need all the help she could get.

Kate had to tell him.

Now that she had the job for sure there was no way she could keep it from Ty. He deserved to know. In fact, she should've told him earlier in the week or perhaps yesterday when she'd been grilling him.

But she'd been scared. Terrified of losing what little time they had left, petrified he'd accuse her of using him right from the start. And now that her feelings had developed into something deeper…

She had no other option but to come clean and pray to God the guy who valued honour above all else would understand where she'd been coming from.

Taking a deep breath, she unlocked the front door and stepped inside, the sight of her walking-talking fantasy leaning against the kitchen doorframe wearing cargo shorts, a sky-blue T-shirt that matched his eyes and a smile doing little for her false bravado.

'Hey there, gorgeous.'

'You talking to me?' she said, forcing a smile as she closed the door and crossed the room to drop a quick peck on his cheek.

His eyes widened in surprise but he didn't flinch; must be used to subterfuge attacks.

She'd never done anything like that before, but right now she desperately needed to be near to him, needed the physical reassurance he wouldn't run out the door as soon as she told him the truth.

'I don't see any other gorgeous, sexy females in the vicinity. Not that I'd see them with you around anyway.'

'Always the charmer,' she said, kicking off her stilettos and flopping down into the nearest chair, pointing to the sofa opposite. 'Want to take a seat? I need to talk to you about something.'

His smile faded as he sat, a slight furrow creasing his brow. 'Sounds serious.'

'Not really, but it's something I should've told you a few days ago if I wasn't such a chicken.'

Tension etched into every muscle of his body as he leaned back and rested an ankle on his good knee. 'Okay, what's up?'

She swallowed, trying to dislodge the lump of foreboding wedged in her throat. 'You know the article I just handed in? And why I really needed your input? Well, my boss pretty much blackmailed me into doing it in exchange for a huge promotion to Chief Editor. It's something I've wanted for ages and I've worked incredibly hard to get it.'

'And?'

Thankfully, he didn't appear annoyed. In fact, his shoulders had relaxed and he rested an arm across the back of the sofa.

'I didn't want you thinking I used you. You know, your co-operation with the story to get me where I wanted to go.'

He smiled, his bronze tan making his eyes glow an electrifying blue.

'So you used me? Must say, I kinda like your techniques at coercion.'

'You're not mad?'

He shook his head, a slight frown creasing his brow. 'Not unless you tell me that all this week has been about is securing that job for you.'

'No,' she murmured, pain clutching her heart and squeezing till she could barely breathe. Their week together had been so much more than that but she couldn't tell him. He didn't want to hear it. 'I think you know me better than that.'

'I do.'

He stood up, crossed the room and dropped down on his good knee next to her chair, taking hold of her hand and smiling up at her. 'See? It's not that serious. You got a promotion out of the story; we had a great week together. So relax.'

Easy for him to say.

He didn't have a giant lump lodged in his throat at the thought of their week ending right now, considering seven days had passed.

'It was pretty great, wasn't it?' she murmured, squeezing his hand, wishing she could convey half of what she was feeling through a simple touch.

'You bet.'

Leaning forward, he brushed a soft, lingering kiss across her lips and she sighed at the all-too-brief contact. 'I have to get back to the base. My CO called.'

'Oh, okay.'

She nodded, ignoring the sting of tears at the backs of her eyes, wishing he'd stop staring at her as if he didn't want to leave.

Maybe she should give it one last go? Tell him how she really felt?

'You're incredible, Katie, and I'll never forget you, but I've got to hit the road. You know how it is.'

Before she could respond he stood up, grimaced as he straightened his knee and headed for the spare room, leaving her on the verge of begging him to stay.

The sad thing was, she did know how it was. She'd sat back and watched him walk away once before, and if the pain had been devastating back then it was near on unbearable now.

Damn, she'd made a mess of this. She needed to convince him to stay, to give them longer than seven days, to take a chance at something potentially wonderful.

However, before she could form the words he was back, bag in hand, a stoic expression on his handsome face.

'Well, it looks like it's time for this sailor to ship out.'

He sent her a sharp salute and she forced a smile as she crossed the room to stand in front of him.

'What would you say if I asked you not to go?'

The murmured question hung between them for what seemed like an eternity as she stifled the urge to wrap her arms around him and bury her face in his chest when she glimpsed the sadness in his eyes.

'I'd say that's a big ask.' He shook his head. 'I'm sorry. I can't give you what you want.'

You can, she wanted to scream. She wanted to yell and rant and thump his chest for not seeing what was staring him right in the face.

She loved him. She needed him.

And it still wasn't enough.

She bit her lip, struggling to hold back tears as he stared at her with regret in his eyes. He'd read her mind other times; she just prayed he did it now.

'Take care, sweetheart.'

Her heart shattered as he picked up his bag and opened the door.

'Ty, I—'

'Don't make this harder than it already is,' he murmured as he stepped through the door and closed it without looking back.

She sank to the floor and cried, once more than she had in the last six years.

So much for the coping strategies she'd learned from the counsellor after her grandparents' death. She'd just flunked 'Getting a Grip 101' all over again.

Tyler screeched into the car park of the orphanage, gravel flying in his wake. He'd focussed all his attention on the road; driving through congested LA traffic when the roads were rain-slicked was hazardous at the best of times, but in his current frame of mind it could become lethal.

Though he felt like ramming something he didn't have a death wish. Besides, he couldn't kill what was already dead inside and that was exactly how he'd felt ever since leaving Kate's place.

Now, with the engine switched off and nothing left to focus on, the pain flooded back.

How could he have let this happen? Loving her, growing

attached to her, wasn't supposed to happen. He couldn't have ties, couldn't do it to her, yet when she'd asked him to stay he'd almost lost it and agreed.

He'd needed to get away ASAP and couldn't have retreated any faster. Their week was done. They were done. Now all he had to do was put it behind him.

Thumping the steering wheel in frustration, he glanced around, needing to focus on anything but the empty ache in his heart.

This place had been home for so long, since his foster parents had dropped him off one afternoon promising they would return. Almost thirty years later, he was still waiting.

He'd never figured out why two seemingly normal people could adopt a baby, only to dump him a few years later like unwanted baggage.

Until he'd blown his knee. It had all become crystal-clear then; the doc had said in all likelihood he had some kind of arthritis that was probably inherited and he might have displayed some signs as a child. After hearing that it didn't take a genius to figure out that first his mother, then his foster parents had ditched the crippled kid.

It was hard enough battling the increasing pain on a daily basis, but when he'd been with Kate he'd almost felt human again.

She'd crept under his guard and into his heart when he'd been determined to hold his emotions in check. He'd kept telling himself it was just about the sex till she'd opened her arms and welcomed him into her life, her house and he'd fallen head first into an emotional entanglement it would take a lifetime to recover from.

Someone tapped on his window and he looked up, the bleakness in his soul engulfing him till he wanted to thump something in frustration.

'Hey. Are you coming in? The kettle's on.'

He managed a smile for Mary. She'd always sensed when he was down and believed that a cup of tea was the elixir to happiness. He had a feeling it would take a hell of a lot more to cheer him up this time.

Taking a few calming deep breaths, he stepped from the car and she squeezed his arm. 'I've seen the kids look happier after vaccine shots. What's up?'

'I don't want to talk about it.'

He waved to a group of nearby children as they headed inside, something akin to pleasure warming his heart as they smiled back, the innocence lighting up their faces. It was a good sign if his heart could still feel emotion other than the ache enveloping it.

'You and Kate have a lovers' tiff?'

He looked down in amazement. 'How did you know we were lovers?'

She rolled her eyes. 'The air between you almost crackled that day you were here. Besides, I could tell by the way she looked at you. She's crazy about you.'

He watched Mary making tea. She would make someone a great wife one day and he hoped that her life outside the orphanage would start sooner rather than later. He owed it to her, just as he'd promised. If the orphanage could survive this time he would find someone else to run it so Mary could be free to lead her own life.

Yet another promise he needed to make good on.

Suddenly, a terrible thought flashed through his mind. What if Kate didn't run the article on the orphanage? He'd lived up to his side of the bargain and she'd secured her promotion because of it. Would she follow through on her side of the deal now that he'd shunned her request to stay and walked away?

'What did I say?' Mary pinned him with a concerned stare.

She fussed over him like a mother hen, always had, probably always would. He'd pretended he didn't like it as a

kid when secretly he'd loved the attention. Most of the other
orphans had been jealous but he hadn't cared. Mary as his big
sister was just fine by him.

'She is, you know. Absolutely mad over you.'

'Hmm.'

He sipped the tea, scalding his mouth in the process. It just
wasn't his day.

'Don't blow this. She could be the best thing that's ever
happened to you.'

'Or the worst,' he mumbled into his cup, wishing that he
could throw himself back into action in some war-torn country.

At least he'd known where he stood under threat from the
enemy. Now, he had no artillery against the assault of an un-
forgettable woman who had crawled under his defences and
led him to the brink of destruction.

Mary shrugged. 'I hope you know what you're doing.'

He didn't justify her response with an answer. Instead,
they finished their tea in companionable silence before he
brought up the safer topic of the children.

For an hour or so, Mary regaled him with tales of the kids'
exploits, making him forget his own problems. It wasn't till
later, after he'd said goodbye to Mary and the kids and walked
to his car, that the problems resurfaced when he looked up to
find Kate strolling straight towards him.

CHAPTER TWELVE

'HEY, Ty.'

Kate stared at him, those hazel eyes playing havoc with his mind while the rest of her had a field-day with other parts of his body.

He gritted his teeth against his first instinct to wrap her in his arms and never let go.

'What are you doing here?'

She'd changed into a red vest-top and faded denim jeans, both items fitting her body like a second skin, and he thrust his hands into his pockets to stop them from reaching out to touch her.

Her cool glance gave away nothing. If she could sense his discomfort, she wasn't showing it. 'I came to see Mary. I needed to clarify a few details before I write the article on this place.'

'So, you're going to do the article? That's great.'

She sent him a confused look. 'I said I would. Why would you think otherwise?'

He shrugged, knowing he was making a mess of this, but in a way maybe getting her mad at him would make walking away easier?

'I thought you might be angry about me refusing your offer to stay.'

She flushed, a slow blush that crept up her neck into her face and doing little to detract from her beauty.

'I'm not that petty,' she said, the gold flecks in her eyes glinting in the waning sunlight. 'Besides, I must've been crazy asking you to stay when I know you're the king of running away.'

'What's that supposed to mean?'

Surprised she'd partially guessed the truth, he wanted to know more even though she had no idea why he'd spent his life running away and was judging him for it.

'Come on, you ran away six years ago and you're doing it again now. Whenever things get too good or a little too close for comfort, you bolt.'

'We both agreed to end it back then,' he bit out, hating how close to the truth she really was and not willing to have this conversation, not here, not now, not ever.

She rolled her eyes. 'Yeah, but you started withdrawing the minute I popped the question. I know, I know, SEALs aren't around much, are in danger constantly, et cetera…et cetera…et cetera… I bought your excuses because I was young and naïve and wanted to make a name for myself just as much as you did, but you know what? This time was different. I wanted to see you again. I wanted to see if we still had sparks. I wanted…'

She trailed off and dropped her gaze, her hands clenched so tightly he could see her knuckles standing out.

'What?'

He fisted his own hands to stop from reaching out to tilt her chin up, to make her meet his gaze. He couldn't touch her. It would undo him completely.

'Never mind.'

He barely heard her whispered words as his mobile phone rang, breaking the escalating tension, and he cursed the bad timing.

The news from the end of the line added to his all-round bad day and he grunted his responses, snapping the phone shut before thrusting it back into his pocket.

'This is getting us nowhere,' he said, eager to escape before the wall around his heart crumbled and left him more vulnerable to this woman than ever. 'I have to go.'

He could've sworn he glimpsed the sheen of tears in her eyes as she nodded and turned away.

'You do what you have to do,' she said, her voice tight and high and totally unnatural.

Despite his anger, his bitterness at himself for letting him get this attached, he wanted to give her some small comfort before walking out of her life for good.

'I just got a transfer. I really do have to go.'

It was totally untrue but maybe this way she'd remember him for doing what he always did—putting his career first—rather than running away because of how deeply she affected him.

In reality, his medical results were ready, and he needed time to prepare himself to hear them before he went for his physical. Meanwhile his heart still reeled from the fact he had no future with Kate.

Sending her a brief salute, he slid behind the wheel of his car and gunned the engine, deliberately not looking back.

Kate watched Ty drive away, tears spilling over and rolling down her cheeks. Angry tears, frustrated tears, useless tears she swiped away while silently chastising herself for being a fool.

She'd had an inkling he'd run to the orphanage, the only place he'd ever called home, after their confrontation and now as she cried enough tears to fill the Mojave desert she wondered if she should've done more to convince him to stay.

However, the second he'd mentioned the transfer she'd known the score. He was running back to his precious SEALs as always, just as he'd said at the start, and nothing she could say or do would change his mind.

'Would you like to come in?'

She turned towards the soft, tentative voice, the concerned

look in Mary's eyes reaching out and drawing her in till all she wanted to do was bawl again.

'Thanks.'

She wiped the tears away with the back of her hand, knowing she must look a fright but not giving a damn, and followed Mary into the kitchen, once again marvelling at her petite stature. No wonder Ty loved her—her fragility just screamed 'pick me up and cherish me'. Even as a woman, Kate almost felt compelled to protect her.

'Would you like a drink?'

'Coffee would be great.'

Kate looked around the kitchen, noting the homely touches that Mary must have instituted to help the orphans feel welcome: the mismatched plates on the dresser, the monstrous cake tin in the shape of Mickey Mouse, the bright mugs arranged in delightful disarray. The last time she'd been here she'd been less observant, too busy watching Ty's reaction to Mary.

Mary placed a mug of steaming coffee in front of her in record time and took a seat opposite.

'You're not having anything?' Kate gestured to the empty table in front of the other woman.

'No. I just had a cup of tea…' Mary trailed off, looking as if she'd made the biggest gaff of all time.

'With Ty?' Kate asked, knowing the answer and wondering why she'd asked the question.

Mary nodded. 'Tell me to butt out if you like, but what's going on with you two?'

Kate wanted to confide in the other woman. Hell, she needed to talk to somebody at this stage. But how could she talk about her feelings for Ty with a woman she hardly knew?

'You can talk to me. Though I love him dearly I won't tell him we spoke.'

Something shrivelled up and died inside Kate. Mary had just confirmed what she'd only suspected to this point.

'Don't you hate me?' Kate asked, admiring Mary for maintaining such a cool façade in the face of her would-be opposition.

Mary looked startled. 'Hate you? Why?'

'For loving Ty.'

There, she'd said the words and they sounded so much more pitiful than when she thought them.

'So you do love him?'

Kate didn't understand the satisfied smirk on Mary's face. She'd expected unsheathed claws, not a knowing grin. 'Yeah, not that it's done me much good.'

'It's not too late,' Mary said, a conspiratorial gleam in her eyes.

As dusk descended the kitchen took on a surreal glow and for a moment Kate thought she'd been trapped in a time warp, having a conversation that didn't make any sense. 'What are you talking about?'

'Go after him. Tell him how you feel.'

Kate was seriously starting to doubt the other woman's sanity; must be all that time spent talking to kids. 'But what about you?'

'Me?' Mary's eyebrows shot heavenward. 'Tyler won't mind. He's used to me interfering in his life.'

'Don't you love him?' Kate asked the redundant question again, her mind a mass of whirling confusion.

Mary's eyes brightened as if a light switch had been turned on. 'Of course I do.'

She paused and Kate's heart sank. 'As a *brother*.'

Ty had said as much and though Kate had believed him she'd thought Mary might have harboured feelings for him. Her memory replayed the way she'd seen Ty and Mary interact and admittedly there had been nothing sexual in it, yet she'd read more into their teasing because of her own insecurities. Yet another blunder in her disastrous week.

'I thought you might have feelings for Ty.'

'God, no!' Mary's vehemence lightened the mood. 'So are you going after him?'

'I can't. He doesn't love me. I tried to talk to him out there but he couldn't wait to get away.'

His image rose before her, the quickly masked hurt in his eyes when she'd accused him of running away.

She'd wanted to shock him, to make him react, anything to get him to look at her with some emotion in his eyes rather than cool control. Instead, it had only served to drive him further away.

'I think Tyler feels a lot more for you than he's letting on.'

A spark of hope flared within Kate. 'Did he say something to you?'

'Just that you were lovers.'

Mary's response quickly doused the spark that had threatened to combust into a bonfire with the right encouragement and her face fell. 'Sex isn't the same as love.'

'I know that and so does Tyler.'

'I don't have any siblings but I know for a fact that if I had a brother I wouldn't be discussing my sex life with him.'

'I know Tyler. He's not that type of guy.'

Kate admired Mary's loyalty but thought her adamant stance in this case was misplaced. 'Did he tell you we were once involved? Engaged?'

'Engaged?' Mary leaned forward, shock written all over her face. 'Are you serious?'

'Guess you didn't know.'

'Tyler mentioned he had a special woman in his life about six years ago but it didn't work out. I haven't seen him date anyone seriously since and I used to rib him about it all the time. That was you?'

Kate nodded, not feeling very special at the moment and wishing things could've been different. 'Uh-huh.'

'So you're the one…'

'The one?'

Suddenly, Kate wished she'd stuck around to face Ty when he'd returned from his first mission. After he'd left she'd thrown herself into her own job, determined to make it to the top. Ironically, she was almost there now and it didn't hold half the appeal it had when she'd been young and ambitious.

'I remember him being pretty cut up at the time and I've never seen him like that again. Till now.'

The impact of Mary's statement took a second to sink in.

'I know he cared about me back then. We both cared. But none of that matters any more because I asked him to stay and he said no. He probably thinks I'm still hung up over my job.'

'Well, are you?'

'No. Sure, I love my job. It's about all I had till Ty walked into my life again.'

'Then tell him.'

Kate shook her head. 'I tried but he didn't want to hear it.'

Mary winced. 'What is it with guys?'

'I don't know. The one I love doesn't want to have anything to do with me.'

'Try bringing them home to twenty kids and see how long they stick around.'

Kate admired Mary for her self-sacrifice but didn't understand it. 'Why do you do it? Look after the kids, I mean.'

'It's my way of giving something back to this place. If my mother hadn't dumped me on the doorstep here after I was born who knows where I might've ended up? Helping out is a small price to pay in return for being raised here.'

Mary's face glowed while she spoke about the orphanage and suddenly Kate wished she could do more than just write the article.

'Ty feels the same way too, doesn't he? That's why he wants to save this place so badly.'

'Yeah, though he's also fixated on a promise he made me when we were teenagers. He said that he'd get us both out of here, to make a life for ourselves. He did it, I didn't and that makes him feel guilty. What he doesn't realise is how much I love working here. I wouldn't do it if I didn't. Besides, it's giving me a good grounding in what I ultimately want to do, which is social work.'

Kate's admiration kicked up another notch. They should rename the orphanage 'Saint Mary's'.

'That's great. Don't worry about Ty. He's out to save the world and everybody in it.'

'And isn't that one of the things you love about him?'

Great, Mary had a talent for reading minds just like Ty.

'You're right.' Kate thought there were a lot of things she loved about him and he would never know.

'Which brings me back to my first point. Go after him. Tell him how you feel. What have you got to lose?'

Everything.

Though she didn't say it, that one word scared her more than anything else.

'He's being transferred. What good would it do?'

Unless she wanted to follow him to the ends of the earth, which she didn't, there was little use in declaring her love. Her knight would ride off into the sunset just as he'd planned. Why did the ending of her fairy tale always suck?

'Make him change his mind.'

Kate stared at Mary in horror. 'And make him hate me for the rest of his life because I made him choose between me and his career? No way.'

'Then go with him,' Mary said, as if it were the easiest thing in the world.

'You think?'

'Why not? If it's happily ever after you want, go for it.'

Kate needed to make a cool, calm, rational decision, not some spur-of-the-moment one based on a love that was probably one-sided, and having Saint Mary egg her on wasn't helping.

'He could be going as far away as Timbuktu,' she muttered, totally floored she could even consider giving up everything for a man who still might walk away any time he fancied, just as he'd already told her many moons ago.

Mary stood up. 'Look, I'm sorry to end our chat but I've got to organise the children's dinner. Think about what I've said. Life's too short not to take chances.' She squeezed Kate's arm as she walked to the stove. 'You owe it to yourselves to try and make this work.'

Kate stared at her, amazed at the camaraderie that had sprung up between them and feeling suitably chastened for all the nasty thoughts she'd harboured.

'Thanks for the coffee and the chat.' She paused for a moment, struggling to find the right words. 'I owe you one.'

Mary smiled. 'Just run the article on this place to keep the doors open. Then we'll be even.'

Kate snapped her fingers. 'The article! I needed to get some info from you. Do you mind if I come back tomorrow?'

'Sure. Maybe you'll have come to a decision by then?' Mary's eyes twinkled and Kate had a feeling they would become firm friends regardless of the outcome of her relationship with Tyler.

'Let me sleep on it.'

Kate knew, though, no matter how many hours she took to dwell on the matter, there were no easy solutions when it came to sorting out the mess with Ty.

Then again, since when had she ever settled for easy?

CHAPTER THIRTEEN

IT HAD been a long couple of days for Tyler. First walking away from Kate and then learning just how badly his knee had deteriorated, then waiting for the physical that could change his life one way or the other.

The docs had given him the usual spiel about success rates and percentages of post-op knees, but in his case they hadn't been encouraging. The cartilage had worn down to the bone and it would take a minor miracle for him to stay in the Navy.

Facing the fact he'd probably never be part of his beloved SEALs again wouldn't be so bad if he could get his head around what had happened with Kate.

What happened to his last fling at fun before he made any life-changing decisions? He'd been determined to hold her at arm's length, flirt with her, have some fun, and enjoy her stimulating company before exiting her life.

Instead, it had blown up in his face like some undetonated bomb and the fallout was just as damaging. He couldn't eat or sleep, her image haunting his mind, and when he did manage to block her out he'd turn a corner and see something to remind him of her.

Take today, for instance. He'd walked past a news-stand and seen the latest edition of *Femme* sitting there. He'd averted his eyes but it was too late and before he knew what was happening he'd bought a copy. Totally sick. He'd never bought a glossy magazine in his life so what was he doing with one lying on his coffee-table now?

The guys on the team were right. Love was a bitch. And now he knew it firsthand.

He glared at the magazine as if it were a venomous snake about to strike. However, the longer he avoided the inevitable, the more he wanted to do it.

Finally, he pulled the tab on a soda, sat down and picked it up. He'd never understood women's obsession for magazines; give him a good thriller novel any day. He flicked open the cover and turned the pages, paying scant attention to the advertisements for make-up and perfume.

There it was. Page nine.

Some of the tension he'd been holding in his gut slowly unwound as he stared at the larger-than-life photo of Mary and the kids at the orphanage.

So Kate had done it.

He read the short piece advertising the upcoming article on the orphanage in next week's issue, complete with address, phone number and web site for donations. As for the feature on the two of them and the auction, he skimmed over it, trying not to notice how she'd blended the skilful words perfectly, outlining the reason behind the man auction, his role in the Navy, painting an accurate and heart-rending picture of the place he'd once called home, the story far surpassing his expectations, and for one second he glowed with pride.

The woman he loved had done this.

Then reality set in.

He tossed the magazine onto the table, tired of rehashing the same old thoughts in his head. Kate was history and the sooner he realised it, the better. Focussing on his physical, adjusting to life as a civilian and finding a new career would be a huge challenge and healthier than pining for a woman he couldn't have.

Padding into the bedroom, he packed his kit, mentally ticking off items as he followed the method he'd used since joining the Navy. Just as he zipped up the first bag he heard a knock on the door, knowing it had to be one of the boys.

'If you've come to give me grief, Bear, save it…' He trailed off as he opened the door to find Kate standing there with a small suitcase in hand.

'Can I come in?'

'Sure.'

He swung the door wider and took a step back, not wanting to brush up against her as she walked in for fear of touching her and finding he couldn't stop.

He needn't have bothered as her signature gardenia fragrance wafted over him and created havoc with his senses as surely and swiftly as her touch would have.

'What are you doing here?'

He gestured to a chair, studiously avoiding looking at her suitcase and what it might imply.

She didn't answer his question. Instead, she placed the suitcase on the floor, picked up the magazine and flipped it open. 'Did you like the article?'

'Yeah, and it looks like the follow-up on the orphanage in the next issue is going to be a winner.'

She shrugged and he watched the way her green ribbed top rode higher to display a tantalising glimpse of tanned, flat stomach beneath and it took all his will-power not to cross the room and haul her into his arms.

'I did what I had to.'

The unreadable expression in her eyes gave him little clue to why she was here though he wished she would stop staring at him as if he'd grown two heads.

Swallowing, he turned away and walked into the kitchen.

'Can I get you anything?' He opened the refrigerator. 'I've got beer, beer and beer.'

When she didn't respond, he looked up and almost jumped; she'd snuck up on him, moving with the stealth of one of his recruits.

'Can we talk?'

The beseeching look in her eyes had him backing away before he knew what he was doing.

'Haven't we said enough?'

He filled the sink, reaching for a pile of dirty plates. In fact, reaching for anything concrete that would keep his hands occupied and away from giving in to their first instinct to touch her.

'I don't think so.'

Her calm voice contrasted with her fiddling hands, which were busily tidying the mail he'd left strewn across the kitchen-top.

'Yeah?' He scrubbed the dishes with particular ferocity before stacking them to dry.

'At least hear me out.'

He glanced over his shoulder, noting her downcast eyes, her wobbly bottom lip. Hell, if she cried he'd never be able to resist taking her into his arms. Emptying the sink in record time, he dried his hands and pointed to the living room. 'We can talk in there.'

She nodded and he resisted the urge to pull her pony-tail as it bobbed. He liked her hair up like that; she looked like a teenager, almost like when he'd first met her. Damn, so much had happened since then.

He waited till she sat down and chose the chair opposite. No use in getting too close.

Kate took a deep breath and plunged straight into her speech before she lost her nerve. 'First up, I'd like to apologise for what I said about you, about running away all the time. I was way out of line.'

'You don't have to do this.'

He stared at her, those familiar blue eyes boring directly into her soul, a place that was empty without him in her life.

'Yeah, I do.'

He shook his head, his too-kissable lips compressed in a hard line. 'Whatever you say won't change facts. We're over. You've got your whole life in front of you. Make the most of it. Move on. Be happy.'

'Not without you,' she murmured, convinced that her thudding heart would drown out her words.

She didn't want to move on. She'd been wrong to agree to only a week, to close the book on their story. From where she stood they had a whole lot of chapters left and she'd have her happily ever after if it killed her.

'I can't give you what you want. We've already discussed this.'

He leaned forward, rested his elbows on his knees and dropped his head into his hands, not looking at her.

She allowed herself the luxury of scanning his bare legs, noting the lean muscles and imagining how they would feel under her hands again. She loved him in shorts. She loved him in anything. She loved him, period. Now all she had to do was convince him of the fact.

'And you still think you can't give me what I need?'

He shrugged, his casualness cutting her to the core. 'I'm sure there are any number of guys just waiting to give you what you need.'

'What do *you* need, Ty?'

He glanced up, his solemn gaze locking with hers across the room, and for one brief second she thought he'd say the word she wanted to hear.

You.

She wanted him to say how much he needed her, how much he loved her despite all that had happened between them, despite the wasted years apart.

But he didn't speak. He just sat there, staring at her with that serious look, not blinking, not flinching, and showing no emotion whatsoever.

Tell him you love him.

Instead, she did the one thing guaranteed to capture his attention, to get some sort of a reaction out of him.

'Well, if you won't tell me what you need, how about I show you?'

Mustering the last of her fleeting courage, she stood up, pulled her top off and shimmied out of her skirt.

No more playing it safe. She would take control, show him what he was missing out on and convince him that they needed each other. For ever.

Tyler's eyes bulged. He couldn't believe that Kate was standing in his living room wearing the sexiest, briefest scraps of lace he'd ever seen. Though what impressed him more were the tempting curves that filled the lingerie and his hands just itched to free them.

'Someone's been to Victoria's Secret.'

It sounded stupid but he had to play it cool till he figured out what the hell he was going to do.

'So what do you think?'

'Nice lace.'

He almost salivated at the thought of peeling the scraps of material away, leaving her creamy skin exposed.

'What about what's inside the lace?'

Her hands slithered down her body and she started playing with the elastic of her panties, driving him insane in the process.

'You'll have to show me.' He forced himself to sit still, wondering if she would take up the challenge.

She did and notched up the level of torture she was inflicting to unbearable.

He watched her push the panties down, step out of them and kick them away. They landed on the coffee-table with a soft plop, pooling in a tempting little heap of black lace, and her bra followed suit as she unhooked it, slipped out of it and threw it at him.

'Great catch,' she said, her husky voice filling the room with promise as he reflexively caught it.

'So, what's the verdict?'

She stood in front of him, wearing nothing but a coy smile.

'Better than the lace. Much better,' he growled as he leaped off the sofa and reached for her.

This was not a good idea.

They were finished and this wouldn't change a thing. He should push her away, send her packing and remember every reason why he had to walk away from the best thing to ever happen to him—while he could still walk.

Closing his eyes, he prayed for control as she moved towards him, driving him to the brink of losing it. Every thought he'd ever had about keeping his distance from her, about walking away and not looking back, almost flew straight out the window as she touched him.

'No.'

He pulled away, his breathing ragged as he marched to the other side of the room, putting some valuable space between them.

He didn't know what had possessed her to come here like this, but he knew that whatever happened he would never forget the sight of his beautiful Katie standing before him wearing nothing but a smile.

As she stared at him the uncertainty in her hazel eyes tore him apart and he gritted his teeth, knowing this final goodbye would be the hardest mission he'd ever faced in his life.

'I think you should get dressed.'

Kate closed her eyes, drowning in mortification. She'd never stripped for him before and strangely hadn't felt self-conscious with the appreciation evident in his eyes as he'd watched her.

However, her act hadn't had the desired effect. Instead of reaching for her and offering her a one-way ticket to wherever he was being transferred he kept his hands firmly planted to his sides while she stood there like a fool in her birthday suit.

She'd taken control hoping to show him what he was missing out on and what had he done? Rejected her touch, put space between them and told her to cover up.

So much for knocking him dead with her body. She would've done better knocking some sense into her head by bashing it against the wall.

Silence engulfed them as she picked up her clothes, trying to muster whatever dignity she could—which wasn't much considering she was stark naked.

'You can get dressed through there.'

He pointed towards the bedroom and walked into the kitchen without a backward glance, leaving her mortified and more alone than she'd ever felt in her entire life.

Struggling to hold back tears, she stumbled towards the bedroom. She couldn't help but notice the two bags lying on his bed, one neatly zipped, the other packed to overflowing. Glancing around the bare, stripped room, she suddenly had her answer.

Nothing she could do or say would change Ty's mind, no words of love, no demonstration of it.

Love might have temporarily blinded her, but the blinkers had well and truly come off now.

Ty didn't want her no matter how much she was willing to give him.

He was ready to move on and who was she to stop him?

CHAPTER FOURTEEN

ONCE she'd dressed and composed herself Kate walked into the living room. Ty looked up from the magazine he held, though she knew he hadn't been looking at it unless his skills extended to reading upside down.

Good. She hoped he felt as rattled as she did.

'When do you leave?' Her voice stayed remarkably steady for a woman who was falling apart inside.

'Tomorrow morning.' He looked at her without quite meeting her eyes.

'You never mentioned where you were going.'

'It's not important.'

Not important? He was walking out of her life for good come tomorrow morning and he didn't want her to know where he was going? Guess it wouldn't be important if he didn't care about her and if his actions weren't enough to convince her of that sad fact, his callous words were.

'A mystery destination? In that case, I don't think I'll be dropping in if I'm ever in the area.'

She forced a smile, knowing her attempt at humour sounded pathetic but grasping at anything to hide her humiliation. And her breaking heart.

'You take care.' He stood up and walked towards her, sending her pulse skittering into overdrive.

'You too.'

Though her mind willed her legs to move, to get out with what little dignity she had left, the message didn't get through. The bleak expression in his eyes jammed all her circuits, rooting her to the spot.

She held her breath as he brushed her cheek with the back of his hand.

'You better go,' he said softly, cupping her chin in his hands, scanning her face with an intensity that suggested he was trying to imprint every last detail into his memory bank.

He leaned towards her and she placed a hand on his chest to stop him, feeling his heat through the cotton and wondering how she could ever live without him again, touching him, smelling him, loving him.

'Don't kiss me, Ty. This is hard enough as it is.'

'Okay.' He sounded shaky and for the first time she thought he might actually care more than he let on.

She picked up her suitcase and walked towards the door, steeling herself not to look back.

'What's the suitcase for?'

She didn't break stride. 'I thought I might be going away but I've changed my mind.'

Or in reality he'd changed it for her the minute he'd shattered her heart by rebuffing her last attempt at making him see they belonged together, and as she pulled the door shut behind her the decisive click rammed home the fact she would never see Ty again.

Striding to the car, she kept her emotions in check till she'd reached its confines, swearing this was the last time she would ever cry over Tyler James.

Tyler watched Kate walk down the path, get into her car and drive away.

Out of his life.

For good.

He should be thankful that he'd had one last glimpse of the best thing that had ever happened to him.

The best thing?

Hell, he'd always been prone to understatement. Kate stimulated him on every level: he admired her drive, her ambition, her zest for life. And as for their physical compatibility—no, he wouldn't let his mind drift off on that tangent.

He needed to think straight, at least for the next few minutes. Something she'd said niggled at his brain and he couldn't quite remember. Was it from before her hot striptease act had driven every sensible thought out of his head?

Every way he looked at it, every angle analysed, all things considered, she was right for him in every way.

Yet he couldn't have her.

Suddenly, it hit him. The suitcase. She'd muttered something about going away and changing her mind. Why would she arrive on his doorstep with a suitcase unless she'd planned on going away with *him*?

Once the wheels started turning his mind shifted into overdrive. If she'd been prepared to go away with him that probably meant she'd put her job on hold. And if Kate had been willing to put her prized promotion on hold to follow him to wherever his fictitious transfer was that meant she loved him more than anything. It was the only answer that made any sense.

Mentally kicking himself and cursing profusely, he grabbed his keys and mobile phone before heading out the door.

His instincts had never let him down before. Maybe it was time he trusted them again, starting with a very important phone call to his commanding officer and the doc.

* * *

Kate needed to get away. Immediately. She couldn't function, let alone think.

So her plan to follow Ty to the ends of the earth hadn't worked out. So what? She could still use the time off.

Hadn't worked out? Not only had her plans backfired, but she'd made an idiot of herself in the process.

Lord, what must Ty think of her? His last impression would be of a woman who was quite happy to come into a guy's house the day before he left town, strip off, offer him her body on a plate and walk away.

'Real classy,' she muttered as she pulled into the LAX car park.

Grabbing her suitcase, she stabbed at the car remote and headed into the departure terminal. She'd been thinking about this for a while and Ty's reappearance in her life had prompted her to seriously reconsider her priorities.

She hadn't been back to Australia in years and what better place to mend a broken heart than home?

Besides, she hadn't spoken to her mum in ages and, though they'd never been close, if there was ever a time she needed a mother now was it.

Before she could chicken out she walked up to the nearest counter and booked a seat on the next flight to Sydney. Doris didn't usually like surprises yet Kate hoped she wouldn't mind this one.

Finding the nearest payphone, she placed a call to work, notifying them of her change of plans. Henry had thought she'd been crazy taking a month off as he was about to announce her promotion, but she'd convinced him that a little 'R and R' was in order, especially after she'd come through for the magazine.

Luckily she hadn't thrown in her job as her first impulse had been to do. Sure, she'd been ready to follow Ty anywhere, but had wisely decided to test the waters of their relationship first before doing anything as drastic as leaving *Femme*. Who knew, maybe she'd jeopardised her chances at the promotion anyway as Henry didn't take kindly to 'flighty' females.

She abhorred his outdated views, but it had never affected her and she'd played his game to ensure her precious job was safe.

Not that it mattered any more. Nothing did. If she didn't have Ty in her life everything else just wasn't enough.

Once she boarded the plane and it took off she snoozed, eager to catch up on some of the sleep she'd been missing the last week. When Ty hadn't been there in the flesh he'd haunted her restless dreams, making any type of rest impossible. Hopefully, the soothing sound of the ocean at Bondi would lull her to sleep for the next few weeks. She needed all the help she could get.

It seemed as if she'd barely closed her eyes before a flight attendant shook her awake, requesting that she return her seat to the upright position for landing. Glancing out the window, she watched the sparkling Sydney city lights reflect off the harbour, the impressive Harbour Bridge and Opera House clearly visible.

It had been six years since she'd seen her home city and now she was here her stomach churned with excitement. Though she adored LA she knew exactly how Dorothy had felt landing back in Kansas: there was no place like home.

After checking into a boutique hotel in Bondi almost metres from her old home she freshened up and headed out, determined to ignore the possibility of jet lag and eager to see everything her old suburb had to offer.

As she strolled along the teeming streets filled with trendy boutiques and vibrant cafés the tension of the last week slowly slipped away. So much had changed here yet the familiar scents of sea air, fish and chips and lattes infused her with a calm she hadn't felt since she'd first seen Ty's name on that damn auction list.

A couple of weeks here would be good for her. Sydney was as far away from LA and Ty as she could get and the perfect place to deal with her memories and move on.

Speaking of memories...she found her feet unconsciously treading the well-worn path to her old home and, though she wasn't ready to face her mum just yet—another few days should psyche her up for that auspicious occasion—she stopped outside the house, hiding like a fugitive behind an old oak on the opposite side of the street.

Narrowing her eyes, she peered across the street, more than a little surprised at the changes wrought: box hedges perfectly trimmed, terracotta pots filled with palms flanking a new leadlight door, an ornate porch light switched on. The house looked welcoming, in stark contract to her memories of it being a prison as she trudged up the same path every day after school and later after her internship at *The Sydney Morning Herald.*

She'd hated this house, hated the fact her father had abandoned her here and left her with a mother who obviously resented her as a constant reminder of the man who had messed up her life.

But maybe that wasn't true. Now that she'd loved and lost herself, maybe her mum had been doing the best she could while trying to mend her broken heart and raise a curious kid at the same time.

And she'd been curious, always asking questions about her father, about America where he came from, practically rubbing her mum's nose in it. It hadn't been intentional, but in hindsight she was surprised her mum hadn't told her to shut up rather than answering her questions with pursed lips and a disapproving frown.

She'd blamed her mum for a lot back then, convincing herself that her mother's parenting had made her the way she was: desperate to escape, happy to travel halfway across the world to do so and silly enough to fall for the first guy to look her way.

Pretty ridiculous, considering her mother hadn't made the decision to leave home, fall for a guy in record time and want to marry him. She'd done that of her own accord, made her own decisions, and it was time to recognise her mistakes, accept it and move on. Without acknowledging the truth she'd never be able to let go and stop loving Ty.

Time to put the past to rest and face the future, in all aspects of her life.

Turning away, she headed back to the hotel.

Maybe it was jet lag catching up with her, maybe the sentimentality of being back in Bondi, maybe the realisation that Ty truly was her past, but whatever it was she had the distinct craving for a long, hot bubble bath followed by several mind-numbing daiquiri chasers.

Tyler was a man of action who hated procrastination in any form so when he made up his mind to do something it had to happen—like yesterday.

However, pursuing Kate took time: he spoke to his doc to push back the date and details for his physical, and he survived his commander's bawling out for requesting extra leave before focussing his attention on the main goal.

Convincing Kate that he was the man for her despite everything he'd said and done to the contrary.

However, when he arrived on her doorstep pride in hand he discovered she'd gone away. That seriously dented his confidence. Perhaps she had been going away when she'd dropped in on him? Or worse, perhaps he'd read a lot more into this than he should have?

Doubts plagued him before his resolve settled. Whatever her motives, he knew what he had to do. If he could find her, that was.

He contacted her office and spoke to Di, her assistant. Their conversation was short and sweet. If he'd thought his commander had been tough he'd been dreaming. Di gave him a tongue-lashing for what he'd apparently done to her best friend before dropping the vital piece of information he'd been after: Kate had taken off to Sydney for a little R and R.

That threw him.

Either she'd planned to go to Sydney all along or she'd run away, as far from him as possible.

There was only one way to find out.

CHAPTER FIFTEEN

FOR a born and bred Sydney girl it was only natural Kate loved the beach so she found herself attending a twilight surf carnival on her second night in Bondi. Nothing like the sight of a few half-naked bronzed Aussie guys to take her mind off her troubles.

Plonking down on the sand, she sipped her take-out latte while listening to the pop-cum-reggae of a local band, content to people watch.

Kids squealed with delight, splashing each other in the shallows while teenagers strolled hand in hand along the water's edge. Tourists posed for photos with surf life-savers while a busker imitated a robot on speed, but it was the cosy couples that eventually got to her with their locked gazes, tight clinches and inane smiles.

Finishing her latte in record time, she dumped the cup in a bin and headed up the beach, hoping a quick stroll would clear her head.

The waves broke around her ankles in swirling foam as she wandered along the water's edge, leaving the carnival revellers far behind, trying not to think past the serene beauty of a balmy Sydney evening.

'Excuse me. Could you give me a hand? I seem to have lost my way.'

Her feet froze, sinking into the soft sand as she turned slowly, wondering if she'd drunk one too many daiquiris before dinner.

'Think you can help a sailor with a lousy sense of direction?'

Her heart pounded as she stared at Ty, watching his lips move and hearing the words but not quite believing he was real as her gaze drifted to the yellow board-shorts, Hawaiian shirt and striped surf cap he wore.

'Not to mention lousy dress sense.'

The man of her dreams was standing less than two feet away on Bondi beach and that was all she could say?

Way to go, Kate.

He stared at her, his gaze dropping to her waist. 'Yeah, well, at least I'm not wearing the local vegetation.'

She noted the appreciative gleam in his eyes and her body responded in predictable fashion, a deep, burning heat spreading through every muscle and bone, melting her brain in the process. The carnival had a luau theme so she'd worn a grass skirt at the insistence of the hotel concierge to join in the fun. However, right now the fronds tickling her legs made her feel downright naked.

'Though what I wouldn't give for a lawnmower right now…' He trailed off, the intensity of his stare leaving little doubt in her mind as to what would happen to her skirt if he had one.

'There's a law against destruction of the local flora,' she said, wondering what the heck he was doing here while fighting the urge to fling herself into his arms.

He raised an eyebrow. 'Who said anything about destruction? I'd merely cut back a bit to display the beauty underneath.'

She tried to ignore the glow that blossomed at his words. Nothing had changed. After all that had happened between them, here they were exchanging quips as they always did.

'What are you doing here?'

She cut to the chase, afraid that if they continued their

banter she'd do something stupid like beg him to give them a second chance. Now that would be stupid, considering she'd already tried and he'd ended it anyway.

'I came to see you.'

She folded her arms and tried to focus on the reason she was here, to get away from the man standing in front of her, acting as if nothing had happened. 'Why?'

The darkness hid the expression in his eyes. 'I have an assignment for you.'

Disappointment flooded her. So what had she been expecting?

A declaration of undying love? As if.

'Can't help you. I'm taking a break from work.'

He flashed the familiar killer smile, the one that made her knees shake. 'I'd make it worth your while.'

If he expected her to melt at the sight of his pearly whites, he had another thing coming. Steeling her traitorous body against reacting further, she shook her head.

'Sorry. Not interested.'

He reached out, running the back of his hand down her cheek. 'Don't you want to hear what it's about?'

Her resolve unravelled in an instant as her skin tingled from his brief touch.

'No.'

She held her breath as his fingers trailed along her jaw-line before cupping her chin and tilting her head up.

He stared into her eyes and all the feelings she'd managed to suppress the last few days flooded back, rendering her helpless.

'I have a friend who needs help. He just made a really bad decision about a woman he's crazy about and is feeling a tad uncertain about what he should do next. What do you think he should do?'

Her pulse raced as his thumb reached up and stroked her bottom lip, sending excited shivers skittering down her spine.

'Depends how crazy he is over the woman,' she managed to say, quelling the urge to nip at his thumb.

'He's totally loco. Stark raving mad. Can't eat, can't sleep.'

'Sounds bad.'

Her breath hitched as his thumb slid perilously close to her mouth for a second and she knew in an instant that she'd stepped right back on their personal roller coaster and couldn't do a damn thing about it.

His eyes widened as he continued in a husky voice. 'Should he tell the woman how he feels?'

Kate took a step back, breaking the contact between them. The ride was rocky enough without their ever-present, all-consuming physical attraction wreaking havoc with her senses. She couldn't think straight when he touched her.

'Sure. Why not take a chance? What does he have to lose?'

'His mind. His sanity. His heart.'

Their gazes locked and held as silence enveloped them, heavy with expectation and untold truths.

Tyler took a deep breath and exhaled slowly. Nothing had prepared him for this. He'd trained for every eventuality in his job, had accepted his diagnosis from the docs, yet felt powerless when pinned beneath the stare of the woman he loved. It totally unnerved him.

He'd been mad to follow her out here.

Why couldn't he have waited till tomorrow when they could have met in the safety of a hotel bar? Instead, he'd called in favours from an Aussie commander he'd met once to locate her hotel, then, having spotted her walking away from the carnival near the hotel, he'd been stupid enough to follow her onto a deserted section of the beach, lured by a glimpse of her sexy legs beneath the ridiculous grass skirt and the promise of more delights underneath.

He shouldn't have touched her. As soon as he'd caressed her skin, all logic had fled and he'd been instantly ruled by his anatomy rather than his brain. Rather than stating the truth from the start he'd resorted to some childish word game, knowing she would see right through him, and now he waited like a condemned man praying for a pardon.

When she finally spoke, he almost shouted, 'Get it over and done with.' Instead, she fixed him with that tell-tale glare.

'Are you saying he loves her?'

'Yeah.'

The noose slipped around his neck and tightened. So much for a pardon.

'Enough to give up his transfer? To stick around?'

He heard the incredulity in her voice even though the darkness hid her expression.

'There is no transfer. He hid behind that to avoid telling the truth, which he'll get around to if she gives him another chance. As for sticking around, he'd be in it for the long haul this time, if she is.'

'What do you mean no transfer?'

Taking a deep breath, he launched into the explanation that would make or break them one way or the other.

'This guy has a secret. Several, actually. There is no transfer because he's having a physical soon to determine whether he is still considered fit to serve given the state of his knee. Though he pretty much knows it's the end of the line and the results of the physical will get him booted out of the Navy. He couldn't tell the woman he loves because he didn't want her hanging around him out of pity so he did the only thing he could. He walked away. He'd already made a promise to himself never to have to depend on anyone and, being a big, macho SEAL, he always kept his promises. The only problem with this one, though, was that he hadn't counted on how much he loved this woman.'

He paused, wishing she'd give him some sign of encouragement, some indication she believed him.

'When he returned from his first mission where he couldn't stop thinking about her, he weakened and looked her up, but she'd gone. Which was fair enough, he told himself. They'd both agreed on a split. And after all, a promise is a promise. He's gone through the motions the last six years. And then she shows up just over a week ago around the time he's scheduled to go in for the physical that will probably end his career and rather than push her away he's selfish, takes what he can get for the week, ready to walk away at the end.'

She didn't blink, move a muscle or give him any indication she was listening to any of this but he ploughed on anyway, needing to explain why he'd treated her so badly.

'His plan was working out just fine till she showed up on his doorstep, suitcase in hand, and it wasn't till he'd pushed her away for good this time that he realised what she was trying to do. He thinks this woman loves him, that she was willing to follow him to wherever in order to give them another chance, but he was still too scared. In all probability he won't be anything more than a washed-up ex-sailor in a few weeks; the docs have already more or less confirmed it. Why should a vibrant, beautiful, career woman be stuck in a dead-end relationship with a guy like that? Then it hit him. He owed her the truth if nothing else. He didn't want to face his future, uncertain as it is, without telling her how much she means to him, how much he loves her, how she's the best thing that ever happened to him and that none of this is her fault. It never was.'

Tyler exhaled, a vice-like pain gripping his heart as Kate stepped away, putting more distance between them.

'Tell your *friend* he has a lot of work to do.'

What was that supposed to mean? Did he have a chance or not? Had she heard a word he'd said? Had she absorbed the implications?

She shook her head, a sad expression on her face. 'The

woman he supposedly loves has no idea what goes through this guy's head. He pushed her away years ago and is still pushing. He pushed so hard she gave up. And now he tells her the truth, something he should've done before, and expects her to take him back? What makes him think she'd even consider it?'

'This,' he said, covering the short distance between them in a second and reaching out to her.

His lips crushed hers, stifling any further protest she might make as he claimed her mouth, ravishing her in a long, deep kiss. He'd wanted to do it since the first minute he'd seen her again and, now that he had her in his arms, he didn't want to hold back and sure as hell never wanted to let go.

She squirmed against him as his hands wandered, touching her everywhere. Her silky skin teased his fingertips and he couldn't get enough of her, sliding his hand up her bare thigh, over the curve of her hip, across the smooth expanse of stomach and finally coming to rest, cupping her breast.

'I love it when you wear bikinis,' he murmured.

She leaned back, offering herself to him like a tempting sacrifice for a feasting god. 'Sweet talking won't get you anywhere this time.'

Her fingers wound through his hair, tugging him closer, urging him to taste, to savour. However, he didn't stop there. He rained moist, deep kisses all over her exposed skin, trailing along the tempting hollow at the base of her throat, relishing her delicate skin and the light, salty taste from the sea spray.

'Ty, we're on a beach,' she said, the sinuous writhing of her body belying the conservative logic of her words.

'And there's no one around down here.'

He drew back to look at her, noting her swollen, slick lips and flushed cheeks, highlighted by the soft moonlight.

God, he loved this woman, heart, body and soul. And how did he show it? By pawing her on a public beach?

His conscience told him to pull away, to take it slow and convince her of his feelings, but his body had other ideas.

Kate decided the argument. 'I've missed you,' she whispered against the side of his mouth as she kissed him.

'Same here, kiddo,' he ground out, barely managing to keep from taking her on the spot.

Kate's heart flip-flopped at his smile as her brain warred with her heart. This was crazy. She'd put time and space between them to get over exactly what she was feeling at that moment: floundering, yearning, wanting him more than ever.

'We should stop this,' she said, stepping away from him. 'This isn't supposed to happen.'

He traced her face with his fingertips, skimming her skin in a feather-light touch. 'You're right. I wanted to talk, to try and work things out between us.'

'You really did all this because of some weird promise to yourself?' She whacked him on the chest. 'What were you thinking?'

Wrapping his arms around her, he snuggled her close. 'SEALs are about honour and integrity and loyalty but a promise means more to me. When I was growing up it's all I focussed on. I promised myself I'd get out of the orphanage, I promised to make something of myself and I promised I'd give something back to those who helped me along the way, like Mary. However, I'd been let down by people I'd loved too many times growing up and I made a promise not to depend on anyone, not to get emotionally attached to anyone ever again.'

'So why did you get involved with me back then?'

A slight frown puckered her brow and he resisted the urge to lean down and smooth it with his lips.

Holding her close, he knew he had to make her believe him. 'Because I fell in love with you, because I wanted to build a family with you, a family of my own, a family that I never had. Yeah, it was quick and it took me by surprise, but I'd been virtually alone my whole life, lived by strict rules both at the orphanage and in the Navy, and for once I wanted to make an impulsive decision, one that involved my heart and not my head. Unless you count the fact I lost it over you.'

'Then why did you agree to end it?'

He'd been kicking himself over the very same question for the last six years.

'Because you were young and I didn't want to take advantage of you. Sure, I was crazy about you, head-over-heels crazy, but I knew that first love can fade as quickly as it comes and I wanted to give you time, see if you still felt the same way after you wised up, after I came back from a long absence.'

Her expression softened but she still looked at him with a quizzical look in her eyes. 'Okay, that explains why you quit first time around. Why push me away now?'

'It's the whole washed-up thing. I didn't want you tied down to a guy like that. I *don't* want you tied down to a guy like that, but I had to set the record straight after the way I'd treated you.'

'That's nonsense. You should've asked me what I wanted rather than making decisions for me.'

He captured her face in his hands and stared deeply into her eyes. 'I may end up a grouchy ex-sailor who can barely walk. Do you know what that means?'

The sheen of tears sparkled in the moonlight and he brushed away a lone tear as it trickled down her soft cheek.

'Give me some credit,' she said, turning her cheek to rest it against his hand and gazing up at him with apprehension in her hazel eyes. 'I'm a big girl. I can make my own choices and I know what I want. What do you want?'

'I want to take care of you.'

He spoke so softly, the sound of the waves crashing against the shore almost drowned him out.

'What's that supposed to mean?'

'Damn it, Kate. Do I have to spell it out?'

'Yes, you do.' She barely paused, the words tumbling out in an angry rush. 'After an amazing week you've done everything in your power to push me away even after I hinted at how I feel and asked you to stay. Then you follow me halfway round the world, spin me some story, which I assume is the truth, then skirt around the issue all over again. Don't you get it? I'm in love with you, you moron.'

There, she'd said it and he hadn't moved an inch, not even a flicker of an eyelash.

'Your declaration could do with a little work,' he said, the corners of his mouth twitching as a big, sloppy grin spread across his face.

'I hate you.' She pummelled his chest, her fists barely making a mark before he stilled her wrists.

'No, you don't. You love me as much as I love you.' His grin widened as she stared up at him, speechless. 'What? Nothing to say? That's got to be a first.'

She reached up, cradling his face in her hands as she pulled him towards her.

'Shut up and kiss me,' she said, marvelling that the man of her dreams had finally come to his senses.

'Is that any way to talk to your future husband? But just to let you know, this time I'm doing the asking and, this time, it will be for ever.'

His lips brushing hers saved her from responding. Besides, he knew her answer anyway. She'd always been his from the very first minute they'd battled wills all those years ago.

'You'll always be my Odd Bod, you know. For the rest of your life. Inside and outside the bedroom, for better or worse, and all the rest of that jargon.'

He caressed her cheek, his touch achingly familiar. 'I'm all yours…boss.'

EPILOGUE

'I ALWAYS wanted a beach wedding.'

Kate turned in the circle of Ty's arms and smiled up at her new husband, the clear blue Bondi sky reflected in his beautiful eyes. 'That's because you're obsessed with water. Once a SEAL, always a SEAL.'

Ty shrugged, his broad shoulders tugging at the tux jacket that fitted his body so perfectly. 'Hey, you can take the boy out of the Navy but you can't take the Navy out of the boy.'

Kate's smile waned as she reached up to cup his cheek. 'Do you miss it?'

His blue eyes clouded for a moment, as if lost in some precious memory, before he shook his head and grinned, the same cocky smile that captured her heart so long ago.

'Honestly? I miss the guys, but my new job keeps me too busy to spend much time reminiscing on the good old days.'

Kate kissed him on the lips, soft, lingering, the type of kiss that needed no words, the type of kiss that told him exactly how amazing he was.

'I'm so proud of you. Any other guy would've wallowed in self-pity after your physical didn't pan out a year ago and you had no option but to leave the Navy. But not my guy, uh-uh. Instead, after a painful knee replacement and months of rehab, you throw yourself whole-heartedly into establishing a youth centre at the orphanage and give Mary some much-needed time out to follow her own dreams.'

She sighed, snuggling closer to him. 'That's my guy, just as much of a hero as he ever was running covert ops or bringing in the baddies.'

'You think I'm that good, huh?'

'Oh, yeah,' she said, leaning into him with her hips, loving the naughty gleam in his eyes as her pelvis made contact with his. 'You're very, very good.'

He laughed, a low, intimate rumble of laughter that enveloped her like a warm blanket on a cold night. 'Watch it, Mrs James, or I might decide to skip the reception part and whisk you over those sand dunes to have my wicked way with you.'

'Promises, promises,' she murmured, her hands skimming his back and coming to rest on his butt where she gave a gentle squeeze.

'Hey, you two! Cut it out! Save it for later.'

They laughed and pulled apart, grinning like a couple in love as they turned to see Bear with an equally goofy grin on his face.

'Great timing as always, Bear,' Ty said, slipping an arm around her waist. 'And I'd expect better of you, Mary. You're supposed to be keeping this big lug in line.'

Mary rolled her eyes. 'I have as much chance of keeping him in line as I did with you all those years growing up.'

Kate sent Mary a wink, knowing exactly how demanding living with a big, brawny, alpha guy could be. 'If Bear's as much of a pussycat as Ty, your job must be a piece of cake.'

'Pussycat? *Pussycat*?' Ty's splutter of indignation had them all laughing. 'Did you hear that, Bear? A guy leaves the Navy for two seconds and he's demoted to pussycat status. Man, that sucks.'

Bear shrugged and draped a protective arm across Mary's shoulders, the big guy towering over the petite woman. 'Take it from me, TJ. Never argue with a woman. Works for me.'

Mary elbowed him in the ribs and chuckled at his mock double-over. 'As if.'

Kate smiled and made a T sign with her hands. 'Okay, guys, time out. This is our wedding day. Time to get the party started.'

'Too right,' Bear and Mary said in unison before turning to each other as Bear swung the laughing woman into his arms and planted a huge lip-smacking kiss on her mouth. 'Later, you two.'

Ty shook his head. 'Tell me again why I introduced them.'

'Because you love Mary, you love Bear and they're a match made in heaven.'

'And you're too much of a romantic,' he said, dropping a kiss on her lips before returning his attention to the couple as they sauntered away, arms wrapped tightly around each other's waists. 'Though I have to say I've never seen Mary so happy. She's revelling in the social work course and dotes on Bear. As for him, he deserves his fair share of happiness too considering his heart's as big as the rest of him.'

'My husband, the matchmaker.'

Kate smiled up at him, oblivious to the sun, sand and four-piece jazz band just starting up in a nearby pavilion where a seafood buffet was laid out for them, oblivious to everything but the incredible man staring at her as if she was the best thing he'd ever seen.

The tenderness in his eyes left her breathless as he drew her close again.

'You know, none of this would've happened if you hadn't run that article on the orphanage. Mary would still be trapped there if that international conglomeration hadn't come up with the funds to keep the place open and to hire new staff. So in a way you're the matchmaker, not me.'

'Fine, I'll take all the credit.'

She smiled and traced a lazy finger down his cheek. 'It's great how everything's come full circle, isn't it? We're reunited, you've kept your promise to Mary and you're back at the orphanage doing something you love. Pretty amazing if you ask me.'

'Speaking of full circle...' Ty sent a pointed glance over her right shoulder and she half turned in time to see her mother flash a tentative, shy smile before taking a champagne flute from a passing waiter. 'I think Doris has wanted to talk to you since the ceremony ended but we've been caught up.'

'Nothing wrong with being wrapped up in each other,' Kate said, giving him a quick kiss on the lips before reluctantly slipping out of his embrace. 'But you're right. I need to have a quick chat with Mum before the festivities get under way.'

'Don't be long.'

Ty's subtle tap on her butt, combined with the naughty quirk of his lips, left her in little doubt that her sexy husband wanted her by his side as much as possible, exactly where she wanted to be.

Kate blew him a kiss and headed for her mum, who was looking extremely elegant in a lavender dress that accentuated her figure and took years off her. Kate had always thought of her mum as wearing drab clothes and a perpetual frown, but thankfully those memories had been clouded by Kate's own unhappiness. Now that she'd come to terms with her past, she saw her mum in a whole new light.

'You look great, Mum.'

Kate reached out and laid a hand on her mum's arm, pleased when Doris turned and her face lit up.

'And you make a beautiful bride, dear.'

They hugged and Kate blinked back the sudden sting of tears, thinking of all the years she'd missed this, grateful they'd managed to patch things up despite their time apart.

'You did a great job co-ordinating things from this end, Mum. Organising a Sydney wedding from LA with the deadlines I've had to meet would've been a killer if it hadn't been for you.'

Doris smiled, a glimmer of tears in her eyes. 'It was the

least I could do, after the botched job I did of being a real mum when you were growing up.'

Kate held up her hand. 'Uh-uh, enough. We've been through all that. You were doing the best you could with a broken heart and I was being a selfish brat blaming you for Dad running out on us. It's in the past.'

She smiled and squeezed her mum's hand. 'Besides, look at our futures.'

They turned in unison to see Ty chatting to Percy Robertson, Doris's new partner, a debonair seventy-year-old who doted on her.

'We're so lucky,' Doris said, slipping an arm around Kate's waist and hugging her close.

'We sure are.'

Kate sighed, content to stare at her new husband all day. However, Ty looked up at that exact moment and smiled, the irresistible magnetic pull between them a force even at this distance.

'I'll see you later, Mum.'

Doris laughed. 'If I had a guy look at me like that I'd go running too.'

Kate smiled as she slipped off her sandals and headed in Ty's direction, her gaze fixed on her husband who was already halfway across the sand to meet her.

'I missed you,' he said, capturing her in his arms and taking her breath away with a swift, thorough kiss.

'I missed you too.'

Her heart expanded at the adoration in his eyes, the sexy smile playing about his delicious lips.

'We've waited a long while for this wedding, Katie. Let's go have the time of our lives.'

'I'm with you all the way,' she said, slipping her hand into his, eager to take the first steps towards the rest of their lives, together.

BEDDED BY ARRANGEMENT

BY
NATALIE ANDERSON

Possibly the only librarian who got told off herself for talking too much, **Natalie Anderson** decided writing books might be more fun than shelving them—and, boy, is it that! Especially writing romance—it's the re-alisation of a lifetime dream, kick-started by many an afternoon spent devouring Grandma's Mills & Boon® novels… She lives in New Zealand, with her husband and four gorgeous-but-exhausting children. Swing by her website any time—she'd love to hear from you: www.natalie-anderson.com.

This book would never have been written without my super support crew: Mum/Nan, Nanny June, Aunty Margaret, Karla, Julia and Jude. Thank you.

CHAPTER ONE

EMMA had been frowning at the spreadsheet since six in the morning and now, almost twelve hours later, the glitch still troubled her. And instead of being able to stay on and fix it properly, she had to go and be social with work colleagues she couldn't exactly count as friends.

She stood, stretched, then opened the window, letting the gentle breeze blow the gauzy curtains about her. Fresh air. She breathed deeply.

The conversation from the courtyard below floated up without hindrance. High-pitched female voices that carried far in the still, warm evening.

'Do you think she'll come?'

'She wouldn't know how.'

The women snorted with laughter. Emma recognised them as Becca and Jules.

'Hell, yeah, the woman needs loosening up.'

'I'll say. I don't know what's stronger, her grip on the purse strings or the lock on her knickers.'

She stiffened as waves of cold then hot humiliation flooded through her. They were talking about her. The financial controller for Sanctuary, she was the one with the purse strings. And the lock on her knickers? Ouch. Just because they spoke the truth didn't mean she couldn't feel hurt. There was a lock—of sorts, but more through circumstance than choice. She'd been too busy on her career path. Most of the time she was still too busy to care, but this very second she'd give a lot to change the situation.

They were still talking. And she, foolishly, was still listening.

'I kind of feel sorry for her. All she does is work. Talk about out of balance.'

'Sorry for *her*? I don't. She's a slave-driver. Just because she wants to work like a dog doesn't mean she has to make the rest of us. I want a life, thank you very much. She's only twenty-six and she's hard as.'

Well, that was what you got for eavesdropping. Like reading someone else's diary, you invariably learnt all the things you didn't want to—about yourself.

And now she had to go to the bar to mingle with these women and the rest of the staff of the exclusive hotel who probably all thought the same thing: that she was a workaholic with no life. And wasn't it true? Yes, she worked hard and, yes, she expected others to. That was how she'd been raised. She'd followed her father's rules: you work hard, you get the rewards—the praise, the attention and maybe even the love. So why wasn't she quite as happy as she should be given her career success? The fighter in her charged her weapons, but she had to admit she was a little lacking in ammo.

As quietly as she could she shut the window. She'd heard enough. She wasn't going to let them get to her—much. But she did want to prove them wrong. Was she coming? Hell, yes. Some time. Somehow. She'd go to those drinks and smile and laugh and act interesting even if it killed her.

She checked her perfectly applied lipstick and ensured there was no stray wisp of hair escaping her immaculate French roll. Appearances were everything. And after all, the perfectionist retentive look was what they expected.

She paused on her way out to bend and take in a whiff of the white hyacinth in the single-stem specimen vase that sat on her desk. It was the only personal item to feature in her self-imposed clean-desk policy. A little revived by the fresh scent, she tossed her head high and pretended she didn't care.

Once she was at the bar her resolve fragmented and she gravitated, as usual, to Max as soon as she arrived. In no time at all they were locked in work discussion. Work on the refurbishment of the hotel was due to start tomorrow and there was a myriad of issues surrounding it. A workaholic, Max saw her in the same mould. He'd taken her on as a graduate and through his mentoring she'd rapidly progressed. Working all hours, she'd more than met the challenge. Now he'd sold the hotel to a larger chain specialising in unique boutique hotels—hence the refurbishment. Not far off retirement, Max had taken the opportunity to cash in, but he predicted a glowing future for her. The chain had hotels in several cities and if she played her cards right, she could have her pick of any of them.

Problem was, she didn't know if she wanted to go through with that. Bigger hotel. Bigger hours. And she was beginning to think she might like more of a life. She'd spent all of it so far fulfilling the expectations of others. And she wasn't sure the results were worth it. But she couldn't tell Max that, not when he'd given her such an opportunity, not when he was one of those people she felt compelled to please.

She glanced over to where the other women were grouped—giggling, guzzling lurid-coloured cocktails and flirting with the bar staff. Here she was, still talking shop with the sixty-five-year-old boss and sipping slowly from the dry lemonade in her hand.

Dull, dull, dull. Those women were right. Depression weighed in her stomach. She'd been working so hard—and for what? Whose dream was she chasing?

She excused herself and went to the bar, getting the bartender to add a splash of gin to her glass. Taking a sip, she turned and glanced away from her colleagues and out across the bar. It had yet to really fill up; a few patrons sat at tables and across the way a couple of guys were playing pool. She couldn't help but watch the one currently taking a shot. He had his back to her and was providing a great view of a particularly great butt. Just because she didn't get to play, she could still look and appreciate. His long legs, slightly spread, were clad in denim. His white tee shirt pulled tight across broad shoulders and muscular back. He held the pool cue with an easy, practised hand and as he bent over the table the whole effect of beautiful-bodied male was magnified.

He took the shot and sank it. His mate groaned. One more shot from the same angle and the game was his. The player rose and walked around the pool table to collect his drink and that was when Emma really stared. She knew that face. And well she knew the cheeky smile that so often graced it.

Jake Rendel.

The depression evaporated and a childlike joy filled her. She hadn't seen him in years, but he'd always shown her a friendly face. And a friendly face was the lift she needed right now.

She forgot the fact that as a teen she'd scarcely been able to look at him without blushing because she'd had such a crush on him. She was so pleased to see him that without thinking she marched straight over, beaming. 'Jake Rendel. How are you?'

The look of shock on his face would have been enough to send her scuttling back to the corner fast if it hadn't been replaced so swiftly by the gorgeous smile that had always knocked her pulse way off kilter. That lock on her knickers rattled.

'Emma Delaney, what a surprise.' His voice was as warm as his smile.

Her pulse skipped another notch higher. She'd forgotten how handsome he was. She had another quick sip of her drink and somehow got the guts to smile back.

She glanced behind him and saw Jules and Becca staring at her. She seized the ammo. She'd prove she could have a conversation with a gorgeous guy and it not be about work. They didn't have to know she'd known him all her life. She widened her smile, looked right back into Jake's eyes and said in the sassiest way she'd ever attempted, 'It's been far too long.'

He blinked. 'It certainly has. You're all grown-up now.' His gaze skittered over her. 'And definitely as successful as you were always going to be. What are you doing here?'

'Work drinks. You?'

'Similar.' His mate seemed to have slunk off leaving them in the corner by the pool table.

There was a pause. Emma struggled to think what to say. Struggled not to stare at him. He'd done some growing up too in the last few years. That fit teenage boy had turned into an even fitter, broader male. Was it possible for a man to be beautiful? If so, Jake Rendel was the definitive example.

The silence was bordering on too long and she became aware he was staring at her as much as she was him. She ran her tongue across her lip, the way his attention was focussed on her mouth, she thought something must be out of place.

Finally Jake elaborated. 'I'm working on a building contract at the hotel nearby for a few weeks.'

'Sanctuary?' she asked, relieved the conversational ball was rolling again.

He nodded.

'I'm the financial controller there.'

He grinned. 'So our paths will be crossing some more. Excellent, you can introduce me round.'

She could. And then stand back and watch as the women queued up. She looked over to where they stood, sorry the fantasy that she'd been flirting with some hot guy would be shattered so soon. He'd be at work tomorrow and they'd know she'd just been talking shop with him tonight.

'You've always stayed in Christchurch?'

She looked back to Jake and answered his conversation-filler question. 'Never left the place. School, then uni, now the job at Sanctuary. It's what I know.'

She'd been packed off to boarding-school from age six. Christchurch was far more her home than the country town where her parents and Jake's mother lived in neighbour-ing properties.

'You look beautiful—very much the professional city slicker.'

Beautiful? Visions of his old girlfriends leapt into her mind and dampened her smile. She wasn't his kind of beautiful.

'We are what we are, Jake,' she said a little ruefully,

wishing her life wasn't all white-collar work. Still smarting from the opinions of her co-workers.

'Well, sometimes we're what we're required to be,' he answered.

She looked at him, disconcerted. The comment was a little close to her own doubting thoughts for comfort. His smile was still easy, but his eyes were astute. She decided to try to keep up the sass, play it light and cool as Jake himself always seemed to. 'You think? What are you required to be, Jake?'

He took a moment to reply and when he did light danced in his eyes and the slow grin revealed his rascal-like humour. 'Well, I can be anything you want me to be, Emma.'

He seemed to have moved nearer, with his body now blocking most of the room from her view, making it feel as if there were no one else there. His voice dropped and she had to lean a little closer herself.

'Is that so?' Her voice had dropped in pitch too. She glanced over to where the others were standing. They were still staring. Glancing back at Jake, she discovered that somehow he'd moved even closer.

'Sure. Anything you'd like. Got any suggestions?'

She couldn't stop the twist to her lips. She could think of a few off the top of her head and not one of them could she utter aloud. Not in this universe. If she were starring in an X-rated movie—maybe. The crush she'd had as a teen came rushing back. She liked him. Always had. Of course, so had the rest of the female population and he'd liked them right back. But not her; he'd only ever been that scamp of a boy living next door who once was a friendly ear that day in the park. Since then she hadn't been able to look at him without turning the colour of an overly ripe tomato. The tomato effect was happening right now, she could feel the heat. Her suggestions? Secret dreams destined to remain silent.

Her silence didn't seem to bother him. 'You know what I'm thinking?' He was looking inspired. 'I'm thinking I should have given you a "hello again" hug. Seeing it's been so long.'

How long had it been? Must be at least eight years. But she was vaguely aware of what he'd been doing in that time. Her sister Lucy was his sister Sienna's best friend. So she knew he wasn't married—chances of that seemed minute. Jake played around. Everyone knew that.

'A hug?' Her attempt at a confident social persona slipped a little.

'Yeah, or maybe even a kiss.'

She tried to look away. She really did. She even managed it for a split-second before she gave up and stared back into those beautiful big blue eyes twinkling at her. Daring her.

'A hello kiss? Just friendly?' She was thinking peck-on-the-cheek friendly, but she wasn't so sure Jake was.

'Sure. Friendly. Maybe we could see how friendly. What do you think?'

Think? How could she think when he seemed to be getting ever closer, his voice lower? Invading her space, spellbinding her. He'd had the reputation for being fast back then. Clearly it was deserved.

She glanced away again, not focussing on the girls that time; she was looking inwards as her heart hammered. Jake Rendel had just asked to kiss her. Maybe today wasn't so bad. Becca's words came back to haunt her—'she wouldn't know how'; 'needs loosening up'; 'hard as'—that was the one that hurt most. The pain pushed her into crossing her own boundaries.

'OK.' Totally breathy, not remotely sassy and not the answer she'd meant at all. She was supposed to have laughed the suggestion off.

Too late. He edged nearer the wall, eyes glittering. The rest of the room disappeared. She stared up at him. One teen dream about to be realised. What would he be like? Hell. What would she be like? Embarrassment overcame her. The heat in her cheeks was at boiling point and her nerve failed. She was no good at this sort of thing, those women were right—she didn't know how and she was about to make a colossal fool of herself. But just as she went to duck away and escape he leaned in, brushing his lips against hers. Ever so gentle, ever so light. She froze. The sensation was soft and warm and she couldn't move away.

He brushed again. Now she didn't *want* to move away. Her lips parted slightly as she breathed and instead of brushing lightly the third time, he lingered. His mouth moved over hers, slow, warm, increasingly insistent. And without thought, without will, she opened to him.

His response was immediate yet still slightly measured, a gentle exploration that teased and tantalised and held the promise of sensual secrets. No other part of their bodies touched. It was as if he knew she felt flighty and he was giving her every opportunity to take off if she wanted to.

She didn't want to.

And inside things really began to happen. As he increased the pressure and depth of his lips and tongue on hers she felt a tingling rise from the depths of her belly to her breast and then it seemed to run through every vein to every part of her body. Like a flower given water she began to blossom, a seductive sensation caused by the six-foot-one pack of gorgeousness in front of her.

Her fingers curled tighter around her glass. And running through her head was the mantra that this was Jake Rendel and he was kissing her. And then even that last thought began to slip away as excitement overwhelmed her. Hesitantly she kissed him back. Then less hesitantly as the taste of him drugged her, made her want more. Hunger. She moaned as she realised the beginnings of a dream. She lifted one hand to his chest. The heat of his body through the cotton tee shirt was as welcome as a roaring fire on the frostiest night. She wanted to get closer to it, uncaring of the risk of burning her fingers. The pressure and depth magnified. His faint stubble teased her soft skin; his masculine scent dizzied her mind. Her body swayed towards his and she only just held her balance.

He lifted his head away. She rocked back on her heels, blinking several times, and saw him studying her expression. Utterly muddled, she tried to look back with what she hoped was cool aplomb. Jake Rendel had been the most popular boy in town and he'd gone through every single one of the beautiful girls that had thrown themselves at him.

He knew what he was about.

She didn't.

He took the glass from her fingers and set it on the table that stood conveniently near. Things always worked that way for Jake. He stepped near enough for her to feel his energy but not close enough that they were actually touching. A sliver of electric-charged atmosphere separated them.

'Going for more than friendly now, Emma,' he warned her.

She didn't reply—was incapable of speech; she thought

she'd just had more than friendly. She wasn't sure she could handle the next level of Jake. What had started as a friendly hello was now a situation rapidly slipping out of her control. Jake Rendel in full force and taking no prisoners.

Jake held back to watch as her blurry eyes widened and he inwardly chuckled. Who'd have thought that shy little Emma Delaney would grow up into someone quite like this? Someone who could kiss quite like that? Outwardly uptight, but in action? Not uptight at all. Body-burning. How intriguing. He breathed in to catch her scent: floral, fresh. She looked like a strict schoolmarm but she smelt of spring.

He'd never really thought about kissing Emma Delaney before, but then he'd never noticed that soft, full mouth before either. Not 'til she'd popped up right in front of him tonight with a sensuous half-smile and smoky eyes.

His five weeks in Christchurch might be more fun than he'd envisaged with her working at the hotel. An interesting possibility. Different.

He was about to investigate further, wanting to kiss her again, when he saw it—another glance over his shoulder. Her glazed look sharpened into deadly accurate focus. He knew for that second her mind was miles away from him.

It was on someone else.

Red alert. Emma Delaney was playing him off. Only interested in seeing someone else's reaction. He shelved plans for a five-week fling and backed off. Stepping away, his smile wiped. This party was over before it had even begun.

He had her attention again but her confused look didn't move him. With a level of discipline that would impress army recruiters, he managed not to spin round and glower at the bloke she was obviously so concerned about. 'Who is it you're watching, Emma? Have you made him jealous?'

'What?'

'Whichever guy it is behind me you're so interested in.'

The shock in her expression had him wondering if he'd just made a huge mistake, but then he saw the flicker of guilt. He'd been right. She was focussed on someone else. Her face coloured instantly.

'I don't like to be used, Emma, and I'd never have picked you for one who played games.'

She opened her mouth and closed it again.

Adrenalin surged through him, making him feel as if he'd powered out on a sea kayak and wrestled with the waves for hours. Instead it had just been a kiss—one that had started out tame enough, but that had ended with him contemplating much more. And he knew she had been too, he'd seen the look in her eye, tasted the hunger in her lush mouth. Had she been honest, he'd have done it again and again. As it was, no, thanks, there were plenty of other fish to fry.

Her skin had yet to return to its normal creamy colour and she was obviously trying to think what to say. He saved her the trouble. 'See you 'round, Emma.' He walked away, leaving her standing there.

Emma watched him rejoin his friend and knew she couldn't leave things like that. He'd gone from devastatingly flirtatious to coldly remote in a blink. He had it partly right but she hadn't been playing him off against some other guy. If she weren't in such a whirl she'd have laughed at the absurdity of that thought. But she was too thrown by the kiss, and she couldn't bear for him to think badly of her.

Sure, she'd acted up initially because the witches had been watching, but within seconds she'd been under his spell just as she'd always been. And amazingly he'd been conjuring it all up for *her*. Not some beautiful bimbo like he'd usually hung with back in the days when their paths had crossed. No, the fact was she couldn't have cared less about anything or anybody once his lips had touched hers. Good grief. This was what she'd been missing?

Then again, she'd always had a thing for Jake. Gut instinct had been so right. And now gut instinct was telling her to come clean to him. She followed him, knowing her face must be completely beetroot. 'Jake, for what it's worth, it wasn't any *guy*.'

He stood silent.

She took a deep breath. 'It was a couple of female work-mates. I'd overheard them earlier talking about me. About my, uh, non-existent love life.' She couldn't bear to look at him at that moment and she pressed on, desperate to get over that most awkward bit. 'I admit it was nice to be seen talking to a guy like you and…um…' Stammering and not quite sure where she was heading, she finally dared look into his face. His expression was lighter.

Then he helped her out. 'A guy like me?' He waggled his brows.

'Yeah.' She tossed her head up, her confidence growing. The lift from his kiss bolstered her decision to be honest. 'You know, Jake. Women only take one look at you and know you'll be fun to play with. And now I know why.'

His amused look deepened. 'I *think* that's a compliment.'

She smiled back, relieved he was no longer angry. She wanted to make things better. 'You really do know how to kiss.' Oh, my God. She hadn't meant for that to slip out.

She knew her cheeks were really glowing now—and not just her cheeks. An all-over body blush.

'You think so?' He ran his hand over his jaw and the smile that tugged at the corner of his mouth was definitely wicked. He lowered his voice and leaned closer. 'Well, if you want a repeat, you just let me know.'

Impossibly she coloured even more, feeling the blaze in her face. She lifted her hands to block her cheeks from sight. Positively frizzling—hot enough to fry an egg on. He must think she was such an idiot. The world's biggest nerd—earnest Emma caught out at trying to be flirty.

A repeat? Well, that would be just fine if his impact on her weren't quite so overpowering. A playful kiss for him was an earthquake event for her. Quite why she'd thought she'd be able to handle saying yes to Jake Rendel was beyond her. He played around and she'd never been any good at team sports. Too embarrassed and tongue-tied to reply, she turned to leave, but his hand shot out to grip her arm.

'I don't mind playing games, Emma, but the games I play have only two players who both know the rules…' He stepped closer again and, like the rabbit caught by the glare of the headlights, she wasn't able to move.

'Rules?'

He nodded, leaning down to whisper in her ear, his voice low and sexy as hell. 'No audience. No ulterior motives. And…' he paused, and the wicked gleam in his eye flared to a full-blown inferno '…no clothes.'

At his sudden smile she knew he'd heard her soft gasp.

Jake Rendel had always been popular because of his good humour, his easy charm. Popular with women. Beautiful women.

She glanced over to where Becca and the others stood,

still staring from behind their drinks. Their less-than-subtle laughter ate at her confidence. She looked back at Jake. He'd followed her line of sight and was smiling at the group of women unashamedly watching them. She saw the assessing sparkle in his eye, the appreciation. And then the reality hit her. If she hadn't come over to him initially, and if she wasn't standing here now telling him about her sub-standard social life he'd be over there working his charm on the whole bunch of blondes.

She was Emma. Geek girl. In no way was she anything like Jake's old girlfriends and, if the attention he was currently bestowing on her co-workers was anything to go by, he didn't appear to have changed too much.

He must have wanted to kiss her out of sheer curiosity. To see if she even *would*.

He looked back at her and his smile widened. Jake was amused. But if he was laughing, he must be laughing *at* her, not with her, because she wasn't laughing at all.

She stepped back as humiliation drowned the last of the delight she'd felt from his touch. She'd been pretending she could flirt and, boy, had she been wrong about that. She couldn't match him. Was hopeless at the whole thing. He'd think she was even more pathetic than when they'd last had a conversation. Jake Rendel messed around. She never did.

She pulled her brain back to business, hiding the fluster. She had a big day on the job tomorrow. She needed to be on top form for that—couldn't let Max down, wouldn't let herself down.

She reverted back to the formal politeness that served her so well. 'Nice to see you again, Jake. Take care.' She knew the platitudes sounded ridiculous after the passionate way she'd just kissed him. She graced him with one of her trademark polite-yet-distanced smiles and left. She didn't look towards her work colleagues at all.

Jake Rendel. The hottest guy she'd ever known and she'd just made a complete fool of herself. He'd never been interested in her. Would never be interested in her. Especially now she'd proved she was the social slow top everybody thought her. She hoped she wouldn't see him again for a long, long time. Except in her dreams.

And then she remembered.

CHAPTER TWO

EMMA arrived at work even earlier than usual—hoping like crazy the builders wouldn't be on the job yet. That Jake wasn't there yet. The fact that he was going to be working in the hotel had gone in one ear and out the other in the excitement of seeing him. Then he'd kissed her—in front of everyone. And she'd humiliated herself—in front of everyone. Especially *him*.

Now Becca and her cohorts would have something different to talk about. Something even more cringe-worthy than her lack of social life: her *disastrous* social life. She didn't want to meet their eyes. And she sure as hell didn't want to see Jake.

Max buzzed her, asking her into a meeting. He greeted her with a wink as she entered the room.

'Emma, I wanted you to be in on this.' He nodded for her to sit. 'You've met Thomas, the boss over at White's Construction.'

Thomas was the same generation as Max. Emma smiled at him as she took her seat.

'I wanted to tell Max in person.' Thomas's smile widened. 'I've handed over the reins. Fresh blood taking over the firm to see it well into the future, just like what's happening here. We've been bought out by a bigger, better company.'

Judging by his pleased expression, Emma knew it was safe to offer congratulations. 'You're retiring?'

'Yes, more time on the golf course coming my way. But this is the man taking over. You have any problems with the builders, you talk to him.' He gestured behind her.

She hadn't realised there was someone else in the room. She turned to see a tall figure leaning against the window and smothered her gasp with a grit of her teeth.

Jake looking totally unlike the Jake she knew of old—the one who hung out in jeans or shorts, and a casual tee shirt. This Jake was in an impeccably tailored charcoal-grey suit. The shirt a bright white, the navy tie classic and understated. Freshly shaved, he looked crisper than she'd ever seen him. He looked like a complete stranger but the imp in his eyes was still there.

Her blush was uncontrollable.

She'd thought he was one of the workers. She hadn't realised he was the boss!

She winced. So much for hoping to avoid him. He'd be in on all the meetings, overseeing the whole damn project.

'You were in the bar last night, weren't you, Jake?' Max filled the gap. Emma glanced at him in horror. His expression was one of wild amusement. 'You already know our Emma here.'

'Yes,' Jake replied, looking at Emma in a way that wasn't reducing the scale of her blush. 'We go way back.'

'Yes, you looked kind of friendly.' Max beamed.

Emma knew her discomfort was obvious and that the Machiavellian streak in Max was loving the whole thing. What Jake made of it, she had no idea. She hoped the whole subtext was going right over Thomas's head. She'd have it out with Max and Jake later. Separately and in private. Wait a second. She didn't want to think about private with Jake. No audience? She didn't want to go anywhere near those three rules. Humiliation territory—she'd had enough of that in the last twenty-four hours.

Instead she chimed in as coolly as she could, 'Actually, we hadn't seen each other in a long time.'

'Oh, well, that explains the warm greeting, then,' Max said with such a benign expression Emma wanted to throttle him. 'Maybe you could show Jake round the place and reacquaint yourselves at the same time. He's only seen the hotel on the plans—take him on a tour now if you like.'

Thus dismissed, she had no choice but to obey. She could hear the chuckles of the two older men as she and Jake left the room.

'Are you embarrassed?' he asked as soon as the door closed behind them.

'No.' Yes. Utterly.

He grinned.

'Where do you want to start?' Focus on the job, not the fit body. Uh-huh. She kept her eyes on the carpet ahead, but secretly concentrated on the peripheral view of him as they walked side by side down the corridor.

'A bedroom's always good.' She heard the teasing lilt.

She had to ignore it. Had to. She was already under his spell and he was *just joking*—knowing she was mortified and turning the screws for a laugh. That kiss had meant nothing to him. 'Let's go to the kitchen area, as that's where you're starting on the refurb.' Brisk, no nonsense, she glanced at him with as much frost as she could muster.

He did his best to look crestfallen.

At that she couldn't help but laugh.

His small smile widened into the full beamer that show-cased strong white teeth and emphasised full sensual lips. Her own reaction was unstoppable. The glow inside, the spark of heat, the broad smile back.

'You're impossible, Jake.' Impossible to stay mad at. Impossible not to like. Impossibly dangerous for her.

'I'm sorry about last night if it makes things difficult for you.'

'It doesn't matter. It was my own fault.' The damn blush rose again. She walked quickly, deciding to get the tour over with as soon as possible. 'You saw how much Max was enjoying it. He doesn't mind what goes on so long as the work gets done. I think he quite enjoys "watching the young ones", as he puts it.'

'The "young ones"?' Amazed amusement.

'Oh, you know, bell-boy flirting with the second-chef, waiter falls in love with housemaid. When you've got thirty-odd young staff in hospitality working funny hours, things are bound to happen.' Just not to her.

'Bound to,' he said blandly.

She shot him a look, but retreated when he laughed aloud. She swallowed her pride. 'Look, can we just forget about last night? I'm really sorry and I am really embarrassed.'

'I'm not about to forget it, but we won't talk about it again if you like.'

From the way his attention seemed to have snapped to their surroundings she was fairly sure he was well on the way to forgetting about it.

Right. Great. Determined to forget about it herself, she focussed on showing him the hotel, pointing out the areas where the bulk of the work was to take place. His teasing manner had vanished completely and she was intrigued to see his professional side. She stood back and watched as he inspected the rooms, running an expert eye over the ceiling, smoothing a hand down a hairline crack in the wall. His hands were large and capable and yet he caressed the satin finish with a light finger.

He'd worked wood from an early age—his grandfather had been a carpenter and before he died he'd passed on all his knowledge to Jake in the workshop that overlooked Emma's backyard. She'd known he'd gone into building but hadn't realised he'd taken over a huge firm like White's. She looked at his suit—made to measure. Bad idea, because then she became aware of the body it clothed and the memory of that body so close to hers for those few moments last night. Big. Strong. Heavenly.

He looked up and caught her staring. He smiled, a wickedness stealing into his eyes. She cleared her throat, looked away and led him through to Reception.

They stood looking at the atrium lounge where major alterations were to take place. She was just explaining the rationale when he surprised her by stepping nearer and fixing her with his gaze. She broke off mid-sentence and stared back at him. His wicked look of minutes before had returned full force and intent had come with it. Before she knew what he was doing he slid his fingers through her hair and pressed his lips to her forehead. They stayed, slowly brushing across her skin.

She stood immobile in the light embrace. Confused, but conscious of wanting more. 'Uh, Jake, what are you doing?'

'Cementing your new reputation.'

'What?'

He whispered in her ear, and she tried to concentrate on

the words and not the sweet wind of his breath on her temple. 'Is the woman on Reception one of the ones from last night?'

'Yes.'

'Thought so.'

She started to turn to look at Becca, but he stopped her by taking her hand, closing his other arm around her body and guiding her to the elevator, pulling her close as they walked. Trying not to enjoy the entire sensation, she allowed the whole thing to happen.

'She was watching, all bat ears and owl eyes.'

'Jake, it doesn't matter.'

'Yes, it does; it matters to you. They hurt you.'

'Only because I was having a weak moment.' She was having another now, standing with his arm supporting her. If he removed it she just might topple over, yet if he didn't remove it she was going to be in pots of trouble.

'Nothing wrong with weak moments, Emma. Even you're allowed them sometimes.'

The lift doors slid open and he ushered her in. He then proceeded to push every single one of the floor buttons.

She braced her back against the wall. 'Jake, what are you doing?'

'Buying time.' He grinned. 'Not that this will give me much—there are only five floors.' He turned to face her. 'I've got a proposition for you.'

'What sort of proposition?' Business, it had to be business. That didn't stop the acceleration of her heart.

'Sorting out your image.'

Not business. She'd kind of guessed that. 'My image.'

'Yeah, you know, the workaholic spinster thing.'

'Spinster?'

He stepped closer, still grinning wolfishly. 'Come on, let's show them that you're really a foxy man-eater who knows how to keep a man dangling.'

His proximity was making her brain function poorly. The ability for rational decision-making skipped out the window. 'Are you offering to dangle?'

The doors opened on the first floor. Thankfully no one entered and Emma didn't have the will to exit—even though she knew she should.

'Sure, I can dangle real good.' He winked outrageously. 'Come on, I'll be around here for, what, five weeks? Let's give them something new and exciting to talk about. Show them that they had you read all wrong.'

The way he could switch from super-professional to complete clown amazed her.

'I am not going to make out with you in the reception area all day, if that's what you mean.' Was that what he meant? Her heart thudded faster.

'Just a couple of hours?'

'No! Be serious.'

'I am being serious. It'll be a laugh, no harm can come of it.'

She wasn't so sure about that. It might be a fun charade for him, but her hormones were doing silly things and he hadn't even started yet. Have a pretend affair with Jake Rendel? 'Why do you want to do this?'

'I saw the look on that woman's face, Emma. I know what she thinks and she is so wrong. I know the type.'

Jake would. Jake would understand every type and have experience with them all. He clearly read her doubts. 'Come on, it'll be fun. A look here, a touch there. They'll be riveted. You said yourself Max won't care.'

A look? A *touch*? 'What about your rules?'

'Ah. Kissing's different. We don't have to kiss for this.'

Didn't they? She stamped out the spark of disappointment. 'But you kissed me just then.' She could still feel it on her forehead.

'That wasn't a kiss. That was a friendly peck.'

If that was a friendly peck, then she was in big trouble.

'Come on,' he wheedled. 'What are old neighbours for? We help each other out. Let's show them your deep, passionate side, hmm?'

His expression was suddenly one that brooked no compromise. 'You know you want to.'

An electrical charge rippled through her as she saw his determination. He was right. She wanted to, and for all the wrong reasons. She ought to be saying no. She ought to be giving him the kind of polite yet firm brush-off she reserved for the much older, usually married, guests who sometimes asked her out. But some of her just couldn't resist the idea of proving a point to those girls.

She'd always been the hard-working geek. The quiet one who could answer all the questions in class. The only reason a Becca at school would talk to her would be to copy her study notes. The whole men thing came easily to women like Becca. Emma knew a beautiful girl like Becca would net a guy like Jake with a snap of her fingers.

A guy like Jake. And the fact that it was him made the whole silly scheme irresistible. Gorgeous. Fun. Impossible to say no to. She could do this safely, couldn't she?

Wouldn't it be fun to be in on the joke for once, not on the end of it? Despite the nagging feeling that this was going to cause huge problems, the answer just slid out. 'OK.'

Another thrill shot through her as his eyes danced with

satisfaction. 'So you can take a challenge, Emma. Maybe we could even work on your wardrobe.'

Her wardrobe? 'What's wrong with my clothes?'

'Nothing.' He was quick to back-pedal. 'They're very…tailored.'

'Tailored.'

He laughed. 'Read uptight-looking. Maybe we could loosen them up a little.'

'I am not going to start wearing sexy clothes at work, Jake.'

'OK.' He raised his hands pacifically before speaking smoothly. 'You don't need clothes to come across sexy, Emma.'

'Have you started already? Because there's no need. There's no one in the lift but us.'

'I speak the truth.'

'You're a silver-tongued devil, Jake Rendel, and I so shouldn't be doing this.'

Amusement shook him. 'Look, we make out like we're having a flaming affair for five weeks and then you crush my heart under your four-inch heels.'

'I don't wear four-inch heels.'

He laughed again. 'I know.'

'Well, anything higher than an inch is impractical and uncomfortable.' Her heart thudded. She shouldn't be taking this from him. He was a tease. He might be a man of experience, but who was he to criticise her clothes? They cost a lot of money. Indignant, she decided to challenge him. 'You think you're enough of an "eligible bachelor" for this?'

His smile broadened. 'You said it yourself, Emma—women like to play with me. What can I say?'

'We can say you've an ego!'

'We can let slip a few more appetising facts if you want, make me more of a catch.'

'Such as?'

'I own my own business with an annual turnover in the millions. I own three properties, including a beachfront home in Abel Tasman National Park that's only accessible by boat or helicopter.'

'Good imagination, Jake!'

He looked at her blandly. 'It's all true. Layabout boy made good, Emma, didn't you know?'

She shook her head. 'Helicopter?'

'With licence.'

'Boat?'

'Three. Sail, speed and a dingy, which is so ancient it shouldn't really count, but it floats so let's say it does.'

She stared at him, unable to believe she didn't know this about him. But then his mother didn't brag quite the way her father did. Eligible bachelor wasn't the word. He should be featured in one of those women's mags. Drop-dead gorgeous, wealthy and funny. 'So why *are* you single, Jake?'

'You said it yourself, Emma. Women like to play, and I like to play along with them.'

Well, at least he was up front.

'This isn't real though, Jake. This is just pretend, *OK*?'

'Sure thing. It'll be a blast.' He leaned against the back wall of the lift next to her, side on, smiling. She felt as if she'd been hit on the head with a mallet and concussion had set in. Was that why she was acting so crazy?

Just pretend. Jake watched her as she slipped back into Max's office. What was he doing? He'd just taken over this company, and had a big contract to fulfil. He was here only for the duration to oversee it and find a new local manager so he could head back to Auckland. Yet here he was setting up a juvenile ploy. But he'd seen the expression of the woman on Reception. She'd given him a come-hither look when he'd arrived with Thomas. He knew she'd recognised him from the night before with Emma and he knew her type all right. The type keen to steal a man from another woman just for the fun of it. She'd see Emma's strait-laced attire and hard-working attitude and miss the hot light underneath.

To be honest *he'd* missed it 'til now. But this time things were going to be different. By the time he was done they'd all see Emma as the sensual temptress he was quite sure she was capable of being. The woman who'd have a man on his knees before coolly discarding him. From the way he'd felt when they'd kissed last night, he knew it wasn't too far-fetched. She packed a powerful punch and he wanted to go for another round. And with a twinge of guilt he recognised that that was the whole point. He wanted to get his hands on her again—test out that seismic reaction. Right off the Richter scale. But her discomfort when they'd met this morning had been obvious to everyone. He wasn't going to get anywhere with her in frozen mode. So he needed to lighten it up. Make it fun—and he was pretty good at that.

He pushed the lift button to ground again and looked to the back of the lift where she'd just been standing. He smiled at the memory of her hazel eyes widening in indignation when he'd teased about her clothes. It surprised him she didn't wear much in the way of heels; most women he knew did—even the really tall ones. A slip of a thing like Emma would usually want the benefit of a few extra inches. He liked it though, liked having to bend to reach her pouty mouth. Liked the fact he could put his hands round her waist and almost touch the tips of his fingers.

Emma Delaney. He hadn't thought about her in years, but there had been nothing else on his mind these last twelve hours. Natural grace, natural beauty, natural talent. And yet she'd always worked like a dog. No matter what she did, the targets she set and achieved were never enough—not for her father. His sister Sienna had talked about the hoops and hurdles Emma and her sister Lucy had tried to leap. Until one day Lucy had simply stopped and Emma had doubled her efforts. As her father had once told him, she was destined for big things and to be in charge of the money in this place at her age was extremely impressive.

There'd been a price, though. How had she phrased it last night? Her 'non-existent love life'. He smiled again at the recollection of her lips clinging to his. He could help her out with that. He really could. Just for a few weeks, have some fun, and give her the confidence and a reputation that would have them flocking. The doors opened and he strode past Reception, flashing a smile of genuine amusement at the blonde behind the counter.

Emma called in to Max to report back. She hoped the colour in her cheeks had died down enough to look less suspicious. Max eyed her speculatively. 'Seems a nice man.'

She decided to play dumb. She couldn't believe she was about to have a conversation with Max about her personal life. Not because they didn't discuss personal things, but because she actually had something of a personal life. 'Jake?'

'Yes. Nice. Successful. Interested.'

'Max, I don't think we should go there.' She sure wasn't. Jake was only interested in having a laugh with her. The whole thing was a joke from start to finish.

He smiled broadly, the twinkle in his eye quite alarming. 'I forget you're young, Emma. You should be wanting to settle down and have a family.'

She sighed. Settling down and family were so far off her agenda and she didn't know if they were ever going to be on it. She was too busy forging this career. And the rest of her time was taken up with her favourite hobby. 'Not in the next few years, Max. I've got a career to build.' She just needed to be sure it was the right one.

He looked at her with his shrewd old eyes. 'You're the most driven person I know, Emma.'

'I'm taking that as a compliment.'

'It's meant as one. I just want you to be sure you're driving yourself in the direction you really want to go.'

She was surprised. She'd never have expected Max to pick up on her doubts. He never seemed to notice much regarding her, except if the numbers weren't going in the direction he liked. 'Max, I've worked hard for this and I want it. Sometimes I get tired, but everybody does.'

'Don't miss out on the fun in life, though, will you, Emma? You can work hard, but you can play hard too.'

She always worked hard; it was the play bit that was new to her. Jake knew how. Her father had commented on it— a talented youth wasting his brain and energy. Emma knew firsthand her father didn't approve of anyone wasting their brain or talent on things he didn't consider were worthy. Clearly Jake knew how to work too—even her dad would have to admit that if he saw him now.

But playing was something Jake excelled at. And, while

she couldn't resist joining him in this caper, she couldn't let it affect her professionalism or the quality of her work. Five years ago Max had given her the opportunity of a lifetime. And with his mentoring she'd risen to the challenge and she owed him. 'I'm not going to let you down, Max.'

'I never thought for a moment you were.'

CHAPTER THREE

JAKE strolled back into the hotel having changed into his on-the-job clothes and saw the receptionist trying to catch his eye. She smiled as he headed over.

'You must be the contractor in charge of all the changes.'

He nodded. 'Jake Rendel.'

'Becca.' The smile was wide and inviting, but strangely all he wanted to do was find Emma. With perfect timing she walked out of the office door behind the reception desk. Excellent. Time to put the plan into action.

He smiled directly at her, telling himself the uplift of his heart was from the buzz of the laugh. She blinked, clearly surprised to see him. Surprised and a little cool. He didn't like that so much, and his risen heart lowered a little.

'Jake—' a set smile accompanied it '—I didn't realise you'd be on site so much.' Definitely cool. Too cool for this project. She'd walked around the desk and as she passed him he reached his hand out to touch her arm. She nearly jumped out of her skin and he had to cover the moment with a cough.

'This is the first contract the firm is doing since I've taken over and it's a big one. I want to ensure it's done properly. And it gives me the opportunity to look for a manager while I'm here.'

She wasn't really listening. She was edging away from him, obviously eager to escape. He didn't like it and it was doing nothing for her planned image overhaul.

'You like Christchurch?' Becca piped up.

'Yeah, being here means I get to catch up with old friends,' he answered, giving Emma a meaningful look. It was wasted as she could hardly seem to meet his eye. She'd retreated into a blush again. Not good. He'd liked the hint of sass she'd shown last night and in a couple of her comments in the lift today. It was unexpected, but it wasn't unnatural to her. He had the feeling there was more to be found under the surface. A whole lot more. And he wanted to help her find it. He was doing her a favour, wasn't he?

But he had his work cut out. She was running away.

'Can you have those stats for me by the end of the day?' she asked Becca. The woman bristled but answered in the affirmative.

Jake only got a vague nod and she was off, her slim figure moving as fast as possible away from him. Ignoring the smiles Becca was flashing his way again, he headed in the direction Emma had taken.

Emma hurried to her office, needing some breathing space. The speed with which he worked was frightening—too much. She couldn't go through with it. Not when he unsettled her so easily. She'd nearly had heart failure coming out of the office downstairs and seeing him in the tight tee and jeans that showed off the length and strength of those legs.

She hadn't realised quite the bog she'd got herself into. Hadn't registered that Jake being in charge meant that Jake was going to be on site eighty per cent of the time and she was already overdosing. Their relationship was a charade but her physical reaction was real—sparking.

One minute later the man himself appeared at her doorway. He stepped in and shut the door behind him.

'Emma, this isn't going to work if you freeze up every time I come near you.'

'Jake, this isn't going to work at all. Let's just forget it. The whole idea is dumb.'

'Too late now, the show's on the road. You have to run with it.'

'Jake—'

'You need to relax, that's all,' he overrode her. 'I think we just need some practice.'

'Practice?' What was it about him that had her blankly repeating everything he said? Why wouldn't her brain work as well when he was near?

'Yes, practice. You need to be comfortable with me being near you.'

Comfortable? Oh, sure. When he looked like that the mercury was bursting out of her internal thermometer.

'Let's just start with the basics. Like if I come and stand next to you, don't go ramrod-straight on me, just take it easy.'

Easy? This? He wasn't standing next to her, he was merely millimetres away and she could feel his entire length. Problem was, the nearer he got, the more he felt too far away. So she had to go ramrod-straight to stop from leaning into him and closing the gap completely.

'Take your jacket off.'

'What?'

He sighed. 'Emma, it is twenty-eight degrees out there and just as warm in here and you're all buttoned up like it's the middle of winter. More than that there isn't any skin. We need skin.'

'Skin?' Parrot in action again.

'Contact. Lovers like to make contact, Emma; that's the whole point. No one will believe we're a hot item unless there is some contact going on.' He rolled his eyes. 'Just take it off.'

Wordlessly, slowly, she unbuttoned the black suit jacket. She did take it off sometimes, but only when she was in her office behind her desk. She always wore it when walking through the hotel. It looked professional, and she only had a simple white cami-tee on underneath. That was it—combination underwear and top that she hadn't intended for public display. He stood stock-still, watching as she revealed the front of it. She hesitated, her arms still in the jacket sleeves, as the edges of his mouth lifted into a grin that sent her mercury even higher.

He tilted his chin. 'Off, Emma. Get it off.'

When he spoke like that she wanted to get it on—with him. Practice—that's all. Keep it under control. She let her arms slide out of the sleeves and the jacket hit the floor.

'OK.' He cleared his throat. 'Now, let's get started. I might come up to you, like I did earlier, and run a finger down your arm.' He proceeded to do exactly that. 'No, don't jump and look at me like I'm about to shoot you. You're supposed to welcome my touch, want it, want more.'

Oh. Want more.

She forced herself to stay still, to relax, to think about something mundane.

'Better.' His voice was lower, softer. Way too sexy. His finger slid up again, then traced down the side of her strap, gently nudging it aside to bare her shoulder completely. 'Much better.'

Fascinated, she watched the blue in his eyes darken as he followed the trail of his finger across her collar-bone. Then the fire from that finger hit her and her lungs shorted out. She snatched in a sharp breath.

He jerked his head up and refocussed.

'OK, look at me like you think I'm some really hot guy.'

She was. He was. This was a nightmare.

He dropped his hands from where they were both now stroking her shoulders and sighed. 'Just think of your ultimate fantasy and pretend I'm him, OK?'

Not hard. No pretence necessary. Right now her ultimate fantasy stood right in front of her. And the problem was it *was* a fantasy.

'*That's* better. Keep looking me in the eyes.'

She couldn't look away if she tried. He stopped issuing instructions. She must have been improving. He lifted his hand to frame her face. Just lightly. Then he stroked a finger down the side of her cheek. She wondered if her eyes looked as large as his did. Then her sight was blocked as he lowered his head and replaced his finger with his lips. Gently nuzzling across her forehead. Slowly, teasing down the side of her cheek. She couldn't help but angle her head into his to feel his warm breath across her cheekbone. Couldn't help but turn slightly so his lips moved ever so much closer to her own.

'Uh, Jake.'

It was so easy to close her eyes and imagine it was real. But while his lips were dangerously close to hers they weren't coming closer. Then she remembered his rules. No ulterior motive—not for a kiss. And there was a motive here—practice. Nothing more than a silly flirtation for show. This was meaningless for him, a favour for a friend. And really she wasn't even that.

She clawed back her sanity and reminded herself she was nothing like his girlfriends. A good three inches shorter than the average and brunette, not blonde. And it didn't matter if the bra was ultimate, über, wonder or super, she was never going to be buxom. Hell, if she were completely honest she knew she didn't really need to wear a bra at all—and often didn't, like today.

So, no, he wasn't interested. He was just helping out the 'girl next door' whom he'd never see in a sexual way. Hell, he probably still thought of her as the scrawny kid he'd come across in the park crying that day.

She pushed him away. 'Enough practice, Jake. I think I've got it now.'

He moved back a pace immediately, a faint flush visible on his cheeks. 'Yeah. Right.'

They stared at each other in silence. He stood, hands deep in his pockets, as his gaze flickered over her. She struggled to keep a lid on her ragged breathing. She didn't want him to know how badly he affected her. She needed him to leave now or she'd humiliate herself completely. She aimed for his kind of lightness. 'See you out there on the playing field.'

He was silent a moment longer as he looked her over once more. Then he stepped away. 'Sure.'

As the door closed behind him she shivered. Looking down she saw with embarrassment the clear outline of her nipples. So much for twenty-eight degrees. She picked her jacket up from the floor where she'd let it fall. She was in way over her head—already. How on earth was she to get out of it when such a large part of her simply didn't want to? Living a fantasy. It really shouldn't matter what Becca and the others thought, it really shouldn't. But Jake was right: she'd been hurt. People seemed to see her in 2D— that all there was to her was a hard-working suit. Frozen up inside, and until now she had been. Bitterly she laughed aloud. She was so far from the man-eating temptress Jake envisioned. Then again, wasn't it the bigger the lie, the more likely people were to believe it?

She just had to keep on top of her attraction to him. Had to remember that it was a game. He wasn't touching her because he was interested; it was all fluffy fun for him. But the response *she* felt was real, and somehow she had to keep it in check.

Her phone rang. She picked it up and heard the strains of a twanging guitar. 'Hi, Luce.'

Lucy, her classically trained, country-music-loving, vio-linist sister, whose best friend happened to be Sienna, Jake's sister. 'What's happening in Wellington?'

The pair of them were completing their honours degrees in Music there this year.

'Exams are over. Now we're unemployed and soon to be homeless.'

'Uh-huh.' Emma couldn't stifle the giggle. She should be strict, but with Lucy it wasn't worth it.

'We're going on a jaunt before the big parental party. Might call in on you. That OK?'

'You know it is. Any time.'

'Sienna says Jake is headed to Christchurch some time soon. You might see him.'

Emma rolled her eyes heavenward. Why hadn't Lucy called the day before? Then she could have been warned and not surprised into doing something crazy like kissing him last night. 'Maybe.'

'Gotta go—Sienna has the engine running already.'

'Don't do anything I wouldn't do.'

The gust of laughter was mildly offensive. 'Sister, you leave me no option.'

The line went dead. Emma put the phone down and stared at it, a small smile on her mouth. Dad had frowned on the friendship between Lucy and Sienna, thought Sienna was a bad influence. If only he knew it was the other way round. When Lucy had slipped off the rails, it had been Sienna who had steered her back on course.

Emma sat and got back to the troublesome spreadsheet of the day before. Only the amount of concentration she could put to it wasn't quite the level she'd achieved yesterday. She smoothed her hair back into its chignon and tried to ignore the flames still flickering at her shoulder where he'd touched her. Tried to stop wondering where in the building he was now, when she was going to see him again, and what he was going to do when she did. And she tried to stop wishing about what he might do if he really were interested and the audience disappeared.

She hid in her office most of the day.

Finally, she had to go and get some papers from Reception—no delaying it any longer. She couldn't progress without them. She went to button up her jacket and suddenly stopped. Skin. She could manage a hint with the suit undone.

'Have you got those stats for me, Becca?'

The grimace on the other woman's face gave her the answer she hadn't wanted.

'I really need them tonight.'

'We've been run off our feet the whole day.'

Emma wasn't interested in excuses. She just wanted the info.

'Becca, I told you I needed it by the end of today.' End of Becca's work day that was; her own had a couple more hours left in it.

'Why not first thing in the morning?' If it weren't for the weight of his arm as he slung it over her shoulder, she'd have hit the ceiling with her startled jump. 'It's not like you're going to be getting much more done tonight.' Jake pulled her closer to him, speaking low and slow, his expression intimate, his eyes dancing.

She would have been very angry if it weren't for the surprise she was in and seeing that shock mirrored on Becca's face. The other woman masked it quickly, but it struck a nerve. She felt unable and unwilling to argue with him—not with the less-than-subtle pressure his fingers were exerting on her tense shoulders. She had to fight the urge to look at his hand as if it were some invading Martian.

'Come on, honey, it's home time. No more tonight, OK? I have other plans.' The way he said it, no one could be left in doubt as to the naughtiness of those plans. How he could get away with being so up front without being sleazy was a mystery to her. Well, she knew how, it was all part of his charm, the teasing, humorous light in his eye that had every woman in a fifty-mile radius smiling with him. Only Emma knew the tease this time was doubly strong. His fingers had stopped squeezing and were now smoothly stroking and, despite the material of her jacket, she could feel the heat, and relived the memory of the afternoon's 'practice' session.

Becca was standing there with her mouth ajar, and Emma summoned a smile—it wasn't huge, but it was a smile. 'First thing possible, Becca? I really will need it first thing.'

'Absolutely.' The receptionist had a reprieve and she appeared to be taking it both hands wide.

Jake's arm slid back across Emma's shoulders and down her arm—where he snagged her hand with his own. Warm and firm, he gave her fingers a gentle squeeze. She felt a matching contraction in her heart and lower belly and she wished she could extricate herself as soon as possible. All this touching was doing crazy things to her insides. None of it was real. She had to remember that.

He turned and spoke, his attention so focussed on her, as if he'd forgotten Becca was even there. 'I'll see you back here in ten, OK? I've just got one more thing to sort out.'

Keenly aware of Becca and her open mouth, Emma had no option but to nod. Jake's eyes were brimming with laughter and she couldn't wait to get him alone to tick him off.

Jake. Alone.

Bad thoughts.

She escaped to the lift and found herself shutting down her computer and packing her briefcase without a second thought of completing the work. She could do it in the morning. She was ahead by anyone else's standards—but she liked to finish well in front of schedule.

Back in the reception area exactly ten minutes later she found him waiting for her, jacket slung over his arm, brilliant smile in place. Becca was handing over to the night receptionist and watching. They left together, Jake holding the door for her as they exited.

He was still beside her five paces down the street and away from the hotel windows.

'What are you doing?'

'Seeing you home.'

'You don't have to. That was just for the benefit of Becca.' Wasn't it?

'No, actually, I really want to see you home.'

Her pulse picked up a little and it wasn't from the walking. 'It's about a ten-minute walk.'

'Really? So is mine. Which way are you?'

Realising she wasn't going to get rid of him, and secretly pleased about it, she set forth in the direction of home.

'Are you in a motel?' she asked. 'You didn't want to stay at Sanctuary?'

He shook his head. 'Needed space from the job. I'm in a serviced apartment. Hagley Towers.'

She knew the building—it was only five minutes' walk from her own place. Several storeys high, it was directly opposite Hagley Park—Christchurch's answer to New York's Central Park. She spent a lot of time walking there and visiting the botanical gardens housed in one section of it, especially at this time of year when the flowers were in bloom. 'Got a nice view?'

'Sure.' He grinned at her. 'Right over the park. And it has a swimming pool, sauna and gym.'

No wonder he looked so trim.

'Where are you?'

'Straight down here and to the left.' She pointed ahead down the busy road.

'You like living so centrally?'

She nodded. She found it handy when she worked such long hours to be within walking distance of the hotel.

'Me too. I have an apartment in the middle of Auckland. A stone's throw from some of the best restaurants in town. Makes deciding what to have for dinner damn hard, doesn't it?' He gave her the grin of a co-conspirator acknowledging a naughty habit.

It was a timely reminder of how different they really were. Of course he'd want to live right in the city so he could make the most of the high life—the bars, clubs and eateries. She bet he had as much trouble deciding which entry in his little black book to invite along to dinner. She just liked being near work. It confirmed her current self-view of boring workaholic. She wished he hadn't wanted to walk with her. He was so attractive, but the more time she spent with him the more she saw how different they were. And how this stupid caper was going to be hard for her. Her discomfort increased with every step as they walked past exclusive boutique shops and cafés.

'We should meet for coffee here some time,' he said chattily. 'You can tell me which of the cafés makes the best brew.'

'How do you like it?'

'Black. Strong.'

Of course. He'd need the hit after those long nights on the town. He'd think she was a complete cream-puff with her decaf soy latte with vanilla shot. Her despondency grew.

Thankfully they arrived at her street. It was an interesting mix of new modern apartments—mostly white and built from combinations of wood, concrete block and plaster. Nestled in and around were a few remaining examples of the old wooden cottages that had once dominated the area entirely.

She turned into her gate. He stopped and stared.

'This is your place?'

She nodded. She'd been extremely fortunate. She'd mortgaged herself to the hilt as a student to snap it up, but had been paying it off at an extremely fast rate—the accountant in her keeping her on the straight and narrow. It needed a lot of work, but it was hers.

She followed the direction of his gaze, taking in the façade. 'Don't you like it?'

There was a postage-stamp-sized garden in the front. Wisteria grew up the veranda pole and across decorating half the tiny cottage with stalactites of lavender petals. Chipped, lichen-covered terracotta pots crowded the ground and had fragrant blooms spilling from them. The air was heavy with the scent of sweet peas and roses.

'Sure I do, it's great. It's just…unexpected. Wow. You're sitting on a gold-mine, you know.'

She did. Developers would demolish the building and have two apartments on the tiny square in no time.

Jake was still looking intrigued. 'I thought you'd be in one like those.'

He pointed over the road to the three units in a row. Sterile, flat-roofed modern boxes. She thought of them as microwave houses. She didn't dislike them—part of her admired the clean lines, and the simple monochromatic landscape architecture using native grasses, shrubs and river stones. But she loved her old cottage and its English-country-style pot garden with its richly scented and deeply coloured flowers.

He was looking at her thoughtfully. His eye ran over her

suit again and she suddenly saw what he was thinking. That her clean-lined dressing style was far more suited to the clean-lined architecture across the street. That the slightly crumbling old wooden cottage with its trailing wisteria was a tad too soft and sweet to be hers. He saw her in 2D too—up 'til now she'd thought he didn't, had wanted to think he saw more in her than the stereotypical frigid workaholic Becca had her pegged as. Obviously not. It hurt.

He loitered by the gate. 'Aren't you going to invite me in?'

'Um.' There were things in there she didn't want him to see. Didn't want anyone to see. And she needed to escape his presence for a while. He was used to the casual, relaxed, have-a-laugh type. She was intense. Right now she needed a glass of cool white wine and some time to work on her project and not think or feel—to stamp out this crazy desire that had her body on edge. Her muddled head needed space. So did her heart.

'Actually I've got some things I need to get done. Maybe another time?'

It sounded insincere and cold and she couldn't make it otherwise.

Did she imagine the flash of disappointment in his face?

No. She hardened. He was new to town. It wouldn't be long and he'd be adding names to his black book and he'd lose interest in her and her image. And that would most definitely be for the best. Pretending she didn't care was something Emma was really good at.

CHAPTER FOUR

'LET's have dinner.'

Jake was determined to get Emma to say yes. He'd been there almost a week and, while he'd seen her several times a day, it wasn't enough.

He went down to the hotel even when he didn't need to—just on the chance he might catch her. Spent the time he was there in a state of anticipation. Told himself it was because he wanted to further develop the 'story' of their relationship, but really he just wanted to further things full stop. He wanted to get to know her. There seemed to be a whole lot more to her than met the eye. Trouble was, she was too good at hiding it.

Each time they passed he looked at her, and took the opportunity to touch her, finding even just the slightest brush incredibly stimulating. Tempting him to want more. But the closer he got, the more he pushed it, the bigger the distance seemed between them. And he found himself caring less and less about whether anyone was watching. He'd already done the job for her. People saw what they wanted to see. He'd read the speculation in the eyes of the other hotel workers. As far as they were concerned, he and Emma were one hot item. Increasingly Jake wished it were true.

She was looking as if she was about to refuse—again. In private she was holding him at arm's length. Then he saw the flash in her eyes, the hint of passion. And he thought for the thousandth time of the kiss they'd shared less than a week ago. She'd let a part of her slip out that night—one he hadn't known was there. Fresh, exciting and wild, and he wanted to find it again. He was pretty certain he could in the four weeks he had left with her, but he knew he needed to take care. She was like a wild flower, beautifully tempting to pick but fragile. Too much force and she'd wither away from him. So he restrained himself—not touching her this time, giving her some space. Hoping she noticed and missed the contact.

'Come on, Emma. Let's just grab a bite and catch up on old times.' The old neighbour approach might be the winner. God, he wanted to win her.

He heard her sigh, and saw her soften. 'We could go to The Strip.'

'The Strip?' He raised his brows suggestively, unable to resist the tease. Old habits died hard.

She coloured. 'It's what they call the area of bars and restaurants down by the river.'

He knew perfectly well what it was and where it was. He just enjoyed seeing how much he could make her blush. It was surprisingly easy. But it wasn't fun; it was arousing. He'd love to do all kinds of things to make her blush.

'OK, let's do The Strip.'

She flashed a look at him and he gave her his best smile of innocence. Neighbourly. Just a hint of naughty.

'Pizza, pasta, rack of lamb?' She gave him the options.

'You choose.'

They walked out of the hotel together as they had done

each night that week. Only instead of parting at the street corner to their own places, they walked in the opposite direction to the river. He breathed in the warm wind and glanced at her. She wasn't wearing her jacket, and was just in shirt sleeves. It was nothing like that figure-hugging white number he'd made her reveal the other day, but it wasn't bad. The soft fabric clung to her slim curves. He put the brakes on his thoughts—he needed to play it slow. She felt the attraction but she was cautious. He was counting on her being curious too. And he'd reel her in, nice and gentle.

They sat at a table outside with the warm wind gently teasing wisps of her hair. She always used to wear it up, her pony-tail swinging, a rich brown—the colour of the darkest chocolate. He'd only seen it loose a couple of times and he'd hardly recognised her. More grown-up, more relaxed. He'd love to see her hair out now. Only she tied it all up so he couldn't see even the length of her pony-tail. His fingers itched to test its silkiness. Loosen it. Loosen her.

She toyed with her drink, waiting for their food, waiting for him to say something.

'Remember that day I found you in the park?' He hadn't really intended to sit and reminisce, had been planning more of a charm offensive. But he wanted to talk to her about that day. While he hadn't thought of it in years, in recent days he'd remembered it often. It made him think there was more to Emma than met the eye.

It had been one of the first days of summer. The kind of hot, dry day you dreamed of the entire winter. Sixteen, he'd been down at the park skateboarding with some mates, living it up before the fruit-picking season started. And he'd spotted her sitting camouflaged in the grasses by the creek.

Crying. Something about seeing her with her hair scraped back into its usual pony-tail, her face streaked with tears, had pulled at him. He'd been unable to walk on by. The slump in her shoulders had struck him. She'd looked as if she'd carried a burden no kid in their early teens should have to bear. He'd thought something terrible had happened. That someone had hurt her. And in a way someone had.

He'd told the others to go on ahead, not wanting to draw attention to her. He'd slipped back once they were out of sight.

She'd just finished her first year at high school and she'd come home for the holidays, report card in tow. And that was what she'd been upset about. She'd been heartbroken over her report. He'd nearly laughed—report cards had usually been a source of amusement for him. Not life-and-death dramas.

He'd asked to see it and had nearly died when he'd read the results. They'd been awesome and yet she'd said they weren't good enough. She hadn't come first; she hadn't got the best grades across the board. And she hadn't wanted to face her father.

'He said we'd go on a beach holiday if I got top. But I only came top in Art and that doesn't count and so we won't go.'

'Of course you will. He was just trying to encourage you. You've done brilliantly. Far better than I ever have. That Art comment is fantastic.'

Her tears flowed again. 'I'm dropping it next year. Dad thinks it's a waste of time.'

He tried to joke with her, make her see that in the grand scheme it really wasn't that important. That her father would be proud of her no matter what.

But he wasn't and she was right. They hadn't gone on the holiday. Instead she'd been packed off to a maths camp.

Her father had stuck to his word. And Jake had wanted to shake some sense into him.

Emma didn't look up, but kept playing with the stem of her glass. For a second he thought she hadn't heard the question, but then he noticed the gentle tide of colour in her cheeks.

'That day I got home from school, you mean? When I was crying?'

'Yeah.'

She looked embarrassed. 'I was so pathetic, wasn't I? Crying over a report card. You must have thought I was such a geek.'

'No. I felt sorry for you.'

He had. He'd even put his arm around her to give her a reassuring hug as he would Sienna. And incredibly he'd felt a pull of attraction. Ripping through his torso, right in his gut. He'd dropped his arm pronto.

In hindsight he knew it to have simply been a touch of lust aroused by physical closeness. The intensity hadn't been because it was her, but because it had been the first time. Not long after he'd discovered girls who would talk back, smile, flirt and then offer a whole lot more.

He hadn't gone back to school after the summer of the report card. He'd had to get out and work—Sienna had needed his help. If he worked then Mum could have more time caring for her and he could help earn the money for her medical treatment. His father had died prematurely from a heart complaint that Sienna had inherited. He hadn't been going to lose her too. And that had been when he'd had his own run-in with Emma's father. Discovered for himself the height of his expectations. And discovered his own desire to prove the man wrong.

Emma cleared her throat. He looked up to find her eyes on him. A shy honesty peeped out of their greeny-brown depths. 'You were nice to me that day. Usually you threw water bombs over the fence.'

He chuckled. True.

She smiled. 'It was like living next to Dennis the Menace.'

'I wasn't that bad.'

'Not far off.'

He loved the teasing glint in her eye and felt warmed by her relaxation. He leant forward and began a 'do you remember' tale of epic proportions and maximum laughs.

Emma lingered over her dessert, but her mind kept flipping back to that earlier conversation.

I felt sorry for you.

She'd never have expected him to remember that day. She sure as hell hadn't forgotten. That had been the beginning of her crush. Until then he'd been the boy next door who played pranks. Suddenly he'd turned into a real person.

He'd stopped. He'd listened. He'd cared.

No one had done that before. No one had since. No wonder she'd had a thing for him—and still did. One act of kindness that had probably meant nothing to him had affected her for years.

He'd put an arm around her and given her shoulder a squeeze. And she'd wanted to lean in to him. His body hot and damp from the skateboarding. Strong, tanned, already muscular from holiday work spent picking fruit. She'd wanted him to put his other arm around her too. Then she hadn't really known what she'd wanted, she'd just wanted it to last. But it hadn't—he'd let her go abruptly, and she missed the contact immediately. He hadn't stayed much longer. For ages after she'd sat in the grass, not crying any more, not thinking about her grades, but thinking about Jake, and how attractive he'd suddenly become.

She'd rarely seen him after that—she'd been away at school; he'd been working. The odd occasion she had seen him in town he'd always been accompanied by some beautiful, buxom blonde. And she'd never been able to compete.

He'd felt sorry for her. He still did. Great. So that was why he'd suggested their fake fling. Any fantasy of that first kiss having more meaning fled. It wasn't that he was attracted to her. He was just the cool guy helping the ugly duckling do the transformation to pulling princess—but only 'til midnight. The clock was ticking and soon enough she'd be the ugly one again. She was mixing up her fairy tales, but this wasn't a fairy tale. There wouldn't be a happy ending here.

Humiliation killed her appetite. She shouldn't have accepted his dinner invitation. But she couldn't say no any more. She was too tempted and too teased by the touches of the past week. She'd spent those days on tenterhooks, waiting, wondering when he'd appear round the corner next. She'd taken to wandering through the hotel completely unnecessarily—telling herself it was to check on the building work, but that was a complete lie.

And when she did see him it unsettled her so much it was all she could do not to run in the opposite direction. He had that smile just for her, would catch her eye, would stand close and take advantage of the opportunity to touch her—a stroke down her arm, a hand on her shoulder, a brush across the back of her neck. All of it designed to show their intimacy. All of it increasing her desire for more.

She wore short sleeves or sleeveless shirts daily. Her

jacket hung gathering dust on the hanger upstairs. And she worked hard to preserve her equilibrium—trying to hide the impact of his actions. It wasn't that she didn't enjoy his attention. She enjoyed it a little too much and she didn't want him to know. That was why she'd kept it short and light, declining any invitations to spend any longer than five minutes with him. More time than that would be too much of a test. But by her agreeing to the scheme to beef up her image, their relationship had already leapt to one of greater intimacy. Them against the others. Sharing secrets, sharing history, sharing a laugh. It made him all the more attractive. That silly teen crush had returned with a vengeance.

And if he knew? He'd felt sorry for her then—he'd feel even more sorry for her now. Socially inept girl fell for guy who was only out to offer a helping hand.

Four weeks to go and, while she didn't want it to end, she couldn't wait 'til it was over.

'Shall we go on and hit the dance floor?'

That was an invitation that had to be refused for more than one reason. She didn't hit the dance floor. Ever. Especially not with the gorgeous guy who already felt sorry for her. If he saw her trying to dance he'd fall in a heap laughing. 'I have a load of work to get through tomorrow.' Work she should have been doing tonight.

'Well, it'll still be there tomorrow, Emma. What about some more fun now?' With that voice and those eyes he could tempt a nun into nudity.

'I'm no good on the dance floor, Jake.'

'Really? I don't believe you. All girls are good on the dance floor.'

All *his* girls would be. But she wasn't. Uncoordinated. It was the geek gene. No avoiding it. She couldn't do the curvy hip-wiggling, boob-jiggling thing. She was too angular. 'You like dancing?'

His eyes were dancing right now. 'Yeah, I like all kinds of dancing.'

He didn't need to say any more. She knew exactly what he was thinking.

The atmosphere thickened, temperature rising. If she let herself, she could believe he was flirting with her. No audience, no ulterior motive. For real and not just neighbourly.

Her whole body seemed to be melting and she suddenly wanted to push it. Test out her intuition. Was he really sending those signals to her? Or was she woolly-headed, merely imagining he was because she wanted it so bad?

She spoke, the breathiness coming naturally. 'What's your favourite?'

He didn't move a muscle, didn't look away, his attention wholly focussed on her. The intensity burned. 'Sometimes I like fast, spontaneous. Other times more leisurely.'

'And if you were dancing with me? What style would you go for then?' Almost bold, but her mouth was dry and inside her heart jack-hammered her ribcage.

'With you?' There was a silence. Neither of them moved, not even an eyelid. 'I'd want to try every which way with you, Emma. But if you're not so sure I might have to start slow, smooth. I'd have to hold you close.'

At the rush of adrenalin she knew she had to step back from the game—she was no match for him. She cleared her throat, hoped the breathiness had gone and that humour replaced it. 'Tango, then.'

He met her banter immediately. 'Shall we find a rose? You can hold it between your teeth.'

She'd been thinking of doing other things with her teeth, lips and tongue. 'I'm not a rose person.'

'No? What are you, then?

'A daisy.'

'No way.'

'I am. A particular daisy, though.'

He raised his brows. 'You have me intrigued.'

'Yep, and you're a tulip. Red tulip.'

He laughed outright then. But she knew things he didn't. She smiled at his relaxing demeanour. The scorching moment had passed and now she couldn't be sure if it had happened at all—if the message in his eyes had been the one she'd wanted to read.

A gang of slightly worse-for-wear party-goers wandered past along the road. They tried and failed to gain entry to the bar. It reminded her how late it was getting.

'I really should get going. I do have a lot to do tomorrow.'

'All right, Miss Conscientious. I'll walk you home.'

'You don't need to. It's still light, I'll be perfectly safe.'

'No, I'll see you there.'

'It's out of your way. Your place is nearer.'

'Unless you're planning on staying the night at my place, I'm walking you home.'

The desire to be brazen resurged, but she hoped the dusk would hide her heated cheeks and played safe. 'It's a nice night for a walk.'

His teeth flashed white in his wide smile.

She tried to suppress the tickle of pleasure and failed.

The wind had dropped, but the temperature was still warm as they gently strolled alongside the river. He walked near enough to her that their arms brushed ever so slightly every now and then, sending sparks through her. She wished they were lovers, so she could touch him as much as she wanted at any time and not have to rely on these accidental moments. She wondered if he was as aware of her nearness as she was his. Daydreaming.

Her nerves tightened with every step towards home. Would he ask her to invite him in again? He had been flirting with her; he had. But this wasn't a date. This was a dinner with an old friend. Not even that, an old neighbour. OK, her pretend lover. Confused about what they were doing—what was real and what wasn't—she opened her gate and found him hot on her heels right up the garden path.

She paused by the door feeling uncomfortable, and made a show of fossicking in her bag for her keys so that she could delay looking up at him. Her breathing was shorter. They'd kissed once and she wanted to again. She could hardly believe how easily that had happened that first night. Now it seemed impossible.

She turned and put the key in the door, battling with the rattling lock.

He stood right behind her, so close she could feel the heat from him; there must only be an inch between them. She leaned a little closer to the door to stop herself leaning back against him.

'What's the problem?'

'I'm having trouble with the door handle. It keeps coming off.'

'I'll fix it for you.'

'It's OK.'

'It's a security issue. I'll fix it first thing.'

First thing? Would he still be here then? She fumbled some more. He stepped around her, to rest against the wall of the cottage, still temptingly near.

She looked at him, the 'you don't have to' dying on her tongue as she saw he was waiting for her to say exactly that. So she didn't. Instead she smiled. 'Thank you.'

His expression revealed his surprise, and his amusement. 'It was fun tonight, Emma. It was nice spending time with you.'

She looked away, her smile dying. *Nice*. Almost as bad as 'I felt sorry for you.' This *was* dinner with an old neighbour.

'Right. Same. Thanks for dinner.' She wished she had the chutzpah she'd had only a week ago. To flirt in the way that had prompted him to instigate that kiss. But the more time she spent around him, the more she wanted him, and the less able she felt to put herself out to get him. For him it was all fake. But she couldn't help her reaction to his proximity. Her gaze dropped to his mouth.

'Goodnight.' He spoke briskly. She looked to his eyes and saw his intent, serious expression. It was almost a frown and she was about to ask what was wrong when his lips twisted into a smile that was a shadow of its usual brilliance. 'See you soon.'

He quickly stepped away, hands jammed in pockets. She stood on the deck listening as his unwavering footsteps grew fainter, wondering why a goodnight kiss hadn't even been anywhere near the agenda, and telling herself she wasn't disappointed.

She rose early as usual, despite the fact she'd taken for ever to get to sleep. Unable to get the image of Jake from her mind—his teasing comments and devilish nature—she'd lain and looked at her ceiling for hours. She might not have that much experience, but she wasn't a complete idiot and Jake had been making a play for her. Right up to her front door when everything had stopped. As if the brakes had been thrown on.

She tried not to make too much of it. Of course he'd flirted. That was what Jake did. He couldn't help himself. It didn't mean anything. He was just carrying their act on a little—giving her some more practice. Being charming. Flattering. And it definitely was fake because if he'd meant it, he'd have kissed her right there on the doorstep. Instead he was careful not to. She guessed he didn't want to lead her on. More humiliation.

She pulled on some clothes and went to her studio to do some work, to make the most of the soft morning light and to banish the moroseness that came with the knowledge that Jake wasn't interested.

Two hours later it was barely past eight and someone was banging the knocker on her door repeatedly. She jerked her head up, having been concentrating so hard on the page before her she hadn't seen anyone come up the path. Whoever it was wasn't going away.

'OK!' she called out, hoping it wasn't some life-or-death emergency, but the way the knocker was being abused she began to wonder. She slid back the chain and opened the door.

Jake, in those faded blue jeans of the first night, hair still damp, unshaven and edgy. Energy almost bursting from his skin.

'I said I'd—' He broke off, his gaze trailing over her— top to toe and back. Then again—this time stopping just above her middle. Then he looked up to her face. 'You look really different.' His voice sounded froggy.

Incredibly aware of the fact she hadn't bothered putting any underwear on, she went for diversion. 'It's my hair.'

She hadn't done it. Just pulled on top and shorts and settled straight to work. So it hung loose, shaggy, the fresh-out-of-bed look. She went to pull it back and tie it with the elastic band on her wrist.

'No, don't. Leave it.' He spoke briskly and she stopped, her arms mid-air. His eyes burned into her. 'It looks nice.'

Nice. Again. But the meaning seemed different this time.

She lowered her arms. The silence was small but sultry and she felt the change. As if the wind had shifted from a chilly easterly to warm nor'west. The wind of madness.

There was nothing neighbourly about her feelings right now. He looked too intense, too tempting, and her response was too terrifying. She looked at the large box his hand gripped tightly. He followed the direction of her gaze.

'A man never goes anywhere without his toolbox.'

'Is that right?' Her soft whisper was more of a challenge than she'd intended.

He answered with a slow, seductive smile. 'It's always good to be prepared.'

'I'll bear that in mind.' Still soft, sort of sassy and slightly cynical. She congratulated herself on keeping cool.

His smile widened and the tease flashed in his eyes. 'I said I'd fix the door first thing. You can fix me some food after to say thank you.'

There were other, more exciting ways of saying thank you. Every one of them flashed through her mind. Her cool persona evaporated. She blinked. 'OK.'

He put the toolbox down and bent at the knees to open it, showcasing muscular thighs. She stood for a moment taking in the god literally at her feet, then slipped inside and made a calming pot of tea. Holding the mug in her hands, she couldn't resist loitering in the hallway to watch as he started work on the door. Framed in the light, he looked like every woman's handyman fantasy. His shirt was open and he had a white singlet on underneath. She wished it were three hours later and five degrees warmer so he'd take the shirt off. He glanced over and saw her watching, saw her drinking.

He walked down the little hallway towards her. 'Can I have some?'

Some what? Some of her?

He took the mug from her fingers and had a sip, not taking his eyes from her. Then he frowned. 'Hell, what is this muck?'

She laughed. 'Herbal tea. Good for your brain.'

'Got any coffee? *Real* coffee?'

'What's that good for?'

'Energy. Lots of energy.'

He was joking with her again. She liked it—the tease of one shimmy forward, one step back. A little flirty dance and, sucker for punishment that she was, she shimmied. 'You need more energy?'

'I'm thinking it might come in handy.'

The provocation in his eyes warmed her already steamy thoughts. She'd have the energy for anything he was up for—with or without the coffee. A kiss would be a good start. She stared at him, at the generous curve of his mouth. Did she just lean forward towards him? Offer him her mouth? Take his hand and lead him straight to her small bedroom at the back of the house? What would Becca do? Simply say, 'Hey, how about it?'

She wished she had the confidence to do all that and more. Wished she could just tell him. Instead she stepped back. 'I'm just going to nip to the shop round the corner for some things for breakfast. Back in ten, OK?'

Jake nodded and forced his attention back to the door handle. He'd managed to spin a fifteen-minute job into forty. She looked stunning. Stunningly different from her weekday wear—the buttoned-up suit. Today she wore a pair of ancient-looking shorts that revealed her slim legs. And a skimpy singlet top—hot pink with splashes of who knew what on it. Skin, skin, skin. Acres of it and he wanted to touch so bad. He tried really, really hard not to dwell on the fact that she wasn't wearing a bra, but it was like a neon sign flashing in his head.

And her hair. It hung to her shoulders framing her face looking more beautiful than he'd imagined, and he ached to touch it. Could imagine it brushing his face as she leaned over him. How he wanted her.

It hadn't been that long since he'd been with a woman— it was never long for Jake—but he had a hunger in him that was growing every day. And aside from the crippling physical attraction, he liked her company, plain and simple. She was bright, humorous and fun to be around, and there was nowhere else he wanted to be right now than in her little cottage doorway, just hanging out.

Except in her bed.

He watched as she walked out the gate and turned down the footpath, out of sight, infinitely more relaxed. She was talking back to him, a cute little sass that he loved. Had it been his imagination or had she almost leaned forward for a kiss in the hallway just then? Talk about wishful thinking. But with her lips parted, her face illuminated, there had been invitation in her eyes.

Then it had gone.

So, so close, and he'd be damned if he was leaving her house today without some sort of contact.

CHAPTER FIVE

THE walk to the shop and back provided Emma with some essential oxygen to the brain. Enabled her to think. She strode out, trying to grow her confidence with every step. She wanted to be like any other red-blooded woman and have an affair with the really hot guy she'd had a thing for since her teens.

She gave herself the pep talk. Don't over analyse. Don't worry about what may or may not happen. Why not just have fun? Flirt. Just do it.

She tried to swallow the performance anxiety.

He had a wealth of experience. She had nil.

He was used to curvy blondes. She was an ironing-board brunette.

But the spark was there. And she was going to blow on it. Be normal. Go for something she really wanted. Jake. Just once. Just for herself.

Although she'd yet to figure out quite how.

He was sitting on the bottom step of the verandah when she returned. She carried the tray of two large, strong black coffees and two decaf, soy lattes with vanilla shot, and had the carrier bag of groceries looped over her arm. She paused on the step and offered him one of the coffees.

He took it with glee. 'You're an angel.'

'I didn't think you'd want any of my instant decaf.'

He looked appalled. 'Hell, no.'

He followed her inside and into the kitchen where she set about preparing their meal.

'So no *real* coffee, you don't smoke and I'm betting you don't drink that much—apart from wine, which we both know doesn't count.'

She smiled. They'd grown up in the heart of the wine country of New Zealand where the wine practically flowed out of the kitchen tap. Even so, cheap drunk was the phrase to describe her.

'Don't you have any vices? No secret indulgence?'

'Chocolate. Clichéd but true.'

'I'm guessing the real seventy-per-cent bitter stuff.'

She giggled. 'No. Caramello actually. A bar a day. Vitamin C.'

He came and leaned against the bench where she was working. She concentrated extra hard to keep her hand steady as she wielded her large kitchen knife. He stood so close she could smell his musky scent.

'Can I help at all?'

It would help if he'd keep just a wee bit more of a distance. Either that or no distance at all. This so-close-but-not-actually-connecting thing was doing her head in.

'No, it won't take a minute. You just sit and watch.'

He didn't take the hint. Didn't sit. Stayed right where he was—right beside her. If she waggled her elbow just a tad she'd touch him. Not nearly good enough.

Intensely aware of his scrutiny, she deftly cut the

Portobello mushrooms into thick slices, halved the toma-
toes and separated the small breakfast sausages. She turned
away from him, breathing out in relief, and put the large
frying-pan on the hob. She splashed in some oil and a
decent knob of butter, allowing it to melt before putting in
streaky bacon from the fridge and the just-chopped food.

He breathed in deeply. 'That smells so good. I never
imagined you'd eat like this. You're like a short-order cook.'

She smiled, poking at the mushrooms with a wooden
spoon. 'I love a cooked breakfast. It's my speciality.'

'Really?'

'Yeah, it's what I serve up if I'm having people over to
dinner. It's the only thing I can really cook.'

'I don't believe that.'

'OK, it's the only thing I really like to cook. Fast.
Satisfying.'

While the food in the fry-pan sizzled she whisked a few
eggs with a fork, adding a grate of cheese and a dash of
milk to the bowl. 'I cheat, though. I scramble the egg in
the microwave and the hash browns are from the freezer.'

'Looks pretty good to me.'

She put some bread in the toaster and pushed the lever
down. Two minutes later she was spreading the hot toast
with butter and piling scrambled egg on top.

'I thought you'd be a cereal and skimmed milk person.'

She snorted. 'Cardboard. Breakfast is my most important meal.'

'You have this every day?'

'Not with all the trimmings. But a good breakfast, yeah.
Sometimes I don't get time for lunch.'

'You work through so it's just a bar of Caramello.' His
glance stabbed.

She laughed. 'Don't look so disapproving. It's not like you don't work hard.'

'Yeah, but at least I have some balance in my life.' Vitality, virility, she knew his kind of balance.

'I have balance.' She might not be out dating a different man every other night, but she did have her own passion in life. She just kept it to herself, that was all.

In the ten minutes since she'd walked back in the door breakfast had been prepared, cooked and was now plated up on the bench in the kitchen, waiting to be demolished. She grabbed cutlery from the drawer and picked up one of the plates.

'Let's eat on the verandah.'

She led the way as he snagged the other plate and the tray with the remaining coffees. Out on the corner of the verandah in the shade stood her table and two chairs. An old but super-comfortable sofa sat under the window. Pots full of flowering plants decorated the border. Their perfume rich but not overpowering. She took one of the chairs and watched as Jake sat and started consuming with enthusiasm.

'Now I know about this I'm thinking about breakfasting with you every day, Emma.'

She paused, fork halfway to her mouth, as she imagined the scenario. Breakfast. In bed? With what on the menu—her?

She had to stop these thoughts. Everything he said she managed to read a hidden meaning into.

He slowed as he reduced the pile of food, sighing happily. 'It's a great place you have here. You like living alone?'

She looked out at the pretty garden, the stunning backdrop of architecturally designed town houses. 'Yes. I work long hours. It's nice to come home and be able to relax, do my own thing.'

'What do you do to relax?'

She looked sideways at him, but he seemed genuinely interested. It wasn't a tease. 'This and that. Potter in my garden.'

'Yeah, it's beautiful.' He reached out to the pot nearest his leg, touching the petals of the hyacinth it housed.

She watched the softness of his stroke. 'It's small, easy to manage.' Truth be told, all she had to do was water it. The beauty of a pot garden was it didn't need weeding— a good thing as she didn't have time; she was too busy on her this and that.

She sat back, replete and warm in the morning sun, determinedly looking away from him. Ordinarily she'd make like a cat, curl up on the sofa and doze for ten. But today an extreme quantity of adrenalin ran through her veins. She might want to go to bed, but sleeping wasn't on the activity list once there.

Out of the corner of her eye she saw him lift his arms, pointing his elbows at the sky while his hands fisted at his neck. He stretched, curving his spine to one side, then the other. He groaned. 'You gotta help me burn off some of this energy. Two coffees and all that food.'

So the meal hadn't made him sluggish either. Did he want to burn it up in the way she wanted to? 'What did you have in mind?'

He stared into the middle distance, seemingly transfixed by a purple iris. 'How about a walk round the park?'

Curbing her disappointment, she fixed a bright smile on her face. 'Sure.'

He picked up the plates and transported them back to

the kitchen while she kicked off her flip-flops and laced her trainers. She stepped into the bathroom and was about to tie up her hair before she thought better of it. She dragged a comb through the worst of the tangles and then simply used her fingers to smooth it. She turned away from the mirror—not wanting to see the heightened colour in her cheeks, the anticipation in her eyes.

After checking the curtains were shut in her workroom and the door was closed tight she went into the kitchen to find him just finishing the dishes and wiping down the bench.

'Thanks for that—you didn't have to.'

'Least I could do after that meal. It doesn't take a minute. I always did the dishes for Mum.'

He would have too. Loyal. Protective. He might not take his relationships with women seriously, but Emma knew there were two women in his life he'd do anything for. Had done everything for—his mother and his sister. After both his father and grandfather died Jake was the man in the family—age sixteen. It hadn't been long after that he left school. For all his joking around there was another side to him. The man who took those responsibilities seriously, especially Sienna, the sister he'd nearly lost. He was looking at her questioningly and she realised she'd been staring. 'Let's go,' she said, quickly leading the way out.

Saturday morning and Hagley Park was busy with runners, rollerbladers and parents pushing prams. The last of the bluebells could be seen in the meadow across the road. They walked on one of the many paths crossing the park, strolling easily, neither of them really wanting to pace it out.

'So you think your women at the hotel are seeing you in a different light?' No smile as he asked.

She was sure of it. So was everyone else. Dan the doorman had winked at her the other day and usually he'd barely meet her eyes.

'Yes. I think they think I'm actually human now.'

'Oh, you're very human.' He spoke softly.

She tried to quell her overly sensitive awareness. 'In that I make mistakes, absolutely.'

'You think it was a mistake? I thought it was kinda fun.'

Her heart dropped. *Was. Fun.* Just a game and over already.

But then he spoke again, low and slow. 'All that touching, flirting, being close.'

'Yes.' She whispered it so softly she was sure he wouldn't hear.

He stopped walking. So attuned to him, she stopped in almost the same instant. She stared up at him and his expression was as serious as she knew hers to be. He reached out and ran his fingers down the length of her arm to take her hand. He pulled her with him as he walked off the path, into the trees. He said nothing. She said nothing. He led her into the shade of a tree, ducking under the large, low branches into the secret space by its strong trunk. He turned and leaned against it, facing her and still holding her hand tightly, keeping her in front of him.

They were protected by the branches and the sound of the traffic was muted, the other park users hidden from sight. It felt as if there were only the two of them in the world. And the spark was enough to send a whole forest in flames.

He looked at her mouth, and then back to her eyes. A rueful expression mingled with the blazing gaze. 'I can't stand it any more, Emma. I'm going to have to kiss you.'

Somehow, even though she was sure she wasn't breathing, she answered, 'What about your rules?'

The pressure on her hand tightened, and he pulled her a little closer.

'There's no audience. No ulterior motives. Just…desire.'

The very same desire rippled through her. And the thrill she got from his admission fuelled her saucy question. 'What about the clothes?'

The corners of his mouth twitched in that delightful fashion that had her wanting to taste them, feel the humour. 'Well, two out of three isn't bad.'

She tried to think of a pert reply. 'But I'm a perfectionist, Jake. I like to get one hundred per cent.' Quite where she got the audacity to say that, she didn't know. Maybe it was heatstroke caused by the burn in his eyes.

He pulled her closer still, his hand relinquishing hers, but only to slide around her waist. 'You'll get one hundred per cent, Emma. Trust me.'

She was incapable of further speech. Her mouth parted as she stared up at him. Riveted by the heat in his eyes, the humour in his expression, she waited, wanting to lean that further fraction forward to bring them into length-to-length contact. But she felt hesitation in him.

He spoke. 'I've been wanting a repeat of that kiss the other night all week. There's no one watching now, Emma. Do you really want it this time?'

Everything inside seemed to have liquefied. A sweet melting sensation that made her want to spread her pliant body over his hard one. There was only one thing to say. 'Yes.'

Her lids lowered as his head bent even as she answered. She felt the increase of pressure from his arms as they tightened around her, as if he were afraid she'd step away.

As if. Instead she stepped closer, tilted her head so she was right there for him.

Contact.

There was no gentle testing of the waters this time. Mouths open, tongues searching, deeply taking. She loved the roughness of his stubble as he moved against her. She raised her hands, threaded them through his thick hair and held him as she kissed him back. Hard. Heavenly and highly addictive.

His hands lifted from her waist, sweeping from her shoulder blades down her body. She felt their fire through her thin singlet top. And even that thin covering was too much. Skin. She wanted it bare.

The warmth in her belly sharpened to a desperate ache. She wanted this so much. But she wanted so much more than this. One hundred per cent.

She pressed against him. His tightness soothed her a little. She pressed again, tilting her hips forward so they ground against him. A wash of heat dizzied her as she felt his erection, large and hard. Her mouth parted further as the moan escaped. She curled her fingers tighter in his hair, fixing him there as she pressed again. Again. And again.

He jerked his head back. 'Stop.'

'What?' Confused, she looked up at him. The flames racing in her veins turned to ice in an instant. Panic. Had she done something wrong?

'If we don't stop now, we won't be stopping at all and we'll get done for indecency.' His fingers dug into her as he grasped her hips and held her away from him. 'Just a kiss with you is lethal. Whatever you do, you really do the best, don't you?'

The way he said it she wasn't sure if this was a good thing or not.

He ran his fingers through his hair—leaving it even more tousled than from when she'd dealt with it. Then he grimaced. 'Let's go back to your house.'

And pick up where they just left off? Yes, please.

'I need to pick up my toolbox before I go home.' He spoke flatly, not looking at her as he dragged a long breath in through his nostrils.

They slowly walked back. She didn't know how to break the silence. Didn't want to do the girl thing and ask to talk about what had just happened. Find out what, if anything, it meant. Find out why she was getting the frosty treatment now. Utterly confused, but she refused to over-analyse, daydream, wish.

He stared straight ahead. His easy humour apparently having gone on holiday. All she knew was she didn't want him to just pick up his box and go. She didn't know what had gone wrong, but she needed to buy some time to make it right. 'Would you be able to do me a favour?'

'Sure.' The automatic response.

'The latch on one of the windows round the back is loose too. Would you mind looking at it?'

The muscle in his jaw twitched. 'Emma, you know what you've just done? You're actually *asking* for help? This has got to be some kind of record.'

She blinked, unprepared for his sarcasm. 'Why do you say that?

'Oh, come on, Emma, you're Miss Independent. You work, work, work and seem like you don't need anything or anybody.'

'I have to work hard,' she replied softly, in contrast to his bark. 'It's expected.'

It was what she'd had to do to get her father's attention. She'd literally had to win his approval. Get an A in Economics and I'll take you to dinner, Emma. Get three A's and I'll buy you a car. Any reward—emotional, material—came from achievement.

He sighed, stretching his fingers from where they were fisted at his sides. 'Yeah, if you don't mind my saying, your dad's real pushy.'

'He wants what's best for me.'

'What you think is best for you, or what he thinks is best for you?'

At that she stopped walking and turned to look at him. 'Who are you to judge, Jake?'

His hands lifted. 'I'm not judging. That's just how it seems. You push yourself to crazy limits to please your father all your life and now you do the same for Max.'

Her jaw fell open. 'Max has been wonderful to me. I owe him a lot.' Why wouldn't she work hard for him?

'Max is your boss and I hope he pays you the earth for the job he asks of you.'

'You think he's taking advantage of me?' She felt stunned.

'Of your type, yeah, maybe. You have to please, Emma. You want people to like you, fair enough, we all do, but you put what others ask ahead of your own wants because it's more important to you to have their approval than it is to satisfy your own dreams.'

'That's rubbish. This is my dream. I've worked damn hard to get where I am. Would I really work so hard if I didn't want it?' Her defence button was well and truly pushed. Where was this coming from?

'Sure, you think you want it. But do you really? Isn't there something else you'd rather be doing?'

She felt the blood rush from her head to her heart. 'What are you on about, Jake? What do you know?'

She saw him do a double take. She realised he'd been shooting in the dark and just happened to hit target. She took a few deep breaths to recover herself. He knew nothing. Of course he didn't. That was impossible. The only person she'd ever shared her silly dreams with was Lucy, and she knew enough of her sister's own secrets to be sure she'd never rat on her. This was just Jake stirring for the sake of it, because for whatever reason he had a serious case of the grumps right now. He must really be regretting kissing her. Anger kicked in her gut. Who was he to kiss her like that and then start digging at her? If he didn't want her, fine; he didn't have to turn into a grizzly bear because things had happened that he didn't like. Hell, he was the one who'd started it.

But she wasn't going to let him know how he'd thrown her. Instead she'd take on his job and lighten things up. Turn the last five minutes into a joke. She racked her brains and then remembered a slogan she'd once read on a tee shirt. 'If you like the look of my peaches, don't shake my tree.' She threw him a tart look, turned and managed a passable saunter away.

Jake watched her sweet rear sashay away from him and couldn't contain the chuckle. The irrational anger he'd felt at his reaction to her was draining. Playful and provocative, she was testing her wings with him and if he was honest with himself he'd say he was happy to be on the flight. More than happy. It was an element of her he'd never suspected. But then, what did he really know of her? Only the achievements her parents had proclaimed to the world, only the hint in her eyes of depths that had yet to be plumbed, only that she was beautiful and when he held her against him she melted and his reason nearly drowned. *That* was where the problem came in. Since when did he seriously contemplate having sex in the middle of a public park in the middle of the day? Since when did he shake with need as he had just then? Since when did he want a woman more than he wanted to breathe? He was familiar with lust—but not like this. Never like this.

And there was more to her. He'd hit on something just then and she'd skirted around it big style. He really wanted to know, had read the panic on her face. Emma the parent-pleaser, the teacher-pleaser…the lover-pleaser? How he'd love to find out. Even more he wanted to find out what would please *her*.

He strolled after her, catching up to her in a few steps. He reached out, couldn't help but slide his arms around her to turn her to face him, only just managing not to haul her close.

He fell back on his humour. 'I wasn't thinking of shaking your tree, honey.'

'No?' She was going for flirty confidence but he could see the uncertain, shy girl in her eye. He loved the mix.

'No, I was planning on making the whole earth move.'

'Really.'

Her soft laugh only made him want her more. Made him want to make it really happen despite the fact that she threatened his self-control completely.

'How were you going to do that?'

'Shall I show you?' Slowly he slid his hands down past

the band of her shorts to cup her bottom. Skin on skin. Her eyes widened. He shouldn't. But there was no audience, no ulterior motive, and he couldn't stop. His fingers burned.

He'd really thought he could just mess around. Have some fun while in town. Could sense that with some encouragement, she'd be keen. He'd deliberately stepped back from kissing her last night—figuring a little time would bring her out more. He had wanted to test his own outrageous response to her—wanted to know he could pull back.

He'd paid the price with a sleepless night and a hard body. He'd turned up first thing because he couldn't keep away any longer. And when he had kissed her just then, she'd turned the tables on him. Reality had slipped. His identity had slipped. He'd forgotten who he was and where he was. Forgotten everything but her, the feel of her, what she was doing and how he felt as she did it.

As with everything she did she set the standard. This game belonged in the Olympic arena whereas he was more accustomed to the social-tournament level. Trust Emma to play with an unsurpassable intensity.

He didn't like it. He'd lashed out at her just now—uncharacteristically unsettled. But he couldn't walk away. Temptation and desire had him caught and all he could do was try to stay in charge—of himself.

He hadn't been joking when he'd said he wouldn't be able to stop. It was only supposed to have been a kiss but his body had raced ahead to the ultimate conclusion. Mentally he'd had her stripped and underneath him.

The silky feel of her gentle curves under his hands caused an acceleration of his heart, making him feel as if he'd just ended a two-hour workout. And he was only holding her. OK, so his hands were on her bare skin, but he was fighting the urge to move them, to slide around and stroke her intimately. He ached to feel her wet.

He stared at her luminous eyes—the dark centre reflecting desire. The electric surge in his body warned him again.

'Later, Emma.' He coughed away the rasp. 'I'm going to have to show you later.'

He nearly threw all caution to the wind. Willing to run the risk of getting caught and prosecuted when he saw her disappointment. He couldn't help but give a gentle squeeze. 'We're playing by *all* the rules next time.'

He felt her responsive wriggle and hastily pulled his hands out, stepping away from her. Walking out of the trees towards the road. And damn well determined there would be a next time. Soon.

It shouldn't be feeling this good.

The latch on the window was old and rusty and wouldn't take a minute to remove. He frowned. 'This is really unsafe, Emma. It's child's play for someone to break in.' The thought of her vulnerability put his anger back on the boil.

He worked on the lock. 'I'm checking all the others before I leave, OK?'

He hardly heard her reply. Glowering, he took his frustration out on the rusty screws. He was shaken by the desire for her, annoyed at the way it had made him lash out at her. She'd been forced to over-achieve, over-please. He'd never much liked Emma's father—hadn't liked the way he'd go on about his daughters. He treated them like performing monkeys—showing off Emma's academic prowess, Lucy's violin-playing. Jake's low opinion had been confirmed after that day he'd found Emma in the park, terrified about the report card any normal person would think was brilliant. His utter dislike had been cemented after he'd had his own brush with him not long after. He'd decided to quit school. Lucas Delaney had come and seen him in the workshop above the garage where his grandfather had taught him to work wood.

He'd lectured. 'You leave school now, you'll be nothing. Picking fruit the rest of your life. Working as a building labourer. Going nowhere fast.'

Jake felt a boy's anger and a man's responsibility. He was nearly seventeen. His mum had been working three jobs, scrimping, saving so she could be there for him and his sister. So Sienna could get the best possible care. Now he was old enough to help out. She needed him. Sienna needed him. And this man had no idea, no understanding of their situation. Having Delaney the Dictator come and blast him was the last thing he needed.

They looked out the window and saw Emma walking across the lawn. 'You see Emma. She knows what she has to do. She's an achiever. She won't be here wasting her talents. You want to go places, you have to put in the work. Quitters don't get anywhere.'

The episode over her report card was still fresh in Jake's mind. It compounded his determination to prove the man wrong, stoking the fire in his belly to get out there and get on with it.

He had a plan and wasting more time at school for nothing wasn't part of it. He knew what he wanted to do, where he wanted to go.

And he'd done it. In a way Lucas had been right—you had to put in the work. Jake had worked like a dog—physically, mentally. Now he had it—the money, the security and the pleasure of knowing his mother didn't have to work ever again unless she wanted to. Of course, being her, she wanted to. He'd paid off her house, paid for overseas holidays. Most importantly he'd ensured Sienna had had the best possible treatment and now had the best possible outlook. He'd even paid her university fees—not that she seemed that thrilled with his interference these days.

He'd never spoken with Lucas Delaney again.

Jake put the new screws in and tightened them hard, then moved on to inspect the next window. Emma had worked like a dog too. All to gain approval. And she'd paid a price. Her lack of social life and her uptight exterior showed that. Surely she wanted more. She worked too hard to have fun and it irritated him beyond belief. He paused, screwdriver in hand, but that was where he could help out—make her have some fun, for real. That kiss in the park had been very, very real. He'd tapped into her sassy vein already. He chuckled again over her peaches, and wanted to shake her tree so bad. Just so long as *he* could handle it.

He walked round to the front of the cottage. The curtains were drawn on the windows on the left-hand side of the hallway. He stared for a moment. Her bedroom was the small room next to the kitchen at the back and the kitchen had a sitting area that she obviously used as her living room. So what was this room for? The builder in him knew it would be larger than the one at the back and it certainly would be the sunniest room in the house. Wouldn't she want that one for her bedroom?

Curiosity lifted its head and sniffed.

He walked in through the front door. Cocking his head, he listened in the little hallway. No sight or sound of Emma. He took another step into the house and saw the door to the bathroom was closed. Luck was on his side.

The scent of fresh flowers was even stronger as he opened the door to the front room. He looked about, his eye taking it all in. Wow. So there was something to know.

CHAPTER SIX

THE room was painted white. The floor was bare—the carpet had been ripped up to reveal the wooden boards underneath, but they hadn't been polished. They were still rough with patches of carpet glue evident. Little furniture. A table against the far wall. A chair.

And in the middle of the room, positioned to catch the light from the window, stood a large easel.

Art.

He closed his eyes a second. Remembering. Her best subject on her report card that day in the park. The subject she'd come top in. The subject she'd said she'd have to drop.

Despite the drawn curtains enough light filtered into the room for him to see the paintings that hung over all the walls. On the table spread out were technical-looking drawings—showing the cross-section of a flower. Then he noticed the paraphernalia next to them. The glass slides, the sharp knives, the magnifying glass. On one corner of the table stood pens, pencils. Under the table stood jars full of brushes, canvas being stretched, more paintings—some finished, some looking as if they'd been abandoned halfway. The faint smell of turps mingled with the blossoms that stood in a vase on the small table the far side of the easel.

He moved to stand in the centre of the room and slowly took in the paintings, also studying the drawings neatly laid out on the table. The contrast between the large, flowing paintings on the wall and the tiny, perfect technical drawings was fascinating. Like two halves of the one, the analytical perfectionist creating photographic-like miniatures, and the emotional, sensual person producing paintings that seemed to catch the soul of the flower. His heart, his body swelled.

He heard the step behind him, the closing of the door. He should feel guilty, he really should, but all he felt was awe.

He turned to face her. She'd changed, out of the pink singlet top that he now knew to have been splashed with paint. She'd replaced it with a clinging spring dress with thin straps. She still wasn't wearing a bra. The attraction to her magnified—overwhelming.

'What are you doing in here?'

He didn't even think to use the window latches as an excuse. 'Couldn't help it. It's the sunniest room in the house. I couldn't understand why you weren't using it.'

She was very pale.

His gaze dropped to her hands. Small, fine, perfectly proportioned. Just like her drawings.

'I thought you gave up Art at school.'

'I did.' She took a breath and then words tumbled out. 'I did Economics instead. But I was boarding and the art teacher was nice to me. And she lent me books and let me work in the art classroom after school hours. Basically she tutored me privately. It was our secret.'

'Your dad never knew.'

She shook her head. 'No one knows.'

'Still?'

She looked defiant. 'It's mine.' She glanced around the walls, anxiety etched on her face. 'Lucy knows a bit.'

He nodded. He'd guessed the sisters were close. They'd have to or else the competition their father encouraged between them would have destroyed any kind of sibling relationship.

'They're amazing, Emma.'

'I never did get past "Still Life with Flowers",' she said sheepishly as she paced about. 'Come on, let's go.' She looked at him and he knew she wanted him out of there.

No chance.

He looked back to study the drawings on the table, determined not to meet her eyes so he wouldn't see the entreaty there. There was a pile of drawings and next to it a loose sheaf of papers with text on them. He picked it up. There was a list of flowers and blurb written underneath. She had scrawled notes next to each entry. He examined it closer, reading, half forgetting Emma's anxiety as he became engrossed.

Emma stood in the middle of the room, heart thundering. Wanting him out of there but not knowing how she was going to do it. He had the look of a man who wasn't going anywhere without a fight and it wasn't as if she could pick him up and eject him physically. Besides, part of her was fascinated, keen to know his view. She swallowed the rising nerves. Eager for his approval.

She blinked back the sudden tears. He'd been right earlier. She did like to please people. Did want people to think the best of her. Needed to be the best—had to be. And that was why she'd never shared this with anyone. She didn't want that pressure. Didn't want to put this out for judgment. It was her escape, her enjoyment. If she wanted to paint the sky purple behind bright orange daisies, she could. And if she wanted to draw a lily with as much exactness as she could then she'd do that too.

'What is it?' He held Margaret's manuscript, flipping through it and reading her notes and then looking at the drawings Emma had laid out in order on the table.

She stared at his back, the broad shoulders that tapered to slim hips. He was strong and suddenly she wanted a part of that strength. So she snatched a breath and told him something she hadn't told anyone, not even her sister. 'My lecturer has written a book about floriography and asked me to provide some sample illustrations for it.'

'Flori-what?' He finally turned to look at her.

'Floriography.' She stepped up to the table next to him. 'The language of flowers. A Victorian thing. They assigned meanings to flowers so they could pass messages to each other by the flowers they gave to each other.'

'Since when does a commerce lecturer write a book about flowers?'

'Not commerce. Botany.'

'Botany? You studied botany as part of your commerce degree?'

'No, I also did a science degree majoring in plant biology.'

'What?'

'I did a double degree.'

'I didn't know that. Surely I should know that. Your father would have told everyone.'

'He doesn't know.'

'What?'

'He doesn't know.'

'You did a whole other degree and he doesn't know?'

It was why she had such a nil social life. She'd spent every waking moment at university running from lectures to laboratories. Her classmates had spent hours in the cafés and bars while she'd worked on through the night to keep up her drawing as well. She would have done Fine Arts if she could. But the demands of the two degrees had been too great. And she hadn't kept up her formal art education at school. Hadn't had the portfolio required. So she'd compromised and done Botany.

She hovered as he leant over the table, studying the drawings, reading the common and botanical names she'd written in a swirl underneath—and the romantic meaning historically assigned. She'd spent hours over them.

She gabbled, wanting him to understand. 'She's selected mostly common garden flowers and included bits on how to grow them and a bit on creating pretty, meaningful displays with them. It's quite detailed. She wants it to be a little coffee-table book, or a gift book, you know?'

He stood up and faced her, eyes shining. 'Emma, this is brilliant. Just brilliant.'

A head-spinning mix of panic, relief and attraction raced through her. 'She probably won't use my drawings, though. She just wanted a sample to send to the publisher so they get an idea of how she sees the layout and stuff.'

'What about the paintings? Are you including those?' He glanced up at the wall to where she'd painted some of the same flowers, a mix of detail and dramatic licence.

Never. She could just cope with sending the drawings by thinking of them as being like the anatomical illustrations she'd done as part of her study. That was why her lecturer had rung her. She'd always got bonus points for the detailed drawings she'd done in her laboratory book. They weren't really 'art'.

Oh, who was she kidding? She'd sweated blood on them, pouring her heart in.

She grasped her hands together and squeezed, tensing the muscles to ease their adrenalin burn. She fought the instinct to fly to her room and hide her head under her pillow.

'No.'

'You should. They're awesome.' He smiled. A full beamer that pulled her happiness level to new heights. And yet she wanted him out of there all the more. She didn't want this part of her life opened up to anyone.

But he was asking questions, looking at everything. 'So every flower has a meaning. What did you say I'd be? A tulip?'

She winced. Saw him run down the list. Saw him stop. Saw the smile.

Perfect lover.

He lifted his head and looked her straight in the eye. 'You think so, huh?'

Her anxiety about him seeing her work melted away in the heat of his gaze. When he looked at her like that all she could think about was how much she wanted him. Mesmerised, she wanted to answer. Wanted to say 'maybe' in a sassy, challenging way that might encourage him. But she couldn't peel her tongue from the roof of her mouth.

He tossed the draft onto the table and stepped nearer. 'You want to put it to the test?'

It was what she'd been thinking about all week. Dreaming of. Her body was coiled for action yet her tongue still wouldn't budge.

But something must have given her away because his

face lit up, and his smile was small but sensual—just the corners of his mouth teasing upwards. He made another move closer.

'I think we should. Don't you?'

Her lips parted but still no sound came, so she just let her body talk instead, leaning towards him as he took the final step to close the gap. He caught her and pulled her home. Her lashes lowered and she tilted her head, relaxing into his body. But he didn't kiss the mouth she offered. His fingers combed through her hair, sweeping it aside to reveal her neck, and it was there that his warm lips descended. Starting at the ultra-sensitive spot below her ear and slowly slipping down and a little cry escaped her. His arms tightened, his hands warm through the thin fabric of her dress. She wanted to kiss him, taste him, but he was out of reach, kissing her collar-bones while his hands gently rocked her against him. Her head fell back, eyes closing; all she could do was rest against him and let the sweet sensations slide through her.

His lips trailed across her, sparking flames across every painstaking inch he covered. As her breathing accelerated so did her desire and her need for more than this. As if he'd sensed the subtle shift he lifted his head. His hands held her tighter to him. She opened her eyes and took in his flushed features.

'Not pretending any more, Emma. This game's going up a level and we're playing for real now.'

Real, but still playing. Could she handle it? She blinked slowly, knowing he could offer her the night of a lifetime. But that was all it would be. There was going to be nothing permanent about this. He was only here for a few more weeks and anyway he played hard and moved on. She didn't know what would happen later; all she knew was that right now she couldn't stop.

'Yes.'

He expelled a large breath, stepping back, taking her hand, heading straight to her bedroom. Confident, in control and not giving her any chance to change her mind. In the centre of her room he turned to face her and she tingled at his expression, at knowing the desire she saw there was real. He pulled on her hand, drawing her to him like a dancer guiding his partner towards him into an embrace. She lifted her face but he still didn't take her lips. Instead he kissed her face, neck and shoulders, his hands firm as they moved over her body. She heard the swishing sound and realised that her dress had just slipped to the floor and all she now wore was a pair of panties.

He lifted his head and stood back a fraction, his lashes showing long on his cheek as he looked down, down, down the length of her.

As she stood there, exposed to his scrutiny, all her inadequacies came to the fore. It was all right when they kissed, when he touched her. She forgot everything then. But having him stand and look at her that way, all she could think was how she could never measure up to the bevies of blonde beauties she'd mentally attached him to. 'I'm not exactly…'

His lashes swept up, the heat in his eyes lancing her. 'Perfect. You're perfect.'

She didn't believe him, self-conscious as she saw him gaze at her bared breasts. 'I'm not very big.'

'Who needs big?' he muttered. 'All you need is enough to do this…' He stepped forward as he spoke, bending and taking her nipple and the softly swollen flesh around it into his hot mouth. She gasped, her legs losing the ability to support her, and his arms tightened, holding her up as he licked and sucked. Pure want shot through her. He still hadn't kissed her mouth and her desire for that grew desperate. She called to him, whispering his name over and over. She watched from half-closed eyes as he continued to torment her.

He guided her back against the bed, lifted his head, and with a gentle smile that teased he gave her a little push, tumbling her backwards. He followed immediately and they landed together on the mattress. Her insides totally turned to mush as her body took on the weight of him.

With his arms either side of her, enclosing her in his warmth, he finally bent his head to kiss her lips. She met him eagerly and her passion exploded as the depth increased. She held his roughened jaw between her palms, holding him in place as much as he pinned her. The kiss grew crazy. Hot, feverish need made her want to speed things up. Having him braced above her like that, all it made her want to do was part her legs—wide. She wanted him, *all* of him.

Then he moved away and the disappointment was like a kick in the gut. He lay on his side, propping his head on his hand, and that teasing smile had widened. 'Time for some fun, Emma.'

She wasn't sure what he had in mind. The only hint that he was as affected by that shattering kiss was his faint breathlessness. It made her realise this was so much more for her than for him. She was about to baulk when his fingers played a scale down her stomach. The touch set off a symphony of sensation. He bent forward and his mouth followed their trail and down he slid. He slipped his fingers under the waistband of her panties, ran them around the edge, pulling at the elastic. He looked up at her with a smile that was wickedly lusty and so infectious. Heat washed over her, sudden and intense. He wanted it and she wanted him to do it. Now.

He somehow got the message. Maybe it was the impatient flex of her hips towards him. He knelt, slipped her panties off her hips, down her legs and off. He flung them away and turned back to her with an expression of extreme anticipation. He slid his widespread hands firmly from her ankles up her calves to her knees and then thighs, pushing them apart with ease. She lay back, watching him as he looked at her, excitement tightening as the pressure of his fingers increased as did the almost feral glaze in his eye.

'I'm sorry, Emma, I can't wait, I just have to…' And he bent his head and tasted her core, once.

She exhaled, not realising she'd been holding her breath. Should she be embarrassed about how turned on she was? How wet she was?

'Emma.' He lifted up from her. 'You have no idea how much I want this. Want you like this.' The look he sent her was viciously searing. Then he was back, burying his mouth and tongue into her, like a man starving, a man who couldn't get enough of her flavour. Licking, sucking as he had her breast only this was even more sensational. Gently, then harder, then gentle again, he teased her. He hooked her legs over his shoulders, settling between them, his hands under her buttocks lifting her so she was utterly available to him. And all she could do was lie there and try to absorb the sensations, the delight, and try to stay cognisant. The flush in her cheeks was intolerable and she flung her arms wide across the bed. He was taking control and giving her the freedom to do nothing but feel. The faint abrasiveness of his lightly shadowed jaw tickled her thighs as her tension rose. She wanted the release but she never wanted this torment to end.

Reason tried to claw its way back to the surface, but she was sunk again as he nipped at the tender skin of her inner thighs.

He soothed with his lips. 'Do you like that?'

Her breathing was short and her answer came in a barely audible puff. 'Yes.'

He did it again. 'Keep saying that, Emma. That's all I want to hear you say to me; just keep saying yes.' The strain in his voice excited her more.

'Yes.' Any other response was impossible. Her fingers curled into the bedspread as she tried to control her reaction. But with every caress that control crumbled. Reality slipped away. Her focus slipped away. All she could do was feel him, the heat of his breath, the firm stroke of his tongue, the suck of his lips and the hard grip of his fingers on her hips, keeping her where he wanted, not letting her pull back, but fuelling the journey to ecstasy.

Her breathing turned ragged; another few licks and she was gasping. Her hands lifted and she grasped his hair, whether to push him away or keep him there she wasn't sure.

He lifted his head a millimetre to mutter, 'Don't fight it. I want to taste it. Let me…let me.'

She pushed his head back down and bucked upwards to meet him, crying aloud as he sucked again and again until every muscle in her spasmed. The 'yes' she screamed was barely recognisable. For seconds her body was locked rigid until finally the tension snapped and extreme pleasure washed through her—waves in which her consciousness almost drowned.

She lay, eyes closed, breathing deepening and she felt his finger gently trace through the wetness at the top of her thighs, and then gently slide right into her. Her eyes flew open as desire jerked through her again and she found herself staring into his blazing face. 'Jake.' She didn't care how much of a beg it sounded.

He moved, coming to lie on her, his jeans rough against her skin. His hair mussed from where she'd driven her fingers through it, gripping him as he'd pulled her through the fire. Their eyes met, his stormy and his breathing rough. 'Are you still saying yes to me, Emma?'

She curled her legs around his waist, rubbing against the taut denim. 'Yes.'

'You're ready for me.' Part question, part statement of fact.

'Yes.' Soft and supplicant. No way was there any other answer.

He bent to kiss her and suddenly all that mattered to her was getting his jeans off. He rolled off her, lying on his back as he ripped open the belt and yanked them down.

And then he froze.

She stared. 'What?'

'I don't have a condom.' He swore sharply. 'Please tell me you have some.'

He whipped his head round at her silence. 'Please.'

'You don't have one in your wallet?'

His fingers raked through his hair as he cursed.

She figured he must have forgotten to replace it last time he used it. She pushed away the stray thought. She didn't have any. Had never had the need. Even more embarrassingly, wouldn't know how to put one on. Colour ran high and doubts came flying in. What was she doing?

'No, you don't. Don't go cold on me.' He moved fast, taking her hands in his and pinning them at the sides of her head while he kissed her hard and deep until she was thrusting up against him, that squirming, desperate mass again.

'We both want this. You have no idea how badly *I* want this.'

She did. She was the same.

'What about your toolbox? You were the one who said about being prepared.'

'Screwdrivers, yes; condoms, no.'

He moved off to rest beside her and they lay together in frustrated silence.

'What about asking your neighbour?'

She was mortified. 'As if. It's hardly like asking for a cup of sugar, is it?'

He started laughing so hard and she mock-punched him on the arm. He immediately tussled back, flipping over her, pressing against her and suddenly so, so, close—the only thing separating them the strained cotton of his boxers. Their eyes locked.

He suddenly looked as serious as she'd ever seen him. 'I don't have a condom with me because I wasn't expecting this to happen. Not yet anyway.'

'But you did expect it?'

'I've been wanting it to happen all week.'

I've been wanting it to happen for years.

She slumped down in the bed, half in frustration, half in despair at her own desperation. She'd thought she was finally going to get somewhere. He'd wanted her. And now that moment was lost. She pulled at the sheet, wanting to cover her cooling body.

Suddenly he was out of the bed and pulling his jeans back up, struggling big time with the zip.

'Where are you going?'

'The service station. There's one round the corner from the park. I can run, be back in less than ten. Don't move. Do. Not. Move.'

He kissed her again—pressing her down into the mattress, leaving her lips bruised but bursting with pleasure. Then he was gone, pulling the tee shirt over his head as he exited the room. She lay staring after him, and lasted about thirty seconds.

The front door flung open just over ten minutes later. He looked at her and sighed. 'You moved.'

She looked at him and nearly melted on the spot. Every whisper of doubt fled again at the sight of him. His intention was obvious. He puffed slightly, a light sheen of sweat beaded on his brow. He clutched a small box. It wasn't even in a bag.

'Have you changed your mind?'

She couldn't answer vocally, still too unsure, so she shook her head just a fraction.

'Well,' he said with a philosophical tone as he strolled towards her, 'I guess it means I get to undress you all over again.'

She stood still. Didn't run, didn't move towards him. Just stood waiting, wanting. Tipped her head back the second he was in range. Mouth open, damp everywhere.

His arms wrapped around her and he lifted her up. She curled her legs around his waist and he walked through the tiny cottage to her bedroom. All the while their lips sealed, their tongues dancing and their arms locked about each other.

His hand slid up her thigh and he lifted his head and grinned at her as he discovered her lack of underwear. She'd been so wet, still was. Putting panties on would have created unnecessary laundry.

He lowered her to the ground and disposed of the dress. His shoes, jeans and tee rapidly followed and at last the searing contact resumed—full-on, fast, frantic.

He broke his mouth away from hers. 'We have to slow this down.'

'Why?'

His grunt of laughter was muffled against her shoulder and he fell back on the bed, pulling her with him. They landed on the box of condoms he'd tossed down a moment before. He ripped it open and had one on in less than a minute.

He paused and looked at her.

She swallowed hard at the sight of him. At the size of him.

He seemed to sense her nerves. 'Slow, smooth, close.' He echoed the words of the conversation of only last night. It seemed for ever ago.

Dancing with Jake. Already she hoped she would get to do it again. Dangerous territory. But the worrying thoughts vanished—along with all others—as he moved, settling over her. The speed of seconds ago was gone. Instead his actions were gentle, deliberate. His hands held her head. He wouldn't let her break eye contact. Her barely acknowledged fantasy of half a lifetime was about to become reality.

Slowly, smoothly, he got close and she'd never felt so excited. Her eyes widened as her body stretched to take him. She wanted it more than she'd ever wanted anything. She took a deep breath. 'Please don't stop. Please don't stop.'

His fingers came over her mouth. She was silenced by them and by the sudden flare in his eyes. He squeezed them shut. 'Concentrate. I *have* to concentrate.'

She lay still, as did he, for the beautiful moment they became one. His eyes flashed opened again and she saw his pupils huge and glowing. He lifted his fingers away from her mouth, replacing them with his lips. Then he smiled at her.

'Don't worry, I'm not going to stop. We've barely started.'

And then he did start, his hands, mouth and hips working together to cause an overdose of sensitivity in her limbs and soul.

She started too, understanding, giving back. She kissed him, ran the tip of her tongue down his neck to taste him, and used her hands to urge him closer. She couldn't contain the cries of delight. Moving with him to create exquisite sensations until with a harsh groan he reared up onto his hands, arching back above her. The muscles in his arms rippled, his chest golden and broad. He ground against her, driving deeper. The edges of her vision darkened, she could see only him, feel only him. She was hardly aware of her moans, the sounds of pleasure just escaping. Effortless joy.

There was nothing slow about it any more. And it felt fantastic. And suddenly she was gone—he'd sent her to some other galaxy, a state of bliss.

He dropped to his elbows, gathering her to him as her body shook. They couldn't have got closer. She heard his groan and felt the hot way he muttered her name over and over as he powered everything into her.

She lay, laxness seeping into her bones. The weight of him welcome in her lethargy.

'I'm not too heavy, am I? Can you breathe?'

'I'm fine.' Cocooned in his arms, still connected, she was more than fine. She wanted this moment to last for ever.

As soon as she'd thought it the reality struck at her. It wasn't going to be for ever. A trickle of chill flowed into the warmth of a moment before. It became a flood as the madness lifted and cold sanity returned. She'd just slept with Jake Rendel. A life-changing event for her, but she was just another girl for him.

She hoped it had been OK. If it had been half as good for him as it had for her then she was in the clear. She felt tears spring to her eyes and she wriggled underneath him, suddenly needing to step back.

He kissed her ear swiftly and whispered, 'We really need to do that again.'

Yes, but she needed to shore up her defences first. 'I'm just going to nip to the bathroom.'

She slid from the bed and looked for something to wrap around her while he rustled in the bed. She heard his mutter, then she heard his shout.

'Emma!' Startled, she looked at him. 'Why the hell didn't you tell me you were a virgin?'

CHAPTER SEVEN

'DOES it matter?' Emma looked at where he'd pulled back the sheet to where the evidence stared them hard in the face. The look of shock on his face as he computed the info wasn't encouraging.

'Of course it matters. What are you doing giving your virginity to—?' He broke off. His frown deepened. 'I could have hurt you. Did I hurt you?'

'No.' She sighed. 'OK, just a little to start. Then it was, it was…' *Mind blowing*, but she couldn't quite say it. 'I was ready, Jake; you said it yourself.'

With relief she watched him pull the sheet up. It was hard for her to concentrate on the conversation with him lying in all his magnificent naked glory. She'd started to want him all over again—but still wanted that mind space too.

'Why didn't you tell me?'

'Would it have made a difference?' Would you have stopped? She hadn't wanted to run the risk. She'd wanted him too much.

He stared at her darkly as he pondered that one. Then, 'I could have made it better for you.'

Hysterical giggles weren't too far away. Better?

Impossible. At least he hadn't said it had been a mistake—yet.

He continued to lecture. 'It should have been more special. Were you waiting for marriage?'

The look of terror that crossed his face as he asked had her determined to straighten him out.

'Jake, stop being so old-fashioned. It had to happen some time. Hell, according to some magazine I read most women kiss twenty-nine men before they get married!'

'Twenty-nine?' He glowered. 'How many have you kissed? What number am I?'

She knew her colour was high and no way was she going to tell him he was her first in all departments. 'What does it matter? And you know what number you are in bed, so you can be pleased about that. I was ready for this to happen and why not with you?' The best form of defence was attack. 'I bet you can't even remember what number I am for you. At least it meant one of us was a pro.'

He sat bolt upright and frowned at her. 'Well, that's charming. Who do you think I am?'

'Well, you said yourself you're a playboy.'

'Ok, I'll be honest. I'm not exactly celibate, but I'm not out on the pull every night either.'

Her scepticism must have been clearly evident.

'I'm not. I have one girlfriend at a time. With a gap in between. We spend time together, have fun, move on. I'm up front. She knows, I know.'

'How long do they usually last?'

'A few weeks.'

'Is that what we're doing?'

Silence. He glowered at her before huffing back down on the bed.

'I don't know what we're doing.' He lay rubbing his hands over his eyes. His forehead creased.

She watched him cautiously. He really didn't seem to be taking this too well. She hadn't thought it would matter that much—or not to him, at least.

Fists clenched, he let out a roar.

She jumped. 'What?'

He flung back the sheet with theatrical panache. 'Look at me. God, I wanted you all over again and now even more so. There are just so many ways we have to do this together. So much I have to show you. You haven't had sex standing up, on top…all kinds of ways.'

She stared at him. Stared at his body. The tension even greater than before, he was the epitome of raw, ready man, muscles bunching, and she knew he was about to pounce. Excitement started to flood out her doubts again. 'So what, now you're going to be my coach?'

'Hell, yes.' He gave a wicked laugh. 'You know, for a beginner you have an outstanding level of natural ability. You're going to be a star pupil.'

'Always am, sir.' She batted her lashes at him. Keep it cool, keep it light. Take advantage of one incredible lover and try not to get your heart smashed in the process. She could handle this. She could. 'OK, but first I have a shower.'

'Not without me, you don't.'

He was out of bed and grabbing a condom from the box before she'd taken a step.

She turned and ran for the bathroom, giggling as he lunged after her. Worries whisked away in the chase.

'Would you believe I'm starving?'

They sat in the kitchen. She'd slipped her dress on again and he lounged in his tee shirt and boxers.

'Yes, because so am I. I've got steak in the freezer, oven chips and mushrooms I can make a sauce with.'

'Anything green?' His eyes twinkled.

She wrinkled her nose. 'Some chopped tomato and a bit of lettuce on the side?'

'You're such a carnivore.'

She smiled.

'Where do you put it all?'

She shrugged. 'Fast metabolism, I guess. I like meat.'

He sliced the mushrooms while she put the chips in the oven and prepared the steak.

'Is it too early for a drink? Got anything to drink?'

'Wine.'

'From home?'

'Of course.'

They carried the plates outside and sat on the verandah again.

He'd demolished half his steak when he caught her eye. 'I can't believe you were a virgin.'

She swallowed. 'Why?'

'You're twenty-six.'

'So?'

'You don't think that's a little unusual these days?'

'We're not all at it like rabbits from the age of, what— sixteen?'

The rascally grin appeared. 'You can't tell me you've never been hit on by anyone. What about university?'

'What about it? I was so busy I just didn't have the time.'

'You didn't go to all the start-of-year parties? End-of-year parties? All-year-round all-night-long parties?'

'I studied. If you want to come top you don't go to parties.'

'Emma, I didn't even *go* to university but I still went to the parties.'

'Why am I not surprised?'

'What about the hotel?'

Getting fed up with the conversation, she pushed her plate away. 'Sure I get asked out. They're always much older. They're almost always married.'

He chuckled. 'You're a victim of your own success.'

Success? Hardly. 'What do you mean?'

'You intimidate guys your own age. You probably earn more than most of them. You're incredibly efficient and good at your job. You have them all shaking in their boots. Whereas older men appreciate your power.'

She rolled her eyes. He was just being generous about a pathetic situation. 'You're not that much older than me. You're not intimidated?'

'I earn more than you.' He looked smug.

'And if you didn't?'

He winked. 'You don't scare me, Emma Delaney.'

It was a complete lie. She terrified him. The last few hours had been the most intense of his life. And his head couldn't quite catch up with it all.

'You won't tell anyone, will you?' She looked anxiously at him.

'What, that you were a virgin?' Who on earth was he going to tell? Ten years ago he probably would have carved it into a tree somewhere, but he was beyond that now— maybe.

She gave a weak smile. 'No. About the room.'

'Your paintings?'

She nodded, not looking at him.

Her worry confused him. 'Why not?'

'I just don't want people knowing. It's nothing.'

'It's not nothing, Emma, they're incredible. You should be proud of them.' He was still in shock about it. In shock about everything. That no one knew about her paintings was astounding; that she'd studied a whole other degree and not told her parents was bizarre. The irony got him. Her father would have been even more proud of that.

'Jake, I really don't want to talk about it. And I don't want you going in there again.'

He looked at her, not sure he could promise either.

'You don't want to talk about it? You must—you never have. Talk to me, at least talk to me.' He didn't want her to shut the door on him on this. Now that he was in, he didn't want to be turfed out.

'There's nothing to say. It's just a hobby, that's all.'

He knew it wasn't. She put hours into it. All those paintings were evidence of that.

'Why don't you show them? You should at least hang some in your house. People would be so interested.'

Her frown got bigger with every word he spoke and he couldn't think why. She had talent—in spades, as usual. Why on earth wouldn't she want to share it?

'I don't want people to be interested.'

She looked like a petulant schoolgirl, but then she bent over her plate and he couldn't help but notice the gentle curve of her breast as her dress slipped. No schoolgirl here; she was all woman. Petite and perfectly formed.

She glanced up and caught the line of his gaze and her lips curved up.

Sexy. Sultry.

Jake blinked. She might not have that much experience

but she sure knew how to push his buttons—a single-touch direct-dial to his hotline.

He gripped the cutlery. He'd discovered all of Emma's secrets today. At least he hoped he had all of them. He didn't know if he could handle much more.

Emma gave up on the last of the steak. Being with Jake did dangerous things to her. Her appetite for food seemed to have disappeared. But her hunger for him was growing minute by minute. She was in danger of keeling over from famine any moment. Fainting at his feet would be too uncool.

She wanted him to forget about her paintings. He was never going to understand why she needed it to be hers and hers alone. He hadn't had to deal with the level of expectation she had and wouldn't understand the bliss of being able to do something badly if she wanted. With no one judging. But while she couldn't make him understand, maybe, just maybe, she could distract him. Make him forget. She stood up from the table but couldn't hide the wince.

'Sore?' His voice was low and chocolatey rich.

She felt the colour rise in her cheeks. 'A little.'

He stood and took the plate off her, setting it down on the table. 'Let me see if I can help you loosen up. Ease away the aches and pains.' In a smooth, effortless move she was off her feet and in his arms.

'Jake!' But she didn't mean the indignation. To be carried as if she weighed nothing more than a feather made her feel incredibly feminine.

He headed straight to her bedroom and her blood started pumping.

'I really need to kiss you again, Emma. Everywhere.'

With his arms so firm around her—what could she do but let him?

Some time later she lay, naked, spread-eagled and sated—for the moment. He lay on his side next to her, head propped up on his elbow, grinning at her wickedly.

'Better?'

Much. But she didn't like this one-sided business.

She sat up and leaned over him. Shyly bold. Pushing up his tee shirt and tracing a finger down his chest. Bending over to let her lips follow its path. Down, down, down.

Then he lifted his hand and stopped her.

'No.'

Startled, she looked at him.

'I don't want you to.'

She had that horrid hot-then-cold feeling. 'Why not?' She glanced down for reassurance and got it: the bulge in his boxers was enormous.

'I don't want you to feel you have to.'

'I don't.'

He smoothed his forehead with his fingers. 'You're always doing things for others because you think you're obligated to. I don't want you to feel that way with me.'

'I do not. I'm not.' Why did he think this? Why couldn't he see that she made her own decisions for herself? Inexperience made her feel inadequate. 'Are you scared I'll do it wrong?'

He laughed. 'Honey, there is no wrong.'

She sighed. He had *her* all wrong—didn't he?

He stared at her with eyes that were dark and unfathomable. 'Tell me.'

'What?'

'Tell me why you want to. Prove it's not because you think you have to.'

She froze. Embarrassment washed over her. That was certainly something she'd never done before. Tell him what she really wanted? *Why* she really wanted it? She couldn't remember when she'd last done that in any area of her life. Open up those secret desires? She looked at him and saw the challenge. It's a *game*, she reminded herself, just a game. And she could make up the rules if she wanted to. A smidgeon of confidence at that thought enabled her to answer.

'I'm not doing this because I think you want me to. Hell, it appears you don't. I want to for *me*.' She coughed, tried for a little more volume, but still didn't make it much past a whisper. 'OK, I've never…touched a guy this way. Maybe I'm curious. Maybe I want to learn. Maybe I want to make you feel the way you do me—I want to know I can do that.'

She felt burningly awkward. But then he was the one who said he'd be her coach.

He sat up, took her chin with a light touch and tilted her head so he could kiss her—gently, so sweetly. He lifted his head and stared hard into her eyes. She held the gaze, feeling herself growing more excited by its intensity, feeling her want for him grow even more. Suddenly he pulled the tee shirt over his head. 'If you insist, who am I to stand in the way of a decent education?' His mouth broke into that magnificent smile and she had the urge to just kiss him and climb aboard. But she wanted to discover him first. Inch by glorious inch.

She smiled, shyly excited. 'I *want* to explore you, Jake.'

He lay back, screwing up his eyes. 'I don't think it's going to take much, Emma. This conversation alone just about has me exploding.'

She rose to all fours and bent over him. Just looking at first. Then touching. First with her fingers, then with her tongue.

Her shyness disappeared as experimentation took over to find what would make him shiver, what would make him tense, what would make him groan.

She achieved it all, loving his reactions, and when he suddenly gripped her shoulders she looked up at his face. His eyes were open now, intensely fixed on her actions.

'OK?' she asked.

His head jerked in the affirmative. She figured the flush in his face was a good sign. She bent her head again.

'Emma, Emma, Emma!' His hands slipped under her arms and he pulled her up the bed. 'Please tell me you're not too sore now,' he asked as he frantically donned a condom.

'Not too sore.' She smiled as he pressed onto her.

'You're ready?' His breathing broken.

'Yes.'

CHAPTER EIGHT

AT 7:30 A.M. Emma walked into her office and stopped mid-stride halfway across the floor. In her single-stem specimen vase stood a perfect red tulip. She glanced around, half hoping someone was there to witness the biggest smile she'd ever worn at that time of day. No one present. Then she slapped herself. Idiot girl.

She was unable to concentrate on the screen at all; her gaze kept darting to the flower. She wriggled on her seat as she kept re-living parts of the weekend. Not a good idea. Intolerable heat alternated with moments of sheer panic. She had the sinking feeling it had meant a lot more to her than Jake. And more than was good for her, given his record of nil-commitment. But she'd known what she was getting into from the start—some fun. Short-term. He was only in town a few weeks anyway. She was just going to have to get over it.

But that didn't stop her dreaming.

She pushed away her keyboard and pulled out a blank piece of paper. Opening her drawer, she selected a couple of lead pencils. She picked up the specimen vase. She just wasn't going to get any work done till she'd satisfied her creative itch. She studied the flower, carefully touched its silky petals, ran her finger down its strong, smooth stem. It was a magnificent example.

She set it down on her desk and started to draw it.

She marked precise, sure lines on the paper, added curves and shading, and soon the tulip looked back up at her in 2D. She smiled, her tongue poking out the corner of her mouth.

Self-mockery curved the smile further as she thought to add something else. She curled a second stem around the straight stem of the tulip. Then the head of a smaller flower took shape. Her daisy.

Her door opened and she looked up guiltily. Max came towards her. 'How are you getting on with that report?'

She glanced at the clock on her computer—nine a.m. Hell, somehow she'd just wasted over an hour on a doodle.

'It's taking a little longer than I'd expected.'

Mortified, she berated herself. She should have worked on it at home in the weekend. Most certainly she should have been working on it now—in work time! Instead she'd been daydreaming about the boy next door. How pathetic.

Max was looking across the room at her through slightly narrowed eyes. 'You'll have it for me tomorrow though, won't you?'

'Of course.' That meant working hard at it from this minute on. She was not going to lose her concentration—or her career—on a fling. Max turned to leave. She snatched up the sketch and tossed it at the bin. Focus, focus, focus.

'Morning.'

She lifted her head so fast she almost gave herself whiplash.

Jake stood in her doorway, smiling hello and stepping aside for Max as he passed on the way out. Max turned and gave them both a look that Emma was wary of interpreting.

As soon as Max was out the door Jake shut it behind him. Throwing her a wicked look, he turned the lock.

'Ever had sex on your desk?' He laughed. 'Oh, no, of course you haven't.'

'No, and I'm not about to.' But her body thought different. It was already warming up and anticipating the action.

'You don't think?'

She walked backwards, hands out—half defending, half beckoning. 'Jake, no.'

'Jake, yes.' He'd undone the top buttons of his shirt as he walked towards her. She stared at his chest, every carnal thought of the last few hours re-entering her head and priming her body.

'Jake.' Rational thought was slipping away.

His grin was utterly wicked as he stepped closer. 'Jake, yes.'

'Yes.' He was with her now. And she was wrapping around him.

They kissed and then he lifted his head to look at her accusingly. 'You taste of Caramello.'

She laughed. 'Good thing you like it too.'

'Tastes even better mixed with you.' He bent and kissed her again. She pressed into him. The hours apart felt like years and she couldn't wait to feel him again. He'd gone back to his apartment after spending Saturday night with her. A night where they'd put in hours and hours of study together. Study of all things physical and pleasurable in each other. Until she'd been exhausted and he'd declared himself utterly spent. They'd cooked breakfast and then he'd gone. He'd needed to work. She'd needed to work. She had intended to. Instead she'd lain on her sofa on the verandah in the sun and struggled to believe it had all actually happened. If it hadn't been for the all-over body ache she would have thought she'd dreamt it.

Now, twenty-four hours later, he was scrabbling with her shirt and she was frustrated with his seemingly glued-on belt. He lifted his head from her collar-bone and growled. 'You do the buttons because I'm all thumbs and I'm going to rip it off if it's not open soon.'

She lifted her hands and swiftly dealt with them.

'I'll do the skirt.'

She chuckled as he simply pushed it up, dropping to his knees to slide her panties down. He loitered over the task. Her giggles became gasps.

'Jake, take care of the condom.' She could hardly get the words out.

He stood and pulled one out. 'I have one in every pocket now.' It was on in seconds, she was on the desk and he was on her, in her and they were away together. She looked up at him and knew her face mirrored his excited expression.

'I can't believe how good this feels.' He growled in her ear as his hands worked through her hair, messing it from its clasp.

'I know,' she whispered, curling her legs around him and arching up. She couldn't get enough of him. Couldn't get enough of this crazy ride. In the hours apart from him her body's excitement level had been building and it didn't take long to reach explosion point. She grabbed some material of his shirt sleeve between her teeth to stop the screams.

She felt him nuzzling and nipping at her neck and knew it was for the same purpose.

Minutes later she floated down from the heights and absorbed the flaming madness of their actions. Since when had she ever acted so crazy? Since when was she so willing to abandon anything and everything for a few lust-fuelled moments? She'd never let her wants overrule her obligations before.

It was then she noticed that her stapler was digging into her back. He pushed away from her, standing up from the desk, and, taking her hand, pulled her to her feet.

Embarrassed, she bent and retrieved her panties from the floor.

'You often have sex at work?' The wildness that had overtaken her was more than a little terrifying.

He pulled his belt though its loop. 'Actually no, this is a first for me too.'

He didn't quite meet her eye, and she could almost believe he was embarrassed too. Surely not.

The phone rang. Eyes wide, she answered, hoping she didn't sound too breathless. Becca. Reminding her of an appointment.

She hung up, desperately pulling her clothes right. 'I'm late for a meeting. I'm never late.' She smoothed down her skirt, thanking the stars it wasn't linen or the creases would be unbelievable. 'Do I look OK?'

Jake surveyed her and inwardly cringed. Did he tell her? He hadn't meant to do it, but he'd been trying to be quiet and nibbling on her neck had stopped him from letting the shouts of lust out. OK, so he'd done more than nibble, he'd been sucking long and hard like some starving vampire. He couldn't get enough of her. And now she had the love bite to prove it.

It was one thing to touch an arm here, throw a look there and give the impression of an affair to her workmates, it was another to thrust such an obvious mark of passion in their faces. Anyone else and he'd have laughed. But this was Emma and Emma was not tacky and he didn't want to upset her. Then he figured a solution.

'Let your hair out.'

'What?' She put a hand to her hair.

'It's all coming out anyway.' He gestured. 'Sorry.'

She took it out of the clip and shook her head. It tumbled down round her neck. Perfect.

Her face glowed and her eyes sparkled and he'd never seen her so beautiful. And he wanted her again already.

'You go. I'm going to stay and get dressed.'

She hightailed it out of there. He watched, unable to take his eyes from the gentle sway of her hips as she walked. Bad move—very bad. He pulled his shirt together and worked the buttons with terse actions.

You'd think he'd be able to keep away from her for twenty-four hours, but no. Apparently not.

Despite his fondness for fun he was professional and when at work, he worked. He'd never have got as far as he had if he did otherwise. And yet, here he was, first thing Monday morning seeking her out and tumbling her on a table with very few preliminaries. He'd just needed to. Needed her. Needed that sweet, warm body wrapped around him, letting him in. He'd needed another of those life-stopping orgasms. Utterly addictive.

He tucked the shirt in. Took a few deep breaths to rebalance. He looked at her desk. The tulip made him smile. He'd found out where the commercial flower markets were and had been there before six that morning to see if any growers had any. They hadn't been going to sell him just the one, but had been happy to when he'd given them enough money for several dozen.

Turning to go, he noticed a piece of paper on the floor that had just missed the waste-paper basket. He bent to put it in for her, but stopped as he saw what was on it. One of her drawings. He studied it—two flowers precisely drawn in pencil. The tulip on the table. His heart lifted; she'd liked it. Then the small daisy wrapped around the tulip, their stems intertwining.

His lips twitched. She'd drawn them. Intimate—as they had been only minutes before. An idiotic amount of pleasure surged through him at the knowledge she'd been thinking of him—of them. Then it dampened as he considered—what was she doing throwing it out?

He carefully folded it over, making sure the paper didn't actually crease. Holding it between forefinger and thumb, he exited the room. He strolled to the room assigned to him and the team and spread it flat again, tucked it into a file and put it in his bag. All the while his out-of-control brain worked furiously to figure out a way to get her alone again.

Emma didn't see him the rest of the day—largely because she hid out in her office hiding her face, flashing at the memory of the morning, of the past weekend. He appeared in her doorway at the end of the day. He stood in the open door, not venturing nearer. She looked across to him and excitement raced through every cell. When was this going to burn out?

'I'm done for the day. What about you?'

With regret she gestured to the pile of files on her desk. 'Got a way to go.'

He nodded. 'Come to my place once you're through. I'll cook you dinner—I owe you a couple of meals.'

A couple? Was he thinking breakfast as well?

'Come into my parlour said the spider to the fly,' she murmured.

He looked at her slyly. 'You think I want to eat you all up?'

She kind of hoped so and the newly released sass in her couldn't help the flirty reply. 'Don't you?'

'Oh, yes.'

She was so tempted.

'We can have a barbecue; it's a warm night.'

'You're in an apartment building; where's the barbecue?' A teeny obstacle and she knew it.

'I have a very large, very nice balcony.'

She was about to say OK when he threw in the trump card. 'And I have a prime piece of meat just for you.'

She looked at him sharply but his expression was innocent—it was only her mind in the gutter and the only prime specimen she wanted was him.

She shouldn't, she really shouldn't. 'I have a lot to do on this report. I might be pretty late.'

'I don't care how late you come just so long as you come.'

And she really wanted to. 'OK.'

'Text me when you leave the hotel.'

She nodded, not looking at him again. She needed to focus on the spreadsheet, not the sex on toast standing in her doorway.

It was after nine when she logged off from her computer. She stood, shaking off the stiffness that had settled in from hunching over the machine for so many hours. She picked up her mobile and mentally debated for a nanosecond. There really was no question. She pushed the buttons.

'Coming now.'

She smirked. She was getting as bad at the innuendo as he was.

It was another hot night. The wind stirred her hair as she walked. Maybe that was the source of her folly—the wind that drove people to commit crazy acts and literally sent the dogs barking. She walked into the lobby. The attendant looked at her. 'Ms Delaney?'

Full marks for service.

He summoned the lift for her. 'Just step in and I'll send you up.'

The attendant must have phoned to let Jake know because he was waiting in his open doorway, looking sinful. Long shorts and close-fitting tee, bronzed muscles on display above and below the material. He smiled and her answering one radiated out from deep within.

'Dinner's just cooking. The sooner we eat, the sooner we get down to furthering your education.'

'You've been putting some thought into that, have you?'

'Uh-huh.' He winked at her and her heart accelerated into attack territory. 'But first, we need sustenance. A bar of Caramello isn't going to be enough.'

Good grief. She could hardly walk for the excitement. Blow the main course, bring on the main event.

He led the way into the kitchen. She looked about. It was your typical soulless serviced apartment. A couple of extra prints hung on the wall to try to give it a cosy feel, but it still looked like a hotel room. There was nothing personal of his evident other than some files on the table, and his laptop.

Empty.

Temporary.

She needed to remember that. 'What happened to the barbecue?' she asked, preferring to look outside than at the reminders of his transience. Pain pricking already.

'Too windy up here.'

Out the window, she saw the branches of the trees down in the park waving wildly. She breathed deeply.

'Smells good.'

'Fillet of beef.' He pulled the tray out of the oven. She moved to lean against the bench and watch as he efficiently served up some hassleback potatoes, letting the meat rest. Then he sliced it. It looked beautifully cooked. She snaffled a stray piece from the plate. Melt-in-the-mouth tender.

He winked at her. 'And a token bit of green, just for show.' Using tongs, he placed a few asparagus spears, drizzled with dressing. 'Getting to know you, aren't I?'

She smiled.

They sat and talked—of the hotel, the renovations, the city, the wine from home. Pleasant but meaningless. As far as she was concerned they were stocking up energy and filling in time.

He cleared the plates. She sat back. Main-event time and she could hardly wait, was burning ready.

But he disappeared into the kitchen for a while, eventually coming out with a stainless-steel bowl and a spoon.

'Pudding.' He answered her silent question. 'Caramel chocolate mousse.'

She could almost cope with having to delay being with him for some of that. 'What's in it?'

'Caramello. Cream. Butter.'

She smiled at the richness—of the pudding and his voice. 'Decadent.'

'Very.' He put the entire bowl in front of her and the solitary spoon.

'Aren't you going to have some?'

'Oh, yeah, I'm going to have some.' The way he said it had her on red alert.

His eyes had lit up with that humorous light that had a huge dollop of lust included. Heartbreakingly attractive.

'What aren't you telling me?'

He said nothing. Pulled up the chair next to hers and sat, close. She swivelled in her seat to face him. With his finger he scooped some of the mousse and painted it on her lips. She flicked her tongue to taste both the sweet and him.

He leant close. 'Told you I was going to eat you all up.' And he kissed her. The chocolate goo warmed and tasted divine, as did the pressure of his mouth on hers. She felt him apply more mousse to the hollow between her collarbones and decided she must have died and gone to heaven.

He pushed her hair out of the way and kissed the side of her neck. 'I'm sorry about this. I didn't mean to.'

'Didn't mean to what?'

He lifted his head and looked at her. 'The mark on your neck.'

She put her hand there, mouthing the 'oh'.

'It's already fading.' Warily he watched her.

She started to laugh. 'Was it obvious?'

He shook his head. 'Not with your hair down.'

'Shame. You couldn't even get a glimpse of it?'

He looked puzzled. 'Maybe if you moved your hair.'

'Wish I'd known, I'd have given them a flash.'

The light in his eye dimmed and he looked away from her.

She put her palm against his jaw and pushed his face back to her, gathering some mousse with the fingers of her other hand. 'Jake, I am going to have to get you back for that.'

'Are you now?'

'Mmm.' She leant forward.

His smile returned.

They lay half under the table, the bowl of mousse on one side, clothes all around. He kissed away another smear from her belly. 'Why is it that the things that are so bad for us always feel so good?'

Like the creamy chocolate? *Like him.*

'Everything is OK in moderation, I guess.' She swirled her finger in the mousse and licked it off.

'I don't do moderation.' He paused and blew warm air across her chocolate-daubed nipple. 'And neither do you.'

She arched up as he took her into his mouth. He was right—he worked hard, he played hard. And she? She just worked hard. And ate chocolate, lots of chocolate.

And there was nothing moderate about how he made her feel.

The first thing she saw as she opened her eyes was his suitcase standing next to the wardrobe. It reminded her there was nothing serious about this either. He didn't do serious—had told her that from the start. All this could be was a fierce affair for a few weeks and then he'd move on.

But the way she felt right now, she didn't know if she'd ever be able to.

CHAPTER NINE

CUP DAY. Punters and partiers descended on the city to go to the races. Emma mentally harangued Max, who thought it would be fine to refurbish the hotel in the middle of Carnival week when they were fully booked. But the vibe from the street was invigorating, giving her a much needed energy boost. She was living on adrenalin, Jake and chocolate. The hotel was full and it was all hands to the deck. Although that didn't mean the staff weren't determined to enjoy it.

'You want to go in the office sweepstake, Emma?'

Emma paused; she'd never been asked before. Becca was actually smiling at her—well, a slightly knife-like smile, but a smile nonetheless.

'Umm, OK.'

'I have a list of the entrants here.'

Cynically Emma noted how Becca seemed to find it difficult to get spreadsheet data for her when she requested it, yet she could whip up a complex sheet capable of figuring payouts for trifectas and quinellas in no time. But she refrained from commenting.

She heard Jake come into the reception—her sensors

acute at detecting his presence. He came and stood beside her. 'Can I play too?'

'You're always playing, Jake,' Emma said blandly, before shooting him a sideways glance, encountering his to her. They swapped smirks.

He studied the sheet.

'Oh, look, this horse is called Foxy Lady—you should definitely pick that one, Emma.'

She threw him an evil look. 'Do they have one called Complete Clown for you?'

'Ouch.' He looked at Becca and winked. 'You know, she's gonna break my heart.'

Emma's skin prickled, knowing it wasn't *his* heart in danger.

At three p.m. they all congregated in the small bar off the lobby to watch the race.

Jake walked in and sidled up next to her. 'You know, we could bet with something other than money.'

'What were you thinking of?' She forced her concentration on the big screen, not on what she wanted to do with the hunk next to her.

'Hmm. My horse wins, you're on top. Your horse wins, you're on top.'

The laughter burst out of her and several staff turned to glance at them.

Jake's horse won.

'Lady Luck is on my side.' He gave her a saucy glance and she felt her cheeks heat. On top. Nice idea.

'Are you going to come out with us tonight?' Emma supposed Becca was asking them both, but it was Jake she stared at.

Jake's lazy gaze flickered over the blonde receptionist

and in a moment of pique Emma wondered if her presence was still actually noticed. Then he looked at her and winked. 'Sure thing, eh, Emma?'

'Sure.' It was the last thing she felt like. She just wanted to go home and have Jake all to herself.

Instead, once she'd logged off and Jake had returned from a meeting they joined the masses out enjoying the crazy wind and warm night. The city was alive with people everywhere dressed to the nines.

'I'm hardly going to win best-dressed tonight, am I?' She frowned down at her black suit and white shirt combo. It was hardly going to compete with the stylish ensembles that some of these women had planned for months in advance so they could stand in the Birdcage at the races and be judged. Even those not competing wore stunning dresses with their perfect tans and hair. Emma was so pale even with fake tan on she still looked as if she were made of milk.

'Oh, I don't know. I've kinda got used to the sexy schoolmarm look. I like being the only one who knows the damn sexy underwear you have going on under the knee-length skirts and plain tops. Or lack of underwear,' he teased.

He always knew the right thing to say to make her feel good. Feel attractive. No wonder he was never for long without a girlfriend. His practised charm would have them queuing up. That combined with his good looks and over-flowing bank balance. Mr Popular—never single for long.

The buzz his comment had given her disappeared.

They went back to the same bar where they'd met again. Jake couldn't believe it had been less than a fortnight ago. Couldn't believe he had only three weeks to go. He pushed that one to the back of his mind. Instead he watched her.

Watched her fight to maintain conversation with the women from the hotel. She clearly didn't feel comfortable in these group situations. Centre stage was not her thing. She'd rather be sitting at her table at home working on her art, or talking shop with Max. He could relate. At times he found all the obligatory corporate events tiresome. Often there was nothing he'd like more than to be in his offices. Or just be home and working with some wood, as he had as a kid with his grandfather. There was something peaceful about it. Like her, he enjoyed creating—but his was nothing on the scale of hers.

Right now he couldn't be bothered being in the bar at all. He just wanted to be in bed with Emma, making the most of it before it faded. It always did fade, this crazy rush of exhilaration—the delight of physical closeness and fulfillment. Admittedly, though, this was extreme. He felt almost desperate for her company. But they were on a time limit anyway. And given the way she distracted him from his work, this was a good thing.

She looked as eager to leave as he felt. He winked at her when she caught his eye and he saw her melt, saw her sparkle back. It made him want her even more. He'd always had the ability to make a joke, make people laugh—even if it was at his own expense. But he'd never enjoyed being able to do it as much as he did with her. He loved to make her smile, to see her soften, and most of all he loved it when she came right back at him with corny lines of her own.

She went to the bathroom and he kept a watch for her return. He met her halfway across the bar. He couldn't keep his distance any longer.

'Come here and kiss me.'

'Gosh, Jake, what happened to your rules?' Her smile was as wide as it got.

'Screw the rules.'

'You want to screw the *rules*?' She paused. 'Or?'

'Or?' He looked at her face on. Turned on as he saw she was relaxed and confident and letting her flirty self loose. 'Are you about to start talking dirty to me?'

'What if I am?' She tossed her head back and raised her brows at him, hamming it up.

He reached for her, pulling her to him. 'You just go for it, honey. Say your worst.' He wished she would. He wanted into her mind as much as her body.

But she giggled and said nothing, inviting him to make better use of her mouth.

He heard the wolf-whistles and managed to lift his head before things got too crazy. 'We've been here before, Emma—enough of a floorshow already.' So much for not being centre stage. He waved a hand in farewell at the hotel staff and led her out of the bar. Her crimson cheeks brought relief to the unexpected knot of anxiety in his chest. He didn't want that kiss to have only been for show.

They walked to her place, passing throngs of people intent on having a good time. He intended to have a good time too and he didn't need them to do it. His good time was walking right beside him.

'I'm in need of a snack—you?'

He wanted more than a snack. But he didn't mind waiting for a bit. He liked to think it meant he did have some control over his ravenous lust for her. 'All-day breakfast?'

He was rewarded with a kiss.

She pushed away and went to the fridge to get the eggs and bacon.

He opened the freezer to hunt out the hash browns and laughed. At least ten bars of Caramello stood in a stack smack bang in the middle of the shelf.

'What's with the chocolate in the freezer?'

'It goes funny in the fridge.'

He snapped off a piece from the opened packet on the top, popping it in his mouth and slamming the door shut. He moved to steal another kiss as she stood by the pan.

'Now you're the one tasting of Caramello.'

'Had some of your freezer supply. That OK?'

'Perfect.'

The sizzle in the pan was nothing on the sizzle between them. Water on hot oil, the heat spitting in all directions.

They ate standing up, fully aware it was nothing more than a pit stop—a moment to get some fuel in before the endurance rally started. He for one was primed and he had the feeling her engine was revving too. But there was something else he wanted from this evening.

He took his opportunity when she went to shower and change—only just winning over the desire to join her there. He fobbed off her look of surprise by saying he'd do the dishes while she was in the bathroom.

He wanted to check out the room again. He'd ensured he'd charged his phone enough to be able to take a few pictures and maybe even a video. He could email it through in the morning. She might say she didn't want anyone to know, but he didn't buy that. Why was she producing pieces for a possible publication if she didn't want people to see her work and know it was hers? He could help her. He had contacts. And he, as always, had a game plan.

The curtains were drawn so he flipped on the light. He figured he had a good fifteen minutes. If he knew anything, he knew women took their time in the shower—even ones as lacking in vanity as Emma.

He ruffled through the manuscript, made a mental note of a few of the flowers and their definitions. Then he took some footage of his favourite paintings.

He heard her footsteps and put his phone in his pocket.

'I thought I told you not to come in here.' She wore a robe, her hair damp around her face, her eyes challenging him. 'Don't you know the story of Bluebeard? Curiosity? Cats? You'll get in trouble.'

From the look on her face he had the feeling the trouble might not be that bad. 'What are you going to do? Punish me?' He grinned wickedly. What would his sweet siren do about that challenge?

She picked it up and ran with it in a way he'd hardly dreamed of. 'Absolutely.' She turned and closed the door behind her. Then he heard the sound of a key turning. She spun round to face him. 'You're locked in here now. This is my room, my secret, my fantasy. You want to be a part of it? Then you have to do as I say.'

His mouth went dry. Her fantasy? 'Sure.' He choked the word out.

For a second she hesitated. Then she crossed the room to stand right in front of him. He itched to pull her that inch closer. 'Go and sit by the window.'

He did as she said, no question. Sitting down, he watched as she rearranged things to her liking. She took the drop cloths and spread them, piling them on top of each other to create a large cushioned area.

His body signalled its approval of her actions. Of her

robe as it gaped slightly as she bent to her task. But this was her room, her idea and he wasn't going to interrupt. She was opening up to him fully at last.

She picked up the vase of flowers, taking each stem out carefully one by one and placing them around the pillowy sheets. Gently shaking each flower as she lifted it, spreading the scent. He watched, rapt, as she moved with gentle grace, and precision—just as she moved with him. As her picture unfolded he felt himself falling deeper and deeper. And the lust kept the panic at bay.

Emma stood and with a degree of nerves turned to look at Jake. She'd been so engrossed in creating her tableau she'd forgotten that he was here in the flesh, and not just in her dreams. Reality intruded and embarrassment rose. He must think she was an idiot. He sat silently, his eyes huge blue pools, and his focus travelled down her, taking in the scene she'd set and her in the heart of it. Then he spoke, his voice soft but slightly raspy as it broke into the silence of the room. 'Your fantasy.'

She had lost her tongue and just nodded.

Carefully, without breaking the eye contact, he rose and walked across to where she stood at the edge of the floral bed she'd created.

'What do you want me to do?'

Her mouth was dry, making speech seem impossible.

His intent look didn't lift.

She'd totally lost her nerve.

'You started this, you have to say what you want. Tell me.' He leant forward and whispered in her ear. 'If you don't ask, you don't get.'

Her eyes half closed. 'Take your clothes off.'

His tee shirt flew over his head and was tossed into the corner in a second. He stood and looked at her.

She looked back and as she took in his broad chest her confidence picked up. 'All of them.'

He scuffed his sneakers and socks off, kicking them into the corner after the shirt. His hands went to his belt. His jeans were under so much strain it was almost impossible to get the zipper down. She couldn't take her eyes from them and felt the ripening as he yanked them down to reveal his boxers. He slipped them down too and his body sprang upwards, freed from the tight material.

She stared. He really was magnificent. She walked around him marvelling at the perfection of his body. Feeling bold enough to reach out a finger and trace the indents of muscles on his back, his skin warm and smooth.

She came to stand in front of him again. Stared up at his motionless face, the intensity in his blue eyes trapping her.

She lost her tongue again—aching for him to touch her. Why couldn't he? He knew exactly how to touch her— what was he waiting for?

He grinned, seemingly able to read her mind. 'How am I to know what to do for you unless you tell me?'

'You already know; you've already done it.'

His smile broadened. 'You don't need to be shy around me any more, Emma. There isn't a part of your body I don't know. Let me into your mind as well. I want to know your fantasies. I want to *be* your fantasy.'

He already was.

'Will it help if I tell you what I want?' Her stomach tightened at the sound of his voice dropping to that low whisper. 'I want to touch you here.' He gestured to her belly. 'I want to taste you here.' He gestured lower. 'I want to play with your nipples; I want to see them harden even more as you get excited. And I want to hear your cry when I move into you.'

The fire of embarrassment in her cheeks flamed anew with desire. She let her robe drop to the floor.

The corners of his eyes crinkled as he saw her reaction. He was encouraging her to be bold, and he was succeeding. 'Fun, Emma. Tell me. It'll be fun.'

He was right. After all, the whole thing was a game. It didn't really matter. She could do anything, ask anything. 'I want you underneath me.' She wanted to feel his strength between her legs. Wanted to be on top of all that power. She wanted to master his body as he had mastered hers.

He lay down on the makeshift mattress. She knelt, one leg either side of his muscular thighs, and took in the view spread before her. His hard, flat stomach, his golden tanned chest fanning out to broad shoulders. She lifted her gaze to his face; he was looking as serious as she felt.

She picked up one of the violets and shook it over his chest, sprinkling scent and dewy droplets on to it. She traced her finger where the water had landed, tossing the flower in favour of him and him alone.

'Do you want me to move or do you want to set the pace?' His body was taut and anticipation glowed in his eyes.

'Let me.' She inched higher to sit at the apex of his thighs.

He smiled and she played, pressing her body against his. Enjoying the freedom to feel his harnessed strength. She knew his potency, knew that if he let it loose she would be sunk, an unthinking mass only capable of feeling. This time she was enjoying the conscious experimentation. Wanted to see how far she could push him, could push herself.

The energy of restraint rolled off him. She moved closer,

kissing him with her mouth, then with her most intimate part—gently rubbing, half sliding onto him before slipping away again. His hands rested on her bottom, not guiding, not trying to control the direction she took, but squeezing slightly, just letting her know he was there and that he was letting her take the lead.

For a few moments.

Then they squeezed harder, became more authoritative, wanting her to take him. She wiggled away and shook her head. He sighed. 'Emma, I can't handle much more.' Tension furrowed his brow, sweat beaded on his chest.

She smiled, the vixen in her finding her power, and she relentlessly continued.

He expelled a harsh gust of air. 'You're playing with me.'

'Yes.'

A grunt of laughter and he conceded defeat. 'OK, I'm happy for you to play with me.'

She continued working, her hips teasing as she slid home, her hands toying with his nipples, then toying with her own, and she watched with satisfaction as he almost lost it.

'Emma.' His head was back on the sheets, his eyebrows pulled together and his eyes shut tight as he so obviously fought to keep control.

It was then she tossed her head back and laughed delightedly. Awareness of her own power dawned on her.

His eyes shot open. 'Oh, I am so going to get you for this.'

'I do hope so,' she answered playfully.

He smiled at her then. And she smiled back, a smile that reflected her realisation of just how much fun this was. How good this felt. He was right—it was fun. She'd shared one of her deepest desires and he'd made it happen for her.

And then he surprised her by swiftly sitting up. The shift brought him even deeper into her. She gasped. He looped his arms around her, holding her tightly to him so their chests were sealed. Their warm bodies combining to create a blazing heat. And in a split-second he reduced her to that shaking mass again, only able to enjoy the sensations he created as he rocked against her. The friction it caused at her nub was unbearably arousing and her head fell back as she moved with him to get closer, ever closer. He kissed the length of her neck, muttering half-sentences she hardly heard.

After, he carefully lifted her off, cradling her beside him. And then he picked up one of the violets, trailing it across her body, the petals cool on her hot skin, beautifully scented. And with a smile he took her fantasy and extended it, making it better than she'd ever imagined. The ecstasy he gave to her was the most addictive drug and she didn't know how she was ever going to give it up.

When she woke she found he'd won the race back to consciousness. He'd pulled back the curtains and the early-morning light flooded the room. It was her favourite time to paint—the quietness of the street, the freshness of the sun's glow. He stood, unashamedly naked, surveying her paintings. She surveyed him.

After last night there were no secrets any more. She knew she could tell him anything. Ask him anything.

She could trust him.

And, oh, boy was her heart going to get mangled when he went back north. But it was far, far too late to pull back. She couldn't say no to him. Couldn't say no to herself.

'These really are fantastic, Emma.'

'I'm glad you like them.' The only person she'd shared her body with and the only person she'd shared her art with. And she'd never regret it.

CHAPTER TEN

'I HAVE to go back to Auckland for a few days. Flying out in an hour.' Jake put his bag at his feet. Emma's face fell and as a result his out-of-control, irritated heart lifted. He walked over to her and she came round from behind her desk, lifting her mouth for his kiss. It was dangerously exciting to be able to have her, even just for a kiss, at any given moment.

She rested her head on his chest. 'I'm so comfortable with you.' She'd spoken softly and he only just caught the words.

Comfortable. For some reason it really rankled. Like an old cardigan you just wore around the house. He didn't feel comfortable with her. In fact, the more time he spent with her, the less comfortable he became. He felt challenged. Physically and mentally.

Emotionally.

And he didn't like it.

He pulled out of her arms, managing a tight smile. 'See you when I get back.'

He turned away from the confusion that sprang in her features, telling himself he was glad he had to go to Auckland. He really needed to get his laidback mojo back. He liked the carefree nature of his relationships—easy come, easy go. But he felt an insatiable intensity with

Emma. An uncontrollable need to seek her out. Be with her. He needed to get on top of it. Going home would help because when he was in the same city as her, he just couldn't keep away.

Emma sat at her desk and stared blankly at her computer screen. Then she shook her head, determined to clear out the dreaminess. She was not going to sit here and moon over his absence. Certainly not going to wonder what he was doing with his time—with his nights. She put her head down, willing herself to get on with it. She'd developed a legendary ability to focus and she needed all of it now.

She spent the latter part of the afternoon in meetings— a helpful distraction from the melancholic awareness that she'd be sleeping alone tonight. On her return to her office she stopped, another surprise on her desk. The tulip still stood in her vase, its bloom widening slightly with age, but tucked in beside it was a tiny blue flower—a forget-me-not. She didn't know how he'd done it. But he had. Underneath his easygoing, jokey nature lay a core of iron. When Jake wanted something, he got it. Including her. For as long as he wanted.

Thursday morning Jake gave instructions to his PA, snapped his phone shut and frowned as he headed towards the building site. He felt off. Definitely a case of wrong-side-of-bed-itis. Or maybe it was a case of alone-in-the-bed-itis. There was a cure. His frown deepened. He couldn't stop thinking about her and this was not a good sign. He was screwing up here and he knew it. Emma Delaney was a good girl. She always had been. And here he was, self-proclaimed commitment-phobe. He'd shouldered enough responsibility in the early part of his life to last him the rest of it. He loved his mother and sister to bits and would do anything for them, but that was enough. He didn't need a serious girlfriend or—heaven help him—wife and kids. He just wanted to have fun. And the women he went with were the same. While Emma might say she was up to the game, it didn't feel right. So he should quit it now. But he couldn't. The dilemma tossed his insides in turmoil.

He looked over at the newsagent's and read the placard advertising the lead story in the day's paper. Despite his brain telling him one thing, his libido was telling him another and this idea was brilliant. His moment of guilt instantly shoved to the side.

Not long into the afternoon of the slow-motion day, Emma took a call from Becca on Reception—'I have a courier parcel here for you. Do you want me to bring it up?'

'No, thank you. I'll come and get it myself.' She needed to stretch out. Use some muscles. Other muscles were begging to be used again, but that wasn't about to happen soon. She wished they'd go back into dormant mode; it made life less difficult.

The slim package bore Jake's company logo in the sender box. She glanced at Becca, who was watching with interest. She gave her a small smile and turned away, managing to make it into the lift before ripping the parcel open.

An airplane ticket and a hastily scrawled note. 'Come with comfortable walking shoes, I have a surprise for you—Jake.'

She read the details on the ticket—flying to Auckland on Saturday morning and back Sunday afternoon. She leaned against the wall of the lift. She needed to finish the last of the drawings for Margaret and get them to her by next Wednesday. She had another raft of data to analyse and prepare for Max. Enough of a workload for three people—she'd need all weekend to try to get on top of it.

She read the note again. No please, no negotiation—but no way could she say no.

Friday was the longest day she'd ever had at work. He'd texted her—confirmed she'd got the parcel, confirmed she was going to board the plane. She hardly slept that night. Mocking herself for being like a kid on Christmas Eve, she tried to work in her art room but it held too many hot memories and she had as much chance of concentrating as a dog being told to sit and stay when a juicy bone was merely a bound away. In the end she sat with wine and chocolate and late-night TV.

He was waiting by the arrival gate, gorgeous as ever. She vaguely took in the fit body clad in usual jeans and tee, but she couldn't look away from the smile in his face and the heat in his eyes. The kiss was wild.

Both breathless, he pulled away. 'Rules. We have to stick to the rules.'

He took her carry-on case. 'Anyway, I have a surprise for you.'

She giggled at his steely grey convertible. 'Jake, you're a show-off.'

He winked at her. 'Boys and their toys, Emma. You know how it is.'

She sure did. She knew full well she was his current plaything. And that was OK. Sure it was. She was grown-up—she could cope with the game.

He drove out of the airport and turned away from Auckland city, heading towards Manukau instead. She looked at him in query.

'Surprise, remember?'

The traffic was heavy even by Auckland standards. Then they passed a sign—'Ellerslie International Flower Show'. She looked at Jake again and caught him grinning at her.

'Really?'

'Sure.'

Her smile blossomed.

They passed a marshal directing people to parking spots. Jake flashed a piece of paper at him and they were waved through to the front.

Emma raised a brow at him.

'Contacts, darling, contacts,' Jake drawled. 'I forgot it was this week,' he added, 'and it's perfect for you.'

She looked at him and couldn't keep back the glow in her heart. 'Thank you.'

He looked at her and smiled and she wished time would stand still because in that very moment she was happier than she'd been in her life. He was totally focussed on her, on doing something nice for her, and she ignored the fact that he was a player used to spoiling his women. She just imagined it was all for real. For ever.

Or at least for today.

But she knew she was looking through a prism, not seeing reality, but a beautiful version of it.

He reached out and stroked her pony-tail, a soft smile tugging at his mouth.

She broke the spell by looking away. She had to keep just a part of herself back or she was going to end up seriously squashed.

They joined the throng at the entrance gates. Jake relaxed and walked beside her, laughing as her enthusiasm bubbled over.

'I can't believe you got tickets. This is awesome. I've wanted to come but never got round to it.'

Ellerslie: New Zealand's premier flower show and Aotearoa's version of London's Chelsea Flower Show. Design and beauty to the fore. Most of all it was a fun day with crowds turning up to take it all in, picnic and be convivial.

They stood in one of the stalls where visitors could purchase plants to take home. She followed as he walked through the displays.

'Look at that one.' He stopped by a delphinium. He looked at her; it matched the colour of her top perfectly. 'You are *not* a daisy.'

She grinned. 'Yes, I am.'

'You're not common; you're like one of these exotic-looking things.' He pointed out the pink-tinged white petals of a moth orchid.

'Not an ordinary garden daisy, but another.' She looked about and soon spotted the one she meant. She picked up the pot and held it out to him. He looked at the small reddish-brown flower with scepticism.

'Smell it,' she instructed, waving it towards his nose.

He bent and sniffed. 'That smells like…'

'Chocolate. Perfect, isn't it?'

'That's amazing.' He smelt it again and laughed. 'Only you would find a flower that smells like chocolate.'

'Chocolate cosmos daisy. Sweet, isn't it?'

'Very.' He looked at her rather than the flower. 'So what does it mean?'

She frowned. 'Did you have to ask?'

'Yes. Tell me.'

She sighed, putting the flower down and turning away. 'Daisies usually mean innocence.'

He laughed even louder and reached for her. Ignoring the fact they were in a crowded tent in the middle of the morning, she leant into him. His lips came within a hair's breadth of hers.

Then she fluttered her lashes at him and gave him a coy look. 'Rules, Jake.'

He let her slip out of his grasp. 'Honey, you're not that innocent. Not any more.'

She waggled her hips at him as she walked ahead. 'Come on, let's go see the winners.'

They headed out to the large display gardens, looking for the medallists. He took her hand. She told herself it was just so they wouldn't be separated in the crowds. Trouble was, she increasingly felt as if she didn't want to be separated from him at all. He was too much fun to be around.

After almost three hours she was in serious need of sustenance. They headed to the little lake that was surrounded by stalls selling tempting food and crafts.

He seemed to know she was flagging. 'I'll get something; you sit and save a spot.'

She sat in the shade, watched him as he moved from stall to stall, clearly deciding which would provide the best fodder. He moved with lion-like fluidity. Long legs striding out casually, but hinting at the strength and speed available should he set his mind to it. She knew how strong he could be, knew how well defined the muscles covered by the tee were. Her body flared at the memories. She was having a wonderful time, but the need to get Jake alone and out of public view was becoming insistent.

He came back carefully balancing a plate and two filled glasses.

He flashed a victorious smile. 'Found a place with French cutlets.'

She laughed as she saw the stack of them. He offered her one of the glasses and then sat next to her. The plate between them, they sat cross-legged and gnawed on the delicately flavoured chops and sipped the wine, listening to the jazz band in the distance playing mellow tunes. They reached for the last cutlet at the same time.

'It's yours.' He laughed, holding his hands up in surrender. 'I saw a Danish ice-cream place just over there.'

She ate the last cutlet with relish. 'Jake, you know exactly how to please me.'

The atmosphere thickened as their eyes met. She put the cutlet bone down, forgetting it in the sudden heat.

He leaned towards her, whispering, 'You know how I wish I could please you right now?'

'How?'

His eyes flashed. 'I'd lie back on the grass, have you straddle me... Why aren't you wearing a skirt? You should be wearing a skirt, because I'd slide my—'

She needed him to stop. She placed her hand over his mouth. 'Jake, don't torture me.'

He nibbled on her fingers. 'Why not? You've been torturing me all day walking around in your tight jeans, wiggling your hips—'

'Jake Rendel! I didn't ever think I'd see you here. Didn't think flowers were your thing at all. You never once gave me one.'

Emma jerked her hand away. The clanging tones of the intruder buzzed in her ears. Her fingers suddenly feeling cold after the warmth of his soft kisses. She looked up and took in the vision standing in front of them.

The creature gave a little pout and laughed, a silvery, tinkling sound. Flat stomach, slim hips, large bust, long blonde hair. An up-to-the-minute dress that clung to her curves. If she wasn't a model, she should be. Type-A model for Jake. The sinking feeling clawed at Emma, pulling her down. The woman oozed confidence. Someone so sure of her worth that she had no compunction about interrupting a couple obviously involved in an intimate moment.

Jake didn't look remotely flustered as he lazed on the grass. 'Emma, Carolina. Carolina, Emma.'

Emma smiled politely and suffered in silence as Carolina gave her the once-over. She knew she was sizing her up as the competition and was sure she didn't stack up. Saw her take in her navy silk top that had a simple shoestring halter-neck tie.

'Emma likes flowers,' Jake said simply, giving the Carolina woman an indolent smile.

'Oh,' said Carolina. 'Lucky Emma.' She gave Emma another look and then focussed on Jake. 'Haven't seen you around lately, Jake. Where have you been hiding?'

'Christchurch, on a job. Working with Emma, actually.'

'Oh.' She visibly preened. 'Well, give me a call when you can. I'm always up for a night out.'

I'll bet. Emma took a quick sip of her drink to stop herself saying something catty.

Jake just smiled and said nothing very much. Emma no longer wanted to listen. If Carolina hadn't got flowers, Emma wondered what he had given her. Done for her. He might not be serious, but he was a generous and thoughtful lover.

She sat quiet as they said their goodbyes. She was not

going to let it cast a shadow over the day, but meeting Carolina opened old insecurities. Emma was nothing like Jake's usual girls. He wouldn't even have been interested if it weren't for the fact he'd felt sorry for her, if she hadn't practically thrown herself at him in the bar, looking for someone to rescue her from her frigid-spinster image.

Jake watched Carolina walk away and wondered why on earth he'd ever dated her. Pretty—sure. Nice—sure. Knew how to party—sure. But she was nothing on the woman beside him now. He'd wanted to take Emma straight home from the airport and have his wicked way with her as soon as possible. He'd fought it. He liked her, liked her company, walking and talking with her, and he'd wanted to be with her as she walked around Ellerslie. He'd be damned if he was going to give in to his body's demands and do nothing but be in bed with her at every opportunity. She deserved more than that. They both did.

He had a need to get to know her better, in her head as well as her body. And it had been fun, lots of fun. She'd shown him how to look closely at the plants—something he'd never bothered with before. She was full of interesting facts and they'd discovered they preferred the same designs. He still could hardly wait to get alone with her, but just being with her was enough for now.

He reluctantly glanced at her. She'd know, of course. No hiding the fact Carolina was an ex—Carolina couldn't have made it plainer. Or that she'd be open to resuming a relationship. It bothered Jake, but, worse, he wanted to know if it bothered Emma. Childishly he couldn't help hoping she would feel jealous. Which was stupid because this was just another of his freeform affairs that would come to its natural conclusion when he did return to Auckland for good. But the thought of her with another man made the reddest mist swirl in front of him and he suddenly ached to know if this was like that for her too.

She was watching Carolina depart. She smiled blandly at him. Her eyes were veiled. It was as if she'd drawn the blinds so she could see out but no one could see in, least of all him. Now he really needed to be alone with her, because when they were alone together she opened up to him and that was what he wanted.

'Let's get that ice cream and get out of here.'

As they walked through the displays he took her hand loosely in his, restraining the urge to grip it tightly. He had the crazy urge to haul her close and tell her how utterly meaningless every relationship he'd ever had had been. A damn stupid thing to want to do—hell, she probably couldn't care less.

They got back into the car and joined the snaking line heading back to Auckland city.

'Where are we going?' She sounded perky. He felt lower.

'I want to show you my apartment.' He was just about fit to burst. He wanted to see what she thought of his place. He didn't share it with many—usually preferring to overnight at his current girlfriend's house rather than his. That way he still had his space—distance and privacy. But he had surprises of his own he wanted to show Emma. And he still wanted it to matter.

The drive took a little longer than usual and she seemed content to let the wind blow through her hair and watch Auckland skate by. His apartment was smack bang in the middle of town. One of the newer high-rise buildings, it boasted floor-to-ceiling windows showing magnificent views across the city to the water. But it wasn't that view that stopped her in her tracks. She stared at the walls.

'Is that a McCahon?'

She stared at him and he knew she was blown away. He smiled. 'Yeah. Do you like it?'

'It's not a print?' she answered herself, shaking her head.

He watched as she slowly moved to inspect the next painting, then the next.

'You collect art.' She didn't sound as pleased as he'd hoped she might.

He stepped after her. 'It's not a huge collection, just a few pieces that I really like.'

A few pieces. More like several that were worth a small fortune, but despite his joking manner he wasn't usually one to brag. They were all Australasian artists. 'A friend of mine runs a contemporary gallery in the city. She keeps an eye out for me.'

He watched for her reaction. Would she be interested? But the bland, veiled look was back and he had no idea what she was thinking. It certainly wasn't the open delight she'd shown when they'd arrived at the floral festival. He was going to have to tread carefully. But he was still going to tread. He still couldn't see why she was so secretive about her work.

Then his attention was caught, again, by the sway of her body as she moved around the room. She looked stunning in jeans and a top that revealed a fantastic portion of her back—her pale skin calling for him to touch. He forced himself to focus—ask the basics and hope for the answer he wanted.

'Want to go out to eat or stay in? I had thought about Sky City, but maybe we could just scale the heights here instead?' He waggled his eyebrows outrageously so she'd laugh at the innuendo and pick the latter.

She stepped out of his reach, only a hint of a smile on her face. 'Actually, do you mind if we go out? I haven't hit Auckland in a while.'

Surprised, he tried to mask the disappointment and came up with another offer. 'Sure. Shall we shower and change first?'

She nodded. 'Do you have a guest bathroom?'

The disappointment was a stabbing pain this time. 'Sure.' Why was she holding him at arm's length? Why more interested in seeing some restaurant than seeing him? It niggled—was it heading for the end already? Not if he could help it.

She paused, looking at one of his wooden sculptures. 'This is nice.'

Pleasure surged through him.

'You mind?' At the shake of his head she reached for it, her fingers running over the smooth wood. Then she glanced around and saw some of the others. The hand-carved fruit bowl, the block off an old rimu fencepost that had simply been polished on one side, the rest left natural. Understanding dawned. 'You made these.' She studied the carvings on the fruit bowl. 'They're really good.'

'They're not.' He laughed. 'I used to like whittling a bit of wood. Picked it up from the old man.'

His grandfather had been able to make anything from wood. Had used to enthral Sienna with little dolls he'd been able to conjure out of any old stick. Jake hadn't made anything for ages but there was something relaxing about taking a piece of natural beauty and making something more out of it. Slowly carving out something special. But where he was a tinkerer, Emma was a professional—or she could be. Her fingers stroked the wood again and he watched as she then curled them away.

* * *

Emma took her overnight bag with her into the bathroom and splashed cold water on her face the minute she had shut and locked the door. She'd needed a wake-up call and, boy, had she got it.

She really didn't want to be here. The scene of all his conquests—the likes of Carolina. Jealousy raged in her. Ugly and unwanted. Unstoppable.

She took out her comb, tugging it through the twisted mess of her hair. As the car had raced along from Ellerslie she'd let the wind blow through it, whipping it into a tangle around her face, and she'd wanted it to blow away the bad feelings. Then she'd walked into his magnificent apartment and had the ground cut from under her again. He was an art lover—a serious collector, no less. And she was such an amateur. She hated being less than the best and she knew her paintings were so far from perfect. He must have been laughing the whole time.

She felt crummy, no two ways about it.

Standing under the shower, washing the travel weariness away, she tried to harden up. She knew he was a player. Had known that from the start—that there had been many before her. And, yes, it mattered. But not enough to stop her from being the next in line. She wanted him. And, if she faced facts, his knowledge of women was a plus. Surely it was the reason he could make her feel so good. Why with just a few touches he could reduce her to a heap of sensation—a woman desperate for the ultimate intimacy. She should take the experience and make the most of it. But she needed just a little longer to build up the defences around her heart again.

She slipped on her slimline satin dress, not bothering with a bra as it had such thin spaghetti straps. Besides, it wasn't as if she was going to do herself permanent damage. She tried not to think about how Carolina would fill out a little black dress. As an ego-boost she pulled on a pair of pretty panties. She looked at her reflection. If she really was a bold siren she'd go without the underwear altogether— but, while she could do that at home, in a crowded restaurant it was just one step too far out of her comfort zone.

A few touches of make-up and some shine serum on her hair and she was done. She tipped her chin at her reflection—*deal with it.*

Back in his lounge that intention started to crumble immediately. It screamed wealthy bachelor and, as pathetic as it was, she just couldn't stop wondering how many others had been here. She gazed at the sofa. Large enough to lie on, it looked damningly comfortable.

Frustrated with her bitterness, she looked at the paintings on the walls again, only to feel even smaller. He'd seen her paintings and they were so gauche compared to these. Embarrassment washed over her. The day that had started so beautifully was turning into a nightmare.

'Where are you?'

She started.

He walked up to her, looking sexy as hell in dark trousers and linen shirt, his hair damp and slightly wayward. He stood way too close and the bad feeling began to be swallowed by desire. 'You've gone away from me. Where?'

He so didn't want to know. And she sure as hell wasn't going to tell him. Revealing her jealousy of his ex-girlfriends would reveal more than she wanted him to know. She'd gone into this with her eyes wide open—he'd told her right from the start he liked to play. And a woman like

Carolina wouldn't let such a small thing as an ex-girlfriend bother her. Hell, it seemed she didn't let a thing like a current girlfriend bother her. Emma was playing with a pro and he was used to worldly types and she wasn't going to get all amateur and upset about previous competition. 'Just thinking about one of the displays today.'

He looked as if he didn't believe her, but shrugged. 'I'm glad you enjoyed it.'

'I did.' Right up to the point when Barbie appeared.

'So what do you fancy to eat—shall we go to the local steakhouse?' He was teasing her, and that tempted her. She found it hard to resist him when he was like this.

But no. She squared her shoulders and decided to up her game. She was not going to get psyched out. She was in it for the duration, could damn well learn to play hard, and maybe she'd end up a winner. 'Let's go up-market.'

His gleam of humour broke into a full grin. 'Sure.'

CHAPTER ELEVEN

THE humidity level in the evening air was high. Storm clouds threatened but when they'd walked to the club Emma hadn't been afraid of a downpour—it might've soothed her heated body. Saturday night, the start of summer and the city was alive. Not that she paid that much attention to it.

Jake had been staring at her the entire meal. She'd had to fight to stop squirming as she'd seen his attention wander over her body, to her mouth, her neck, her breast, and she'd known exactly what he was thinking, what he wanted. Exactly what she wanted. The time away from his apartment had relieved her jealousy. His undivided attention, his attraction showing so clearly, was a balm on her aggravated senses—even if that attraction was only physical and temporary. They'd said little through the meal, commented on the flower show, complimented the food, circling the real issue—the flare between them that was threatening to blow up again. Time to go home.

Then he spoke, a low voice that she still heard with clarity despite the music in the trendy club. 'Come dance with me.'

She stared back at him, with regret, not wanting to see the blaze in his eyes dim. 'I told you, I don't do dancing. I'm no good at it.'

It didn't dim, it intensified, and his lips curved as he insisted, 'We're not talking ballroom. We're talking bump and grind and I *know* you can do that.'

He took her hand and pulled her to her feet. Despite the sizzle in her fingers, her heart sank. This so wasn't going to end up like in the movies where the guy leads the girl into an applause-inducing spin on the dance floor. Where couples parted and stood back to watch in awe. More likely people would watch and laugh. The place was heaving with bodies moving in sync with the deep bass. She felt awkward. Eager to escape the sweaty couple beside her, she moved forward and trod on Jake's foot. 'See, I told you I was useless.'

He laughed, releasing a little of the pent-up energy she sensed in him. 'Come here and lean against me; I'll do the moving for both of us.' He wound his arms round her waist and drew her into length-to-length position. He nudged a foot between hers. Her lashes drooped as her senses suffered Jake overload. She couldn't say no to him, just wanted to touch and be set ablaze.

Then he moved, gently swaying her, as his strong hands guided her hips, rocking her against him, with him, to the relentless beat.

After a moment of statue-stillness as she absorbed his nearness, she gave herself over to it. Fitting in to him. The closer she got, the last lingering doubt and jealousy disappeared. Then she relaxed completely, while another tension deep inside began to tighten. The steam rose as her body softened and his became hard. A few beats later he pushed his thigh between hers and it became her support as she rode it. A temporary substitute for what she really wanted.

Breathing suddenly got really difficult. Her lips parted as she tried to get more air in. His hands weren't guiding her any more; her hips were moving of their own accord, back and forth in tandem with him. She could hardly see his face in the dark of the dance floor, but the flashing lights were reflected in his eyes as he didn't take them off her. Glittering. He lifted one hand from her back and then she felt his fingers slip beneath the hem of her dress.

This wasn't dancing. This just about wasn't legal. But it was so, so right. Thankfully the room was crowded and there were so many others on the dance floor, all intent on their own partners, or finding a partner, no one was going to be watching them.

Her hands scaled his chest and she felt the muscles tighten under her fingertips. He bent and kissed her neck as his hand slid up her thigh. He kissed her collar-bones and started to head further south while his fingers went further north. She moaned. In that instant it changed from dangerous dancing to all-out foreplay. He pulled her tighter to him as he lifted his head.

'We need to finish this in private.' His arm firm around her waist, he strode off the dance floor and she half skipped to keep pace with him.

This time as she entered his apartment she couldn't care less about who might or might not have been there before her. All that mattered was now and getting enough of him. She turned and faced him, her hands holding the hem of her dress, teasing it up as her legs parted, ready and inviting. He slammed the door behind them and tossed the keys onto the table with such force they skittered right off and onto the floor. He strode to her, stripping his shirt off at the same time. 'This is insane.'

* * *

She woke nestled in his huge bed, him half sprawled across her, his thigh heavy on her own, his arm around her, holding her close. She turned to his face and, consigning her cares to future contemplation, she woke him in the most intimate way she could.

An hour later and the sun was starting to rise high in the sky.

'I have another surprise for you.' He traced a finger down her torso.

She looked down from where she sat straddling him.

He cleared his throat. 'It means we have to get out of bed. You OK with that?'

'Do we have to?' She leant forward and smoothed her palms over his shoulders, loving the breadth, loving the freedom to touch him however she pleased.

'Yeah,' he groaned. 'It'll be fun.'

'Nothing's as fun as this.' She bent her head.

His fingers tightened around her and he lifted her away. 'Let's do this in the shower. Two birds, one stone.'

They didn't take the car, going on foot instead.

'I'm taking you to meet a friend of mine. I think you'll like her.'

Her. Emma's previously soothed hackles rose. How many of Jake's ex-girlfriends was she going to have to meet this weekend? Her blood ran even colder as he steered them into a contemporary art gallery.

'Hey, Jake.'

Emma warily watched the woman approach. She was older than she'd anticipated, dark haired with a large grey streak at the front. The epitome of urban cool, slim and wearing black, black, black. Emma thought she was not unlike Cruella de Vil. Maybe Jake had gone off-type more than once.

Then a younger woman clad in matching black, with close-cropped purple-tinged hair, came over to join her. She slipped her arm around the older woman's waist and squeezed her close. They swapped an intimate look.

Oh. Emma rebuked herself. Clearly it was possible for Jake to have female friends who weren't ex-girlfriends. Lesbian ones. She surreptitiously pinched her arm hard for being so catty.

'You must be Emma; I've been looking forward to meeting you.'

Emma blinked. Since when? She'd never heard of this woman.

'Jake emailed me pictures of some of your work. I'd be very keen to see some of them up close for myself.'

Emma froze. 'Uh.'

Jake stepped in, his hand heavy across her shoulders. 'Emma, this is Cathy. She owns the place. She's the one I told you about who keeps an eye out for me. But this time I've found something for her. I sent her photos of a few drawings and then a couple of the paintings.'

He what?

'Your drawings are superb, technically outstanding. Painstakingly detailed, but it's the paintings that really caught my attention. You use your skills, but then they're imbued with such emotion. Wonderful stuff.'

Emma was floored. She tried to turn her brain's engine on, but it appeared the battery was dead. Jake had emailed pictures? When? How?

Cruella was waffling again about the depth in her

painting. Emma had never been one for art-speak. Switching off, she glanced at Jake. He was beaming at her.

'I told you they were brilliant.' He looked as if he'd done something marvellous and she wasn't able to inform him otherwise. Had he paid Cathy to go on like this? Was this whole thing a set-up?

'Are you willing to send some samples up to me?'

'I, um…' she stopped and swallowed the high-rise-sized lump in her throat '…I'd never thought much about showing them in public.'

'Well, that's why you paint, isn't it?'

Actually, no. She painted because she enjoyed it. It made her feel good. It was *hers*. And no one was judging her on it. Not until now. But a lifetime's conditioning dictated her response. Be polite. Never be rude to people you just met who are being nice to you. Don't let them down. Aim to please—others not yourself.

Cathy smiled at her silence. 'Jake told me you were shy about it, but you shouldn't be. Many artists are the same: they like to paint, but they struggle to put it out there and then stand back in the corner and hide. It takes courage, but I'm sure you're a courageous person, Emma.'

Oh. She had the whole psychology thing down pat. Emma smiled weakly. Did she have the courage to turn this woman down? Did she have the courage to tell Jake exactly what she thought of this stunt?

'Why don't you take a look around and see what you think of the kind of work I like to display?' Cathy gestured down the cleverly lit, wooden-floored space. 'We're a successful gallery. I'm pretty good at spotting talent and we sell a lot—to clients with good taste, of course.' She laughed and winked at Jake.

Emma felt nauseous. This was so humiliating. Hot sweat covered her body and quickly turned cold. She walked away, slipping ahead of Jake so she could fix her polite mask in place. She folded her arms tight across her chest. Despite the warmth of the late-spring day, she felt as icy as a winter storm. She stopped at a large painting, blown away by its scale and execution. She could never compete with something like that—didn't want to. She wasn't a real artist, she just liked drawing flowers, for heaven's sake. She hadn't asked for this.

The soft tread of Jake's sneakers meant she didn't hear him until he was right behind her, slipping his arm around her waist just as the young woman had slipped hers around Cathy's when they'd arrived. Intimate. Knowing. But Emma was unable to swap the look of lovers.

'Fantastic, isn't it?'

Was he talking about the art or the situation? She decided to answer about the painting in front of them. 'It's beautiful.'

Melancholic, she stared around the walls. She'd been driven to succeed almost all her life and she didn't want to have to succeed here. His eyes were on her, waiting, questioning, but she couldn't give him the response he was looking for.

They slowly walked the perimeter, looking at the various works displayed.

'Will you send something?' Cathy asked as they came back to the reception area.

She tried to explain. 'I don't really do it for others. I just enjoy it.'

'Why not let others enjoy it too?' the younger woman piped up for the first time. 'It's not a competition. No one's really judging. They'll either like them or they won't. And who cares if they don't?'

Jake's arm tightened around her. 'That's what I say.'

'People would get a lift from them,' Cathy encouraged and Emma felt overwhelmed by their three-pronged attack. Railroaded into smiling and acting as if she were pleased.

The young woman spoke again. 'You'd be surprised how much we sell and how much people pay. You just have to be careful because the tax implications can be a nightmare.'

'Not a problem for Emma—she's an accountant.' Was that pride she could hear in Jake's voice? Hell, it was like her father rattling off all her accomplishments to whomever they met. Emma, the performing poodle. She glanced at him as he smiled and chatted. Did he have any idea what she felt about this? For a while there she'd thought Jake understood her. Obviously not.

Cathy handed her a card. 'Think about it. If you do decide you want to show, give me a call. I'd be interested in helping you.'

Helping? Or taking over? Setting the agenda: commissions, deadlines, orders—*pressure*. Emma didn't want to fail at this, so she refused to compete.

Walking back in the warmth of the sun, she felt frozen through to her marrow. Her art was a part of her that she'd locked away. And now Jake had come and opened it up— not just for himself, but for everyone, and she didn't like it.

She felt him look at her but she couldn't talk. She didn't know what to say, where to start. He'd gone to a lot of trouble to set up that meeting for her and part of her didn't want to knock him back for it. The pleasing part.

She stopped in her tracks as she realised what she was doing. She'd worked so hard all her childhood to please her father, now she worked damn hard to please Max.

But it wasn't supposed to be like that with Jake. Jake was for fun. Being with him was just a game—right? She was with him because it pleased *her*. The same reason she painted—for her alone. Only now he was messing with it, interfering, changing the dynamic. And she felt forced to perform—for him.

She couldn't let it happen. She couldn't let what he thought, what he wanted, matter that much. Not when this was a temporary fling. Until now he'd given her unfound freedom. By making it a game she'd been able to do whatever she wanted, say whatever she wanted and be more brazen than she'd ever dreamed. He couldn't change the rules now.

No audience. She wanted none for her passion. Except him—and he wasn't her audience, he was her playmate.

He closed the door to his apartment behind them and swung back to face her. 'You're mad with me.'

She turned to the windows, trying to keep calm. 'How did you photograph my paintings?'

She watched his reflection as he walked towards her.

'You're really mad with me.' So he did know her feelings. He did see into her—at least some of the way.

'How?'

He answered the question. 'With my phone.'

'When?' She stepped forward again, away from him. She wanted him, she'd always want him, but right now she didn't want him to touch her. She wanted to keep in control.

'The other night before we, ah…before we slept in there.'

Before she'd totally opened herself up to him. That was why he'd gone in there. *No ulterior motive?* Even if he'd thought it a good one, it still hurt her. Awfully, tears threatened. She wanted to hide.

He saw in the reflection and turned her back to face him, his hands cupping her face. 'Look, honey, I know you're scared, but your paintings are brilliant. And I'm not just saying that because I want to get in your pants. I don't know much, but I know a little about art and you have talent. You really do.'

It wasn't about talent. It was about protecting what was hers and hers alone.

'Cathy can see it too and she really does know her stuff. She wants to sell them for you.'

'I don't want to sell them.'

'At least exhibit them. You should be proud of them, you should want people to see; you should be out there promoting this.'

Should, should, should.

She didn't want him to go there—started to build the wall of reserve to cover the rawness. 'No, Jake.'

'Why not?'

'I just don't want to. Can we not talk about this any more?'

Through her anxiety she saw his frustration.

'No, we need to talk.' He sighed as she brushed his hands away and walked towards the window. 'You can't tell me you're not interested in letting people see your stuff when you're doing illustrations for a book! You can't have it both ways, Emma.'

The book was different. They were technical drawings, as exact as photographs, only more delicate. The paintings she'd done with passion and exuberance and sheer joy because they didn't matter, they didn't have to be perfect.

It finally registered that the phone was ringing and had been for some time.

'Are you going to get that?'

'No. This is more important.'

The click as the answering machine switched on stopped her from speaking.

'Jake, it's Samantha. Heard you're back in town but I can't raise you on your mobile…' Emma tried to block her voice but the words, the dulcet tones, dropped into her head like stones tossed in a shallow pool. Splashing, stirring up the mud and staying. She could just picture her—Barbie Mark II. She looked at the machine. The red indicator flashed that there were another three messages. Multiple Barbies. Bitter jealousy resurged and oozed from every pore. It tipped her balance, fuelling her anger to an irrational level.

Jake seemed not to have heard the call at all. Intently focussed on her, his argument laced with passion. 'Why hide away, Emma? Why don't you want people to appreciate your gift?' He stood next to her, talking to the side of her face. She maintained an impassive exterior and he growled, annoyance mounting. 'It's like you have this split personality. You crunch numbers by day and create amazing art at night. Everyone you work with thinks you're some workaholic icicle when you're actually this insatiable, sensual woman.'

She jerked to look at him, stunned by the even more personal direction he'd gone in. Insatiable? Sensual? Didn't he realise that was only with him?

'Why can't the world see all of you, Emma?'

'It's a hobby, that's all.'

'Bullshit. You spend hours on it. This matters to you. You told me yourself you're a perfectionist.' He swore. 'You haven't even told your parents. How can you have kept this secret from them?'

Her blood ran cold. 'I don't want them knowing, Jake.'

'Well, don't worry about me telling them.'

Given he never spoke to them, she knew there was little danger of it. 'You really don't like him, do you?'

He hesitated. 'He's your dad.'

'Yeah, but you don't like him.'

He shrugged. 'He's pushy.'

Yes. Even she could admit that—hell, the old man would admit it himself and defend it to the hilt. It made her even madder that Jake judged him like that. She knew what her father was like and she was the one who had to live with it. Not Jake. 'He is and that's the point. I don't want him or anyone else pushing expectation on me with my paintings.'

'Well, what about Margaret—aren't your drawings for her doing exactly that?'

'But that's on my terms, Jake. *My* terms. You had no right to show anyone my paintings. Why can't you understand that?'

'Your talent is too great to be shelved, Emma. Someone has to get you out from the rock you're hiding behind!'

Silence. She struggled to take in his attack. Hands on his hips, he scrutinised her. She glared back, resentment burning. For Jake everything was simple—you wanted something, you went for it. It wasn't so easy for her.

Jake was in her life temporarily but his actions—all of them—would have a permanent effect. She needed to stop him in his tracks now.

She curled her fingers into fists and fought to keep cool. Why couldn't he see that some things were for public and some for private? She didn't want to have to let him down, but he was ramping up his expectations of her. Insisting she put herself out there. Wanting her to do something she simply wasn't capable of. She locked down and called on every ounce of self-control. She breathed out slowly, quietly.

'I'm not going to change my mind, Jake. Maybe it's time you took me to the airport. I don't want to miss my flight.'

He blinked at her change in direction. 'Are you kidding?'

She turned and tried to stop him with the coldest vibe she could send his way. 'Should I get a taxi?'

It was his turn to look frosty—his face hardening, eyes shuttering.

She moved away before he answered, going to gather her belongings and toss them into her overnight bag. She glanced around his room and could scarcely believe that only a couple of hours earlier she'd lain in his bed so carelessly. Why did he have to push when for once she'd been having such fun?

He was pacing, fidgeting with the car keys in his fingers when she returned. 'Come on, Emma. Let's talk about this.'

'Leave it. There's nothing to talk about. It's my hobby, that's all. I'm not going to send them to any gallery.'

'Since when were you such a chicken? I thought you were the bravest person I know. And I can't believe I'm wrong.'

Why on earth had he thought that? She'd never been brave. She'd never stood up to her father. Never gone for what she really wanted. Only reached for her dreams in secret. Until now when she'd played out her desire for Jake in public—uncaring who knew. Not such a great move.

'I can't believe you're going to fly out of here and not sort through this with me.' He looked frustrated.

That was exactly what she was going to do. She'd opened up to him—he knew everything about her. She'd trusted him with her secrets—those of her body and her art. Thankfully she hadn't openly given him her heart.

At the airport she fiddled with the luggage label on her bag. He walked up to her, stopping too close. She looked no higher than the stripe on his casual cotton tee. He took the bag from her, peeling her fingers from the handle with a firm hand. The electricity jolted through her. Those hands could touch her ways that made her lose her mind, made her forget everything but the pleasure to be had with him. But she didn't want to let that happen now. He'd have her under his spell and she'd be saying yes—but he'd asked her something she didn't want to say yes to. She clamped down the hum of desire that ran at a constant when he was around.

'You're mad with me. OK. But let's not forget the important things, huh?' He pulled her stiff body towards him and firmly planted his lips on hers. She tasted his anger and her own and even more annoyingly it made the kiss even more divinely fiery. She felt him settle in closer, ready to drown her resistance. Only just, just, did she manage to keep under control and pull away hard. She grabbed her bag and headed through the security check before he could stop her. She heard him call her name but kept walking.

The *important* things? She'd already lost sight of them and that meant nothing but trouble.

As her plane landed she realised she didn't know when he was returning from Auckland. She rode in the taxi and couldn't stop thinking about him. Her. Her art. Her life. The way her past achievements had stifled her own aspirations. The way her upbringing had conditioned her to obey and dutifully fulfill obligations in public while keeping what mattered most a guilty secret.

The minute she was in her cottage she walked into her art room and took the key out of the door. No longer needed. She swished the curtains back. No longer secret. Jake had seen to that. She stared at the paintings. As a kid she'd dreamed of being an artist. Of living a bohemian lifestyle where she could spend her days doing her favourite thing. Of going to fine arts school. Of travelling and seeing the Masters.

She'd been told it was impossible—laughable. Her father had done just that when as a kid she'd confessed her dream to him. He'd scoffed—did she think she was going to live some romantic, idealised life in a garret in Paris? He'd told her to wake up—you go to university and study something useful. You build a career with hard work, he'd insisted. That was how you got anywhere. That was how you earned approval—his at any rate.

Why couldn't she have been like Lucy and done it anyway? Lucy who'd kept up with her music, defiantly doing what she wanted. Refusing to follow the path their father tried to keep them on. And he still loved her, didn't he? Sure, he hassled her, but he was proud of her at the same time.

How had she got things so muddled?

Margaret's book had been like a secret gift. It had tapped into her youthful secret desire. And wasn't it enough? It was Margaret's dream—Emma was only doing some sample illustrations for her to pitch it to the publisher. She wasn't really putting her heart on the line. Showing her paintings wasn't something she'd ever felt she could do. If you were going to do something, you were going to be the best at it—that had been her mantra. And she didn't have the confidence to take the risk here.

But Jake had come along and encouraged her to do whatever, whenever—with him at least. Freeing her of anxiety by making it all a game. All the fun with him was careless—or at least meant to be. Once she was on the court with him all qualms were kept at bay by the magic of his touch. He was such a pro. She wished she could be like that for real. Wished things didn't have to matter so much.

And now, she finally admitted, *he* mattered to her— more than anything. And what he thought mattered, and what he wanted. And he wanted her to open up and he didn't realise how vulnerable she'd be if she did that.

Damn.

She stormed into the kitchen and pulled her laptop from its case. She had mountains of work to do and she had to get it done. For once she looked at it bitterly, resentment rising. She'd far rather be on the end of a paintbrush right now. But she'd told Max she wouldn't let him down. And nor would she.

Monday came and went with no word from Jake. She worked through and spent the evening on her drawings. Margaret phoned, wanting them midweek.

All her deadlines were hitting at the same time.

After nine on Tuesday night, she heard the knock on the door. His knock. She was stressed to the extreme. She had only the night to get the drawings finished and she still had work on Max's report to get through first. She pulled on the guy ropes of her helium-filled heart. She was not going to fail to complete it because of her silly crush, even if he did provide the best—and only—sex of her life. But in interfering with her decision to keep her art to herself he'd crossed the boundary and she needed to shove him back over it.

He walked straight over her threshold talking, taking the bull by the horns, excited glint in his eye. 'I've been thinking about it. So you're shy about the paintings, sure. But you could exhibit and sell them under a pseudonym—until you have the confidence to come out. Why not just send a couple and see how they do?'

He still hadn't got it and she had too much to be getting on with to go in circles. 'Jake, I told you the other day, I don't want to and I don't want to talk about it any more.'

He swept his arms around her. 'Come on, have dinner with me. Come and have me.'

Oh, she wanted him, but she wanted not to want him more. Trapped, she told herself her work was the reason. 'I can't, Jake. I have too much to do.' She pulled away, pointed at the table overloaded with papers. 'I shouldn't have gone away in the weekend.'

'Emma, you're allowed some time off.' Just like that his easygoing veneer slipped to reveal the same frustration of two days before. Neither of them had got anywhere.

'Not when it conflicts with work I have to do.'

'Why kill yourself meeting deadlines for other people? Why not show people what you really love? You haven't even shown the people you love the most!'

Hadn't she? She'd shown him—and he hadn't understood at all. He hadn't seen how important it was that painting was her private thing. And now she could only hope that that wasn't all he hadn't seen.

She desperately hoped he hadn't seen how important

their affair had become to her. How jealous she'd felt when meeting Carolina, how crazily she wanted him every moment. How badly she'd fallen for him.

In love.

She had to cover up. Had to push him away, scrape a little dignity and count down every long minute until he left Christchurch again for good—to take her heart with him.

In the moment of her silence he'd hit boiling point. 'You're twenty-six years old, for God's sake. Why not just do what you want to do? Why spend your entire life trying to live up to other people's expectations? Show your paintings. You want to, Emma, I *know* you do.'

Sensory overload as his words ripped her open. This wasn't a side of Jake she could cope with. She wanted the easygoing, humorous one, not the iron-willed one prying into her deepest feelings and fears.

He must have seen her stricken expression because his manner softened. 'Come on. Come out with me. Have dinner. Relax, we can talk, eat meat if you want, drink some nice wine…'

He'd been driving her in directions she wasn't used to and suddenly it was all too much. She fought. 'Stop pushing me. Who are you to push me around like this?'

He jerked up in shock. 'Emma, I'm just concerned for you.'

'If you're that concerned for me, you'll let me get on with my work—I'm going to be up all hours to get it all done as it is.'

'What? You can't.' His volume rose with every word. 'You can't spend an entire night on these reports, then try to finish the drawings before putting in another twelve-hour day. That's crazy.'

'I did it for enough years at uni—I know what I can do when I push hard enough,' she yelled, more than matching his decibel level. 'I'll get the drawings to Margaret, and Max needs the data and I mean to give it to him. I won't let him down.'

'He says jump, you say how high. No matter how impossible the demands, how much it impacts on your life, you do it. When are you going to learn to say no?' In her face, eyes blazing, he was wild.

'I'm saying no to you!' Not as wild as her.

The silence was sudden and deadly. They both breathed hard, but strangely she couldn't hear the air as they dragged it in.

She watched, mentally distanced as he stepped back, nodding to himself. 'So you are.'

His footsteps sounded as curt as his voice. The door slammed behind him.

She'd got her way but it was game over. Nil all.

CHAPTER TWELVE

THE hours ticked long into the night as Emma finalised the report for Max. She forced herself to focus. Once she was free and on to the drawings, she entered the 'zone' she usually loved so much when creating. But tonight was different. The scene with Jake replayed on auto. Over and over. Ugly. Pain growing with each repetition. Together with the nagging feeling that he might have been just a little bit right. That she might have been more than a bit wrong.

He'd said she was scared. OK, she admitted it—he was right about that. She was afraid—but of what? She didn't want to have to meet someone else's expectations. Because if she didn't, if she wasn't the best, she wouldn't be wanted. Let someone down and they wouldn't want you any more— wouldn't give you what you needed from them. So she hid away the things that really mattered because then they wouldn't hurt. What a stupid idea that was. Just because something was a secret, didn't mean it was safe. And wasn't life much more fun when you took the risk and shared?

She rebelled again. Damn Jake—damn him for opening her up and making her think. And feel.

She finally went to bed at six-thirty in the morning. Snatched just an hour before dragging herself from the bed and standing under the shower for even longer than usual, wanting to wash away the tiredness and the ache. It didn't work.

She went into the art room and studied the last of the drawings she'd completed through the night. Not bad. She knew they were good to go. She'd given it her all. She carefully slipped the illustrations into the portfolio together with the clean copy of Margaret's manuscript. She looked at the table, looked at her work on the walls, and with a spark of defiance she lifted a couple of canvases. She wrapped them carefully and put them into the carry case. Phoned the courier company before she changed her mind. They were gone by eight-fifteen and there was no going back.

So there Jake Rendel.

She practically ran to work. She had already emailed the final report through to Max well past midnight, but she wanted to be there to address any questions he might have. She knew he would have been in at work since half seven and would have read it by now.

Her phone rang almost the moment she sat down. Her heart stopped. She answered, breathless, and grimaced at her weakness.

'Emma, it's Margaret. Just got your package. They're perfect, absolutely perfect. I knew you were the one to ask. I'm so confident they'll go for us. Thank you so much.'

It took a moment to switch gears. She'd so hoped it would be Jake. 'Well, we've tried, haven't we?'

'We sure have. The paintings you've included are just fabulous.'

'Oh.' She already regretted that. 'You can leave them

out if you want to. They were just something I was having fun with.'

'Leave them out? No way! They're the icing, they really are.'

Emma didn't know whether she wanted to laugh, cry or vomit. What was she doing? Her nerve hardened. She was playing by *her* rules.

Next call was Max. She forced the air from her lungs. He was happy with the report and scheduled a full staff meeting for late afternoon. She slumped in her chair, running on nothing, and couldn't even face the idea of chocolate. She'd done it. Margaret had the drawings and was happy. Max had his report and was happy. She'd achieved what she'd set out to do—but so what? Was she happy? Crowd-pleasing wasn't all it was cracked up to be when you started to wonder about what ends you were working to. Not her own. She'd always been reliable, capable Emma—efficient and above reproach. Since when had that translated into so thorough, so diligent—so doormat?

Jake tried to stroll casually into the hotel but knew the way his fists were clenched around his jacket and briefcase that it was a dead loss. Muffled thumping from upstairs indicated the boys had begun part of the demolition work for the day. He was waylaid by Becca for a few minutes' meaningless chitchat. As he struggled to extricate himself from her his attention was suddenly arrested by the sight of Emma in conversation with the doorman. He watched as the guy leant forward on his desk, body language all a go-go. Jake tensed. He knew the jealousy was totally a double standard. But he couldn't bear the thought of her getting close up with anyone but him. Ironic when he'd hardly been lily-white. Girls aplenty in his past. But not now. He'd lost his appetite for anyone but her.

She looked relaxed, and certainly didn't look as if she'd been up all hours working her butt off. She sure as hell didn't look as if she'd spent a moment's worry about how things had ended with him last night. He had no idea whether she cared or not and it was eating him up. He wanted her to care. Wanted it all to matter the way it did to him. The pleasure he got from her pleasure was scary. He loved to see her loose and laughing. *Loved*.

Now *that* was scary. His instinct was to fight it—fear confused with anger.

He finally got away from Becca and walked over. He interrupted the conversation and saw the veil pull across her eyes, the smile fade. He glared at the door guy who backed off immediately. Good. 'Did you get it all done?'

She nodded.

Foolishly he couldn't help setting himself up again. 'Are you going to have dinner with me tonight?'

She looked away. 'No, I…'

That word again. The one he hated to hear fall from her—especially so quickly and so casually. She didn't care. He consciously relaxed the muscles in his jaw. So it was game over. He felt like picking up one of the sledgehammers upstairs and knocking down that partition wall himself—blow by blow.

She elaborated—eventually. 'I have to meet with a couple of catering companies for Mum. Their party is coming up.'

He knew the one. 'Second Saturday in December. The highlight of my social calendar.' She frowned at his sarcastic drawl. The Delaney 'Start of summer/Wedding anniversary/Christmas' bash—renowned in the town. Old Lucas had his lawns manicured for it, usually put a marquee out the back, hired a band and invited the world. Everyone came and Lucas stood forth and showed off his beautiful house, beautiful wife and beautiful daughters. Jake bristled.

His mum always went, Sienna too. But he'd never bothered despite his name being on an invite every year. *Jake & Partner*. It had been bad enough seeing it all from his room above the garage as a youth. Lucas and his overt display of wealth and success and his hard-pushed daughters. If only he knew the half of it.

Jake's blood boiled over. 'How can you go home and be the dutiful daughter when they don't know half of what's going on in your life? The things that are most important to you?'

The veil lifted to reveal the fire in her eyes. Flames of anger, but he couldn't help but think he saw desire too. 'Everybody has secrets, Jake.'

'Not like this.'

'I take it you won't be going.' She gave a scornful laugh.

With savage satisfaction he was able to give her answer back to her. 'No. I sure won't.'

'Of course not. Wouldn't want to see my father and me having a good time. It would ruin your perception of him being the ogre and all.'

'Perception? You're the one who's keeping your life a secret. What are you so scared of if it's not him?'

The fire in her eyes flared, that whisker of desire obliterated. 'Maybe it's interference, Jake. Maybe I don't want him or anyone else meddling in something that is my business.'

'You think I was meddling? I was trying to help you…'

Her eyes widened further and, stunned, he saw the

anger in her ignite. 'I don't need your help, Jake. I don't want your pity. You don't have to feel sorry for me. So don't throw your weight around where it's not wanted. Just back off!'

His jaw dropped. He'd never, ever seen Emma as wound up as this and it wasn't just anger he saw, but fear and a hurt, hunted look. Before he could process it his brain ticked over into defence mode. How had this gone so wrong? Did she really think he was that overbearing? It hadn't been that bad, for goodness' sake. She was acting as if he'd committed the crime of the century.

She turned and he watched, too angry to move, as she went to the lift and pressed the button to summon it. She stood with her back to him, no glance back. Interference? He'd been trying to help her—and she needed it. She was hiding away and living some half-life when she should be celebrating and making the most of her talents—all of them. But if she wasn't able to see it, or want it, then fine. He didn't need the grief. He'd head back to Auckland and have some fun. This was just too much like hard work. The breath steamed out of him.

Relax.

Yet kid as he might and tell himself to 'chill', he couldn't because it hurt. The deadlock made his bones ache. Trying to release the clamp in his jaw was mission impossible now. He could smash that partition with his bare hands. He spun on his heel. As he strode past Reception Becca called to him. 'She did it, huh?'

He looked at her, wondering what she was on about.

'Emma.' Becca jerked her head towards the lift into which Emma had disappeared. 'Broke your heart.'

It was a little too close to the bone and every muscle screamed tighter with tension.

'I'm good at repair jobs.' She delivered the blatant invitation with a vivacious smile.

For once he couldn't laugh it off and, ignoring the fact he was supposed to be going to a meeting with his foreman, ignoring the woman leaning towards him suggestively, he walked straight out of the hotel wanting as far away from this mess as possible.

The day dripped by. Emma's blood boiled with bitterness. What had happened to the laid-back game they'd been playing? She'd been such a fool—got too involved, taken it too seriously. And he hadn't taken her seriously enough.

He'd been trying to help her. *Because he felt sorry for her.* So humiliating. Here she was in love with the guy and he was still just being 'nice' to the overly conscientious geek girl. Showing her a little fun—something to while away the time he was down here.

She'd seen him talk to Becca when he came in. All smiles for the blonde beauty. Her strung-out nerves had snapped at that. It would be no time until another woman caught his interest. Well, she wasn't going to hang around waiting to get tossed aside. She'd ended it—saving herself from further hurt and humiliation.

The bitterness grew. She didn't know if it was possible to feel more hurt. She worked up her anger to cover it. His antagonism towards her father and the party was a good place to start. Truth be told, she didn't much enjoy the event either, but she'd always, always show up for her parents—as would Lucy. She might not want to share everything with them at this stage in her life, but that didn't mean she didn't love them. Loyalty was a big thing. He was loyal to his mother and Sienna; of course she was loyal to her parents. Even if her dad was pushy, deep down she knew he only wanted the best for her.

She dragged herself to the staff meeting in Max's office and read through the financial summary for them. Braced herself while Max discussed the progress of the refurbishments. They'd just finished discussing this when Becca spoke. 'Wasn't Jake going to give us an update?'

All heads swivelled in Emma's direction. One of those please-let-the-ground-eat-me-up moments. She tried to look dignified and hoped her blush was more of a four than a ten on her usual scale. She looked to Max for the answer. He too was looking at her, thoughtfully, and she read concern in his expression. He eventually filled the silence.

'I believe he got called back to Auckland on business.'

She knew Becca was still looking at her. She could see the small smile and thought ugly thoughts for a second. Then she thought about what she was going to do. He'd gone, relieved her of the necessity, but she still wanted to escape.

She waited until the others had left Max's office. He looked at her but quickly glanced away, seeming to know she needed a rest from relentless scrutiny. 'What's up, Emma?'

'I'm sorry for the short notice, but do you mind if I take a few days off?'

He tapped something on his computer before asking blandly, 'How long do you need?'

'Just until the end of the week. I'll be back Monday.'

He typed some more. 'So long as you leave everything tied up and detailed notes, then I see no problem.'

She'd just reached the door when he called her name. She stopped and turned back to him.

He smiled at her. 'Have a good break.'

She squared her shoulders, trying to hide the horrendous confusion inside. 'I will. Thanks, Max.'

She stayed late, working to tie up the loose ends and make notes should anything arise in the next week that needed answering. All the while she kept her mind a blank. Focusing on one task and then the next, calmly, methodically, until at last her desk was clear and computer shut down. She was ready to leave.

Only then did she glance at her specimen vase. The tulip and the little forget-me-not were well past their best. Petals withered and about to drop. Beautiful while they lasted, but ultimately doomed to fade. She picked up the vase and tipped the entire contents into her waste-paper basket. Looping the strap of her bag over her arm, she walked out and didn't look back.

CHAPTER THIRTEEN

JAKE frowned at the small-scale building model and pretended he was listening to the architect next to him, all the while mentally beating himself up. It was his own silly fault. He'd set himself up completely. Offered to be Emma's plaything. Only now she didn't want to play. And nor did he. He wanted the real deal and she wanted it over.

He'd always been a champion player and that was how she saw him. But now he wanted different. The realisation was slow and painful and he fought it. He hated the way his feelings for her and the situation he was in were so beyond his control.

He vacillated. It wouldn't work. Couldn't. He didn't do serious. Didn't do commitment. And he definitely didn't do distance. She had a huge job in Christchurch that she loved and put above everything else. And he couldn't move either. People counted on him. He had to forget the idea of her in his future and just keep the memory of a fun few weeks. Now he could move on to something new and exciting.

So why did it feel as if his heart had been skinned?

He gave the architect a set smile and escaped to his car.

He still wanted her and could have sworn he'd still seen desire in her face when they'd parted. If she'd felt that, then he still had a chance. She was just mad with him for forcing her hand.

He hunted for common ground—literally. He didn't have a patch of earth in his penthouse apartment. He frowned. But he did have the roof. He could have a pot garden on the roof. And there were lots of hotels in Auckland—they'd need accountants. His pulse quickened.

Maybe he had stuffed up. Pushed too far. But he'd wanted to help. If he confided in Sienna she'd roast him properly. She was always on at him for interfering in her life. And yet, he couldn't regret it. Maybe he'd gone about it wrong, maybe he should have talked it through with Emma first, but he'd thought going to the gallery and meeting Cathy like that, hearing her evaluation direct, might get through to her better than he could.

It frustrated him beyond belief that this vibrant, warm woman struggled to express her desires. But with him she had. And that was why he'd done it, because he was sure that deep down she wanted to paint, and for people to know it. She was just stuck where she was because she thought it was where she had to be. He hated that she was too busy meeting other people's expectations to be making the most of her talents and maximising her pleasure in life. Many people didn't have that, weren't able to combine career with something they loved, but Emma could if she wanted, and he'd wanted to show her that. When he set his mind to something he could usually succeed and he liked to be able to put that to use for those he loved.

And there was the rub.

It wasn't just some fun affair. A game that went a little further than they'd intended. He hadn't been having sex with her.

He'd been making love.

For the first time.

And, stupidly, he'd only just realised it.

Was it too late? He gripped the steering wheel. It couldn't be. He was in love. A damn awful situation to be in and one he'd never imagined. The ironic laugh jerked out. All this time he'd been off kilter with wanting her. Needing her so bad he could hardly think straight—because at the back of his mind was the knowledge that she wasn't going to be his for long. He'd always said he didn't want to settle—he just wanted to have fun.

Life with Emma was fun.

Life without her wasn't.

The solution hit him like the thunderbolt from the heavens. The only way to cure the discomfort Emma brought him was to ensure Emma was with him for good.

He took in a deep breath. Felt better for the realisation. Then panicked.

How was he to convince *her*? She had no basis for comparison. How did he get her to understand that what they shared wasn't normal—that there would never be better than this? As far as she was concerned they were just playing around with him in the role of her 'get-some-experience' guy. She didn't want or expect serious from him. She'd just shoved his serious intention to help her straight back in his face.

He toyed with his phone, but knew it wasn't the answer. Too complicated—he needed face to face. He cursed his hotheaded decision to blow out of Christchurch and get back to Auckland. But he'd been mad with her overreaction. Hurt that she could switch off from him so easily. Scared that her coldness meant she didn't care.

So if he was to convince her, he had to speak to her in a language she'd understand.

Emma's mobile buzzed. She pulled the car over and flipped the phone open, trying not to be disappointed when it wasn't Jake on the caller display. She so had to get over him. Good thing she'd ended it when she had. It was enough of a killer as it was—her heart punctured by a thousand shards of glass.

She pressed the answer button. Margaret's excited voice burst into the silence of the car. The publisher wanted it. All of it: her drawings, Margaret's text—*the paintings.*

'By rights you should get first billing because without your drawings there wouldn't be a book. Look, I shouldn't be telling you this because the publisher is going to call you direct, but they're already talking about spin-off items. They want to do some stationery and maybe even a calendar featuring your work. He's already asking me if I knew if you had other stuff. Have you got other paintings?'

Emma paused, life at a crossroads.

Should she stay on the straight, flat road or go for the no-speed-limit motorway that led who knew where? A crash on that one could be fatal. But the other option would be fatally boring. Jake's cheeky grin appeared in her mind's eye, daring her to be bold, to say what she truly wanted— to herself and the rest of the world.

She closed her eyes, holding on to the image. 'I've got loads more.'

Twenty minutes later she sat in the café on the coast, the seagulls circling the car park, the decaf latte perfect. She clutched the cup with her shaking hands. Breathing deep, she looked around the décor. Paintings done by a local artist adorned the walls. Signs beneath each one giving title, medium and price. Simple. Little ad hoc sales generating a small, haphazard income. And then a plan began to form. One way of having it all—career-wise at least. She might have lost Jake but he'd never been hers to keep anyway, and maybe she could take something from the experience, what he'd taught her. She could apply the freedom to have fun and still achieve. To relax, be herself and do what she wanted—her own way.

First thing Monday morning after those few days tripping round the coastline, sketching ideas and images, Emma gathered her nerves and wobbly emotions. Clicking on the print icon, she picked up the paper on the way out and walked straight to Max's office before she lost her nerve.

His door was open and she rapped on it lightly to get his attention. He looked up from the documents in front of him and his gaze went unerringly to the sheet she held.

He spoke before she had a chance. 'I've been expecting this.'

His prescience was scary. She looked at him in surprise.

'Is it to travel or is it for love?'

She sank into the chair across from him, knees giving way in the relief that he already knew, and that he didn't appear too hurt or cross. She put the letter of resignation on his desk. 'Actually, it's a slight change in direction career-wise.'

He tapped his forehead with his finger. 'Should have known it wouldn't be the obvious.' He smiled, reassuring. 'I knew I wasn't going to have you for ever, Emma. And nor should I. You should be off chasing dreams.' He leaned back in his chair with a satisfied sigh. 'I'm off to chase mine shortly. On the golf course. Retirement!'

She knew then the phrase 'nobody is indispensable' deserved to be a cliché. He wasn't; she wasn't. The hotel wasn't going to fall over in a heap because the two of them were departing. Fresh changes would probably bring fresh vitality. She warmed. 'You've worked hard.'

'So have you, and in the last few years we've done a wonderful job together.' He stood and headed to his mini bar. 'Drink?'

'At this time of the day?' It was barely after nine.

'Mmm. Right as ever, Emma. Let's go for ice cream instead.' Max had an insatiable love of frozen ices. They walked out of his office and out of the hotel towards the natural ice-cream shop he haunted. 'The company will be disappointed. They know what an asset you are.'

She flushed and shook her head. 'I just crunch numbers. Anyone with the training can do that.'

He shook his head. 'You have a work ethic second to none.'

The waitress had seen them approach and had his wild berry frozen yoghurt ready on the counter. Emma ordered triple chocolate and ignored Max's appalled noises. 'I'm sorry I can't last the distance for you, Max.'

'Don't be silly. I'm lucky to have held on to you as long as I did. Thanks to you I'm leaving on a high—the hotel is in excellent shape, will be wonderful once the extensions are done. It sold for a mint. I couldn't be happier. And now you're off to pastures new. It's exciting for both of us.' He took a giant bite of his cone with his front teeth.

Valiantly ignoring the goose-bumps Emma got on his behalf, she grinned. 'Thanks, Max.'

He winked. 'And what about that man?'

'Which man?' The chill she felt was harder to ignore this time.

'Jake, you know, the one who made you smile.'

She licked her ice cream to delay answering while she tried to think of something noncommittal.

Max got in first. 'He seemed very taken with you.'

Hell, he was getting soppy in his old age.

'I thought you were going to have some fun as well as work hard?'

Emma cleared her throat.

Max sighed. 'Shame, I thought you were well suited. Still, plenty more fish in the sea.'

Just not any Emma wanted to catch.

He left her at Reception as Becca gestured her over.

'Some flowers arrived for you while you were away. We tried calling you at home but there was no answer so we put them in the staff room. They're gone now—the cleaner must have taken them away in the weekend.'

'Was there a note?'

She shook her head.

Emma nodded. Not wanting to meet Becca's piercing gaze, she turned to go back up to her office, but stopped as she thought of something. 'Do you know what kind of flowers they were?'

Becca frowned. 'No, it was all the one type, but I don't know what they were.' She paused. 'Not roses.'

'What colour?'

'White.'

Not tulips either; everyone recognised those.

She went back to her office, determined to forget about it. Now she'd made her decision she'd hoped the days would slide by faster, but each hour seemed to go slower and slower still. She grappled with the simplest of tasks—heart not in it—and counted away the minutes.

Jake stared at the block in front of him and contemplated the night ahead. He couldn't remember the last time he'd been home alone night after night like this, but he really didn't feel up to going out.

A bit of time and perspective usually did wonders, but it wasn't helping in this case. He could kick himself. He should have listened, should have seen the extent of her anxiety. Now he worried he'd broken her trust by showing Cathy her work when she wasn't ready. But he was a man of action. Too much, too soon—the story of their whole affair.

He'd needed some time to get to grips with what was happening and clearly she still needed more. He refused to believe he could feel this strongly and she not. He ached all over. He had to make this right. It had been days and he'd heard nothing. He glanced at his mobile. Silent, still and he was not going to pick it up and press buttons. If she hadn't understood the flowers, he'd find another way. Never a quitter, he always had a backup plan. Trouble was he might need more than one in this case and he didn't know if his heart could handle the suspense. He picked up his chisel. One scrape at a time.

When Emma got home that night she found a beat-up blue car parked outside her cottage. Oh, great. Talk about lowering the value of the neighbourhood.

'Well, if it isn't Tweedledum and Tweedledummer.' Lucy and Sienna sat parked on her veranda, bottle of wine already open. She summoned a grin for them and trudged up the two stairs.

'Hello, Ms Workaholic. We've been here for *hours*.' Lucy raised her glass at her.

Emma looked at the almost-empty wine bottle and the grease-stained fish and chip wrappers. 'No kidding.'

She sat down on the top step, took Lucy's glass from her hand and drained it.

Lucy stared open-mouthed. 'Bad day?'

One of many this last week. Despite handing in her resignation and starting work on a new painting, she couldn't shake the blues. Couldn't stop thinking about Jake. It frustrated her beyond belief. She'd always been a career girl and now she stood on the brink of a new and exciting venture and all she could think about was some bloke.

But he wasn't just any bloke and that was the problem.

She couldn't bear to look Sienna in the eyes. They were the exact same blue as Jake's. Only Sienna had a mass of hair the colour of strawberry-tinted gold, not the thick, black, slightly unruly cut that Jake had.

'We're only here for the one night, sister. OK if we crash?' Lucy poured the remainder of the bottle into her glass and handed it to Emma.

'Sure, where are you headed?'

'Going walking—Milford Track.'

Emma nearly choked on the last of the wine. 'Since when were you two so energetic?' These two were total urbanites. She couldn't help a sideways glance at Sienna. Milford Track was one of New Zealand's most glorious walking tracks—but quite a hike. Because of her heart condition Sienna had been banned from strenuous physical activity almost all her life, until she'd taken up the drums in utter defiance of the medical profession—and her mother. And Jake.

Sienna caught the look and answered the implied question. 'I'm crossing off a few items on my life's "to do" list.'

'Yeah, and I'm on the prowl for gorgeous Scandinavian tourists.' Lucy leered.

'The ones backpacking with their gorgeous Scandinavian girlfriends,' Emma flattened her drily.

'Bah humbug.'

Emma stood and stretched. 'Come on inside. You've had dinner whereas I'm starving.' She wasn't really, but it gave her something to do. She rummaged in the fridge for a pack of smoked salmon and ferreted some crackers from the cupboard.

The two sat at the table and regaled her with tales of club life in the capital, Wellington. It made Emma's head ache and so she halted it with ease—by nagging them about their futures. 'So, what do you do with a music degree, girls?'

Lucy screwed up her face. 'Ugh, don't. You sound like Dad.'

'Or Jake,' Sienna added.

At the mention of his name Emma's hands wobbled. Her heart did more than wobble. It lurched. But she decided to be bold and mention him. Sienna must know they'd seen each other down here. She just hoped she didn't know how much of each other they'd seen. 'I saw him at the hotel a bit but I think he's gone back to Auckland now. Did you want to catch up with him?'

'Hell, no, the last thing I need is him sticking his oar in. He'll be wanting to arrange my career for me—fixing up an interview or something.' She gave a mock shiver.

Emma stared at her.

Sienna laughed at her expression. 'Seriously, you think your dad is bad, he's nothing on Jake.' She sat back in her chair and launched forth. 'Jake fixes things—it's what he does. Buys buildings and fixes them. Arranges deals. Makes oodles of money and keeps foisting it on to us. He's forever going on to Mum to retire when it's the last thing she wants to do. He hasn't learnt he can't do it all for us all the time.' Her fingers beat a steady tattoo on the table. 'Can you imagine his frustration when he couldn't fix *me*?'

Lucy handed her a glass of water but it didn't stop the tirade.

'And now he doesn't seem to realise I'm perfectly capable of achieving something on my own. He still won't let me carry my own bag—if he saw that camping pack he'd have a fit. He thinks he's helping. I know he just wants the best for me, wants it to be easy for me. But he doesn't understand that I want to do it myself—'

'Don't grump, Sienna,' Lucy chided. 'It's how he shows he cares.'

Emma frowned at her salmon and looked up to see Sienna looking at her with an apologetic expression. 'Don't get me wrong. I love the guy to bits and I'll always be grateful for what he's done for me. But I'm grown-up and healthy and he doesn't have to worry any more. I can take care of myself.' She reached for a cracker, but it didn't make it to her mouth; instead it became a quasi-drumstick with a life of its own, beating on the table. 'He's been so busy concerning himself with me and Mum, he's burnt out.'

'Burnt out?' Emma couldn't see that. Jake had more energy than anyone she'd ever met.

'In the sense he won't have a long-term relationship. Goes through girls like you wouldn't believe.' The cracker snapped. 'Two months tops, then he trades them in. And the thing is some of them are actually quite nice.' She shrugged. 'But he says he just wants to have fun. He's always felt responsible for us and doesn't want more responsibility with a serious girlfriend. Then again, maybe he just hasn't met the right one yet.'

For the kazillionth time in her life Emma wished her skin weren't so pale that even the tiniest hint of a blush showed like a stop sign. The right one? How she wished that had been her. But she'd just been the geek one. The one he'd felt sorry for. His interest had come on the back of that. She attributed it to novelty factor—a game going a few steps too far. He enjoyed women, and she was no more special than any of them. She hadn't even gone the usual distance. Two months? She'd had less than two weeks. A huge chunk of her, the naughty, recently discovered live-on-the-edge and take-what-you-want side wanted the six or so weeks she was missing.

Badly.

The rational, protective, sensible part told her she'd had a lucky escape because any longer in his bed and she'd be a complete wreck when he ended it and found someone else.

She suddenly realised Sienna had stopped talking and that she'd been abnormally silent. Lucy gave her a long look but said nothing.

Emma stood and got a couple of bars of Caramello from the freezer. Distraction always worked with wayward sisters and their friends.

'Mind if I look around your cottage? It's so cute.'

Sienna was on her feet and walking down the hall before either Lucy or Emma could speak.

The shriek was instant as she went into the art room. 'Emma, this is amazing! I never knew.'

Lucy shot Emma a look and mouthed 'sorry'.

Emma shrugged. It was OK. It was going to have to be OK because she was going public—in print, no less.

She stepped into the room after Sienna and stared at the half-tubes of paint smeared on her palette—wasted. She'd spent over two hours trying to mix the exact shade of green she was after and had failed. In everything this week, she was off her stroke.

Morosely she contemplated the upcoming weekend. 'You're coming to the parents' party, aren't you?'

'Absolutely.' Sienna's distracted answer came as she studied the painting of the wisteria.

'Wouldn't dream of missing it,' Lucy added bluntly, winking at Emma. 'I hear you've been sorting out some of the catering.'

'You know how it is. Mum wants something splendid. Something from the city that you can't get at home.'

'I had no idea you painted.' Sienna was working her way around the walls. 'These are fantastic. You know, Jake collects art—you should show him.'

Emma stared at the abandoned picture of the gardenia and swallowed the irony.

She set the two of them up in the lounge. They unrolled their sleeping bags happily and said they were in training for the hiking trip. Emma winced. The idea of camping was romantic, but the reality of bugs, hard ground, sand and damp irritated her. Give her a hotel any day. She lay in her bed listening to the muffled sounds as they settled down for the night. It wasn't long before quiet descended over the cottage. She looked through the chink in her curtain at the streetlight.

It's how he shows he cares.

Deep inside that greatest of human traits flickered—hope.

She tried to squash it. Of course he cares—as he cares for his sister. She was the quiet, studious neighbour he'd *felt sorry for*. But images of them being utterly adult flashed through her mind. Had he really been feeling sorry for her then? He wasn't doing *that* to make her feel better.

He'd wanted her. Again and again.

She tried once more to kill the hope—he wanted anything in a skirt. A player enjoying the novelty of a skinny brunette. Heat ran through her as the devilish side asserted dominance—so what? You were enjoying him too. Wasn't it possible just to go back to the game? Ignore the reality of the impact, the consequences of the end result?

Her heart pounded as she dared herself. She just had to get through the party at the weekend and then maybe she'd go and demand the remainder of her two months. Could she do it without more damage to her heart?

What had Jake said: if you don't ask, you don't get?

She'd grown the courage to go for what she really wanted career-wise; could she take the same risk with her passion for Jake? Fight the fear and ask for what she wanted: him—for however long it lasted.

CHAPTER FOURTEEN

JAKE headed UP the stairs with a heavy tread and a heavy heart. This was his last shot. And he was terrified.

Emma's father stood on his deck, lord of the manor, watching him arrive.

'Jake.'

'Lucas.'

'Nice to see you here. You coming to the party later?'

'Maybe.'

'How can I help?'

'Actually I was looking for Emma.'

Lucas stared at him. 'She's not here.'

It was as if a ten-tonne safe had landed on his chest.

'She's gone to get some flowers for the party tonight.'

Jake exhaled, the crush on his ribs easing. The disappointment in that fraction of an instant had nearly caused a cardiac arrest.

Lucas's gaze sharpened and then he looked away. 'You see her in Christchurch?'

'A bit.' Every delectable inch of her.

'She seem happy?'

Jake was stunned into silence. He looked at the older man and for the first time noticed lines—of age and worry.

Lucas gazed into middle distance. 'She doesn't seem too happy.'

Jake's heart-rate picked up. Had she confided in her father? Was he about to get a 'you be good to my daughter' lecture? He half hoped so. Hoped she was as miserable as him because things had gone wrong.

But, no, she'd never have told her father a thing about their affair. Not when she hadn't told him about her art, about a whole other degree she'd achieved.

Lucas sighed. 'All you want for your kids is the best. Want them to do OK, be OK. You try to teach them what's important. And all you seem to do is stuff up.'

Jake cleared his throat; he didn't quite know what to say. Nothing was needed, apparently; Lucas continued without prodding. 'Neither Emma nor Lucy seem as happy as I'd want.'

Hardly surprising. Lucy had spent the latter half of her teens so far off the rails that only now was she straightening out—largely thanks to Sienna. Jake had no idea to what extent Lucas knew of what Lucy had been up to in that time. Probably little. It seemed his daughters weren't exactly open with him.

'You did good, Jake. You work hard, like Emma. You've got money to burn.' He looked him in the eye. 'You happy?'

Jake looked over the gardens and took a deep breath as he thought about his reply. 'There are a couple of things I need to sort.'

Lucas nodded. 'Sienna?'

Jake frowned. Nope, for once in his life he hadn't been thinking about her at all.

'I know how much you've done for her and your mother. Such a worry all those years. But she's OK now, isn't she?'

Jake nodded slowly. Sure, she had a fixed-up heart and the doctors saw no reason to think she couldn't live a full normal life.

The older man laughed roughly. 'I once said you'd come to nothing if you left school at sixteen. Remember?'

He could hardly forget.

'Wrong, wasn't I? Mind you—' he frowned '—I've been wrong about a few things.'

They both stood and contemplated the garden.

'You were just trying to help me, Lucas. You thought you were doing me a favour, but I had to do it my way.' He frowned. He'd been doing to Emma exactly what her old man had tried to do to him. Thinking his way was it, bullying her into showing her paintings when she'd needed to do things her way, in her own time. Knuckle-head. But he was a man so used to being in control and he could control nothing when it came to Emma. Certainly not his feelings. And as a result he'd come down too heavy.

'Emma's OK,' Jake said finally. She would be; come hell or high water he'd do something, anything, to make it work.

Lucas turned to him. 'Can I get you a beer?'

Emma cursed as she lifted the bunch of Christmas lilies into the car. Typical, she'd got yellow pollen from the stamens all over her white tee shirt and down her dark denim skirt. Permanent stains. The story of her life at the moment. Permanent mark on her heart too. Lucy looked at her. 'Are you sure you're OK?'

'Yeah, I'm sure.'

Lucy sighed. 'That's just so not true, but if you're not

ready to talk, fine. I know something's up.' She sniffed. 'Can you lighten up a bit, though? The damn party's hard enough to live through if I don't have you on board.'

They got in and Lucy pulled away from the kerb. 'Is it a bloke?'

Emma said nothing.

'I've never seen you like this so I'm figuring it *must* be a bloke.'

A whisker of amusement slipped from Emma. 'I'll be OK, Luce.'

'I know. You always are.' Lucy checked the rear vision. 'Be good to be more than OK for once, though, wouldn't it?'

Emma struggled to get out of the car without crushing the flowers and making even more of a mess of her top.

Slamming the door shut with her foot, she turned to walk up the path laden with the fragrant blooms.

'Hey, Jake, long time!' Lucy sang out.

Emma jerked her head up to see her father sitting on the top step of the deck, beer in hand. And next to him, beer also in hand, sat Jake. A bowl of cashew nuts sat between them. The party seemed to have started early. And it was more of a shock than if they'd lined up a bunch of geriatric strippers.

Compelled by forces way beyond her control, she looked at Jake, meeting his gaze, and she stood still on the path while he looked her over. Even from the distance between them she could see the glimmer of amusement in his eyes, the gleam of desire. Then it faded and they sombrely stared at each other.

She was glad she was holding the massive bunch of flowers because it gave her something to cling to instead of running and clinging to him. She'd give herself away completely, willing to take anything he offered, just wanting him again and having him for as long as he could offer. It was humiliating. She wanted it, but she wanted it on her own terms and she needed some time to compose herself.

He carefully set his glass down beside him and pulled to his feet.

Then Emma became aware that both her father and sister were staring at the two of them, heads swivelling back and forth like the open-mouthed clowns in the sideshow-stall attraction. And she had the horrible feeling her heart had been written all over her face.

Jake spoke. 'I wanted to have a word, Emma.'

Nobody moved for an instant as the four of them exchanged looks.

Lucy suddenly swung into action. 'Dad, you take the lilies from Emma.'

Her brain not functioning, Emma argued. 'I have to do the display.'

Lucy passed stems to her father, who had walked down to meet them. 'You're not the only one who knows how to put flowers in a vase.'

Jake walked down the stairs and along the path to where she still stood. Lucy carried the flowers past him and inside, flashing him a warm smile. Her father was looking sideways at them and weaving up the path as a result.

Her attention snapped back to Jake. 'What are you doing here?' Work, it had to be work.

'Waiting for you.'

She ordered her heart-rate to slow down; she could hardly think with its beat thumping so loud and fast in her ear. 'But this is the one event on your social calendar you always miss.'

He closed his eyes, blocking her view to his frustration and whatever other emotions he was feeling. When he opened them again the turmoil was blanked. 'Emma. I wanted to see you. I have something for you.'

The fog of shock and confusion cleared and she was able to see him, really see him and take in his appearance. She'd always love him in jeans and a tee. But today he looked a little thinner, needed a shave and he looked tired.

'You've been working long hours.' She realised she'd spoken aloud.

'No worse than you, I imagine.'

If only he knew. And soon enough he would. She planned to tell him everything. Just as soon as she got the guts.

They stared at each other as silence fell again, awkward, unbreakable. She felt the flush mount in her cheeks. Was he remembering the same things she was? The way he felt, the things they'd done? Did he want it all over again as she did right now?

Incredibly she saw an answering rise of colour slash his cheeks. 'I, er, I have it in my garage.'

'Oh.' She pulled her shoulders back and down, willing the wobble in her legs to vamoose. Could he see the shakes she had? The physical impact of his presence knocked her sideways—literally.

She straightened up and put one foot in front of the other, letting him go slightly ahead so he couldn't see her look such an idiot. The garage stood on the boundary between her parents' property and his mother's. Two storeys—a flight of stairs ran up the outside to get to the workshop upstairs, where his grandfather had spent most of his time whittling wood, and where Jake had spent many hours keeping him company. His mother's car hadn't been parked in the garage in decades—it was too full storing bikes and benches and Sienna's old drum kits. She used to practise there—Jake had lined the walls with soundproofing board and Sienna and Lucy had spent hours in there, practising, gossiping and being girls.

With the woodworkers upstairs and the musicians downstairs it was a little shack of hobbyists. And one party that Emma had never been in on.

Jake led her in, heading straight to one of the benches lining the far wall. The gloomier light meant her eyes took a moment to adjust.

'I made you something for Christmas.' For the first time she could recall, Jake sounded vaguely uncertain.

She looked to the bench that held his complete attention. On top of it stood a boxy shape covered in soft cloth.

'It's a little early and not exactly wrapped—sorry.'

He stood aside, waiting for her to step forward, still not looking her in the eye. She reached out and lifted off the cloth.

A wooden box, about the size of a microwave, highly polished. She recognised the wood as rimu—reddish, native to New Zealand. Carved around the edges and sides was a border—a simple daisy chain. The same chain was carved on the top of the lid, but this time as a frame for a carved picture in the centre of the lid. She blinked. Instinctively she lifted her hand and traced her finger in the groove he'd chiselled out with such skill.

She felt the blood drain and her vision blurred as a faint threatened. She knew the picture. It was the one she'd drawn in her office that day—of the tulip and the daisy intertwined. 'I found it next to your rubbish bin.' He looked at her and she saw the defiant look he'd worn many times as a boy. 'I didn't think it should be thrown away.'

She looked down at the carving. Was he just talking about the picture? Her nerves tightened even more. She felt as if she were balancing on a tightrope suspended above shards of glass. She didn't want to slip in case she landed on them and got cut up even more. Didn't want to hope that maybe she'd land on marshmallowy pillows instead.

'It must have taken hours.'

'Sure. But then I didn't have anything else to do with my hands.'

The silence was absolute.

To cover it she lifted the lid of the box, gasping as she saw inside.

'It's for your art stuff.'

There was a removable top layer divided into several compartments of varying sizes. Perfect for pencils, charcoals and brushes. She lifted it out by its handle. The space underneath was divided into large segments. And in each compartment lay a large block or five of Caramello.

She smiled.

'Figured you need a stash to get you through the hours you work.'

Now was the perfect opportunity. She wanted to tell him. She had a Christmas present of her own she'd been planning on offering to him. She opened her mouth and started, wanting to be on the road of no return before she lost the nerve.

'I'm leaving the hotel.'

He jerked his head up, the focus of his eyes sharpening. 'What are you going to do?'

'I'm setting up my own business.'

She read his surprise and she thought she could see concern also. So she battled on, speaking with the same defiance he had moments ago, only more urgent. 'I like numbers, Jake. I like making them work. I enjoy the accountancy. I'd never have worked so hard at it if I didn't. It wasn't all about pleasing Dad or Max. I'm not that much of a sad case.' She sighed. 'OK, that was part of it. But not all. And I love painting. So I'm not going to give either part up completely.' She paused, wondering what he'd think of her plan. He was fixed on her. 'Margaret's book is going to be published using my drawings.' She took a deep breath. 'And some of the paintings. And the plan is to release some additional products to tie in—stationery, a calendar and stuff.'

'With your paintings.'

She nodded.

'There's going to be an exhibition when the book is released.'

He looked staggered. 'That's amazing.'

She continued, not wanting the interruption until she'd explained it all. He was the first person she'd told in full. The one who mattered most. 'I'm selling the cottage and with the funds I'm going to set up a small business as a specialist accountant working for artists, writers and actors and the like—who have irregular income and have to deal with potentially tricky things like royalties and expenses. I'm just going to work on it part-time while developing my own portfolio for the exhibition.'

There. Done.

For the first time since she'd clapped eyes on him that afternoon she relaxed a little. Only one more hurdle. She waited for his response.

'How do you feel about exhibiting?'

She answered honestly. 'Terrified. But, kind of excited at

the same time.' She brushed ineffectually at the yellow stains on her skirt. 'Once you knew, then Cathy at the gallery, Margaret, Lucy and Sienna, I found it wasn't so bad.'

'You've been in touch with Cathy?'

She nodded. 'You were right about her—she is great.' She took in another deep breath. 'It scares me, Jake, but if I think of it as a game it's OK. I'll do it for as long as it is fun and try not to get too uptight.' She couldn't hold the smile back as she said that. 'I've been trying to excel all my life, but I'm going to try and relax over this. Ultimately it's still for me, Jake, and there will always be paintings I paint that will only ever be for me. But I'll give it a go and if I hate it I can stop. I was halfway there anyway, doing the drawings for the book. It's just that you came along and pushed me along faster than I was willing to go.'

He looked pained. 'I'm really sorry about that, Emma. You were right; I shouldn't have. I shouldn't have sneaked in and taken the photos.'

'I know you were just trying to help. I think I would have got to this point eventually, but you just speeded up the process. And Cathy is a fabulous contact.'

'You were doing it yourself with Margaret's book.' He glanced at the box. 'Have you told your parents?'

'Not yet. I wanted…' *to tell you first* '…to be sure of a few things. I've done a painting for them for Christmas.' She stopped, conscious of his hooded stare.

'Do you have to sell the cottage? I thought you loved it.'

She shrugged. 'I'll find another place I love as much. And you were right—its location makes it a gold-mine.'

She paused, suddenly lost for words. The most important ones lodged in her throat and she couldn't quite get them out. She felt the chasm between them and didn't know how to bridge it. She waited, wanting some sign of encouragement but unable to see it.

'That's really great, Emma.'

She couldn't read his expression. His words sounded so final, so 'end of conversation'. Not interested, then. It *had* just been about helping her out—and a fling on the side.

'Thank you very much for the box—it's beautiful.' Stilted, stammering, she turned to head home, staring at defeat and despair.

It seemed as if he was about to let her leave, but suddenly blurted out a question. 'You didn't get the flowers I sent you?'

She turned back immediately. 'No. I was away.'

Heavy-lidded, he watched her relentlessly.

She tried to ask as nonchalantly as she could. 'What were they?'

'Gardenias.'

She'd drawn them only recently and had written the meaning in her neat script beneath. Painted them only the last weekend and destroyed the result because she'd felt such a fool.

I love you in secret.

Did he know that was their hidden message? She was shaking from the inside out. 'Why gardenias?'

She'd never seen him so tense. And then he sighed and the words seemed to come from deep inside. 'You said everyone has secrets, Emma.' He breathed in and as he exhaled his tumbled out. 'I love you. That's my secret. I love you and I always will.'

CHAPTER FIFTEEN

'YOU'RE kidding.' Emma was so stunned she couldn't stop the rudeness of her question.

She watched as for once Jake's was the face to colour. 'Actually for once in my life I'm not joking.'

She glanced up to the ceiling thinking that the roar she could hear was some freak hailstorm. No, it was just her pulse crazily loud, irregular and fast.

He was talking again, just as fast as her heartbeat and she strained to hear every word. 'I'm sorry, Emma. I'm sorry I started this out as just a fling; I'm sorry I took photos of your paintings; I'm sorry I broke your trust.'

'You didn't break my trust, Jake. I've always trusted you. And I know you thought you were doing me a favour.'

'I just wanted to help you because I thought I could and because I wanted you to be happy.'

'Because you care.' Statement not question. But she still couldn't believe the way in which he cared.

'I care. A lot. More than a lot. But I don't care what you do, how much you earn, how successful or otherwise you might be. I'll still love you. I'll still be here for you. I'll still support you no matter what. It's you I love, Emma, you for being you. You don't have to do anything other than be yourself for me. And I know that wanting to please people, wanting to achieve things for them is part of you, but you don't need to do that for me. OK?' He took a breath and continued. 'I don't want you showing your paintings if you don't want to—not because I thought you should or Cathy or Margaret or anyone else. You should only do it if you want to.'

'It is because I want to, Jake. I do. It started as a secret because I was scared of what Dad would say—as a kid, his approval meant everything. Then the fact it was secret became habit. And I felt that people would expect the best from me. I became scared that if I didn't live up to that I'd be rejected. Stupid, huh?'

'No.' A faint smile touched his face. 'I'm glad you held it to yourself for so long. I'm glad it was me that you shared it with.'

She wasn't at all sure they were still talking about her painting.

'So what do you say, Emma? Fancy…' He paused, his tension audible to both of them. He tried again. 'Fancy spending a little more time with me, go on a few dates. Give me a chance?'

'You don't need a chance.' She couldn't lift her voice higher than a whisper and he moved closer to hear her. Not close enough. Her body and soul were screaming out to touch him but she couldn't get the words out of her damn mouth. 'Jake…' She moved towards him.

His face lit up.

'Jake?' Sienna's voice rang out, and she appeared in the doorway of the garage a split-second later. 'Jake, I need you to lift the crate of…'

Emma pulled back, sweeping her raised hand through her own hair instead of reaching for Jake as she'd intended.

'You're going to have to do it yourself, Sienna. I'm busy right now.' Emma had never heard such an abrupt tone from him. Certainly never when talking to Sienna. He grabbed Emma's hand and led her out to the staircase

Emma turned her head to see Sienna standing, mouth open, staring after them. Hot colour flooded into her cheeks as Sienna's burst of laugher rang in her ears.

She matched him step for step as he bounded up the stairs. He let her hand go as he opened the door and she walked ahead into the middle of the room, looking about, but supremely conscious of him shutting and locking the door. Superficially she took in the divan against the wall, the beer fridge, kettle and toaster. An ancient stereo system sat on the ground with a box overflowing with CDs next to it.

The magic of the previous moment had gone and she was so thrown she didn't know if she'd dreamt it. She covered her confusion with a little laugh. 'This is your "man cave".'

His fingers roughed his hair. 'Yeah, I guess. Once I started working I used to sleep here sometimes—if I was home late and didn't want to wake the others in the house.'

'Did you do a lot of entertaining here?' She couldn't help asking.

He flashed a grin. 'Not nearly as much as you think.' She threw him a sceptical look.

'Really. I was talking it up earlier.'

'And now you're talking it down to make me feel better.'

He fixed on her. 'Does it bother you?'

'I'm human, of *course* it bothers me.'

'Good, because the thought of you with someone else makes me so mad I could just…' He stopped and laughed.

'But I'm so not your type!' She quickly walked away, wincing at her needy outburst. The window she stood at looked down on Jake's pool and over the fence to her parents' backyard—the manicured lawn and formal flower beds, the marquee set up for the annual bash.

He followed her, stopped to stand right behind her and her excitement level ratcheted up a notch. *Soon.* But they needed to talk. They hadn't been talking nearly enough and that was part of the problem.

'There is no "type" for me, Emma. There is only you.' He turned her towards him. 'Until now, I could take or leave my girlfriends. Fun. Good friends, even. But nothing that serious. It's so different with you. I can't leave you, Emma. I can't ever leave you. You *make* my life.'

She stared into his eyes, saw the honesty shining out and told him her own secret. 'I had such a crush on you.'

'No-o-o.' His hands dropped to his sides.

'Uh-huh.' She laughed at his shocked expression. It emboldened her to be completely blunt. 'For *years*. Ever since that day in the park when you were so nice to me.'

'Nice?' He stared, lost in the memory. 'I put my arm around you to give you a hug like I would Sienna and suddenly I was on fire. I should have known then that there was something special about you. About us.' His chest rose and fell as he took a deep breath. 'You were into me?'

'I've always been into you. So cool, so funny, so good-looking. You listened to me, Jake. No one had listened to me like that.'

'Yeah, but I stopped, didn't I? I stopped listening right when I should have been paying the most attention.'

'You were just wanting to help me. I know that. And you were right. Sharing things is fun. Sharing things with the people you care about is fun.'

'I like sharing things with you, Emma.'

She smiled, the sauce bubbling forth. 'I like sharing me with you, Jake.' She batted her lashes.

He chuckled and his hands were on her arms again, still rubbing, but drawing her closer, millimetre by millimetre until she was close enough for him to rest his forehead on hers. 'I've been thinking of you every moment, Emma. Waking, sleeping. Thinking of you.' He sighed and lifted his head, looking into her eyes with such a sweet intensity and she felt a crazy calm over her, despite the desire burning inside. It was all going to be OK. 'I saw you standing in front of me in that bar and you're all grown-up and we're out of this town and you had this look in your eye and I thought, Why not? A fun moment with someone a little different.'

Confidence sent the blood flowing in her veins. 'But it wasn't.'

'Nuh-uh.' He shook his head and stroked the tip of his finger across her lips. 'That one kiss wasn't nearly enough. Especially when I found out it was only for show. I wanted all of you all to myself.'

She chased the path of his finger with her tongue and as a reward he stepped even closer.

'I figured I could get close to you, at least fool around just a little. I thought the more I touched, the less I'd want to.' He grunted. 'Wrong. Totally wrong.'

She took the final step closer, bringing them into complete contact. 'You set up our game.'

His face split into that gorgeous grin that he got when

he was having wicked thoughts. 'Good idea, wasn't it? Play at being lovers. But it backfired.'

She raised an eyebrow.

'I couldn't control it, could I? For me it got very serious, very quickly and I knew I was in big trouble.' He looked apologetic. 'I wasn't planning on serious, Emma. I thought it would burn out. But instead all I wanted was to be with you. I wanted to make you happy. And I thought I could help arrange that.' His eyes narrowed in his frown.

'Being happy isn't something you can control for me, Jake. That's something I have to take care of myself. And I'm working on it. I've redirected my career. I've opened up about my painting. There was only one thing I had yet to do.'

'What's that?'

'I'm going to Auckland. Ticket's booked for next week.'

She felt his stillness. 'What are you going there for?'

'You.' She took his face in her hands. 'I wanted more of you. Was coming on the chance you might want more too.' She shrugged sheepishly.

'Sure.' He slid his hands down her back. 'I want more.'

She slid her hands through his hair, curling her fingers into the thick locks. 'No more games, then?'

'The only game I'm planning on playing in the future is Scrabble.'

'*Scrabble?*' She laughed, tilting her chin at him. 'Jake, you are a closet geek.'

'Yeah, well, you're a closet saucy minx so I guess that makes us even.'

She let the minx out of the bag. 'You're still going to play with me, though, aren't you?'

He lifted the hem of her tee shirt and stroked his palms

down her bare skin, pressing her against him. She practically purred as he unzipped her skirt.

'I've just rolled the dice.'

Their eyes met. Every cell in her body in tune, ready. It was the moment she'd been waiting for since she'd seen him on her father's deck.

Finally he lowered his mouth to her upturned one.

Ignition.

He kissed her. She kissed him. Beautiful, rejoicing, tender, and she revelled in his touch. He stroked, smoothed, and slid his fingers, hands and body over her skin.

And he was going too damn slow.

'Jake, please hurry.'

'Why, you got somewhere to be? You got a plane to catch?'

She choked, the gurgle of laughter caught on a sob of desire.

He kissed her, and kissed her again. 'It's all going to happen, honey.'

But it still wasn't enough and the only way to get it was to steal the march. Catching him by surprise, she pushed him onto the divan, stripping him of his tee shirt—at least managing to get it over his head and down as far as his elbows as he lifted his arms up high for her.

'I want you, Jake Rendel.' She kissed him, bruising her lips as she passionately pressed them against his hard muscles. Moving over his chest and up his neck to his jaw. 'Get undressed, dammit.'

Her urgency was infectious. He shrugged his arms free of the tee, lifted her so he could ditch his jeans as fast as was humanly possible. Then he leaned over her, his body pressing length to length. She couldn't think of anything else. Nothing mattered any more. All she wanted was him, in her, all the way. *Right now.*

'Do me, Jake.' She arched up to him, half begging, half teasing. '*Do* me.'

Wicked delight radiated from him. 'Emma, I'm not going to make it if you talk like that.'

'I'm not afraid to ask for what I want any more, Jake. And I want you.'

She pushed up, inviting him, and he took his place with a fierce thrust.

'You've got me.'

And then the dynamic changed completely—frivolity vanishing. She cried out, long and loud as he filled her. He'd plunged deep only a couple of times when it hit, the rapturous waves beating over her. She swept her arms down him as her body locked in ecstasy, screamed out the pleasure. It was the fastest road to orgasm she'd ever been on. She panted, but wasn't given the chance to recover as he kept up the stroke, building her up again. She opened her eyes to watch his answer.

But he didn't come with her. Instead he continued to hold back, working to rouse her again, intensely focussed on her, all traces of humour gone. 'Everything is so raw when I'm with you. You leave my heart so vulnerable. It scares me.'

'Jake.' She knew he heard the love in her voice and then she told him anyway as the sensations crested. 'I love you.'

'Say it again.'

She did and he closed his eyes, opening them again to reveal painful honesty. 'This feels so right. I never thought anything would be right again.'

'It's OK, Jake.'

'I really thought I'd lost you.'

She wrapped her arms around him and hugged him tight to her. 'You could never lose me. I've always been here. We just didn't know it.' And she moved with him, started to drive him, made it faster, harder, whispering to him, voicing her excitement and exciting him with it. But still he held back, his body an instrument of pleasure for her. It wasn't until she'd buckled yet again that he finally spent his love into her.

'Do me a favour.'

'Mmm.' Deliriously happy, giddy from multiple orgasms, curled in his arms, she couldn't move.

'Whatever I ask, you have to say yes.'

She smiled. 'I am not having a threesome.'

'Just say yes, Emma. It's not hard.'

She reached behind her. 'Yes, it is.'

'I'm not kidding.' The tension in his voice caught her. She heard his drawn breath. 'Just say yes.'

She turned her head and looked at him. 'You're serious.' She saw his unsmiling face, unusually strained. 'Jake?'

'Marry me.'

She blinked, the buzz in her ears blocking her comprehension. She whispered. 'I'm sorry, I'm going to have to get you to say that again.'

'Marry me. Please.'

She blinked again. And again—rapidly as the stinging sheen of tears hampered her vision. One spilt over and his hands came to frame her face.

'I really need to hear it, Em.'

She took in a shaky breath and mentally debated her answer. 'Sure.' She managed to say it smoothly and then beamed at him through the twin rivers tripping down her cheeks. '*Yes*. I sure will marry you.'

He shouted and wrapped his arms around her, rolling over and taking her with him so she lay on top of him. Her tears spilt onto his chest.

'No more.' He kissed them away from her eyes. 'No more.'

She buried her face in his neck, breathing in his warm masculinity—the faint stubble of his jaw pressing on her forehead. She'd never imagined such happiness and she shut her eyes fast in case it was a dream—she never wanted to wake from it.

His hand left her back and she felt him reaching for something.

'Emma.'

She had to open her eyes then. He'd pulled a box out of the pocket of his jeans.

'I was going to put it in your art box but I chickened out.' He handed it to her, his expression solemn.

A ring box. Her eyes widened. 'Jake.' Propped up on her elbows, her naked body flowing over his—it wasn't how she'd ever imagined she'd receive a wedding proposal, much less an engagement ring. Her heart thundered as she lifted the lid. Her eyes widened more.

'This is, um…' She stared at the contents. A chunky plastic flower ring, the kind you'd get in the two-dollar store for a four-year-old niece. Bright yellow with white petals on a garish blue circle. Adjustable size and everything. She looked up to see him grinning broadly. He winked.

'I want you to come with me to choose your proper ring—you know, we decide things *together* from now on. But I wanted to have something for the moment.'

He took it out of the box and she held out her hand, laughter lighting between them. 'You want me on my knees?'

'Of course. I want you every which way.'

He snorted as he slid the toy ring down her finger. 'Good thing you have such small hands.'

'Where'd you get it? Christmas cracker?'

He pretended to look wounded.

She fluttered her fingers, admiringly. 'I'll treasure it for ever.' She started to giggle.

'What's so funny?'

'Can you imagine Sienna and Lucy as bridesmaids?'

'Hell.' He shuddered. 'You don't think we should elope?'

'What? And deny your mum the pleasure of seeing her fine son get married? I'd never do it to her. Besides, I want the meringue.' She wrinkled her nose. 'I'm going to have to wear fake tan.'

'Honey, you could wear a sack and you'll still look beautiful to me.'

She cracked up. 'Oh, Jake, you smooth talker.' She ruffled his hair and planted a kiss on the underside of his chin. 'I am going to like being married to you.'

He tipped his head down and suavely replied. 'And I'm going to love being married to you.'

Their smiles melted in the kiss and she felt the flick of fire again, but on hearing the car doors slamming on the street below she lifted her head. 'I'm going to have to go.' The party would be warming up and she needed to be there, taking her place as the dutiful daughter.

'You don't think you're going without me, do you?'

'You never come to this party.'

'As far as I'm concerned it's our engagement party. I'm coming. Besides, your old man isn't that bad.'

They pulled their clothes back on, hindered by the lingering kisses in between each item, the slide of his body into hers.

As they dressed for the second time a question occurred to her. 'What were you going to do if I wasn't here?'

'Send you the art box by courier and hope you saw the message.'

'The picture?'

He shook his head. 'There's a less subtle message carved on the bottom.'

'What is it?'

He just grinned. She flew down the stairs to where the box still sat on the bench in the garage. She tipped it upside down to see underneath and softened in delight. She leaned back, knowing he would be behind her. She lifted her arm around his neck as he nuzzled hers.

Happiness, relief and plain old-fashioned lust glowed.

The box sat, forgotten for the moment, with the little carving in the top left hand corner showing for all the world to see:

J.R. ♥ E.D.

A sneaky peek at next month...

By Request

RELIVE THE ROMANCE WITH THE BEST OF THE BEST

My wish list for next month's titles...

In stores from 15th November 2013:

❑ Her Secret, His Child – Miranda Lee,
   Anne McAllister & Christina Hollis

❑ Untamed Billionaires – Nicola Marsh,
   Ally Blake & Trish Wylie

In stores from 6th December 2013:

❑ Marrying His Majesty
   – Marion Lennox

❑ Christmas Miracle – Caroline Anderson,
   Shirley Jump & Linda Goodnight

3 stories in each book - only £5.99!

Available at WHSmith, Tesco, Asda, Eason, Amazon and Apple

Just can't wait?

Visit us Online

You can buy our books online a month before
they hit the shops! **www.millsandboon.co.uk**

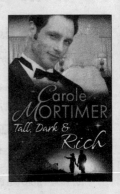

Wrap up warm this winter with Sarah Morgan…

Sleigh Bells in the Snow

Kayla Green loves business and hates Christmas.

So when Jackson O'Neil invites her to Snow Crystal Resort to discuss their business proposal… the last thing she's expecting is to stay for Christmas dinner. As the snowflakes continue to fall, will the woman who doesn't believe in the magic of Christmas finally fall under its spell…?

4th October

www.millsandboon.co.uk/sarahmorgan

Come home this Christmas to Fiona Harper

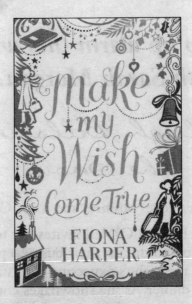

From the author of *Kiss Me Under the Mistletoe* comes a Christmas tale of family and fun. Two sisters are ready to swap their Christmases—the busy super-mum, Juliet, getting the chance to escape it all on an exotic Christmas getaway, whilst her glamorous work-obsessed sister, Gemma, is plunged headfirst into the family Christmas she always thought she'd hate.

www.millsandboon.co.uk

She's loved and lost — will she ever learn to open her heart again?

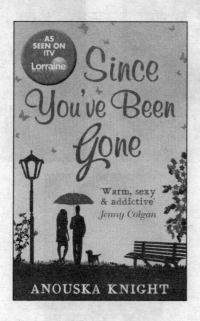

From the winner of ITV Lorraine's Racy Reads, Anouska Knight, comes a heart-warming tale of love, loss and confectionery.

'The perfect summer read — warm, sexy and addictive!'
—Jenny Colgan

For exclusive content visit:
www.millsandboon.co.uk/anouskaknight

Meet The Sullivans...